Mary Kate

NADINE DORRIES grew up in a working-class family in Liverpool. She spent part of her childhood living on a farm with her grandmother, and attended school in a small remote village in the west of Ireland. She trained as a nurse, then followed with a successful career in which she established and then sold her own business. She is an MP and has three daughters.

Also by Nadine Dorries

The Tarabeg Series
Shadows in Heaven
Mary Kate

The Lovely Lane Series
The Angels of Lovely Lane
The Children of Lovely Lane
The Mothers of Lovely Lane
Christmas Angels

The Four Streets Trilogy
The Four Streets
Hide Her Name
The Ballymara Road

Standalone Novels
Ruby Flynn

Short Stories
Run to Him
A Girl Called Eilinora
An Angel Sings

Nadine Dorries

Mary Kate

First published in the UK in 2019 by Head of Zeus Ltd
This paperback edition published in the UK in 2019 by Head of Zeus Ltd

9 7 5 3 1 2 4 6 8

A catalogue record for this book is available from
the British Library.

ISBN (PB): 9781786697554
ISBN (E): 9781786697523

Typeset by Adrian McLaughlin

Printed and bound in Great Britain by
CPI Group (UK) Ltd, Croydon CR0 4YY

Head of Zeus Ltd
First Floor East
5–8 Hardwick Street
London EC1R 4RG

WWW.HEADOFZEUS.COM

In memory of my good friend
Ann Frances Rayment

Mary Kate

Chapter 1

Brooklyn

It wasn't yet nine on a hot Brooklyn morning when Joe Malone the fourth slipped into the high-backed red-leather bench-seat in the window of his favourite diner, Enzo Capaldi's. He had sat in the same seat and ordered the same breakfast every day for the past year, since returning home after being discharged from the marines. Quite literally, he'd taken his dead father's place.

Before stepping inside, Joe Junior had tied up his daddy's old Labrador, Rocket, on the post outside. Rocket had followed the same routine most days for the past twelve years, and it was for his sake that Joe Junior kept it going. 'An old dog can't change his routine any more than a man can,' he'd told his mother as he fastened the collar and lead around the neck of the moping dog the day after his father's funeral.

The diner was shady in the mornings but baked in the merciless heat during the afternoons, which was why Joe

Malone the third had chosen Enzo's in the first place, on Rocket's account. Enzo always placed a large bowl of drinking water just outside the diner for passing canines.

Joe and Rocket had their place, their timing and their breakfast just right. Joe Junior kept an eye on Rocket from the window seat as he lit his first cigarette of the day. His short, dark, slicked-back hair was slightly damp from his morning shower and he still wore it in the style of a marine. Cupping his hands together in a cradle, the cigarette dangling from his thumb and forefinger, he watched as the commuters bustled past and were swallowed up by the sidewalk, descending into subway hell.

The waitress spotted him and with a smile and a nod she yelled out his arrival to Enzo behind the griddle. 'Joe's here,' she called. 'Large sweet espresso and OJ coming up, Joe.' She lifted the coffee pot off the hot ring and poured it, at the same time as she slid a glass under the OJ dispenser and opened the tap.

'Hey, is Joe Junior in already? You're five minutes early, Joe,' shouted Enzo, 'or I'd have had it ready for you. I'll bring it over myself – time for my break.'

Joe raised his hand above the high back of the leather bench in acknowledgement and greeting and opened the newspaper he'd bought from the vending machine situated right outside the diner. He'd checked the mailbox on his way out of his apartment building and was disappointed that there was still no reply from Ireland. It was almost a month since he'd written to the address on the will.

He slipped his fingers into the back pocket of his neatly pressed linen trousers and took out the copy of the will that had been given to him by Mr Browne, his daddy's solicitor. His bright blue Irish eyes, which reflected his short-sleeved shirt of exactly the same colour, scanned once again the instructions written in his great-granddaddy's hand.

Fourth generation, raised in an Irish American community, Joe Junior had always felt more Irish than American. When he'd been forced by his father to attend the Irish-dancing classes held by the church youth club, the music had reverberated from the sprung floorboards of the hall right into his soul, its repetitive rhythm like a drumbeat calling him home to Ireland. His father had only known the country from the stories handed down through the generations of New York Malones, but he'd had a deep longing for the place. Joe Junior truly was his father's son: often, in his dreams, he would find himself standing by a river, surrounded by green fields and mountains. He had once confided this to his mammy. 'You saw *The Quiet Man* too often at the movies,' she responded. 'I told your father it would affect your brain. He's made you as bad as he was. Me, I never want to see the place – why would I? My granny used to write to us and every single letter began with "Oh, God, the rain hasn't stopped." Years, that went on for. Who wants to visit a place where it rains every day? By the time she died, according to her letters it had been raining for fifteen years nonstop.'

Every year, his father used to tell him that he intended

to visit Ireland and that he would take Joe Junior with him. But his business always got in the way; he was too busy living the American dream. The final plot they'd hatched had been the post-marines trip: they would make the journey before Joe Junior settled down to help run Malone's. They'd planned it down to the last detail, had pored over brochures and gone to the movies, had attended the Irish Centre and collected the newspaper and talked of little else. But none of it was to be. His father's heart attack five days after Joe Junior's discharge robbed them of their father-and-son trip of a lifetime.

On his deathbed, Joe Malone the third made his son promise he would make the trip for him. He wanted him to let them know in Tarabeg that the first Joe Malone had never stopped missing them. Joe Junior had sworn his pledge, sitting at his father's bedside in the hospital.

'We can't make our trip together, boy, but promise me you'll still go? Someone has to go back. There's a whole family there, and my daddy was sure one of the original Malone brothers is still alive.' His hand found a new strength as it gripped his son's.

Joe Junior looked into his eyes. 'I will, Daddy. I promise you that.'

The grief at his passing lodged like a weighty stone in his gut, but in those final seconds he vowed to do what his father had yearned to do.

He was still struggling to come to terms with the contents and conditions of the will. He read it every day, expecting each time to discover that he had imagined it. He'd known that the first Joe Malone to arrive in America had died under a cloud of secrecy; few in the family ever discussed it and certainly not with him. Joe Junior was only twenty-five years old and his father's sudden death at forty-seven had brought enough sadness and changes for him as the eldest child to deal with. And then the solicitor, of Messrs Collins, Murphy, Browne and Sons, had, under the terms of the will, enlightened him.

He would remember the moment for all of his life. He'd been seated on one side of the huge oak desk, surrounded by teetering piles of dusty, buff-coloured files tied up in bright ribbons. Mr Browne, a thin-faced man with thinner lips, narrow eyes and retreating hair reduced to four greased strips combed backwards across his pate, had removed his wire-framed glasses and slid a large cut-glass ashtray across the desk towards Joe. Then he extracted a handkerchief from his jacket pocket and wiped at his watery, smoke-stung eyes.

'I'm not sure if you are aware that this will was written by the first Malone to emigrate to America from County Mayo in Ireland.' He folded the handkerchief carefully as he spoke and tucked it back into his pocket.

Joe didn't speak; he simply nodded and drew on his cigarette. He didn't want to reveal that, unlike other Irish American families who celebrated their first generation of immigrants, he knew next to nothing about the first American Malone.

'They were desperate times indeed. The Irish were very poor, and out in Mayo they were the poorest. They suffered the worst during the famine, lived hand to mouth, and it took many years to recover. Of course there was plenty of work to be had here, paying very good money to unskilled men.' Mr Browne replaced his spectacles, allowing Joe time to respond.

Still Joe said nothing. Mr Browne had an air of disapproval about him. He didn't seem at all comfortable, even though he surely did will-readings every day. Something wasn't quite right. Joe was alert, prepared; his marine training came to the fore and he kept his composure. He detected a change in tone as Mr Browne continued. Until that point, everything had been straightforward enough, but he could sense that was about to change.

'There has been a codicil, honouring previous and past wills and continuing forwards from the death of the first Joe Malone his express conditions, instructions and wishes.' He was speaking faster, as if in a hurry to reach the end of something he would rather not be doing or saying. 'There was a condition of time, or should I say, the passing of time.'

The phone on his desk rang.

'Excuse me,' he said, looking irritated. He picked up the receiver.

Joe had never before seen a telephone trimmed in eighteen-carat gold plate. It caught the light reflected from the lamp on the desk and winked at him.

Mr Browne was speaking into the phone. 'I collected it

myself from the safe-deposit box last night. It's in my safe. I will see to it now. You don't need to do anything more, thank you, Miss Carroll.'

He replaced the phone and glanced over his shoulder. 'Excuse me,' he said again and pulled open a drawer in his desk, extracted a key, stood up, pushed his green-leather and oak chair backwards and walked over to a tall, gilt-framed painting on the far wall of the expansive office. It was a portrait of a formidable but dull-looking man in a top hat and cape; he had a walking stick in one hand, a scroll in the other and what looked like a dead fox slung over his shoulder.

Joe looked out of the window. They were on the tenth floor and the view of New York was breathtaking. He wondered how this solicitor appeared to know more about his family than he did. Neither his father nor any of his brothers knew anything about the first-generation Malone. It was a mystery that had burnt away in his father's heart, a yearning, which Joe Junior had inherited but couldn't explain, to understand, to see the place their family had originated from and had lived in for centuries, through the worst of times.

Mr Browne returned, lowered himself into his seat and placed a small box wrapped in purple velvet on the desk. Joe pulled himself back from the view and stubbed out his cigarette in the ashtray.

'Do excuse me. I shall continue. This next revelation may come as something of a surprise to you.' Mr Browne cleared his throat. 'Joe Malone the first was incarcerated in jail for the greater part of his life for his role in an armed robbery.'

Joe gasped; he couldn't help it. His defences had been penetrated. This was the last thing he'd expected to hear.

'This will states that there is a considerable inheritance awaiting you, to the tune of a million dollars, in a village called Tarabeg, in County Mayo, Ireland. More precisely, at Tarabeg Farm on Tarabeg Hill. There is no mention of where this money originated from.'

Joe blinked, then blinked again. He forgot to breathe.

The solicitor leant across the desk, pulled a silver tray towards himself, picked up a cut-glass decanter and began to pour. 'Here. Miss Carroll thought you might need this. It always helps to get the blood flowing after a shock.'

He pushed the glass towards Joe, who took the drink gratefully and downed a large gulp before wiping his mouth with the back of his hand. 'A million dollars?' Joe let out a long, low whistle and realised he'd spoken his thoughts out loud. He cradled the glass in both hands to stop them from trembling.

'Indeed. I don't think it is too difficult to guess how the money was obtained. Joe the first paid the price in prison, and with his life, but he was on the run for over a year before he was caught, and in that time he appears to have made adequate provision in a number of ways. One of the reasons he served so long was because the money was never recovered.'

Mr Browne coughed. Joe sensed there was still more to this than he was being told.

'There is also this.' He pushed the box across the table to Joe. 'We have held the keys to the safe-deposit box on your great-grandfather's behalf.'

Joe set down his whiskey glass on the polished oak, not on the silver tray, causing Mr Browne to wince somewhere deep inside. He picked up the box and studied it carefully. The velvet was soft beneath his fingers. Soft and thick, and it hinted at things other than riches. There was a depth and meaning there, and, it hit Joe in a flash, sadness. He lifted his gaze to Mr Browne, who averted his and once again dabbed at his eyes.

The grey sky had darkened the room and the bottle-green lamp on the desk cast a warm amber glow. Joe leant forwards into the light and opened the lid. For the second time in minutes, he gasped. Nestled on creamy kid leather sat a beautiful emerald carved in the shape of a heart. It was attached to a gold chain. When Joe lifted it into the air, it swung in and out of the light. His skin prickled, the hairs on his arms rose in response and his stomach flipped.

Mr Browne went through the motions of returning his handkerchief, then picked up the will. 'It is one of two. They were originally earrings, separated at the point of theft. One was sent to Tarabeg, the other kept in a safe-deposit box, awaiting today. You now have to look further into the box.'

Joe furrowed his brow and lifted the kid-leather cushion

to reveal a yellow slip of paper. He tried to retrieve it, but his hands shook so much, he failed. 'Could you, please?' He handed the box to Mr Browne and felt his breath leave his body in a rush.

Mr Browne held out his hand, which Joe noticed was also trembling. '"Take me home." That's all it says,' he said with a hint of surprise as he passed Joe the piece of paper. 'I think the emerald may be symbolic. As you know, it's a favourite jewel of the more successful and wealthy Irish ladies in America. I imagine when he wrote this he wanted the two hearts to be reunited. Maybe one represented him and the other his home?'

Joe did not know that rich Irish American women wore emerald hearts. His parents had never moved in circles where people wore jewels.

'The will, which I have a copy of for you, states that Joe Malone the first sent the money back to Tarabeg in a box and received confirmation that it had arrived and was being kept in a safe place. It also states that he didn't expect all the money to still be present. He wanted every-one to benefit.'

'Aren't you supposed to tell the police about this?' Joe spluttered, thrusting the emerald and its chain towards Mr Browne. 'I mean, it's obviously stolen goods – I can't take it.'

Mr Browne flushed bright red. 'Mr Malone, your great-granddaddy was a decent man, a good friend of my own grandfather's, the founder of this firm.'

'Regardless, shouldn't you be handing all this information over to the police?' said Joe, quite stunned by this reply.

'Mr Malone, my granddaddy started this business to assist your great-granddaddy. They were friends and both of them helped Irish labourers who were working on the roads and bridges and were being exploited. The money was no ordinary robbery. It was the payroll of a company that sent terrified men up scaffolding without any protective shoes or clothing or even a safety harness. A company that made men from Ireland work outdoors in temperatures that would fry an egg on the sidewalk, a company that made them work until they were as red as a lobster and dropped dead from dehydration and sunburn. Joe Malone the first, he saw a boy from the same village in Ireland as himself fall to his death, and that was when he decided on revenge. It took him a whole year to organise.'

'Why now? Why is this all being revealed now?' asked Joe as he took out another cigarette.

Mr Browne picked up the decanter, turned over the empty second glass on the tray and poured one for himself. The moment was coming when they were both going to need it. 'Your great-granddaddy robbed a payroll, which was no small crime. He used some of the money to alleviate the suffering of many people. He also explicitly requested that the provisions in his will be carried forwards across three generations, to allow enough time for memories to fade.'

Joe glanced pointedly at the gold-edged phone and then back to Mr Browne. 'Did my great-granddaddy's ill-gotten gains help start this firm?'

Mr Browne looked sheepish. 'That brings me to the last part of the will.' He picked up the glass, took a gulp and once more wriggled in his chair to retrieve his handkerchief. He inhaled deeply, leant across the desk and, lifting Joe's glass, handed it to him.

'This will come as a bit of a shock to you, I think. You, Mr Malone, are now the major shareholder in Messrs Collins, Murphy, Browne and Sons. Which means that you now own the firm. Your dividends have been building up since the firm went into profit. You are a very rich man.'

That had happened a month ago, and this morning, in the diner, Joe Junior was beginning to feel the first pangs of frustration.

The diner was filled with the noise of crashing plates and shouted orders and the smell of crispy-fried bacon. 'Coffee coming up,' shouted Enzo. Joe folded the will, rose slightly from the seat, and slipped it into his back pocket.

The law firm made over $500,000 a year in clear profit, and that was after the likes of Mr Browne had skimmed their dues off the top. Joe had tried to take it all in. The Malones would never know a poor day again. They were a law-abiding, strict Catholic and very successful business family. They were comfortable, though not rich – until now. Malone's Building, Plumbing and Electrics was a medium-sized firm, employed over fifty skilled and unskilled labourers and was run by a competent foreman. It had been founded by his great-granddaddy to provide Irish labour for the maintenance of the Brooklyn Bridge. But where had the money come from to start it in the first place? For Joe Junior, the worst thing was that there was no one he could ask about it in America: the conditions of the will prohibited him from doing so.

'Here you go,' said Enzo as he placed the coffee and OJ in front of Joe. 'Martha's doing the eggs. Any news from Ireland?'

Joe downed half the glass of orange juice in one gulp. He'd told Enzo some of the details, that he was tracing his great-granddaddy's family, but not all of them. His father had sat in this same place and had breakfast with Enzo every day for thirty years. Joe Junior was continuing the tradition and for the first time he looked at Enzo and wondered, did he know? Was Joe Junior really the only person to be told how much money his great-granddaddy had sent back home to his brother ready to be collected when enough time had passed? For some reason known only to him, he had hurriedly posted a cedar box to Ireland via sea mail. How had the Revenue not intercepted it? There were so many questions and Joe Junior had no idea where to look for the answers, which was why he'd thought of Ireland. Maybe someone there knew. Maybe, and he knew it was a long shot, the person into whose safekeeping it had been sent was still alive.

'Nothing yet. Father Francis from St Saviour's has made enquiries, but apparently all the records of births and deaths are kept by the priest's housekeeper in Tarabeg, and you have to knock on her door and ask her. That's the way over there, it would seem.'

Enzo laughed. 'You didn't know that? Every Irishman coming in here who's tried to trace his roots comes up against the same brick wall. It's the way all over Ireland. It depends what the housekeeper is like whether or not you get to find out if you're on the right track or not. Those old crones, they hold the power over there. One of my customers, he told me a few dollars usually sorts it.'

Martha came over with two plates and laid one down in front of each of them.

'Don't you ever cook your own breakfast?' asked Joe as he smiled up his thanks to Martha.

'Hell, no. It doesn't taste the same. I cook that food all day long – I can only eat it myself if someone else cooks it.'

Joe looked down at his stack of pancakes smothered in maple syrup and the heap of crispy bacon on the side. Despite his sweet tooth, he retained the slim, toned figure of a young man who was a regular visitor to O'Hara's Boxing Club, walked Rocket six blocks each morning and went for a run all the way out to the bridge each evening. At night he walked the four blocks to his parents' brownstone, ate his second meal of the day with his widowed mother, and then walked back home again.

'Don't be afraid that they'll be put off in Mayo because

you're American,' Enzo said. 'They live for visitors over there and they love it when the names connect and they realise it's one from their own line in their own village who's come back to trace their roots. You know, when the O'Connors went back home, the whole village turned out to wave them off. Some were even crying when they left. They all knew they would never be back. I always think Ireland is very like Italy – they're just the same over there.'

Joe wiped the maple syrup from his chin with his napkin and took a sip of his scalding sweet Italian coffee. 'It's the opposite problem with me,' he said. 'My worry is that I'll get there and won't want to leave.'

Enzo let out a long low whistle. 'Phew, don't be telling your mammy that, she'll have heart failure.'

'Don't I know it. I know this too – while you were talking there, Enzo, I made a decision.'

Joe looked out of the window at the crowd of people hurrying to work. Some bent and stroked Rocket and then, catching Joe's eye, straightened up and smiled. Rocket, a regular fixture on the sidewalk at that time of day, looked to him for approval before he took the biscuit the lady who passed him every morning had extracted from her pocket. Joe raised his hand and smiled. He had never met the woman – she'd been a friend of his father's – but they spoke in a form of sign language every morning.

The sun was hot, the pavement dusty and the traffic noisy. Joe had no need to work each day. His father had left him and his mother comfortably off. His younger brothers all worked in the business, but not Joe, who had served seven years in the marines. On his return, he'd been made chairman of the company, which took up very little of his time. He knew he was a lucky man. He respected his brothers, who gave their heart and soul to the family business; in turn, they respected him for having given seven years to America.

'I've decided that I'm gonna give it a couple more weeks. And if I still haven't heard back from Tarabeg, I'm going to get on a plane and fly out there regardless,' Joe said to Enzo.

He doubted very much that there would still be a million dollars there, not after so many years, but he really didn't care. He wanted to see for himself what was this place and who were these people his great-granddaddy had trusted so much more than anyone in America; the place where they had chosen to remain when everyone else had jumped on the nearest ship and headed to foreign shores. His great-granddaddy's company was based in Brooklyn, had a huge contract for the maintenance of the Brooklyn end of the Bridge, so why send a wooden chest all the way across the Atlantic and not just to somewhere safe across the bridge? He must have had a reason, and Joe Malone the fourth knew that he had to find the answers. It was a way to try and fill the hollowness in his heart that had been there since the day his daddy had died.

'Do you think you could put up with my mother bringing the dog in every day when I go to Ireland, Enzo?'

Enzo picked up his sandwich, which was dripping runny egg over his hands. 'If it keeps her happy, I'll step in for you at supper, if you like?' he said as he licked each finger in turn.

Joe laughed. Enzo had a soft spot for his mother. 'Just as long as I don't come back and have to start calling you "Stepdaddy".'

He laid down his knife and fork. He was going home, although it was a place he had never even visited. Home, although he knew no one there. Home, where, apparently, a million dollars and an emerald heart were waiting for him.

Chapter 2

Tarabeg

'Is she after coming home for good, is she?' nine-year-old Finnbar shouted through cheeks stuffed full of fresh brack. He ran out of the kitchen and through the Malones' shop, grabbing a bar of chocolate from the counter as he passed, and piled into the waiting car.

Rosie followed him, trying to keep up as she peeled her cardigan off her shoulders. It was only 10 a.m., but the sun was already too warm for comfort for those who lived on the west coast and were more used to wind and rain than a blisteringly hot day. 'Finn, that chocolate will melt – give it to me. And did you ask?'

Finn laughed and turned his mischievous face and chubby cheeks dappled with fresh freckles towards her. His bright blue eyes sparkled. Both Finn and his sister, Mary Kate, had golden-red hair like their late mother, and on a sunny day it shone, flecked with a multitude of golds and silvers, reflecting the light. 'I did. I asked Granny Nola and she said yes.'

'I bet she did not.' Rosie tutted and glanced up the road towards her husband, Michael, who was standing by the display of goods in baskets and wooden boxes on the cinder path outside the shop. He was issuing last-minute instructions to Peggy Kennedy, who would have sole responsibility for the shop while they were gone. Rosie hoped he hadn't heard Finn. It had been a morning of raised voices and she was already exhausted; it felt as though breakfast had been hours ago.

She bent her head to peer through the window of the car. 'Finn, it is speech day, a special day, a day when you need to be wearing clean shorts. Mary Kate is coming home for good today, all the families will be there at the school and she will be wanting you to be looking your best. Please, Finn. Just the one day, will you behave and do as you're told?' She reached her hand through the window, her voice pleading, a tactic that never worked well.

Finn never wanted to upset Mary Kate, the angel in his life. With a sulky expression on his face, he grudgingly slapped the chocolate bar into Rosie's hand, folded his arms and slid into the tan-leather back seat of the car, where he would be sandwiched between Rosie and his Granny Nola for the journey to St Catherine's. They were the only family in the village to own a vehicle for leisure purposes. Michael Malone also owned a van, which he used for transporting goods from Dublin and Galway back to his general store in Tarabeg. Rosie had no idea why he'd bought the car as it was used only on high days and holidays. Most people in the village still relied on donkeys and horses and carts, which seemed to amuse the tourists who were now visiting rural Ireland in increasing numbers.

Rosie looked down and saw only half a bar of chocolate in her hand. 'Finn!' She almost shouted this as she thrust her head inside the car.

'It's gone. Look!' Finn poked out his chocolate-stained tongue for Rosie to inspect.

'You are one little terror,' Rosie said as she withdrew her head.

The car still smelt of new leather. She hadn't really minded Michael buying it – after all, the business he'd built up had become the most profitable not only in Tarabeg but for miles around. Its success was down to Michael's relentless hard work, and Rosie had not complained about that either. Rosie never complained. 'It's everyone else who's a pain,' she would often say to Keeva, whereupon they would both burst out laughing.

Rosie's auburn hair was held back from her face in a blue headband, and as she continued freeing her arms from her turquoise hand-knitted cardigan, she shook it down her back. Her skin was pale and freckled and she kept her arms covered whatever the weather, dreading the itchiness that the sun brought. But the heat wafting out of the car was already overpowering.

She looked over towards the crossroads and saw Nola,

her mother-in-law, deep in conversation with Josie Devlin. Rosie didn't need Bridget McAndrew, the village seer, to tell her what they were discussing: it would be the imminent return of Mary Kate. Mary Kate had been home for the holidays many times since Rosie and Michael had married, but she always ended up spending much of her time at Tarabeg Farm with her grandparents, Nola and Seamus, and her great-granddaddy, Daedio. Somehow she persuaded Michael, against his will, to let her sleep most nights up there, in his old bed.

Rosie was desperate to be the caring stepmother of a happy family but found herself constantly thwarted by Mary Kate's unintentional slights and Michael's unwillingness to challenge his mother or put his foot down. Her friend Teresa Gallagher repeatedly urged her to make Michael do what was right, but how could she? His grief at his first wife's death had brought him down further than most of the villagers had seen any man fall. Michael was entirely unaware that the longest prayers at Mass were still said for him.

Rosie had hoped their marriage would lift him up, restore him to the man he'd once been, the man she could still remember. But the Michael Malone everyone knew had never fully returned, and their marriage had not stitched together the torn-apart family. He was not living a married life with Rosie but that of a widower, and that was how people still saw him: as the bereaved husband of Sarah. Similarly, even though Rosie had been in Finn's life since his mother died when he was only hours old, in the eyes of every single person in Tarabeg he was still Sarah's son, not hers.

Rosie glanced across the road to Paddy Devlin's butcher's shop and bar and saw her friend, Keeva, the Devlins' daughter-in-law, standing at an upstairs window, also watching Nola and Josie talking. Keeva spotted Rosie and shrugged her shoulders. Rosie gave her half a smile back. Rosie was thankful she had Keeva over the road; and her husband, Tig, was Michael's best friend. Between the two of them they spoke a lot of common sense and kept Michael on the emotional straight and narrow. They were Rosie's only advocates in a village that had never stopped mourning Sarah's untimely death, the only ones who acknowledged to her that Michael Malone had changed on the night his wife had died. They were Rosie's true friends and support.

Mary Kate had completed her education at St Catherine's in Galway. She was no longer a girl, and today they would be bringing home a young woman.

Keeva now appeared at Rosie's side, followed by a trail of little boys, who tried to pile into the car with Finn.

'Oi, get yerselves out! Now!' shouted Keeva as she grabbed at legs and shoes and ejected them one by one.

The boys were noisy but lost interest in Finn as soon as Rosie said to him in a voice that brooked no argument, 'Move out of that seat and you'll have your daddy and Granddaddy Seamus to deal with.'

Finn shuffled into place, then stuck his head out the window to watch Keeva and Tig's two eldest scamper off towards the Taramore river. His face was creased with envy and his lips still smeared with melted chocolate.

'Are you off now?' asked Keeva as she folded her arms across her apron and watched one of her sons kick a football high into the air in the middle of the road. She frowned, concerned about the bar's window getting hit.

'Aye, we are. As soon as Michael has finished giving out to Peggy. Eight years now and you would think she started only yesterday.'

Keeva smiled. 'It's a grand day indeed – Mary Kate's coming home. Isn't it just fabulous, Rosie? Mary Kate all grown-up. What a blessing that she loved the school so much. Imagine if she'd hated it, after all she'd been through. Nola would have never spoken to any of us again.'

It had been a plan hatched by Rosie and Keeva to give Mary Kate a proper education, more than Rosie, as the schoolteacher in Tarabeg, could offer. They had met resistance but had won in the end.

'I can't wait to have her back. What a delight she is compared to that lot.' Keeva glanced towards three of her red-headed boys running around in the street and shook her head at the din they were making as they kicked the ball. Keeva had been Sarah's best friend and one of the first to welcome Mary Kate into the world. She liked Rosie, was friends with Rosie and sympathised with Rosie's position – how could she not. Rosie was the schoolteacher, had been a member of their group, though always on the periphery, and had been working part time in Michael and Sarah's shop when Sarah died. But Sarah lived in Keeva's heart also, and, as a result, Keeva loved Mary Kate possibly more than Rosie ever had.

Rosie laughed. 'I know I say it every day, but I don't know what Finn would do with himself without your boys over the road.'

'Come over as soon as you get back and let me know how it all went, and make sure Mary Kate is with you – don't go leaving her behind.' Keeva waved as she walked off, and stopped in the middle of the road to issue another warning to the boys, who promptly ignored her.

'Why is Granny Nola talking so much?' said Finn, leaning out of the car door. He'd climbed over into the front and was now in the driver's seat.

'Get your feet off the seat, Finnbar. You'll have your father giving out to you.' Rosie pushed Finn's boots into the footwell and with her handkerchief began to wipe away the dust left by Keeva's sons on the leather upholstery.

'Mammy…!' Finn wailed, exasperated at his question not having been answered. 'Mammy, why is Granny Nola taking so long?'

'She isn't, Finn, and shush, she's coming now.' Rosie raised her hand to Nola, who was walking towards the car carrying the largest bunch of flowers Rosie had ever seen. Mary Kate had telephoned Mrs Doyle in the post office days ago, asking for Nola to bring flowers to the speech day; they were beginning to wilt in the heat of the morning.

Rosie looked back to Michael to see had he heard Finn shouting. He had, and he was turned their way. As he saw them, the grumpiness slipped from his face and he broke into a smile. To Rosie it was a look of such deep fondness, and there was such love in his eyes, that her heart did a somersault. She blushed, rolled her eyes at the antics of Finn, and melted, just as she always did when Michael smiled that way.

Michael continued staring and smiling for a few moments longer. It had been nine, nearly ten, long years and yet still, whenever Finnbar shouted 'Mammy', Michael's heart expected to see and hear Sarah answering their son. As he looked towards Finn now, in the dazzle of sunlight reflecting off the gleaming paint, glass and chrome of the car, he saw her, fleetingly, just as he always did. Her blaze of red hair, shot through with threads of the deepest gold, flashed in the light. He felt her as much as he saw her. She turned to him and smiled, and because he knew her gossamer image would vanish as quickly as it had arrived, Michael smiled back to her, to the love of his life, his dead wife, his Sarah. He had long since learnt there was no point in calling out to her. He had come to accept these visions as a gift. She smiled back to him and he held the vision, controlling his tears, his eyes spilling out to her all the love in his heart.

And then she was gone, replaced by Rosie, leaving his heart pained.

When Finn called out for his mammy, Sarah always answered. She was forever there, in Tarabeg, had never left, and Michael knew that if she hadn't been, he might not have stayed either. In the darkest days, when he was only just about functioning, he'd been tempted not to return home. On his buying trips to Dublin he had often stood on the bridge over the Liffey and contemplated his own demise. Though Sarah was dead, he felt her presence in their home still, waiting for him; her smell was in her clothes, and if he closed his eyes, he could feel her. At times he was convinced he heard her breathing next to him in bed. It was this that had saved him, made him turn on his heel and walk back to the van, start the engine and head for home. How could he die in Dublin when Sarah had never really left Tarabeg?

It had never felt right to him that Finn called Rosie 'Mammy', but as Nola had said to him, 'Finn knows no other. He was only hours old when Sarah died, so of course he should call Rosie "Mammy", that is who she is to him.' He couldn't argue with her. She was right. Nola was always right. He had married Rosie, and she was mammy to Finn, but deep inside, he felt a loyalty to Sarah that made his heart fold. He would not, could not, confess to anyone that he resented Rosie being mammy to Finn, despite the fact that he could never have managed without her. She'd been indispensable, always there, making the impossible possible.

Michael turned away now from Finn and Rosie and his

vanished vision of Sarah and continued talking to Peggy. 'I've left the feed for Pete Shevlin to collect out here on the path, in the sack.' He pointed to the hessian bag leaning up against the wall.

'Ah, sure, but how will Pete know that one is his?' Peggy asked, her brow furrowed beneath her thick fringe of dark, wiry hair, her hands thrust deep into her apron pockets. Her eyes were dark and brown and gave the false impression that she was wise and thoughtful. But Peggy was far too interested in the shallower aspects of life, hers and everyone else's, to pay too much attention to that which was relevant or necessary. Working in Malone's had been the next best thing to securing a job with Mrs Doyle at the post office, and what Mrs Doyle didn't pick up at her end of the main street, Peggy gathered at hers, filling in the gaps.

Peggy's daily focus was on gathering every bit of information she could about life in America and writing it all down in a book; she'd begun the book five years ago and had reread it many times. At night she worked in Paddy's bar, where she put together a list of addresses in the most exotic-sounding places in America, written down for her by every passing tourist and fisherman with the promise of a warm welcome when she finally crossed the Atlantic. She saved every halfpenny she earned working for Michael during the day and for Paddy and Josie at night into an oversized jar that she hid under the eaves of the cowshed on her parents' farm. She counted down the days until she could escape and head for New York and a life of high heels, fox-fur stoles, sharkskin slips and whalebone corsets.

Michael lifted his cap and wiped away the line of sweat that had formed on his forehead. 'Pete will know, Peggy, because the sack has his name on it, because there is no other bag of feed out here that I can see, and because I'm telling you now. He will be down with the cart to collect it this afternoon.' Exasperated, he had almost raised his voice.

Peggy Kennedy had not been his choice to work in the shop, but the fact was that more people were leaving Tarabeg than were staying. Every year, Tarabeg's population decreased while Liverpool and America saw theirs grow. It had occurred to him recently that there'd been a whole year of his life when almost nothing of any importance had been his choice. Following Sarah's death, he'd lost a good twelve months to grief, alcohol and self-pity and during that time others had made decisions for him, decisions he had since come to regret, one of which was the employment of Peggy.

'And make sure you take the right money for the fishing licences. Captain Carter has put them up to two and six now that the salmon are in, and the day's fishing is to be done by four or the ghillie will charge them double. Do you understand that, Peggy?'

Peggy planted her hands firmly on her hips. 'Michael Malone, do you think I am simple or what? Of course I understand that. You are offending me now. Go and bring Mary Kate back home. Sure, look what I bought her.'

She disappeared inside the shop and seconds later ran back out carrying a brown-paper bag, rather scrumpled. Michael knew this would be because whatever was contained inside would have already been shown to pretty much every resident in the village.

She pulled out a set of lace handkerchiefs with the initials MKM embroidered in the corner. 'I got them done specially, in Castlebar,' she said. 'See here' – she pointed to the blue stitching in the middle and a thatched cottage to the side with a red door – 'that's the river and that's the shop.'

Michael's heart softened with gratitude and guilt at his impatience. Peggy tested him to the limit, but like so many in Tarabeg, she had a heart of pure gold and it was probably true to say had never harboured a bad thought towards anyone in her life. She was a gossip, but a kind one, if there was such a thing.

'She will love them, Peggy,' he said as he put his hands into his pockets and sighed. 'You know she doesn't want to come here, don't you? She'll want to go straight back up to the farm to see Daedio. She spends more time up there than she does in the shop.'

'Oh, sure, that's just because she's so close to Nola, and God in heaven, Nola has been at that school more than she's here in Tarabeg.'

Michael knew this was true. St Catherine's opened its

doors on Saturdays for afternoon tea for parents between three and five o'clock. So Nola had made Seamus learn to drive Michael's car and take her out to see her granddaughter every week. Michael himself was always at his busiest on a Saturday, dealing with the fishermen; the daily routine of their family home was anchored to a business that opened at seven and closed when people stopped ringing the bell. Sister Magdalena, mother superior at St Catherine's, had tried to point out to Nola that she was not Mary Kate's mother, but she was met with a rehearsed and swift rebuttal. 'Sister, her mammy is dead. I am the closest she has to a woman with the same blood in her veins so I will be the one coming to see her, every week that God keeps me alive and able.'

Nola had taken the place of Rosie and it was unspoken that she ranked higher in Mary Kate's world. Rosie had been kindness itself, but the bond between Sarah and Mary Kate permeated every room in the house and every conversation, from the inane to the extraordinary. There wasn't anything Rosie could do to eradicate the ghost of Sarah.

'Morning, Peggy. Is Michael giving out to you like you've never managed the shop on your own before?' said Nola as she approached the two of them. 'Michael, give Peggy a break, she runs the place every single day without you on her back. Go and get your father from Paddy's. He'll be asking you to stop every five minutes for a piddle and making us late if he has any more to drink.

And look at Finnbar, would you, Peggy, what a good lad he is, in the car after going already and not a complaint out of him.'

Nola didn't acknowledge that the cleanliness and readiness of Finn was all down to Rosie and that if he'd been left to his own devices he'd be tearing around the road with the Devlin boys, or down at the bridge watching the water rush and roar, or pestering fishermen further along the river, taunting them with his ability to fish better than they could and daring them to let him have a go.

Michael heeded Nola's warning and hurried across to Paddy's bar, where through the window he could see Seamus sitting at the front counter together with Paddy himself.

Seamus and Paddy both looked up as Michael crossed the road. 'Oh, there ye are, we're off,' said Seamus, picking up the glass and downing the remaining drop of Powers whiskey in one.

''Tis a beautiful day for her to be coming home,' said Paddy.

'Aye, but to which home, Paddy, that's the question. I don't know where Mary Kate gets her stubbornness from, but she is bold, sure she is, and determined. I bet you a glass of the Powers she'll be wanting to come back to the farm with us to see Daedio. I near have to pay her in the holidays to go back down the hill to Michael and Rosie. 'Tis only the pull of Keeva and Finn and the boys that works in the end.'

'Well, she can't do that today,' said Paddy. 'We have the party ready for her. What time will you be back? Everyone's looking forward to it, and would you look at the sun, what a great night it will be. Now, Seamus, don't be telling her. It's a big surprise, remember.'

Seamus looked wounded. 'Well, I'm telling you, I would never let her know about a surprise. Pete is bringing Daedio down at about four, all ready to meet her. Bridget McAndrew is up there with him now. The old bugger, he's the worst.'

Paddy wiped down the bar. 'He's the best,' he said with a grin. 'A creaking gate, he is. I've never known a man as well for his age. Bridget says he's got a lot of life left in him yet.'

The door opened and Michael strode in. 'We are all ready, Da,' he said.

'Quick, here, Michael, take this to fortify you for the journey.' Paddy poured out a glass of whiskey.

Glancing over his shoulder to check that neither his mother nor Rosie was watching, Michael drank it in one. 'That was good,' he said with a grin and a wink to Paddy. 'After half an hour with Peggy, I needed that.'

'Oh, don't you be worrying about Peggy. Tig is back soon and we'll keep an eye on the shop. Away with you now and bring that little colleen back home to where she belongs.'

'Aye, wherever that may be.' Seamus stood and took his cap from the stand. As they left the bar, he gave his son a warm and fatherly pat on the back. The bell above the door jangled as it closed.

'Right, Da, let's go and collect the member of the family who is as stubborn as the donkey.'

Seamus laughed. 'Well, she is seventeen now, she's just finding her feet, but I'm thinking she'll be a woman soon enough – and doesn't she have a woman's ways. If she's anything like her Granny Nola, you won't be able to keep up with her.'

As the car turned out of Tarabeg and onto the Galway road, Rosie dipped her head and glanced up at the bright blue July sky. No one had spoken a word since they'd loaded up and pulled away. She was in the back seat with Finn at her side and Nola on the other end. Seamus was in the front next to Michael. He appeared to be studying the passing hedgerows intently.

Rosie stole a glance at her husband in the rear-view mirror. His chin was set firm and he was concentrating on the road ahead. She sighed as her hand slipped to her side, found that of her stepson, Finn, and felt the warm and welcome embrace of his sticky fingers. She squeezed them lightly and turned to smile at him. He would never allow her to hold his hand in full sight of his father or any man.

'I hope those flowers don't die from the heat in the boot of the car,' Nola said testily. 'Mary Kate gave me very clear instructions as to what she wanted me to buy.'

The words hung in the air and no one replied.

Rosie thought back to the previous evening, when Nola

had come to the house from the post office, having just taken another call from Mary Kate. 'Is there tea in that pot, Rosie?' she'd asked.

Rosie was heaping fried potatoes and bacon onto a plate for Finn, who had not long arrived home from playing out, was starving hungry and was ignoring the conversation taking place around him, his eyes fixed on the frying pan.

'What did Mary Kate have to say?' said Michael as he stole a fried potato from the plate and popped it into his mouth. Grinning, he rubbed his son's hair and turned his attention back to his mother.

'Tell him,' said Seamus, who took a cup of sweet tea from Rosie.

'Seamus, since when have you told me when to speak and what to say?' Nola glared at her husband, who appeared to shrink before Rosie's eyes. 'Oh, well, she was just saying she had a notion to travel, that's all.'

Michael's response was the closest thing to a roar Rosie had ever heard. As he gesticulated, only Rosie knew that the white stains on the backs of his hands were from the limewash he'd been using to brighten up Mary Kate's walls. She herself had sat each night hemming and sewing a new bedspread and matching curtains.

She was brought back into the moment by Nola's voice. 'Michael, will the flowers survive until we get there in this heat? I don't want to be letting her down.'

Michael appeared to have also been thinking about the

previous night's call. ''Tis a hot day, Mammy. I'm going to take Mary Kate to Dublin with me next week. I thought if she wants to travel, I'll take her with me and teach her how to do the buying for the shop.'

'Can I come, Da?' Finn lurched forwards on his seat and put his face in the gap between his father and Seamus.

'You can when you're older. Not yet though.'

Finn sank back again. 'Mary Kate gets everything.'

Rosie picked up his hand and smiled at him. He flopped to the side and, dejected, laid his head on her shoulder.

'I think that's a grand idea, Michael,' said Nola. 'Mary Kate will love that. It will make her feel just the lady too, choosing stock for the shop. Mind, don't let her be too much like her mammy – whenever you took Sarah to Dublin, she always came back with a new dress.' She turned to look out of the window and began to chuckle at her private memory of Sarah.

Finn squeezed Rosie's fingers and looked up at her, understanding, his eyes full of sympathy. She kissed the top of his head and gazed out at the distant hills. Her opinion was not required. It occurred to her that the only person other than Keeva who'd spoken to her in the past hour was Finn. She was a poor second to Sarah. The ghost of Michael's first wife haunted her and that was unlikely to change now that Sarah's double, in looks as well as temperament, her daughter Mary Kate, was coming home.

*

Bridget McAndrew washed up her and Daedio's pots in the sink. Nola and Seamus wouldn't be back until the evening and she had promised to sit with Daedio for part of the day. His bed was adjacent to the fire, and if pushed, she could have spent the day sat in the rocking chair, talking over old times with Daedio. It had been arranged that when Bridget left, Teresa Gallagher would come up from the presbytery to take over.

'Have a sleep now until Teresa gets here,' Bridget said.

Daedio had been quiet, almost withdrawn. Bridget had tried to contact Annie for him, his long-dead wife, but, unusually, she'd failed. As she turned from the sink, he was staring at her back, a look of deep concern on his face. Picking up her hat, she removed the long pin and placed it on her head, sliding the pin back through the tight bun of grey hair. 'Don't be worrying about Annie, we'll have better luck next time. Maybe it's me, Daedio. Maybe as I am getting older, the sight is leaving me, although they say it should get stronger.'

Daedio shook his head. 'It's not that, Bridget. Don't go yet. Pour us a drink of something strong and come and sit here before that woman with a face more pinched than Mrs Doyle's skinny arse gets here. I've something to show you.'

'What have you got to show me you couldn't let me see an hour ago when I got here?'

Daedio slid an airmail letter out from under the blanket on his bed and held it out for her to see. 'Get the drinks,' he said. 'We're going to need them.'

Chapter 3

The convent bells pealed on the hour, an insistent ringing down of the seconds as Roshine thundered up the flight of wooden stairs to the dormitory she'd slept in for the past nine years. 'Mary Kate, Mary Kate, where are you?' She almost flew around the corner, grabbing onto the doorframe to steady herself as she stopped dead in her tracks.

Mary Kate was standing in front of the looking glass on the wall by the bathroom door, fixing her shining gold plaits into place with a sky-blue ribbon.

'What in God's name are you doing up here? People are already arriving and Mother Superior said we cannot be late.' Roshine lived in fear of everyone and everything; she was the absolute opposite to Mary Kate, which was why they had been good friends since the day they'd arrived. Roshine lived in awe of Mary Kate's nerve, and Mary Kate's audacity was tempered by Roshine's cautious and often sensible words of warning.

'Holy Mother, you think I'm going to be late today of all days?' Mary Kate laughed as she pulled both ends of the ribbon tight. 'You don't have to be worrying about me no more, Roshine.' She let her plaits drop and turned to face her friend. Her eyes shone with barely contained excitement and her full smile lit up the room. 'Daddy says I have hair like Rita Hayworth and I've seen a picture in a magazine in Mrs Doyle's – won't it be just the thing when I can style my hair like her and not have to tie it in plaits every single flamin' day?'

Roshine looked shocked. 'Shush now, if they hear your blaspheming, they'll say we aren't fit to be leaving. Here…' She grabbed a piece of paper out of her skirt pocket. 'Here, before I forget, this is the number of my da's surgery. You can call and get a message to me anytime you want. When am I going to see you again?'

Mary Kate studied the piece of paper. There was no phone at home. 'Sure, why do we need a phone here when Mrs Doyle has one in the post office?' her da always said when she asked could they have one. 'The only person we would be telephoning would be Mrs Doyle. Who else do we know who has one?' Keen as she was to embrace modernity, Mary Kate had seen his point: no home in Tarabeg had a telephone. Phoning Roshine would mean that anyone who was in the post office when she made the call would hear every word she said and so she knew she would not be calling Roshine from Mrs Doyle's. What Mary Kate had to tell her could not be heard by others.

'My da comes to Galway to buy stock for the shop once a month – I'll get him to give me a seat in the van and I'll call to let you know when I'm coming. That's if he's still speaking to me when he knows I want to go and live with my Aunty Bee and Captain Bob in Liverpool.'

'Does your Aunty Bee know you want to do that?' asked Roshine. 'You and your notions... Your da will go mad when he finds out – he won't allow it, you know that, don't you? I thought you'd told your Granny Nola that you wanted to live up on the farm?'

Mary Kate smoothed down the front of her skirt and checked herself in the mirror. 'No, Bee doesn't know. I haven't told her yet, because if I do, she will write to Daddy and Rosie to ask their permission and then they will find a million reasons why I can't go. I'd rather be on the farm than in the house, but, Roshine, I'm seventeen now, I'm a grown-up and I've been at boarding school all these years. I am not going back to be cooped up in Tarabeg, not yet anyway. I want to see the world and do things and make me own money. If Aunty Bee was in America, I'd be off there, but if I told Daddy that, I think he'd die of a heart attack right there and then.'

Roshine grinned. 'Liverpool is a wild place – are you sure it isn't the fellas you're after, Mary Kate?'

Mary Kate laughed and poked Roshine in the side. 'No, it is not. I'm not a madwoman. I'm not going to be tying meself down like Aunty Keeva with a football team of boys running around. I want to... you know... do something real and see places. There has to be more to life than Tarabeg and if it was so great, wouldn't everyone who leaves be running back? I swear to God, not one of them does.' Mary Kate looked down to her feet and an expression Roshine had become used to crossed her face. ''Tis Mammy… she's not there at the house, and Aunty Bee, she is a part of Mammy, we both are, she's Mammy's blood too, like me, and I want to go and stay with her. Even Granny Nola said 'tis wicked that Daddy and Rosie won't let me go and see her even for a visit. I've not set eyes on her or Ciaran and Captain Bob since the day she left Tarabeg.'

Roshine gave Mary Kate's hand a squeeze. No further words were needed. Over the years, Mary Kate had opened up and confided in Roshine about the death of her mother and how her father had then gone on to marry the woman who'd been her own schoolteacher.

Mary Kate turned and ran to the window, grabbing the sill to stop herself from hurtling into it. Roshine raced after her, her footsteps echoing on the wooden floorboards.

'Will you take me with you, to Liverpool?' Roshine's eyes were full of hope. The girls' nine years together at St Catherine's had been happy ones, made all the more so by their solid friendship.

'I will. As soon as I get to Aunty Bee's, I will call your daddy's surgery and let you know. All you'll have to do then is get yourself over to Liverpool. Aunty Bee will love you.'

A car rolled into the driveway, closely followed by a

van, the different vehicles reflecting the differing means and livelihoods of the parents collecting their girls for the final time.

'Promise me you will come for a visit at least?' Mary Kate said.

'Look, there's my mammy and daddy.' Roshine pointed at one of the cars, and she and Mary Kate almost jumped up and down on the spot.

'Come on! The time has come – those cars are here to spring us free. Two more hours and we are out of here.'

At the door, the girls both turned and for the last time glanced over the dormitory where they had laughed, cried and shared their hopes and dreams for the future. The iron bedsteads had been stripped of their pink candlewick counterpanes, and the row of sinks against the far wall were already pristine, clear of their wooden toothbrushes, pots of talcum powder, hairbrushes and ribbons, ready and waiting for September and the new girls who would take their place.

'Come on, let's go,' said Mary Kate, breaking the melancholy, and without further hesitation they galloped down the stairs hand in hand, the ringing peal of the bells and the sound of car tyres on gravel more inviting.

'And, finally, you will leave this school as young ladies of education and impeccable manners, you will demonstrate thrift and the ability to manage whatever circumstances life may place before you. I send you out into the world as ambassadors of St Catherine's, and, remember, in all your deeds and actions we shall also be judged.'

Sister Magdalena folded her speech notes and gazed down at the solemn upturned faces of the latest group of girls to depart her care, the leavers of 1963. They were seated cross-legged on the wooden floor, which had been specially polished for the occasion, its mirror-like shine testament to strong-smelling lavender wax, elbow grease and the tears of many a housemaid's knee.

It was speech day and summer and expectation fizzed like static in the air. The freedom of adult life was creeping closer by the minute and even though they were sitting on the floor, the girls were giddy at the prospect of what lay before them, just beyond the boundary walls of the school.

On hard wooden chairs and gym benches arranged down the sides of the hall sat the lay teachers and nuns who had taught and cared for the girls during their time at St Catherine's, penning their pupils in for one last time, on guard against any premature bids for freedom. The school turned out young ladies with the skills to run a home, manage household accounts and cook an array of fine meals made up of things other than rashers and potatoes. Through the years, it also identified its most pious pupils, who would today be transferred to the convent situated directly adjacent to the school in preparation for a life of religious devotion. Mary Kate looked around at the faces whose future that was and her heart melted with pity for them.

The parents sat at the rear of the hall on wooden chairs brought in from the dining room. In the dining room itself, just down the wood-panelled corridor, the long refectory tables had been covered with the white damask cloths kept for religious holidays and speech day. Plates of sandwiches, brack and trifle, prepared by the girls and the kitchen maids, stood ready and waiting for when Sister Magdalena sounded the final retreat.

The hall was now silent as Sister Magdalena folded her glasses and laid them on top of her notes on the green-baize table. The moment of quiet she had left for her words to be absorbed by her young ladies was filled only by the inevitable rumbling of stomachs and shuffling of feet. The sun fell in through the high arched windows and the room was crisscrossed with pillars of light and swirling eddies of fine dust that settled on the tightly plaited and beribboned heads. The girls were poised ready to rise and flee, itching to be on their way, and this protracted farewell in the form of speech day was agonising. There was not one more lesson to take, and the trunks were already piled up in the gravel driveway – out in the open, this year, thanks to the fine weather – ready to be loaded up and driven away.

Most of the mothers present had themselves been through this rite of passage. They knew their position as parents to the young ladies before them gave them no authority here. They were powerless in the presence of Sister Magdalena, headmistress of the school and mother superior of the convent. In the eyes of God, she was the mother of all who were gathered there, young and old. Her shrunken form, bowed from years of work, did not diminish her authority. Those mothers had once sat cross-legged on that same floor and they too feared the wandering eyes of Sister Magdalena landing upon them as she scanned her congregation, feared it as much as their daughters did, sitting like angels, perfectly still, hands crossed in laps, blancoed shoes leaving white smears on the polished floor. Lips were licked, a baby cried, a less patient mother politely coughed.

'Can we go now? My arse is as stiff as a dead donkey's langer on this chair.' A man's hoarse whisper flew over the heads of the girls and reached Sister Magdalena's ears.

A wave of suppressed giggling washed through the hall, Sister Magdalena frowned, and Mary Kate swallowed hard. That voice had belonged to her Grandfather Seamus, she was sure of it. She closed her eyes.

'What? What did you say?' The voice rang out again.

It was definitely Grandpa Seamus. He'd become hard of hearing over the past few years and had taken to talking far too loud. Mary Kate knew without turning round that even though Granny Nola would be equally embarrassed, she'd also be fighting hard to contain her mirth.

Mary Kate's head of red hair lifted sharply and her unblinking blue eyes met Sister Magdalena's gaze. Mary

Kate… Possibly the keenest of all her girls to rise and run, Sister Magdalena thought. It would be you. The edges of Mary Kate's mouth rose in an almost imperceptible smile of defiance and Sister Magdalena felt the familiar rush of blood to her face. Of all the girls that had passed through her school during her fifty years on the staff there, no other had driven her to the depths of anger or heights of admiration in quite the way Mary Kate had. She looked down at the open gaze, at the only girl whose hair was already staging its own rebellion, escaping from its plaits and springing up around her cheeks in soft curls, and a shiver ran through her veins. For fear was a stranger to Mary Kate, and if there was one thing Sister Magdalena knew after all this time it was that fear, and fear alone, kept her girls safe. Fear of the Lord, of sin, of purgatory, of superiors. Before her sat nineteen fearful young women, and one other, who would, hands on hips and without a second thought, always face fear down. She was so different from most of the girls she'd taught, but then so were the circumstances that had brought her there.

The only reason Mary Kate had been accepted into the school was because Father Jerry and the magistrate Brendan O'Kelly had insisted on it. And how could Sister Magdalena refuse; what was she there for, if not to nurture children like Mary Kate? The child's story was written in sin: her mother dead, her grandmother murdered and her father about to be remarried. Sister Magdalena made no comment on the latter – wasn't it just the best kept secret anyway. Every widowered man had to marry, for a man could not live without sex; and every widowed woman had to marry, for a woman could not live without money. 'And who will be paying her fees?' had been the first question she'd asked them.

'There will be no problem there, the father only has the fastest-growing store in all of Ireland. The money runs in laughing through the door of his shop all by itself, so it does,' Brendan O'Kelly had exclaimed, a hint of envy in his voice.

'Well, if that's the case, why bring her all the way to Galway? Why not pay for someone closer to home to teach her? We are a charitable school, bursting at the seams. Is there no National school in Tarabeg? I've been told there are still hedge schools operating in the barns on the bogs and hills and around the west coast, with good Catholic teachers from Dublin thirsty to educate and elevate the people from lives of poverty. A man with good money would be well placed to help his own village and pay for a teacher, would he not? Would ye like some tea and brack?'

Sister Magdalena had given the men a smile and they had both softened in its glow. She'd been sixty-five at the time and still able to make advantageous use of her twinkling blue eyes, her diminutive stature and her love for the Lord, which shone through her every pore.

Father Jerry looked to Brendan, who was fiddling with the hat he'd removed as they'd stepped into the visitors' room, rotating it round and round in his hands. They had failed to plan a strategy or decide who would say what, or rather what wouldn't they say. There was a lot in Tarabeg to hide, and now that they were there, standing before the honest and probing gaze of Sister Magdalena, one thing was clear to Father Jerry: plan or not, they would have to tell her everything.

'Ah now, the hedge schools are long gone, Sister, even on the bogs.' Father Jerry smiled. He was on safe ground here, this he knew. Sister Magdalena had been at the convent since before the turn of the century. She was talking about the teachers who used to travel out from Dublin to educate children in barns or, if they were lucky, in a deserted cottage; teachers who were keen to try and provide the youngsters of poor west-coast families with the skills to better their lives. But these days those who could aimed to better their lives by escaping the seemingly perpetual rain and emigrating to Liverpool or America at the first opportunity.

Sister Magdalena held out a pretty china cup balanced on a delicate saucer to Brendan. The grey wisps of steam obscured his spectacles as he took a grateful sip of the strong, sweet tea.

'Sister, Mary Kate, she comes from the most devoted of families,' Father Jerry began, 'but her mother died in childbirth a year ago, and now the father, he is to marry the woman who has been helping him since the death of Sarah.'

'She was the mother,' interjected Brendan helpfully as

he placed his cup down on his saucer with a clatter. He had drained the tea in two gulps.

Father Jerry took the opportunity of Brendan speaking to fill his mouth with the buttered brack. It was still warm and he wondered would he dare tell his housekeeper, Teresa, how good it had been when he returned to the presbytery in Tarabeg? He often flirted with such a notion, knowing all the while that he would never dare. If Teresa asked him had there been cake and how was it, he would reply as always, 'Ah, 'twas a little on the dry side,' or, 'I was thinking they would benefit from a lesson from yourself now.' Today would be no different.

'You see, here's the thing, Sister. The woman who has been helping the father, Michael Malone, she is also the teacher at the village school.'

Sister shot a look at Father Jerry, awaiting his own explanation. Already she could tell something was not quite right. 'Really? A teacher's job is to teach, not to nursemaid an orphan. How did that happen?'

As Father Jerry pointedly sat forward in his chair and eyed the teapot for several hopeful seconds, it occurred to him that he wasn't really sure. How had it happened? How had quiet Rosie O'Hara become installed in the Malone home so soon after Sarah had died? He knew, they all knew, that Rosie O'Hara had been in love with Michael Malone before he'd left to fight in the war. It was not something she'd ever spoken of, to anyone, but nothing escaped Father Jerry's housekeeper, Teresa, who had after all been Rosie's only friend in those early days. But that had all changed when Michael had returned from the war and within almost hours, to the surprise of everyone, had married Sarah McGuffey.

'She was a good friend and help to the mother who died,' said Brendan.

Father Jerry sighed with relief. Brendan had put it so much better than he would have. A man who took confession was inclined to confess himself and let everything spill out, but that would not be right, not here. Not to a mother superior who had spent her life shielded from evil. How could he tell her of the problems they had experienced in Tarabeg? Problems that had led them to bring the case for Mary Kate to Sister Magdalena's door. That in their own school in Tarabeg, the principal – a man appointed by Father Jerry himself, a man they had all admired, a man they had drunk with in Paddy's bar, fished with, played football with – had all the time been practising his own form of evil on the boys they had entrusted to his care. And who was it who had helped Father Jerry to deal with all of that – hadn't it just been Rosie O'Hara herself?

'More tea, Father?'

Father Jerry relinquished his cup and saucer, which in his huge hands looked like they belonged to a child's china tea set. 'Now that the father is to remarry, it has brought its own problems. It was felt by all that it would be better altogether for the child if she was to continue her education here, in a good school, away from the village.'

Sister Magdalena knew she was lost. How could she refuse? But she still felt that information was being withheld. 'What of the other members of the family?' she asked. 'Is there no one else to step in and help?'

Brendan coughed and looked to Father Jerry as he spoke. 'There is a great-aunt. She left for Liverpool, months ago now. 'Tis a fact that the girl was close to her and, well, there are worries that since the great-aunt left, Mary Kate is finding it hard and 'tis almost as though she's suffered a second loss. The father is worried that she may want to follow, and as she is so unhappy, he may find it hard to refuse her, but... there are reasons why that would be impossible.'

Brendan made no mention of Captain Bob, the man Bee had moved away with and whom everyone knew had a wife of his own back in Ballycroy. He left it to Sister Magdalena to assume what everyone else did, that a childhood in a city of sin like Liverpool was to be avoided at all costs.

Sister Magdalena had placed her own china cup onto the silver tray on the low polished mahogany table. They were Sisters of the Poor in name only. 'Very well, gentlemen. Term begins in two weeks and the fees are fifteen shillings a term, paid in advance. A better education for that she will not receive anywhere else.' She rose to pull the cord at the side of the fireplace for one of the maids to collect the tray and missed the sighs of relief that came from both men.

And now, nine years later, Sister Magdalena looked down into the eyes of the seventeen-year-old Mary Kate and wondered what life had in store for her. She spotted her father with his wife, Rosie, and her brother at the back, along with her beloved grandparents who had never missed a Saturday afternoon visit. Sister Magdalena and Mary Kate had fought their battles over the years, but she did something now that she had never done before during a solemn service: she smiled down on Mary Kate, who immediately smiled back up. It had always been clear to her that if Mary Kate chose to take the veil, she would one day become a headmistress or mother superior herself, but she was sure that would never happen. Sister Magdalena recognised in Mary Kate the qualities of endeavour that others had once recognised in herself, but a convent and the confines of a school was somewhere Mary Kate was heading from, not to.

'Let us pray. Up onto your feet, girls,' said Sister Magdalena as the shuffling rumble and scraping of feet became louder and more impatient.

'Are you going to do it now?' hissed Roshine.

'Mary Kate,' a voice whispered above the clatter from the side of the hall. One of the lay teachers held out the bouquet of flowers that Granny Nola had transported to the school.

Mary Kate took the flowers, walked to the front of the hall with her head held high and a smile on her face, mounted the steps to the stage and placed them on the table in front of Sister Magdalena. 'Thank you, Mother, from all of us. We will try our best to make you proud.'

Sister Magdalena turned to the hall with astonishment etched on her face as the parents and children began to clap in appreciation.

It was only later, as the Malone car was heading towards Tarabeg and the kitchen maids were clearing away the detritus from the afternoon tea, that a novice nun told Sister Magdalena that the flowers had been Mary Kate's idea. The presentation had been arranged following a discreet telephone call to her village post office and all the girls had agreed that, despite Mary Kate's insistence that one of the girls taking the veil should present them, Mary Kate had to be the one to do it.

'Well, I never,' Sister Magdalena spluttered. 'After fifty years, I am taken by surprise.'

'She will spend her life surprising people, that one,' the young novice replied. 'Don't you think, Mother?'

As Sister Magdalena buried her nose in the heady scent of the rich blooms, she wiped away a tear. Of all the girls she had ever taught, that one she would miss.

Chapter 4

Liverpool

'I'm finished at two – we could take a walk up into town and make a start on that list of yours,' Captain Bob said to Bee at 6 a.m. as he tucked into his breakfast. It was the same breakfast he'd had every working day since they'd moved to Liverpool from Tarabeg. Porridge made with water, and a fat rasher, cut with the blade set to number three and sandwiched between a slice of white bread, all swallowed down with two large mugs of strong, sweet tea. Bee always sat with him and watched as he ate every morsel. It gave her as much pleasure to observe him eating in the mornings as their lovemaking did at night, and besides, given that she couldn't work because she had no marriage lines, what else did she have to do?

'I don't know of a man in Liverpool who offers to go shopping without being forced into it. You are a one-off, Captain Bob.' She smiled over the brim of her cup and her

53

eyes met his, which were as blue and twinkly as the day they'd met.

They were both aware that the words 'with his wife' had been missing from her comment. 'A man in Liverpool who offers to go shopping *with his wife*' is what she should have said, what she wanted to say.

'Well, if my little Bee needs a new coat, who am I to argue?' He tilted his head of curly white hair to smile at her.

Bee sat up straight in her chair, pulled the breadboard and knife towards her, laid the flat of her hand on top of the loaf to check it had cooled enough to be cut, and lifted the knife. 'It's not so much that I want one,' she said as she looked up at him, the knife mid air. 'I'm quite happy with my old one, I can tell you – it's just that, well, the fashions in Liverpool are changing so fast and every time I walk down to the river in my long coat I feel like an old Irishwoman. I don't like to stand out so much. Have you seen how some of the girls are wearing their hems up above their knees now! I'm never going to be doing that, but nor am I going to be looking like a cast-off from before the war.'

Bob took the slice of bread Bee held out to him, placed the bacon inside, folded it over and wiped the hot fat from the plate in front of him. He held his sandwich, ready to pounce on it, and realised he had no idea what to say in reply. This recent discontent of Bee's was a new phenomenon and he was sure it had something to do with her son, Ciaran, having left home to join the merchant navy.

Bee had made no attempt to discourage Ciaran, aware that if she tried too hard, he would sneak off like many local boys did. When a ship was in and taking on, young men would slip down to the docks in the middle of the night and sail on the first tide, without their mother's blessing. Bee could not deny that the sea was in Ciaran's blood: he was the son of a fisherman sent to an early watery grave off the coast of Mayo, and now he was influenced by the man who had taken his father's place, sea-captain Bob. 'How could he have chosen any other way?' she had asked herself so many times.

'Are you expecting a letter today?' asked Captain Bob before he sank his teeth into the soft white bread.

Bee received many letters and they were the highlight of her day, the bridges that took her back home. From Keeva in Tarabeg, from the exotic ports where Ciaran docked, from her dead husband's parents out on the coast, and – her favourites – from her great-niece, Mary Kate.

'Well, I haven't heard a thing from Mary Kate for over two weeks. I think she's forgotten about me altogether.'

'Isn't she finishing school any day now? She's probably busy packing up and moving back home.'

'Yes, but home to where, though?' said Bee. 'She's never been keen on staying in the shop since Michael married Rosie.'

Bob picked up his tea and blew the steam away. 'If you're asking me, my guess is she will go straight up to the farm, to Nola and Seamus. She has a fondness for Finn, but he sounds so close to Rosie, it must seem to Mary Kate as though they have two different mothers.'

Bee glanced over to the window as the first pair of boots heading down to the Dockers' Steps stomped past. 'Well, there isn't a lot I can do. Not one of them will let her live here with us, not given our situation. We can fool all of Liverpool, we're good at that, but we can't fool those left at home. They know the truth and they turned us down once. I can't even ask.'

Captain Bob put down his tea and sighed. He saw the sadness that flitted across her eyes. Mary Kate was the closest member of her own family Bee had left. This was the point at which he always became lost for words. He and Bee and Ciaran had fled Ireland, fled his wife and demanding daughters in Ballycroy, and sought the anonymity of Liverpool, a city that allowed them to live together. They were lovers in need of dark shadows in which to hide. He had never regretted leaving the wife who had never wanted him or cared for him. A wife who made him feel as though he was a stranger every time he walked into his own home. A wife who laughed at him, scolded him and taunted him with her frequent hints at how she occupied her time while he was away at sea, who spent more time in the bar, leaving the running of their home to his daughters. His daughters were equally vindictive, all except for Nell, who had been afflicted since birth and the only one he missed and made his heart ache with the guilt of it all.

In the past, he and Bee had been happy to meet one or two nights a week in secret at her Tarabeg cottage, but everything changed the night her sister Angela was murdered by her husband. Bee changed. She needed him, whereas before she had only wanted him. Since arriving in Liverpool, they had masqueraded as man and wife, Bee wearing the wedding band she had never removed since the day her late husband Rory had slipped it onto her finger. Bob had travelled ahead and secured the house, using his own marriage lines as proof of respectable status. He paid a month's rent in advance and returned to Tarabeg for Bee and Ciaran.

Their home was on the dock streets, where the rent was cheaper, because Bob still sent an envelope of money to his wife and now grown children every Friday. Even so, because Captain Bob was a river pilot, they still had far more than any of the dockers' families on their streets, some of whom were Irish immigrants like themselves and had a brood of children to feed.

As Bee helped Bob into his thick black jacket with its oilskin covered shoulders and upper back, he bent and kissed her full on the lips, as he always did. 'When we finish shopping, we'll have a little drink in town, shall we?'

Bee smiled up at him. 'We shall, if that will make you happy.'

Their eyes locked for a long moment. The one thing that would make them truly happy could never be theirs. They would never know married love. She could never call him 'husband', nor could he proudly call her 'my wife'.

'One day,' he whispered and pulled her into him. She hadn't needed to say anything: he saw the sadness in her eyes, was painfully aware that she would never be fully happy until she could hook her arm through his and know they were together in the eyes of God, sin-free and proud.

'Aye, well, you can't go promising something you can't deliver,' she said as she pulled away. 'We may both be dead before she is and she will be the only one of us who gets a place in heaven.'

Captain Bob had no answer to that; it was as true as the day was long. 'We will have that drink after we buy you the nicest coat in Liverpool,' he said to cheer her up as he patted her on the backside before slipping out of the back door.

Moments later, while Bee was standing at the sink clearing away the dishes, her neighbour, Cat, walked in through the back door. Cat hadn't knocked – no one ever did on the dock streets. They both knew it was no coincidence that she'd arrived within seconds of Captain Bob leaving; she would have been standing in her cold kitchen, waiting to hear the click of the back-door latch and the thump of the captain's boots as he made his way down the entry.

Cat was a widow and therefore a woman whom Bee understood, but without being able to let her know why. Having her as a neighbour had been a blessing. When she'd first arrived in Liverpool, Bee had had no idea how to work a gas cooker, having always cooked over an open fire, and was ignorant of city ways, which were so different from how things were done in villages on the west coast. Cat, a native Scouser, had been a willing helper, and from those initial acts of kindness had benefitted greatly from Bee's generosity, and her burning guilt. Women with more inquisitive natures than Cat's, women who asked too many questions – like Linda, her neighbour on the other side – were a curse.

'He's gone then, has he?' said Cat as she closed the back door behind her. 'Is there a ship out at the bar?'

Bee hadn't turned around from the sink and carried on washing the still warm plate Bob had eaten his bacon from. 'He has and there is, Cat. Has Linda's Jimmy gone down to the docks yet?'

Cat sniffed and took a look around the kitchen. 'I don't think so. I feel sorry for Linda – he's such a lazy bastard. At least my old man never missed a day's work. If he had, he might still be here, God love him.' Cat's husband Ben had been killed outright by the hook of a crane swinging through the air and colliding with his skull. An all too frequent dockside fatality. 'You haven't emptied the tea leaves away, have you, Bee?'

Bee sighed. 'No, Cat, I haven't, of course not. I saved a cup for you and there is hot water in that kettle if you want to pour some on.'

'Oh, thank God for that. I'm parched, I am, and we ran out yesterday.'

Bee and Captain Bob had always been a mystery to Cat. Bob was a captain, a pilot, which gave him status, and yet he lived on the dock streets. 'I can smell a river rat a mile off,' Linda had said to Cat. 'I'll find out what's what in there.' But she never had and it drove her to distraction. Cat took everyone at face value, laughed off Linda's pre-occupation with the lives of others, and had never for one moment suspected that the wedding band on Bee's finger was not from Bob or that the two of them weren't married. Linda, though, knew something wasn't quite right and hadn't stopped sniffing since the day they'd moved in next door.

'How much did Captain Bob earn last week then?' asked Cat as she poured the scalding water onto the tea leaves. 'He was out every day, wasn't he? Never had a day off, did he? What I want to know is what is it you two are doing with the money. And with your Ciaran earning now too. Rolling in it, you two are.' She laughed, not aware that she was probing and making Bee uncomfortable.

No question was out of bounds on the dock streets and Bee knew the details of every woman's sex life. She ignored Cat, picked up a cloth and began to dry the dishes.

'I wouldn't mind, but you've not bought something new – ever,' said Cat. 'You're wearing the same bloody coat you got off the boat in, and him on a captain's wage! You don't drink, you don't smoke, you never go down the pub and you've never once set foot in the Irish Centre with the rest of the Irish around here. Don't you ever get sick of the sight of each other?'

Bee placed the plate on the press and sighed. She was used to this. Cat's twenty questions, raised every time she saw Bee, rarely altered. She was as nosey as the others, but she lacked Linda's edge, and a successful inquisitor she was not.

'Actually, Cat, Bob is taking me shopping for a new coat later today, as you mention it. I'm meeting him and we're taking a walk up to Bold Street, to one of the outfitters there.' She turned and smiled at the expression on Cat's face. It was a delight to see her eyes widen, her mouth drop and her brow furrow.

'Bold Street? Jesus. The only time I've ever been up there was when I was a kid, with me da, when he was selling chestnuts on a brazier in the winter. Used to have the spot on the bottom where it meets with Church Street. There was nothing I could afford in any of those shops then, and there wouldn't be anything for me now either. Look at the state of you, living here and shopping up there. I wouldn't even get taken on to work in one of the shops. I'm not la-di-da enough for them.'

Bee instantly felt guilty and sorry for Cat. Cat had helped her more than she had hindered her over the years and now she felt mean. 'I tell you what, Cat, I'm not baking today, but how about I bring you a slice of fruitcake back from Lyons,' she said with a smile.

Cat's face lit up. Bee knew fruitcake was her favourite.

'Would you? I can't afford it, mind. I can't give you any money for it. I don't get me widow's pension until Friday.'

'I'll buy it for you, Cat, as a present, but don't go giving any to Linda. If you feel inclined to give her anything at all, why don't you tell her to get Jimmy up a bit earlier and down to the front of the queue in the pen each morning. I heard Hattie's Jack going past my window at six on the dot this morning, before Bob had even left. He would have been there before the foreman opened the pen gate. I bet he's been taken on every day.'

Cat's face fell. 'I can't tell her that, Bee. The steaming lump is lying there now. Told Linda to bugger off when she tried to move him yesterday – he didn't go in then, either. He was in the Anchor last night and he keeps saying his back is bad. I feel sorry for Lin, I do.' Cat removed the stub of a cigarette from behind her ear. She didn't tell Bee that she'd picked it up off the entry floor before she'd turned into Bee's gate. The stub was still wet from the lips of Hattie's Jack.

Bee knew Cat had come round because her kitchen was the only place she would find a hot cup of tea that day; she loved her tea more than a rare slice of fruitcake. Bee was about to wipe the crumbs from her breadboard, but with a glance at Cat, she cut the loaf in half. 'Here, this bread is going to go stale. I still haven't got used to our Ciaran not being here and wanting half a loaf at night to mop up his gravy. Why don't you take it in for your kids for breakfast? Make a nice bit of toast with dripping. Here.' She placed an enamel pot of dripping on the board with the bread. 'Wrap it in your apron, go on, before the kids leave for school.'

Cat pushed the stub of the still unlit cigarette behind her ear. 'You are an angel, Bee, you really are. If anyone says to me that the Irish are dirty, they get an earful from me, they do. I was blessed, I was, the day you was sent to live next door to me.' She dropped the pot of dripping into her apron pocket, wrapped the rest of the loaf in her apron and was heading for the door in seconds. Cat was a gossip, but she was a mother first, and she wasn't about to choose a natter in Bee's kitchen over the chance to give her children some breakfast. 'Can I take me tea with me?' she said, looking longingly at the mug.

Bee smiled and topped up the tea from the pot. 'Here you go, Cat. Drop the dishes back later.'

'Oh, Bee, you'll go straight to heaven, you will,' and Cat shuffled down the yard in her threadbare slippers, making sure she didn't spill a drop.

It was as Bee was leaving for the Pier Head and closing the back gate behind her that she saw the post-office boy cycling down the entry. She was wondering why on earth she was buying a coat in July – she was so hot already. She missed her shawl, but none of the Irishwomen on the dock streets wore the outdoor uniform of home and she would never be seen in town without a coat, so boil she would.

There was something about the way the boy looked at her as he placed both his feet down on the stone flags to slow his bike. 'Got one for you, Mrs Tooley,' he shouted.

Bee wished he'd kept his voice down, wary of the net curtains on either side of the entry twitching in response. 'You'll wear out your shoe leather like that,' she said, holding out her hand for the envelope, concealing her irritation at his having announced her business to the street. 'What is it?' she asked, frowning. Her envelopes arrived handwritten, not like this, brown and typed.

'It's a telegram. Just came in. It's for Captain Tooley,' he replied as he handed it over. 'Here, you have to sign for it.' He pulled a book out of the basket on the front of his bike; hanging from its metal spine was a pencil on a string. With both legs astride his bike, he pushed up his cap, grinned and passed her the book. 'I won't get a biscuit for me troubles now that I've met you in the entry,' he said.

'You cheeky bugger,' said Bee. 'I'll give you one next time you bring the post.' Her voice tailed off as she turned the envelope over in her hands, looking for the postmark. There was none, just the word 'Telegram' typed along the top in a large, self-important typeface.

The boy hovered, his bike tipping from side to side as his feet didn't quite reach the ground.

'Go on, off with you,' said Bee. 'Have you no other letters to be delivering?'

His face fell and Bee knew why. He was waiting to find

out what was in the telegram, but she would not give him the satisfaction. Looking crestfallen, he gripped the handlebars and, using his feet, shuffled the bike round in the narrow entry to head back in the direction he'd come from. 'See you tomorrow, Mrs Tooley,' he shouted. 'I reckon you're due a letter from your Ciaran any day now.'

'God, you are worse than Mrs Doyle, or Linda, even,' Bee muttered, thinking of the postmistress back home in Tarabeg.

She stared at the envelope in her hand and, glancing towards her back gate, wondered should she step indoors before she read the contents. She opened all the post that came to the house, Bob's too. He had no interest in dealing with bills or the occasional brief letter from his wife demanding more money. Nell was the only one he wanted to know about. She was a loving girl, prone to fits of temper and bouts of strange behaviour, but, given a little encouragement, she always reverted to her loving self in time. Bob's wife knew of his affection for her and had not mentioned her since the day he left.

Bee scanned up and down the entry. No one had emerged through their back gate at the sound of the postboy's bell. From her bedroom window a few minutes earlier she'd seen that almost everyone was out the front, hair in pin-curlers held in place by headscarves tied around the back, ready to be unsprung just before they left for the bingo or the Irish Centre on Friday night. Every docker's wife went out on a Friday night, even if they had to beg, borrow or steal to get there. Cigarettes waved in the air as they chatted and watched the kids playing in the gutters. They sat on hard-backed chairs or leant against the stone windowsills, drinking tea from stained, chipped cups, complaining that it was too hot to do any housework. The lives they led could not have been more different from how Bee's had been as a young mother back in Ireland, but, luckily, having no children at home, Bee didn't need to try and fit in with them.

Cat was at the water pump at the end of the street round the front, pumping the handle up and down until the water splashed all over the naked toddlers who were running in and out of the flow, screaming and relishing the refreshing coldness. 'Come on, one at a time. I can't keep this going – me bleeding arms are aching.' Cat grinned and shouted as she squinted through the smoke from the damp and rapidly extinguishing cigarette dangling from her bottom lip. She was thirty and would very soon look fifty. Bee wondered why, if life in Liverpool was supposed to be so good for the Irish immigrant, these people were so poor and the women always so exhausted.

She could hear the distant screeches of the splashing children and, feeling alone and safe, she tucked her finger under the flap of the envelope, eased it open and pulled out the slip of yellow paper. As she read the contents, she gasped. Her hand flew to her mouth and tears rushed to her eyes.

Bernice Tooley dead – 17 July – Galway Hospital – Contact family immediately.

She read the words half a dozen times before they began to sink in. Captain Bob's wife was dead. Could this be a mistake? No, how could it be.

The consequences of this news made her hands tremble and her knees go weak. They could marry! And, more than that, much more, they could go back home, to Tarabeg. To her own cottage, as man and wife. She would be able to open her eyes in the morning and hear the sound of the ocean, not the dockers' klaxon. Captain Bob, an experienced seaman, could get work anywhere on the coast. Bee gasped. Only upon realising she could return home did she truly recognise how unhappy she'd been in Liverpool for all these long and lonely years, in exile from her family, from the graves of her sister and niece, from everyone and everything she knew.

She heard Cat's back door slam.

'Bee, is that you? Are you there? The postboy just came down the end of the road and he said he had a telegram for you. I'm just in the front, soaking the kids. You should see them! What was it? Not bad news, I hope. Give it here so I can 'ave a read.'

By the time Cat had opened her back gate and stepped into the entry, Bee was gone.

Chapter 5

The journey home from St Catherine's to Tarabeg was cramped and not uneventful.

'I wanted that parquet floor to swallow me when you opened your big mouth. Did you see the look on the nuns' faces? I swear to God that novice had tears in her eyes, so she did. I thought she was about to explode with the laughter. Oh, but the shame. I wouldn't want to be the one responsible for keeping the shine on that floor, would you, Rosie? Seamus Malone, it is now official, you are more like Daedio every day. Would you like a bit of chocolate, Mary Kate? Here, I have some in me bag.'

'No chocolate in this car, Mammy,' Michael roared from the front seat.

'I notice I wasn't offered any,' said Seamus, still smarting from being told off for having spoken out during the graduation speech.

'Oh, stop your sulking, you big baby,' said Nola. 'I can take you nowhere, so I can't.'

They were all laughing at his indignation until he blurted out, 'Well, you can take me to the party tonight. I'm not going anywhere else until this young colleen has been welcomed back into the village.'

Mary Kate had Finn on her knee and he was almost entirely blocking her view through the window. 'What party?' she said, trying but failing to sit forwards under the weight of her brother.

Nola reached over and with half of her usual force bashed Seamus over the head with her handbag. 'God in heaven, you've done it now. What in God's name is wrong with you? Will you shut your big mouth! Michael, would you tell him? Was there ever a more stupid man that lived in Tarabeg?'

But Michael was too busy dodging the flying handbag and trying to see the road through his tears of laughter to answer his mother's many questions and retorts.

Seamus glanced sideways at Michael and rolled his eyes, too afraid to laugh himself.

'Mammy, give Daddy a break – the man only asked you a question during the speeches back there. I'm stopping for a pull on my pipe.' Michael turned the wheel of the car onto the road to Tarabeg and across the magical musical bridge at Bellacorick. The river sparkled in the sunlight and they would follow its glittering path all the way home.

Michael was a happy man. His daughter was coming home. Nine full years had gone by and for the first time it felt as though the ghosts of the past could be laid to rest.

He looked up into the rear-view mirror and froze as the face of Sarah stared back at him. He blinked, he smiled, she was gone. A chill ran down his spine. Something was wrong, he was sure of it. That was twice in one day.

Nola leant forwards. 'Here you go, here's your pipe. I've had everything in my bag today, it'll be all the lighter now. And mind the ash doesn't fly back in through the window, I don't want it all over this hat.'

'Daddy, can we stop and play a tune on the bridge?' said Finn.

Mary Kate, feeling very grown-up, and afraid of sounding childlike, said nothing.

'Go on then,' said Michael.

'Oh good,' said Seamus. 'I'm desperate for a piss after all that tea. Aren't ye wanting one yerself, Nola?'

They all erupted into laughter again as Nola's handbag came down on Seamus's head once more. Even Nola laughed this time. 'You'll poison the fish,' she said, 'the amount of Guinness you put away last night.' And, turning to Mary Kate and Finn, 'Don't be vexing the faeries, now. That's the last thing we want today.'

Mary Kate and Finn picked up stones from the river's edge and, taking up positions at either side of the road, ran the stones along the top of the bridge. Both of them grinned as the bridge played out a tune. The faeries had blessed them: the bridge had sung to them. Nola tiptoed to the riverbank and, removing her hat, dipped her hands into the cool water, shook her fingers and then traced them across her brow. Seamus had disappeared out of view, down the side of the bridge.

Michael was sitting on the bonnet of the car enjoying his pipe, and Rosie was standing next to him. 'Don't you sit on the car,' he said, 'it'll burn your legs. The sun is mighty fierce.'

They both watched Finn and Mary Kate doing what they had always done on the musical bridge. In Michael's eyes, Mary Kate was a little girl of six all over again. She raced Finn along the road but dropped her stone and, according to the family's rules, had to pick it up and go back to the beginning. 'Drat and drat,' she shouted and bent over from laughing too much as Finn dashed ahead.

'We are going to have to make a decision soon,' said Rosie, breaking into Michael's thoughts. 'She has had a grand education, better than my own, and she won't want to be wasting it in Tarabeg.'

Michael tapped his pipe against the wall of the bridge, spilling the last of the smouldering tobacco onto the road, and ground the embers with the heel of his boot. 'Well, she's too young to be going off anywhere else,' he replied. 'I'll take her to Dublin with me, show her the ropes of running the business, or maybe she'll want to join you and Declan teaching at the school.'

Rosie placed her hand over her eyes to shield them from the sun as she watched Finn and Mary Kate but also to hide her thoughts from Michael. 'Aye, you could be right. I'm sure she would be happy with either of those,' she said, all the while thinking that they were about to face a crisis. Mary Kate was bursting with a hunger for life – accompanying her father on his buying trips to Dublin would not satisfy her, and nor would life in a village school, of that Rosie was certain.

When the car finally turned into Tarabeg, the first person Mary Kate saw outside the shop was Daedio, being pushed in his wicker wheelchair by Bridget McAndrew. Mary Kate had attended many a party in Tarabeg, the most notable being the end-of-harvest celebrations, which were thrown on the first full moon after harvest and always carried on through the night. She knew who would be there – it would be the same people she'd grown up with – but there had never been a party thrown in her honour before; this was a first. She beamed with pride as Keeva rushed across the main street from the bar and pulled open the car door.

'Welcome home! My God, would you look at the cut of you. Come on, I have to take you straight over to Paddy and Josie – she's cooking up your favourite pork belly for you, I hope you're starving. Michael, Seamus, Tig has your drinks poured. They phoned ahead from Ballymara to Mrs Doyle as you passed through to let us know you were on your way. Come on now, before Tig drinks them down himself and uses the excuse that he thought you weren't coming. Finnbar, go on, you too, your food and the boys are waiting for you.'

Finn dashed across the road, and Michael and Mary Kate walked over together.

'How was it?' said Keeva to Rosie and Nola, who were unloading their baskets and handbags from the boot as everyone else headed for the noise coming out of the Devlins'. They heard the roar of delight as the door opened and Mary Kate walked into the bar. The light was fading and the new electric lamps were already lit in the bar windows, throwing a yellow glow onto the street.

'It went well enough, if you didn't mind being humiliated by Seamus,' said Nola, folding her arms and trying her best to look indignant.

'Oh, come on, Nola, Josie has an answer for that, and 'tis called a glass of the Powers.' Keeva turned and smiled at Rosie as she took Nola by the arm and steered her across the road. 'Are you coming, Rosie?' she asked over her shoulder.

'Aye, I'll just unpack the bags, as Michael hasn't bothered,' she said, only slightly affronted. 'Is Peggy over there?'

'She is that. She's already dancing with Declan Feenan, I think.'

Rosie grinned as she walked around the back of the shop and into the house. She could hear the fiddler playing, the sound of glasses chinking and laughter floating all the way across the street and she wondered, if she didn't make her way over, if she just put the kettle on, made a nice cup of tea and took herself off to bed, would anyone actually notice?

The drinks flowed, as they always did, and the music

continued without a break, one fiddler or mouth organ taking over from the other as they danced into the early hours. The doors of the Devlins' were wedged open and the party had spilt out into the street. Mary Kate was taking a rest on a hay bale and Declan Feenan came and sat next to her. She had removed one of her shoes and was rubbing her stockinged foot.

Declan had arrived in the village just before Mary Kate left for St Catherine's, employed as the new teacher of the boys' class. Nine years later, everyone still referred to him as 'new'. 'Are you glad to be home, Mary Kate?' he asked as he handed her a drink.

'I am, in a way.'

He clinked pots with her. '"In a way"? And what is that supposed to mean? In what way would that be?'

While the village danced in the moonlight, Mary Kate unburdened her heart to Declan, her tongue loosened to a precarious degree by the porter Daedio had made her drink to mark her end of schooling. 'And so I need a lift to Galway, so that I can get the train to Dublin and then the boat to Liverpool to surprise Aunty Bee. It has to be done in secret, mind. Daddy and Rosie, they would never let me go.'

Declan was shocked. 'What, you would leave without telling Rosie and your daddy? Is that wise? You can't do that. Do you even have any money to be running away, because that's what you're doing, Mary Kate.'

'Sshh, Declan, someone will hear you. I do. Daedio gave

me twenty pounds for my seventeenth birthday, which is an absolute fortune, and when I get to Liverpool, I can earn more.'

Declan whistled. 'Where did he get that kind of money from?'

Mary Kate wasn't interested in that but answered anyway. 'He had a brother – Joe, I think – who went to America, God, a lifetime ago now. He was all into road- and bridge-building in New York and he set up a company or something. He made lots of money and before he died he sent some to Daedio.'

'Is that what bought this land and shop?' asked Declan.

'I suppose so.' Mary Kate had only just been born when the shop opened and didn't know anything of life before Malone's. Changing the subject quickly, she said, 'Declan, after the school here breaks up next week, will you please, please give me a seat in your car to Galway and not be telling anyone? Please, I'm begging you.'

'Are you mad, Mary Kate? I can't do that. Rosie is my school principal – I'd lose my job. And Father Jerry, I'd have to answer to him an' all.'

'Declan, you will answer to no one. If I don't tell anyone and you don't tell anyone, how would anyone but you and I know?'

Declan continued to object, in the strongest terms, but by the end of the party Mary Kate had floored him by threatening to make other arrangements. 'If you don't, I swear to God I'll find the gypsies and ask them for a lift.'

Declan froze. He knew that a local gypsy family had been banished from the village at around the time Sarah Malone had died. But he guessed that Mary Kate didn't know the details. He'd heard the stories about Angela's murder, Sarah's death and the curse on the Malones, all told in whispers. The stories sent shivers down the spines of the hardiest men, and the mad murderer, Mary Kate's maternal grandfather, was still out there somewhere. The gypsies were the last people she should be seeking help from.

He was between a rock and a hard place, and so, reluctantly, he agreed to hang around Tarabeg for a week after the village school closed while she prepared her escape to Liverpool. 'I know Rosie wants the school to have a fresh coat of paint, so I'll be offering to spend a week doing that. But, Mary Kate, promise me you'll think about this. I'll only take you because I want you to be careful, and at least with me you'll get there safely. You have such a determination in your eye – I can see you are hell bent on going.'

'I am, Declan, and that's a fact. I've been thinking about this for a whole year. I am going.'

Declan stared down into Mary Kate's unyielding eyes. She was not to be dissuaded, but he still had time to come up with another plan.

'Chairs on top of desks, please.' Rosie's voice rang out across the classroom as twenty young heads bobbed up from arms folded on desks, some more slowly than others. Rosie was still at work as the school at Tarabeg broke up the week after St Catherine's. She had taken to telling the children to rest their heads on their desks and close their eyes for the last half hour of the day. She did this because she worked them hard and some of the children were white in the face by the afternoon and still had to trek three miles across bog and up the mountain to get home. In the summer months they were then put straight to work on the land until the light faded. The past few weeks had been busy with turf ricking and stacking and it had shown, in both their lack of concentration and their grimy hands.

The classroom filled with the clatter of chairs being lifted onto desks by excited but well-behaved children. It was the last day of term, the weather had been glorious and ten weeks of freedom beckoned. The following term would start late, to allow the farm children to help with the harvest.

'Line up by the door,' said Rosie as she walked along the bench gathering up the exercise books. She made her way to Declan Feenan's door.

His boys were ready, standing to attention and barely containing their excitement at the prospect of no more school and a long summer ahead.

'I'll ring the bell, shall I, Mr Feenan, or do we make them all wait another hour?' Rosie asked mischievously. Marriage had softened her naturally reserved nature.

Declan, who was wiping his blackboard clean, turned

and grinned in response, and the cry went up from both lines of children, 'Oh no, Mrs Malone, please, no!'

Rosie relented. She could keep the smile from her face no longer. 'Go on, off, the lot of you! And behave yourselves. Have a wonderful summer.'

Forty children piled out of the classrooms into the cinder yard and the cacophony was louder than at any other home time of the year.

Mr Feenan came and stood next to Rosie in the porch as Finn kicked a football high into the air.

'You'll be playing for Mayo soon, you will that, Finnbar Malone,' an unexpected voice called out across the yard.

Rosie and Declan turned at the sound of Father Jerry and his housekeeper, Teresa Gallagher, approaching the school gates. Teresa now needed a stick to walk and had taken on extra help at the presbytery. Father Jerry had tried his best to persuade her to retire, but she would have none of it.

Father Jerry sprang forwards, took the ball with the side of his foot and kicked it back to Finn as Teresa made her way up the path to Rosie. In a flash, Mr Feenan had fetched his chair from the classroom and placed it by the door for Teresa to sit on in the sunshine.

'Would you look at that. A fine gentleman, you are,' Teresa said as she sank onto the seat. 'We were just popping in to wish you a good summer, Mr Feenan, before you head off back to Galway. You are staying with your mammy, are you not?'

'He's supposed to be.' Rosie replied for him. 'Aren't you, Mr Feenan? The problem seems to be that he can't drag himself away from the new football pitch.'

Mr Feenan thrust his hands into his trouser pockets and leant against the doorframe as he waited for Father Jerry to join them. He was grinning and blushing at the same time, and was riddled with guilt. How could he tell Rosie it wasn't the football that was making him reluctant to leave Tarabeg but her own stepdaughter, Mary Kate, who was holding him to his promise. 'That's the plan, to head to Galway, but I think some of the boys have other ideas for me.'

'Aye, he's football mad and the boys are loving it. He can do no wrong, and do you know, he was telling me he is using the football and the new pitch as a shameless bribe. If the homework isn't done, they don't get to play on the pitch for a week,' said Rosie as she playfully nudged Declan in the ribs.

Mr Feenan looked down to his shoes, shamefaced but grinning. Captain Carter, who owned most of the land around Tarabeg, the river and the fishing rights, had donated a patch of land big enough for a football pitch at the end of the village. It had transformed the lives of the boys and the fortunes of the school, which now had something other than a small cinder path at the front for the children to play on. It was difficult to work out who had been the more delighted with the gift, Mr Feenan or the children. 'I thought I would wait for another week before I go home to Galway. I promised Mrs Malone I would give the school a lick of paint and I may as well do it now, before I head off. 'Tis true, I have said to the boys that if they want me to organise a few games, I will be on the land every evening, but only if they want to play, mind, and they can get down from the farms.'

'That's very generous of you to give your time like that to painting the school, Mr Feenan,' said Father Jerry. 'If I hadn't seen you running around the pitch like a madman, I would be thinking it was a totally selfless gesture.'

They all grinned at the sight of Declan blushing, even Teresa.

'Right, Paddy has a drink waiting for you. He thought you were going today too and so he sent me to fetch you. Come on, he'll have a Guinness poured ready,' said Father Jerry.

Declan needed no encouragement as he lifted his cap from a nail in the porch.

Teresa tutted. 'Drinking in the day, Father? Surely not.'

'Now, now, Teresa, 'tis no ordinary day. The school has closed for the summer. Paddy and I and a few of the others thought we had to be saying our goodbyes to Mr Feenan here. We'll take the Devlin boys and Finnbar back with us.'

Rosie and Teresa watched as Mr Feenan and Father Jerry gathered Keeva's five sons together and Finn with them. Finn waved to his mother.

'Tell Peggy I'll be home in half an hour,' shouted Rosie, who then turned to Teresa. 'Will the day ever come when you tell the father you have known all along that they all sneak into Paddy's bar for a Guinness in the afternoons?'

Teresa folded her arms in indignation. 'Will I? Never! There's only one person in charge of that presbytery and if he knows I know what he is up to, I'm lost, I can tell you.' She glanced back through the door into Rosie's schoolroom. 'I thought Mary Kate would be in here with you. I dropped by to ask her how she'd feel about starting a Sunday-school class after Mass, given that she is the most learned young woman in the village after her great education.'

Teresa noted the lack of a smile on Rosie's face as she replied, her hands buried in her jacket pockets. 'Well, if you can find her, you can ask her,' she said, her eyes following the backs of the retreating boys.

'What's that supposed to mean?'

Rosie kept her gaze firmly on Mr Feenan, Father Jerry and the six boys as they turned the corner and continued towards the Malone shop and Paddy Devlin's. The boys ran on ahead of the adults, doubtless making for the bridge and the chance to mess around in the Taramore river or just watch the water come crashing down from the hills on its way to the coast. As they disappeared from view, Rosie glanced sideways at Teresa.

'I don't know, Teresa, she's hardly slept in her own bed since she came home. Finds every excuse she can to stay up at the farm with Nola, Seamus and Daedio. The minute Michael headed off to Dublin to buy stock, she found a reason not to go with him, said she'd promised to read to Daedio and was off up the hill. I don't mind, but poor Finnbar, he is feeling it. Thought he was coming home to his sister every night this week, only to be disappointed. One thing I do know, though, is that she won't be staying around here. She's too restless, and that's going to break the hearts of her father and her brother. I wouldn't be surprised if she sneaks off in the middle of the night on a boat to America or something equally dramatic. She's very like her mother.'

Teresa removed her hatpin and then the hat itself. 'I'd say she was more like her father. Wasn't he the one who went to fight in the war for the sheer adventure of it? No, Mary Kate may look like her mother, with her red hair and her big eyes, but she has Michael's daredevil nature. Isn't the sun glorious? 'Tis too hot for a hat.' She picked up the hat and began to fan her face. 'Well, it will break Daedio's heart more than Michael's if she flits off somewhere,' she said matter-of-factly. ''Tis only the poor who emigrate – those with money stay put, and Daedio insists he has money, thanks to his brother, who must have been the hardest-working man in all of New York. They want for nothing up on that hill. Bridget McAndrew was telling me that Mary Kate's homecoming has given Daedio a new lease of life.'

Rosie laughed. 'Well, there's some good news then, although I'm not sure how Nola will feel about it. I swear to God, he will make it to a hundred and more, that man. Do you fancy coming down to the shop with me for a cup of tea? Peggy will be dying for the company.' She stepped back into the classroom and then came out again with her basket. 'I can send a message with the boys for Keeva and Josie to come over and join us, give them an escape from the men. Josie won't be busy in the butcher's now.'

'I will, if you will be so kind as to take my other arm. Don't tell Father I'm struggling on one stick or he'll pension me off to my sister's – I'd rather be in my grave.'

'Don't be talking like that,' said Rosie. 'You and Daedio, you'll be outdoing each other. You know what they say: people live forever in Tarabeg.'

'Well, they used to.' Teresa squeezed Rosie's arm. If Sarah Malone had lived forever, Rosie would still be a lonely spinster; that was a fact, and half of the village knew it. Rosie had eyes for no one but Michael, and when Sarah died, she hadn't let her second chance to capture him pass her by.

No one was more surprised than Rosie to find Mary Kate in the Malones' kitchen when they walked through the back door.

'Ah, she's here at last,' said Teresa. 'Would you look at you! Did they stand you in the vegetable patch all day at that school? You've grown at least a foot since Easter. How did you learn anything at all?'

Mary Kate laughed. 'I'm seventeen now, Aunty Teresa. Rosie, where's Finn?'

'I would think he's down at the bridge with Keeva's boys. Are you home now, Mary Kate?' Rosie's voice dropped on the last words; she half dreaded the answer. Michael would be back that night from his buying trip to Dublin and Rosie knew he'd be delighted to find his daughter asleep in her own bed.

Mary Kate hesitated, but only long enough for Teresa, with the wisdom of advanced age, to notice. 'I am. I'm home now,' she said. Even Teresa didn't notice the fingers crossed behind her back. 'I'm away down to the bridge to see the boys. Nice to see you, Aunty Teresa.' Mary Kate planted a kiss on Teresa's cheek and ran out of the door.

'Mary Kate!' Finn saw her coming before she reached the bridge. Leaving the Devlin boys, he ran towards her and threw his arms around her waist. 'Are you down from the farm, are you staying home?' He looked up at her, his eyes bright and trusting, and Mary Kate's heart folded.

'I am for now,' she said. That wasn't a lie.

Finn grinned from ear to ear. Thanks to the Devlin boys across the road, he was never lonely, and one or the other of them slept over at the Malones' most weekends, but Mary Kate was like a princess to him. He adored the ground she walked on, the only sadness in his life being that she wasn't as close to Rosie as he was himself. 'Come to the bridge – we're throwing sticks to see which survives to the river.'

Mary Kate had played the same game many times herself at his age. The force of the water rushing down from the mountains destroyed most sticks before they made it across the pebbled bottom of the shallow stretch of river. 'I'm coming,' she said, glancing nervously back towards the bar as she stood on the bridge, wondering was Declan good for his promise. She had to speak to him once more before she wrote to Roshine. She was leaving Tarabeg and heading to Bee in Liverpool on Sunday and her source of transport to the train in Galway was Declan Feenan. If it wasn't, she was well and truly stuck as there was no one else in Tarabeg close enough to her in age that she could trust.

Declan had seen her through the bar window and ten minutes later he approached the bridge. 'Hello, grand to see you,' he said as he raised his cap. He knew that what he had promised to do was madness, that he could lose his job and livelihood if he was caught.

Mary Kate wasted no words. 'Are you good for your word, Declan Feenan? Will you still give me a seat in your car to Galway?' she asked, her eyes full of fear.

He had meant to persuade her to change her mind, to find another means of transport, to reconsider altogether her plans to leave. She was totally unlike any other girl he had ever met, either from Galway or in the village. Her education gave her an air of confidence and womanliness, and if he was honest with himself, he was scared to say no.

'Of course I am, but what if I get caught, if Rosie finds out? One word from Rosie to Father Jerry and I'm fired.'

Mary Kate's face creased into a frown and she placed her hand on his forearm. 'I have explained this. No one will know – they will never make the connection in a million years, and if neither of us ever says a word to anyone, how can anyone ever find out? If a secret is kept, a secret is safe. 'Tis only when someone is told that it gets out, because a secret will spread faster in this village than the news that Murphy's pig has escaped again.'

He wondered at her maturity. 'How did you ever work that one out,' he said as he let his breath out in a whistle. ''Tis true, but I have to know I can trust you not to tell anyone, Mary Kate. 'Tis my job and my pay. I don't have another.'

Mary Kate grinned. 'Well, I think I should be asking can I trust you not to try and kiss me when we are alone in the car?'

Declan's heart began beating against his chest wall with the force of a hammer and his face flushed red hot with embarrassment. 'Of course you can trust me. I'm ten years older than you, I'm a schoolteacher, I hold a position of trust – what a thing to say.'

'Well then,' said Mary Kate, 'if I can trust you, you can trust me.' She threw her head back and began to laugh, her hair tumbling over her shoulders.

Declan thought he had never in all his life seen a whiter, prettier throat and he fought back his immediate physical response. He imagined threading his arm around her waist and pulling her into him, kissing that white neck, that freckled nose, those lips. He imagined slipping her dress down from her shoulders, watching her breasts escape the confines of the fabric, and the sense, the feel of her... Swallowing hard, he banished the image from his mind. Mary Kate could trust him not to kiss her on the road to Galway, but only just.

Chapter 6

The Malones spent Saturday evening together at home. Michael had lit a fire to ward off the river mist and they were drinking porter in front of it. Mary Kate was talking to Finn and her father while Rosie sat sewing in Sarah's rocking chair. A painful memory of her mother sitting there winding woollen skeins to sell in the shop flew into Mary Kate's mind.

'You could do worse than train to be a teacher like Rosie,' Michael said.

'Here in Tarabeg, Da?'

'Aye, and why not? Rosie would like nothing better, would you, Rosie?'

Rosie smiled and said nothing. She didn't need a crystal ball to see that this was the last thing Mary Kate wanted to do.

'I've spent years cooped up in a school, Da, enough to last me for the rest of my life. And besides, I want to see a bit of the world before I settle down. Could there be anything worse than leaving school and going straight back into a classroom?' Mary Kate scrunched her hands into her long hair and shook her head in frustration. 'Oh God, what could possibly be worse than that?'

Rosie blushed; it was exactly what she had done. She was relieved that neither of them seemed to have registered that, but then Michael removed his pipe from his mouth and looked up at her. Rosie gave a very slight shake of her head – 'don't bring me into it' was the clear message – and it seemed Michael had taken that on board. 'Well, that's a fine thing to say,' he responded. 'What about Mr Feenan?' Rosie almost flinched. 'He's not that old,' Michael continued, 'still in his twenties, and he's well respected around here.'

By now Mary Kate was playing cards with Finn on the mat in front of the fire. Finn was lying on his belly and Mary Kate was sitting cross-legged in front of the rocking chair. She threw her head back and almost let out a wail. 'Da, I want to go somewhere and do something else with my life. You gave me an education. It's a big world out there and I've only ever been to Galway and Tarabeg.'

'Well, I don't know how you're going to be doing that. You won't be going anywhere alone. The world is a dangerous place. Jeez, I wouldn't let you set foot in Dublin alone, and that's in our own country. Only the poor sail to America, and do you know what they do when they get there? They spend their time writing letters home and crying into their Guinness, that's what. And in their dying breath, every one of them whispers to the priest the name of their village and the name of their mammy, and that's the God's honest truth. Cry for home, they do.'

Mary Kate leapt up off the floor, threw her arms around her da's neck and pleaded with him as she laid her head on his shoulder. 'Da, you did it. You went off to fight in a war on your own and left Mammy to wait for you.' Her eyes burnt with indignation as they held his.

'That was different, Mary Kate. There was a war to be fought and I'm a man – a young man then. 'Tis different altogether now.'

Mary Kate knew there was no point arguing, or mentioning Bee. He wouldn't discuss Bee and Captain Bob in front of Finn and she had heard his objections many times, whenever she brought up the subject of going to Liverpool to visit her aunt. Michael's answer was always an emphatic, 'No, you cannot.' He gave her no explanation, but she had overheard enough conversations to know why. Captain Bob and Bee weren't married, and whenever their names were mentioned, it was done so in whispers and was followed by the click of the rosaries.

Declan Feenan had washed out his paintbrush and was resting on the steps of the school when Mary Kate ran up to the gate.

'Are you done?' she asked. 'I can't stop, I'm going up to the farm, but you won't let me down tonight, will you?'

Declan removed his cap and wiped his brow. 'Are you sure?' He was still hoping she'd rethink her plans.

'I am completely one hundred per cent positive,' she replied, and every syllable carried the weight of her conviction. 'I'll see you there, as arranged. Leave your car boot unlocked, I'll try and get some things in earlier.' And before he could reply, she was gone.

She spent the rest of Sunday afternoon up at the farm, sitting on the end of Daedio's bed reading to him. His eyesight had become so bad, he could no longer distinguish the words himself, and she felt a pain in her heart, knowing how much he enjoyed their time together.

She slammed the covers shut. 'Daedio, why won't Daddy let me stay with Aunty Bee in Liverpool?' He was the only person who would give her an honest answer and he did not let her down.

'They aren't married, not in the eyes of God, anyway. They're not man and wife, and that is a terrible sin altogether now. Your father won't let you stay with them for that reason, although he was no saint himself.'

Nola was standing at the kitchen table making scones and listening. 'Aye, but Michael didn't bring Sarah into this house until they were married, and nor would he have, regardless of the circumstances at the time, which were not easy.'

She wiped flour from her forehead with the back of her

hands and shot Daedio a warning look. No one had ever spoken to Mary Kate about the manner of her grandmother's death or her murderer of a grandfather, and no one was about to, not if she had anything to do with it. Mary Kate knew nothing of the spell the tinker had cast over her mother when Mary Kate was a babe in her arms. To her, Shona Maughan was just a witch of a tinker who was now too old to travel and lived in her caravan miles away, banished from Tarabeg by Father Jerry. She'd been told nothing, and as far as Nola was concerned, she never would be. There was a reason Michael was so fiercely protective of Mary Kate: who knew where the spell would end? Her mother and maternal grandmother had both gone in tragic circumstances. 'Least said, soonest mended' – that's what Nola had told them all. 'Say nothing. Let the spell be buried. Sarah would never have wanted her to know.'

Mary Kate stared down at the crocheted rug that covered Daedio's legs. She tugged at a loose thread between the stitched-together squares of green and purple and frowned. 'If I stay here in Tarabeg, I may never see Bee again.' She lifted her head and looked Daedio in the eye. She wanted him to understand, him of all people, when he heard the news, why it was she had gone.

Daedio pulled the pipe from his mouth, held it in mid air and looked at her as though she'd spoken in a different language. 'Now what would you be talking like that for? Of course you will! What a notion. Bee has a nature for Tarabeg, she's not one for staying away in Liverpool for long. As God is my judge, she'll be back here soon. 'Tis time.'

'Your father is right, Mary Kate,' said Nola. 'I have a great affection for Bee, so I do, but Michael is right on this. Take no notice of Daedio. Bee has made her bed and she's lying in it. I can't see her coming back here. God in heaven, what would she be wanting to do that for, with the life she's been living in Liverpool, graced with all the mod-cons and gadgets I cannot for the life of me even pronounce let alone use.' Nola slammed the door of the range shut and wiped her face with the towel she kept tucked into her belt.

Mary Kate sighed. She was sad that among these people she loved so much there was so little acceptance of Bee and Captain Bob, even after all these years. 'No wonder people move away,' she muttered as she rose and placed the book on the shelf at the side of the fireplace.

She didn't care what people said; she didn't care how Bee and Captain Bob lived. Bee was her link to her mother. They were connected by the invisible bonds of family, and however stretched those were, they still pulled at her every day. By whatever means she could, she would get to Liverpool. Daedio and Granny Nola had been her last hope. She had waited for someone to take her side, understand her need and fight her corner, but no one had. It seemed that her position had been decided on, determined long ago in accordance with the acceptable roles open to a woman in Tarabeg. As long as she had a roof over her head and could contribute to placing food on the table, that would be her lot, until someone took a shine to her and offered to marry her, whereupon the cycle would continue.

The light had faded, and Seamus arrived at the door to take her back down to the village. 'Are you ready, miss? I'll see you out in the old house – Pete's getting the horse ready.'

As Mary Kate passed the end of Daedio's bed, he grabbed her hand. His eyes locked onto hers, and her back prickled with fear. Those eyes bore right into her soul; they were perceptive and wise, and they knew.

'Seamus, here, take these scones to Pete,' Nola said. But he was gone. 'Oh for the patience of all the saints.' Nola sighed, wrapped the scones in a tea towel and shuffled out of the door after Seamus.

Daedio and Mary Kate were alone.

'Come here,' said Daedio, glancing behind him to check that Nola was clear of the cottage.

Mary Kate sat back down next to him, and from under his pillow he pulled out a roll of notes, which she immediately recognised as dollars. There were so many sent from families across the Atlantic, they were taken as currency in the shop and converted by Mrs Doyle in the post office.

'What's that?' she asked, even though she knew.

'It's from the money my brother Joe sent, long, long before you were born. See up there...?' Daedio nodded at his cedar box on the top of the press. 'That will be yours one day, and all that is in it. And that's not all, Mary Kate. There is a secret in this family. One day your father will tell you where this money came from, but there is more, and your Great-Granny Annie, she knew what she was doing when she decided to keep it warm. Can you remember that? There is plenty more where this came from, from where Great-Granny Annie kept it warm.'

He pressed the dollars into Mary Kate's hand and folded her fingers over it. His eyes shifted to the stone above the fireplace, which he'd managed to push just far enough back into place so that anyone looking would be curious enough to look further. He would have given it all to Mary Kate, every dollar, there and then, but that was for Michael to decide.

Joe had left for America to become a builder and had chosen the path of bank robber. Some seventy years ago, a letter from a New York solicitor had informed Daedio that Joe was serving his time in jail; a crate of dollars was delivered to Tarabeg and Daedio had kept the money hidden ever since. It was a long time before Daedio and Annie heard that Joe had died in jail, and during all those years it was as if the money had glowed from beneath the limewashed wall as the two of them sat in front of the fire.

'You're going, aren't you?' he said. The light had left his eyes, replaced by tears. 'I've seen enough run from Tarabeg, off to Liverpool or America, to know that look when I see it. All my family went, every last one. All my precious grandchildren followed them, except Michael.'

Mary Kate bowed her head and kept her own eyes on her clasped hands.

'Here, put that in your pocket before that witch of my daughter-in-law comes back in.'

She smiled and did as she was told.

'Promise me one thing, before ye go,' he said, and now there were tears in her own eyes. 'Remember every word of what I have just told you, and come back as soon as you can. This hill, it is yours. If you don't ever come home—'

Mary Kate made to object, but Daedio raised his hand.

'Stop. Everyone leaves here with the promises of how quickly they'll return falling from their lips, and hardly anyone does. Imagine the amount of tears that have fallen on foreign soil. 'Tis one thing to make your fortune, another altogether to be trapped and unable to return. But you aren't in that position, you have something to return for, more than you can ever earn. For you, 'tis different. Go for the adventure, not for the money.' He tapped her pocket with his hand. 'Keep yourself safe and if I am gone before you do return, remember this: your Great-Granny Annie, she is looking over you. She's standing right next to us now – aren't you, Annie?' He looked up to his side and smiled.

Mary Kate stared at where he was smiling but saw nothing.

'When I've passed, and it will be soon, there will be two of us looking out for you. You might think I'm gone, but I won't be. I won't rest until I know you are safely returned, back up on this hill.'

Mary Kate took a deep breath. The thought of Daedio dying had never entered her mind and she wasn't going to let it do so now. 'Daedio, everyone says that no one dies in Tarabeg – even though Mammy and Annie did.'

'Come here.'

She leant into his chest and he folded his arms about her.

'Bad things did happen here – we let our guard down – but you're right, we are blessed.' He held her away from him. 'They say 'tis the purity of the water and the goodness in the hearts, but I will go and join Annie one day. Just you remember everything I told you, and if you can't get back for the funeral, come and see me in the churchyard. I'll be waiting for you. And give Bee my best. Tell her I miss her.'

Mary Kate's head shot up. 'How did you know?' she whispered.

'Mary Kate, come on!' Seamus shouted from the yard. 'The horse is ready and growing impatient. His harness is on.'

Daedio smiled. 'Annie knows everything. She just told me. I said didn't I, she's watching over you.'

Mary Kate stood and smoothed down her skirt. Her pulse was racing, her mouth was dry and her eyes were full of questions.

'No,' he said, 'don't you be worrying, I won't be breathing a word to anyone. God knows, I have counted the days you have been in school until the holidays came. You light up this place and the thought of you going away is a hard one, but I will bear it. Now run, don't you forget anything I said. Run, before that mad horse and cart takes off without you.'

Hours later, she lay in bed, fully dressed, the covers up to her neck, her heart pounding. She took in the night sounds of the village, isolated them one by one, committed them to memory and packed each one away in her heart. She listened to the rush of the river her da and Tig and Father Jerry poached in, flowing across the seven acres. There was no one poaching tonight, luckily – that would have thwarted her plans, and Declan might have panicked and gone without her. The owl hooted, and she wondered, was it the same owl from when she was a child, when she used to lie in that same bed listening to her mother and father chatting in the kitchen below, or was it an offspring. It hooted again. 'I hear you,' she whispered, 'I'm coming.' The cow snorted in the byre below her window, she would be lying on the straw, the dogs sleeping at her side with one ear pricked, alert. A fox scurried across the yard and the dogs emitted a low warning growl.

Then she heard the car.

'God give me time. Wait for me,' she prayed, knowing

he would. She had already stashed her belongings in the boot of his car, so that he couldn't panic at the last moment and drive off without her.

She swung her legs out of the bed and laid the letter to her father against her washstand; the ink on the buff envelope dark in the moonlight. She opened the drawer on the nightstand and took out the box her father had given her when her mother died. Opening the lid, she felt the familiar sadness as she peered at the emerald heart pendant her mother had always worn. She wondered whether she should take it, but there was no time to ponder; snapping the lid shut, she tucked it into her suitcase. She picked up her brown leather shoes, laces open and dangling, scuffed from scrambling up the hill to Tarabeg Farm.

Out on the landing, she could hear the rumble of her father's porter-induced snores; another sound to pack away. She looked towards his room and the closed door, and another time, another life, flashed into her head: the door open, candlelight flooding out onto the landing, a broken teapot on the floor, pottery smashed. It wasn't a snore she'd heard then, but her father's wails of grief as her mother lay dying on her bed. Now, as then, Mary Kate's heart froze, every part of her paralysed in terror. The past could not be repaired, could not be forgotten; it was always there and she felt now, as she always had, that in Tarabeg the death of her mother defined her life, her days, her nights, her fears.

She turned and tiptoed along the landing, stopping only at Finn's room. His door was open, as always, and he lay on his side, facing her, his eyes closed, his thumb in his mouth, his hair shining in the moonlight streaming in through the window. She felt the stab in her heart. Would he ever forgive her? Would he ever adore her again? She tiptoed over and planted a kiss on his head as she stroked his hair. She placed a second note on his pillow. Her mother's face was in his. The feel of his hair was her father's. The same colour, the same smell. She filled her nostrils with the memory of Finn as, in the distance, from across the bridge, she heard a car engine ticking over, counting down the moments, waiting.

She took the stairs one at a time, missing the ones that creaked, grabbed some ham from the press, opened the back door and threw it over the byre. The dogs knew it was her and had not let her down; the ham was to distract them. Jacko the donkey let out a snort. He had been part of the family before she had even been born. Bending down, she kissed his nose and rubbed her fingers along the coarse hair between his eyes. 'It's just like school – I'll be back. One day,' she whispered. Bid, her one-eyed dog (the other eye having been lost in a fight), came over and licked her hand, a thank you for the ham. 'Thank you for not barking,' she mumbled as she slipped on her shoes and, crouching, tied the laces. The dogs nuzzled her hair and licked her face, and it was these last private moments with the animals that broke her defences. The tears flowed. 'Stop,' she said to herself as she dashed them away with the back of her hand. The dogs, sensing her unhappiness, nuzzled closer, Bid resting his chin on her lap, the bitch licking her face and whimpering.

She rose, smoothed down her skirts and took one last look at the house. In the bedroom window she saw her mother, Sarah, one hand each side of the frame, looking down at her, and a gasp caught in her throat. 'Mammy!' She blinked away the tears, but her mammy was gone. It had only been her mind playing tricks.

She lifted the latch, with almost no noise, and fled.

Declan almost jumped out of his skin as she yanked open the car door. He was fearful and anxious. 'I was counting down in my head – you had twenty-two second left,' he said.

'Declan Feenan, you should have been a comedian,' she said as she wriggled into the seat. 'You have my life in the boot of your car – everything I own, my money and all. You were going nowhere.'

Despite his nervousness, Declan released the handbrake and eased the car back onto the road from the cutaway at the bottom of the bridge. She was right, he would probably have sat there all night and waited for her. 'Maybe not, but, God in heaven, this is the scariest thing I have ever done in me life.' He leant forward and wiped the misted windscreen with the sleeve of his jacket.

'It was easier than I thought,' said Mary Kate. 'Even the dogs behaved, for a bit of rasher.'

Declan pointed into the footwell in front of her seat. 'There's a thermos of tea in the bag there, and some sandwiches I made up. It's a long drive we have. I'm not dropping you at the train in Galway, I'm taking you all the way to Dublin, for the boat. At least that way I'll know you're safely away, given as I'm your partner in crime.'

Mary Kate's mouth fell open. Leaning across the seat, she planted her lips on the side of his cheek and threw her arms around his neck. 'Declan Feenan, you are a saint of a man.'

He grinned and blushed in the dark, delighted at her response. 'God, you are a bold woman, so you are. I hope you keep that under control in Liverpool or you'll be landing yourself in trouble. Did anyone see you?'

'No.' Mary Kate swivelled around in her seat and looked back at Tarabeg receding in the moonlight. 'No one saw me.' The haunting eyes of Jacko, old and wise, the feel of the dogs' fur, the smell of Finn and the sight of her mother at the window, those things would not leave her; they would be the memories that would one day pull her back. 'Not a living human soul,' she said and she continued to lean on her arms and stare as one familiar landmark after another disappeared from view.

Rosie had slept fitfully, waiting for what she had been anticipating and had finally heard. As the latch of the back door dropped, she crept from the bed and padded across the floorboards in her bare feet to their bedroom window. From there she could see up onto the bridge and she caught sight of Declan's car as it slipped away down the Ballina road. She shivered. It was a warm night and yet, as so often, their room felt inexplicably cold. She looked down at Michael. He was sleeping peacefully, blissfully unaware, and she wondered, should she wake him? He would give chase in their car, which was a considerably bigger and grander model than Declan's. He would no doubt catch them and bring Mary Kate back.

She turned to the window again and drew the curtain further back with one hand, allowing the moonlight in. 'Declan, well I never, you dark horse,' she whispered.

Her breath clouded the glass and she lifted her finger and drew the outline of a heart on the surface. As she did so, she remembered Sarah's emerald heart and wondered if Mary Kate had taken it with her. She hesitated. One shake of Michael's shoulder, one word in his ear, that was all it would take. She stood rooted to the spot as the cold ran up her legs and the sound of the car engine faded into the distance.

By the time it had vanished entirely and there was silence once more, it was as if nothing had happened. She stepped back, allowed the curtain to drop into place, then returned to their bed and pulled the blanket up to her chin. She stared at the ceiling as her husband's chest rose and fell in harmony with his snoring.

'Good luck, Mary Kate,' she whispered.

She thought of her futile years of thankfulness. Of her time spent loving Michael, waiting for him to return from the war; watching him with Sarah, marrying Sarah and losing Sarah; waiting for her turn. She wouldn't wish that on anyone. If only Mary Kate had confided in her, she would have been on her side. She would have pushed Michael to let her apply for university in Dublin, never guessing it was the last thing Mary Kate wanted.

She closed her eyes and knew there would be no more sleep tonight. She would wait for Michael to wake. She wondered how she would deal with the fallout once he knew his precious daughter had run away; his Sarah look-alike, his Mary Kate.

Bridget McAndrew heard a car in the distance, but was too distracted by her own thoughts to wonder who it was as she sat by the side of her bed and reread the letter she had taken from Daedio. He had not wanted it left at the farm in case Nola should find it. She had no need to look at Porick to check he was asleep; his snoring shook the heather roof, confirming she was safe to take the letter out of her pocket. Electricity had only been installed in the main streets in the village and they were still dependent upon the fire and candles for heat and light.

Daedio had asked her what he should do and for the first time in her life she had no idea. The letter was typed and she read it again.

A letter written by my great-grandfather while he was in jail has, after many years, been passed on to me, in accordance with the terms of his will. It would be too complicated to enter into the circumstances of the delay; however, my great-grandfather urges that I make contact with you, as he has sent something to you to be kept safe for me.

Joe Malone Junior

Daedio had opened up to Bridget some years ago about the money behind the fireplace and its provenance. 'I bought the seven acres Michael's shop is built on with it,' he'd confessed. 'I've bloody spent enough of the feckin' money. How do I know it's Joe's great-grandson? It could be the great-grandson of someone he was in jail with. Joe never told me about any wife or littl'uns. If there had been some, he wouldn't have sent the money all the way here in a wooden box, would he? I'm convinced it's an imposter who knows where the money was sent. I think we are all in mighty danger. He'll be coming after me with a gun. That's what those American gangsters do.'

Bridget could see that Daedio was worried. 'Let me take the letter. I'll lay some truth herbs on it and see what happens.'

'Aye, you had better, because if Nola finds it, she won't let up until I tell her everything.'

The truth herbs had failed her for the first time ever. Nothing had happened. Bridget was none the wiser. She shook the herbs away, unused to not having been given the answers she was looking for. The spirits had been quiet for days and it occurred to her that something was moving in the spirit world in Tarabeg. There was disquiet. Since Mary Kate had returned, there had been no contact with Annie, and now this.

There was no indication, one way or another, what on earth was behind the letter, but she did make a decision. In this, she would have to help Daedio all the way. She would need to protect him and be there for him or the worry would see him off sooner than he was due.

'I'll look out for him, shall I, Annie?'

She scanned the room for a sign from her best friend, Daedio's late wife, but there was none. That was another first, and the knowledge of it, the loneliness at having been deserted by her spirit guides, filled her with fear. Maybe she was losing her powers altogether. It wasn't just the sight they blessed her with, they protected her too. They imbued her with powers to keep Tarabeg safe from the likes of Shona Maughan and the wicked spells she cast over the village. Shona had not been seen for some time, but Bridget felt her. She was alive and brooding and the whispering messages Bridget received from the other side were troubling. A cold breeze wafted across the back of her neck, something was wrong. She felt a shift as the air beside her was displaced, someone was with her. Annie had finally appeared and the message she brought chilled her heart. Shona's work was not yet done.

★

Rosie wasn't the only one who saw Mary Kate leave. Father Jerry had watched from the dark window of the presbytery. Since the day evil had stalked and wounded Tarabeg, the day Sarah had died, he had been on his guard.

When the rear lights of the car had disappeared out of view, Father Jerry lifted his cloak from the back of the door, picked up the torch from the side of his bed, and crept out of the presbytery and across the road to the door of the church. He clicked off the torch; the moonlight was bright enough for him to see his way.

He decided that he would walk the boundaries of the entire village, passing every door, and as he did so, he would pray. He would encircle the village in a band of protective prayer and at the same time he would pray for Mary Kate and for her return, because she was part of the village, its future and its survival. If it were not so, the wicked spirits would not have preyed on her family as they had. There was a reason her grandmother and her mother had suffered so. The tinkers' spell that had been cast by Shona Maughan on the day Michael's shop opened had yet to be broken, and broken it must be, with Mary Kate.

There was a path already laid for Mary Kate to follow. It was beyond his control. All that was left for him to do was to pray that it would one day lead her safely back to Tarabeg.

Chapter 7

'No! God in heaven, you haven't!' Roshine tried hard not to shout. She'd been called from the house to the surgery to answer the phone and could barely believe that Mary Kate had carried out exactly what she'd said she was going to do.

'Roshine, the first person he will call is you. Please, you have to lie for me – don't you tell him where I am.'

'I don't know where you are! Where is it? You've only told me you're in Dublin.'

'Aye, well, true enough and that's what you can say. That I'm in Dublin. And that I meant what I said in the letter: I will come back, when he agrees to let me live my own life and not keep me prisoner in Tarabeg.'

'Oh God, Mary Kate, that's such a drama. Your da's a good man, he would have let you when you got a bit older. Do you have to do this?'

'Roshine, he wanted me to get the teaching certificate

and then go back to school again, to teach. My father wants me, one way or another, to spend my life in a classroom. I can't do that. Don't even mention the word "Liverpool" to him. Please don't let me down.'

'I won't. But, Mary Kate, listen to me, keep my address and number on you and if you ever need me, make sure you call me right away, do you hear me?'

'I do, and I promise I will. I'll write to you soon anyway and let you know where I am.'

A moment later the pips began to beep in the handset.

'Mary Kate! Mary Kate!' Roshine shouted, but it was too late; her friend was gone. She stood listening to the dialling tone, staring helplessly into the phone.

'Who was that, Roshine?' her mother called from inside the house.

'Oh, just one of the girls from school. She's got a job and she's away to America.'

Roshine tiptoed into the kitchen and picked up the dog's lead from the back of the door. The dog, hearing the familiar sound, was at her side in seconds.

'Which girl? I haven't heard that. What job? When is she leaving? We'll have a party for her, shall we, Roshine?'

Her questions were answered by the sound of the back door slamming.

Mary Kate stepped out of the phone box, which smelt strongly of urine and stale tobacco, and into the fresh briny air of Dublin harbour and the familiar sound of seagulls screeching overhead.

Declan was standing in front of her, looking tired. They had driven through the night and he was holding two bread rolls filled with hot bacon. 'I found this stall over by the ticket office,' he said. 'They sell tea too. There's an hour until the boat leaves – shall we go and have a pot?'

Mary Kate had slept for the past few hours, her head lolling on the back of the leather seat. There was nothing she wanted more than a hot cup of tea. The smell of the bacon was making her stomach roar. They had opened the thermos as they pulled up at the port, but the tea inside had been lukewarm and bitter.

They both looked over at the boat and the activity of bags being loaded and people already forming a queue. Mary Kate would shortly join them with her school suitcase and sail to Liverpool.

Declan's chest tightened. The minutes were ticking away. He had stolen glances, watched her as she slept. He'd needed to stop the car for a comfort break and when he got back in, she was still sleeping. Her features were relaxed and her lips were parted. With one finger, he'd lifted a strand of her hair from the car seat and let its silkiness glide through his fingers. By the time they reached Roscommon, he had feelings for her that he'd never had for any other, and yet there he was, driving her away.

The sky was grey with the sort of early morning mist that favoured the Irish coastline and Mary Kate pulled her cardigan about her. 'Come on then. God, I'm starving.' She bit into the bread as she walked.

The café was nothing more than a wooden hut with tables and chairs under an awning. It was early, but the port was already awake and they weren't the only couple at the tables. Between them sat a large enamel pot of tea and an overflowing ashtray.

Declan, laughing, leant over and wiped away the bacon grease that was trickling down her chin. Lighting a cigarette, he sat back and watched her as she finished her tea. It's now or it could be never, he thought to himself. His fingers trembled and the ash from his cigarette fell onto the wooden table. He flicked it away with the back of his hand and, clasping his fingers together, with the smoke from the cigarette stinging his eyes, he stared out over the bay. His heart pounded and his mouth dried as he made the decision. If she got on that boat and he hadn't said anything, what would he do the minute it sailed? *You would be stood here like a fecking eejit*, he told himself.

She'd been about to swallow her tea, but she lowered the cup halfway to the table as he spoke out of the blue. 'Mary Kate, if things don't work out in Liverpool, will you let me know, will you write to me? Will you drop me a line anyway, to tell me how you're getting on, or get a message to me at the post office?'

'Why?' she asked. 'What for?' And then, 'Besides, if I write to you, Mrs Doyle would know it was me and that would be all.'

He swallowed hard. 'I know this may not be what you want to hear, but I care for you. You've grown up, Mary Kate, and you've taken the eyes right out of me head. Mine and everyone else's, I'd be saying. I would like to know that you're doing okay, that everything in Liverpool is as it should be, as you want it to be, and for you to know that if you ever think you could give an old sod like me the time of day... Don't worry, you don't have to answer me now – I'll wait.'

Mary Kate gulped and placed her cup back on the saucer. It rattled; her hand was now trembling too. In no way whatsoever did Declan Feenan fit into her plans. She immediately regretted having asked him for the lift, even though, if it hadn't been for him, she wouldn't have been able to get away. 'Declan, I didn't know—' She stuttered over her words.

He interjected, to her relief. 'Aye, you wouldn't, why would you. You were just a kid when I came to Tarabeg, and then you were gone. You only see me as a teacher who works with your mammy.'

'She's not my mammy.'

Her response took Declan aback. He had never known Sarah, or Mary Kate before her loss. 'I... I'm sorry,' he said.

'No, sure, 'tis not your fault. Declan, I have to get away. I don't know for how long or when I'll be back.' She left the 'if' unspoken.

His heart sank into his boots. 'Aye, well, if you do change

your mind and come back home, you know there's an old fool in Tarabeg waiting.'

Mary Kate smiled at his self-effacement. Feeling sorry for him and fond of him all at the same time, she reached out her hand and placed it over his. 'Declan, I have to go. Since Mammy died, I've felt as if I don't belong, or only half belong. Maybe if Aunty Bee had stayed and there was some of Mammy, her family, left, it would be different, but there isn't anything I can do about it. Since Daddy married Rosie, my home hasn't felt like home. I feel like a visitor in the village. I have to want to be there and I don't. Maybe being away from home will send me running back, and when it does, I'll see if there's an old fool hanging around in Tarabeg, will I?' She smiled as Declan turned to face her and his eyes held hers.

'You do that,' he said, 'and I'll be there, just in case.' He turned his hand over and, lifting hers, kissed her fingers. There were tears in his eyes. He knew she couldn't understand the way he felt – she was only seventeen. He couldn't understand it himself. For all his adult life, he'd wondered would he ever find a woman he wanted to love. And now he'd discovered that God had kept him waiting because He had the very best in store. He'd fired an arrow into his heart without any warning, had set it on fire, and was now taking her away already. What was God playing at?

The ship's horn blew and a man yelled the final call to board the boat.

'Oh, God, after all this, I'll miss the boat,' she shouted.

They ran together, as a couple, holding hands, Declan carrying her bag, holding tight onto her with his other hand all the way to the bottom of the steps.

'All aboard,' shouted the wizened old sailor over Mary Kate's shoulder as he took her ticket and punched it.

Declan dropped her hand. She took her bag and raised her face and he kissed her in a way that said 'Come back', not 'Goodbye'. Turning, he walked away and left her standing, watching. Her first kiss. Her lips tasted of his salty tears or were they her own? She wiped her eyes with the back of her gloved hand and the man shouted again. 'Oh, God, sorry,' she said and ran up the steps, missing Declan as he turned, his own cheeks wet.

He saw her retreating and then she was swallowed by the dark gangway of the boat. He wondered, would he ever see her again or was this to be it, his one snatch at happiness? A car journey with the beautiful and impetuous Mary Kate and that salty kiss with trembling lips. He shouted her name, but she was gone, and amid all the hustle and noise it was as if she had never been there at all.

Mary Kate stood on the deck with Bee's most recent letter clutched tightly in her hand. She had no idea where to go or what to do and so she read the letter again, to calm her frayed nerves. Her usual boldness had deserted her the moment the gangway banged shut and a crew member yelled, 'Check the bolts.' There was a shuddering, a clanging and then that was it – the boat pulled away from the shores of Ireland and all that Mary Kate knew.

Bee's address was written on the back of the envelope and even though she knew it off by heart, holding onto it gave her some comfort. She was not heading to an imaginary destination; 27 Waterloo Street was a real place and she was not alone, not lost. She was heading to Bee, her mother's aunt, her Granny Angela's sister, her own flesh and blood; she was a part of that pack of women, they were her family, bound together by tragedy and love. She was heading to a woman and a place she had never been allowed to visit, but Bee's message had changed that.

Mary Kate's heart had soared when the letter had arrived at St Catherine's. It had contained a secret message, one that told her to go to Liverpool when she finished school. She was relieved that Bee understood and that her aunty missed Mary Kate as much as Mary Kate missed her. She had written about Mary Kate returning to Tarabeg and had sounded almost wistful, full of her own longing for home. The letter was almost a month old now, crumpled and well read.

I know you have found being at home difficult, since your father married Rosie, but she is a good woman and she cares for you.

I envy you when you tell me you have visited the cottages. I might have known you would take flowers for

Angela and Sarah when you were home. When you have a notion, do call at the empty house. I can see you looking out at the shore, just like your mammy did when she was your age as she sat on the bench weaving her lobster pots. Sit there yourself, Mary Kate. If there is anywhere you can talk to Sarah, it will be there. They will both be there, Sarah and her own mammy, my sister Angela. They'll be your guiding angels. I've been told that so many times by a lady with the sight who lives in the next street to me. You are Angela and Sarah, and in you they live on. She told me to tell you, go and sit on the bench outside the cottage, the place where Sarah spent her hours praying for Michael's safe return from the war and dreaming about you, years before you were born.

Or maybe you'll be paddling in the Taramore in the village with Finnbar. Would you believe, sometimes I would give anything for a moment of the gossip with the likes of Philomena O'Donnell or Mrs Doyle, and I think about Paddy and Josie Devlin and how kind they were to me when Rory died.

I know how you must feel about Rosie. It has hurt me too, hearing how she has taken Sarah's place and become a real mother to Finnbar when that boy has not a shred of her own flesh and blood in him. My heart aches for him.

I shall take the guilt of not being there for both of you to my grave. But it was never to be. I had to find a life for Captain Bob and me to be together and that wasn't possible in Tarabeg. I am so sorry I had to leave you.

You will return home to Tarabeg with itchy feet and big ideas. I swear to God, if your mother hadn't promised herself to Michael before he went away to war, she would have run away to some place like this, to where I have ended up, to Liverpool or America. It would have been Sarah here in Waterloo Street, not me. Just like your mother made her choice to stay in Tarabeg and wait for Michael, you can make your choice now as to what the future holds for you.

Without her even knowing it, Bee had planted the seed of rebellion in Mary Kate's mind. 'She would have run away to some place like this.' Those words had been committed to memory. Mary Kate was her mother's girl. It was a hidden message; it had to be. Bee wanted her to come but knew she couldn't ask. Bee knew all along that Michael would never allow her to sail to Liverpool; this was Bee's way of telling her to come, come here, come away, to her, to Liverpool. And now she was.

We have been here for so long now and I can't see that changing anytime soon. I hope one day to return home and to see Tarabeg again. Don't I just dream of the place every single night. But until that time, I will be here in Waterloo Street. I hope to see you one day soon now that you are leaving school and are all grown-up.

'I hope to see you one day soon' – it very definitely was

a secret message, and Mary Kate had understood exactly what Bee was asking her to do.

She smiled to herself as she read the letter again. She imagined the look on Bee's face when she opened her door, wondered would she recognise her from the child she had left.

Chapter 8

'Hello, love, looking for somewhere to sit?' A tall and kindly lady beamed down at Mary Kate as she stood there on the deck. Despite the weather, the lady was wearing a felt hat. In one hand she held a birdcage covered in heavy fringed cloth, suspended parallel with her ear; in the other, down by her side, she carried a carpetbag.

Nola had told Mary Kate so often, 'You can always trust a lady who wears a hat.' She immediately thought of Aunty Teresa from the Presbytery, whom she had never in all of her life seen without a hat, and realised that Granny Nola was probably right. There was no woman more trustworthy than Aunty Teresa. She folded her letter from Bee and held it tight. 'I am, yes. Thank you.'

'Come on then, I'll show you the best place to sit.' The woman had twinkly grey eyes that seemed to smile of their own accord in her thin face. Her wrinkles appeared more like laughter lines, gathered around her eyes and mouth and leaving her powdery pink cheeks soft and clear. She wore sturdy brown leather shoes, laced up in a neatly tied bow, her skirt was a soft flannel grey and hung to mid calf, and her white blouse was edged with a lace collar and cuffs, its neck fastened at the base of her throat with a cameo brooch. Beneath the loose blouse, her frame looked slender and fragile.

In a matter of seconds, Mary Kate went from feeling anxious to safe.

'That lot there…' The lady indicated the crowds who'd gathered three deep at the deck rails. They were waving – their caps raised high in the air, their white handkerchiefs fluttering – to friends, loved ones and relatives on the dockside, solemn or tearful, or simply bidding farewell to Dublin itself. 'In two minutes, they'll be thundering down the stairs and taking the best seats, so come on, come with me. I'm an old hand, I'll show you the way. You're going to be on this ferry all day, so you may as well make yourself comfortable.'

Mary Kate looked back and wondered if Declan would still be standing on the dock watching the boat sail away, trying to catch sight of her. She knew he would be and she felt a moment of guilt, a sting of pain.

'Come along,' said the lady. And Mary Kate, still under the influence of Sister Magdalena and unable to disobey an order issued by an older woman, followed her, the birdcage and oversized carpetbag down a spiral staircase made of wrought iron and painted dark green.

The steps were wet and looked precarious and Mary Kate clung to the handrail for dear life as the soles of their shoes clattered out their descent, the noise echoing loudly across the scrubbed wooden deck. At the bottom they crossed an exposed section of the lower deck, where the screech of seagulls following the boat was almost deafening, and entered a cavernous room full of wooden benches riveted to the floor. A line of salt-stained port-holes afforded no view of the shrinking Dublin coastline and the room was filled with steam from a simmering urn on a counter in the corner. A man in a sailor's cap leant casually up against the wall behind the counter, reading a newspaper and smoking a cigarette. He didn't look up as they walked in.

'Here we go. Put your bags down there,' said the lady as she placed hers firmly on the end of a front bench. 'I'll put Bluey on the other end, here.' She lifted the cloth of the cage to reveal a very blue budgie, who bobbed up and down in greeting.

Mary Kate did exactly as she was told and sat on the bench, in the middle.

The lady straightened her back and, scooping up a purse out of her bag, folded her arms. 'Now, don't tell me, this is your first time, isn't it?'

Mary Kate nodded and smiled. 'It is. Is it obvious?'

The lady threw her head back and laughed. 'You're a dead giveaway, my dear. Let me tell you why: you have a letter clutched tight in your hand that you won't let go of for love nor money, and you haven't taken your cotton gloves off. You can put your bag on the bench next to you, it doesn't have to stay on your knee – it isn't going to fly away. I can barely see you over the top. And for goodness' sake, don't look so scared.'

Mary Kate warmed to her instantly.

'Now, my name is Mrs O'Keefe, and I'm going to get a nice cuppa and a chocolate biscuit. It's the only thing I look forward to on this journey. You're lucky, the sea's calm today. Some of that lot' – she raised her eyes heavenwards, towards the upper deck – 'will head straight to the canteen. They'll eat a hearty breakfast and then feed it to the fishes long before we reach Liverpool. Shall I bring you one back?'

'Oh, please, let me get you the money.' Mary Kate tried awkwardly to scrabble around for her purse.

'No, you look after my Bluey and my bag while I'm gone and we'll sort that out later.'

Mary Kate took her bag-minding responsibility very seriously. She stretched out her arms and rested one hand on her own bag and the other on Bluey's cage. He bobbed along his perch to take an inquisitive peck at her fingers.

As she turned to look through the porthole, she noticed a dishevelled young man lying along the full length of the wooden bench beneath it. He raised his head slightly and his eyes met hers before his head flopped back down. His hat was on the floor next to the bench and it was obvious to Mary Kate, having seen enough men following a night in Paddy's bar in Tarabeg, that he was worse for drink. Something about his eyes made her uncomfortable and her skin prickled as she looked away.

A few moments later Mrs O'Keefe was back with a pot of tea on a wooden tray and a plate of biscuits. 'Come on then,' she said. 'Budge up and I'll put the tray between us. It's a calm crossing today. If you keep that down, you can try a sandwich at lunchtime, but don't have the spam. Made me ill for a week once, that did.'

Mary Kate exhaled. She could relax. She had done it. So far, she was safe and well, and she'd already made a friend. The rhythmic bumping of the waves against the boat was telling her that she was free, sailing away on the crest of her dreams.

Within minutes, Mrs O'Keefe had extracted from Mary Kate every detail of her escape from Tarabeg with Declan and her plans for Liverpool. 'God, your family will be out of their minds and sick with worry,' she said as she lifted up the small blue milk jug and poured some more into Mary Kate's cup. 'You will make sure to let them know as soon as you arrive, won't you? Liverpool is a big city. Nothing like Galway or your Tarabeg. Not everyone is friendly there like they are back home. Be on your guard, won't you? There are some right scallywags about.'

She inclined her head towards the bench where the drunken young man was now snoring. 'You know, the sailor in the kitchen was telling me that some of them don't get spotted, so they sleep it off until they're halfway back to Dublin on the night sailing out of Liverpool and get off the boat exactly where they got on. Money spent, and they land up back on their mammy's doorstep.' She tittered with laughter.

'Oh, I will be on my guard, of course I will,' said Mary Kate, having no idea what a scallywag was. 'I'm perfectly capable of looking after meself. I've been helping Daddy run the shop since I could walk. You don't need to be worrying about me. I have a good education and I won't have any trouble finding work.' She sat upright and proud and her eyes held Mrs O'Keefe's, who resisted a smile.

Mrs O'Keefe decided not to say any more. Mary Kate had enough on her plate for one day.

The lower deck area had filled up and Mary Kate had pulled her bag a little closer to allow someone to squeeze onto the far end of their bench. She looked about the room, which was now filled with trilby hats, the blue haze of cigarette smoke, men in sailors' uniforms and women clutching the hands of small children.

'They're all leaving for the work,' Mrs O'Keefe confided. 'There's plenty to be had in Liverpool. That's how I met my husband, God rest his soul. Came to Liverpool for work, met me and spent the rest of his days married to a Scouser. He only came for six months, but he stayed forty years. He's buried back in Dublin though, his dying wish, and that's where we've been, isn't it, Bluey? We go once a month to the grave and spend the day there. I give him all the news – you know, the football results and the like. I write the scores of the matches down so that I don't forget when I tell him. He loved Bluey – more than me, I reckon – that's why I take him along. I stay for the night at his sister's and then come back on the morning boat.'

By the time they were several hours into their crossing, Mary Kate felt that there was nothing of importance about her life that Mrs O'Keefe didn't now know, and vice versa.

Eventually, the sound of the engine altered and appeared to slow and there was a lot of shouting and clanging of chains.

'Ah, twenty minutes to go,' Mrs O'Keefe said. 'Now, let me see the address of where you're going, love.' She held out her hand to take the letter, which Mary Kate was still gripping tightly. 'Oh, God, it's on the dock streets. Be careful down there, won't you. It's not far, but if you can afford it, I'd be getting a cab if I were you. You'll hear the klaxon go when the dockers are knocking off and I wouldn't want you to be on the street then, not a girl from a convent school. No, that wouldn't be right. You won't understand half the things they'll shout at a good-looking girl like you. I'm off on the bus in the opposite direction. I have to be back at the house for three thirty to meet my sister, Lizzie. She'll be on the phone to the police if I'm late. Hates me going to the grave, she does. Thinks it's all a nonsense.'

They had chatted for a full twenty minutes about how successful Lizzie was at running her own business, an agency supplying housekeepers, domestic helps and the like to Liverpool's wealthier homes. Mrs O'Keefe was proud of her.

'You could get the bus too, but that will drop you at the top of the Dockers' Steps and that's just where you don't want to be. You're dressed far too nicely to pass unnoticed. And they say the people from the bogs are the ruffians! Wait until you see some of the kids on the dock streets. No, get a cab just this once – do you have enough money?'

'Oh yes. Daedio gave me twenty pounds for my birthday, and then he gave me a lot more yesterday.' Mary Kate stopped speaking – had it been only yesterday?

'Sshh, girl.' Mrs O'Keefe put her finger to her lips and frantically looked about her. 'Don't go telling that to anyone else, do you hear me? That's a lot of money. Keep what you have tight in your purse and keep your purse on you at all times. God in heaven, you innocents from the bogs, you are a gift to the conmen around the Pier Head. And, believe me, most of them have an Irish accent, so don't be trusting anyone just because you think they're from home, do you hear me? The stories I've heard. Promise me you'll go straight to your aunty's house and nowhere else first.'

'I promise.' The purse Mary Kate had placed in her coat pocket weighed heavy against her leg.

They parted at the foot of the landing stage and Mrs O'Keefe pointed towards the taxi rank. 'See over there, that wooden hut, that's where the Crosville buses go from. The taxis are right next to that hut. I can see one now – can you?'

Mary Kate placed her hands over her eyes and squinted at where Mrs O'Keefe was pointing. 'I can see it,' she said, her voice rising with the excitement of being in Liverpool.

'Here, love.' Mrs O'Keefe waved her handkerchief in the air and the taxi driver acknowledged her by putting his arm out of the window and waving back.

'Here's my corpy bus. The taxi will only cost a few bob. Get your money out now and then put your purse away. I'll stand with you.'

Mary Kate did as she was told and extracted the twenty-pound note from her purse.

'Jesus, is that the smallest you have?'

Mary Kate nodded, dismayed. 'Will they not take it?'

'Well, you can ask him first, but it's a lot. It's more than a fortnight's wages for some.'

Mary Kate decided not to tell her that the dollars Daedio had given her amounted to the equivalent of fifty English pounds.

'Go on then, off you go.'

Mary Kate kept the note and her purse in her hand, ready.

'I feel like I should give you a hug,' said Mrs O'Keefe.

'Here, let me write my address down for you. When my husband was alive, God rest his soul, we had lots of girls coming straight from the boat to us from Dublin. We've set more of them up in jobs in Liverpool than I can think, thanks to Lizzie's agency. Hard to believe, but there are more women in Liverpool who employ someone to wash their smalls than you can poke a stick at, and I'm one of them, I'm afraid. Now, take my address in case you should ever need it.'

Mary Kate thought of Declan's words. 'Honestly, I'm much sharper than I look,' she said. 'No one will pull the wool over my eyes. I told you, my da runs a shop.'

'He runs a shop in a village,' said Mrs O'Keefe, her voice loaded with doubt before heading on her way. Mary Kate gave the appearance of being almost too trusting, too friendly, too nice. That was the trouble with the Irish – they thought everyone was a relative, and in a way they were. The generations had crisscrossed over hundreds of years – linked up, got broken, been reconnected, one village, one town, one name to another – which instilled a sense of family and belonging like nowhere else in the world.

The cab driver saw Mary Kate approaching and threw his cigarette butt out of the window. He wasn't sure if the man following behind was with her or not. He folded his newspaper, shoved it down the inside of the car door and jumped out.

'Where to, queen?'

'Waterloo Street, please. Number twenty-seven.'

He took Mary Kate's case in his hand. 'Right, well, that's not far then. Coming for work, are you?' He'd met them all before. The student nurses arriving from Dublin, the navvies, the cleaners, the barmaids, and the prostitutes too. Half of Liverpool was Irish and he prided himself on being able to tell one regional accent from another. He could divide Cavan from Donegal, Galway from Sligo. 'Mayo, is it?' he asked with a smile.

'Yes, it is. Tarabeg.' Mary Kate was loving Liverpool already. Everyone was so kind and friendly. Mrs O'Keefe must have been a very over-cautious type. 'I only have a twenty-pound note – can you change it, please?'

The cab driver whistled and pushed up the brim of his cap. 'No, I can't, queen. I don't get many notes, and if I had to change that, it would clear me out. Tell you what, you wait here, keep hold of the note, and I'll nip over to the cashier in the Crosville hut and ask him if he'll change some of my notes. If not, we can call into the post office on the Dock Road on the way. You will need that changing. You can't buy a bag of chips with a twenty-pound note, queen – you'll starve to death. Let me put your bag in the boot first to keep it safe.'

Mary Kate smiled. Another problem solved. 'Is the cashier far?' she asked.

'No, he's just in the wooden hut there, or I wouldn't be offering, would I – you might run off with me cab and then what would I do?'

They were both laughing as the cabbie moved round

to the back of his car with Mary Kate's luggage in his hand. He pulled open the boot and pushed her case to the back, drew the rug he kept in there over it, closed the lid and came back round to the side of the car. It had taken him all of ninety seconds, but he was too late. Mary Kate was lying on the ground beside the cab, groaning. Her legs were splayed out behind her, her face was a deathly shade of white, and blood was trickling from her temple. She tried to scramble to her knees, had no idea what had happened, but collapsed back down. One minute she'd been standing there smiling, watching the cabbie with her bag, the next she was on the floor with a painful wound on the side of her neck. The twenty-pound note and her purse were gone, and her letter from Bee was flapping on the ground next to her, the wind lifting its corners, threatening to steal that too.

'Oi, you! Stop!' The cab driver saw that the man who'd been following Mary Kate was running away and he gave chase.

Mary Kate flopped against the side of the cab, her back propped up against the door. She recognised the thief – it was the young man who'd been asleep on the boat, lying on the bench behind her. She could see her purse in his hand, but despite his dishevelled state, he was running twice as fast as the cabbie. A whistle pierced the air as a policeman came out of a small wooden hut and also gave chase, but he was even slower on his feet than the taxi driver.

The thief ran out across the tramlines. A tram horn

blasted and cars beeped. In a flash he was gone up Church Street, swallowed up by the crowds of shoppers heading one way and travellers the other. Both men knew they'd lost him. They stopped, bent over, placed their hands on their knees and gasped for breath.

The reality of her situation hit Mary Kate in a wave of despair. She was a stranger in a huge city and she'd been robbed. She was penniless. Everything Daedio had given her was gone. Tears filled her eyes, her heart thumped, and she began to tremble.

'Welcome to Liverpool,' said a man who'd been passing and had hurried over to her. 'Here, let me help you. You've taken a bit of a knock, haven't you.'

Mary Kate felt swamped with dismay. Shocked by the violence she'd just been subjected to, her instinctive reaction was to mistrust this stranger. She pulled back.

'Don't worry about me, I'm here to help you,' the man said. 'Besides, you've got nothing left, so there's no point in robbing you now, is there?' He grinned as he removed his long, grey overcoat, folded it and placed it behind her back.

She felt as though the cobbles were about to open up and devour her. This was as bad as it could be. Every penny she owned in the world had been taken. 'No one can pull the wool over my eyes,' she'd said to Mrs O'Keefe. 'I'm perfectly capable of looking after meself.' And here she was, in Liverpool and already caught off guard and attacked and robbed. And Mrs O'Keefe, a woman she didn't even know, had left her not five minutes since. Thank God she still had her case and Aunty Bee's address. She'd been told it wasn't that far on foot. She could still make it, and Aunty Bee would know what to do.

A woman had trotted over to join them and she squatted down beside Mary Kate. 'Are you all right, love?' she asked. 'I saw him from my office window, just over there – I sell the ferry tickets. It happens all the bloody time, it does, that's why they put the police hut just there, near the bottom of the landing. Honest to God, and it's still going on. I'll get you a tea. Do you think she needs a check-up at St Angelus? That's a nasty mark on her neck, and look, she's bleeding.'

The woman glanced up at the man who'd stopped to help. He had already taken Mary Kate's pulse, and from the pocket of the overcoat folded behind Mary Kate's head he was now removing a stethoscope.

'I'm Dr Marcus,' he said. 'From the Princess Avenue surgery. I was on my way to St Angelus. I can check her over right here. If you could kindly fetch her some strong sweet tea, and I will fetch my car and my bag.'

The woman almost dropped a curtsey. 'Of course, Doctor. I'll go right now. Won't be long, love,' she said to Mary Kate with a sympathetic frown. She scurried away and returned minutes later with the tea and the waitress from the Pier Head café, who carried the pot handle in one hand and the spout in the other.

Mary Kate was bemused to see a crowd gathering. The

policeman was back by her side and had taken out his notebook, and the cab driver was next to him, rolling a cigarette. 'I'm right out of puff,' he said. 'I need this to breathe. Do you want one, love, to calm your nerves?'

Mary Kate shook her head. She couldn't yet trust herself to speak in case she burst into tears and embarrassed herself further.

They all turned as a car pulled up behind the cab. Dr Marcus jumped out with his Gladstone bag in his hand. The lady from the tea hut who'd carried the teapot recognised him immediately.

'Oh hello, Doctor, fancy it being you. I'll pour you some tea an' all.' She was hoping he might take a look at her varicose veins when the drama was over.

Dr Marcus turned Mary Kate's head one way and then the other as he held her eyelids open and shone a light into her eyes. He smiled at her. 'I think you'll live. You've had a nasty shock, though, and you've sustained an injury. He knocked you with some force on the back of your neck, judging by the size of the red mark. It'll be a nasty bruise in the morning and very painful.'

Mary Kate could hold it together no longer. The horrible mugging, the doctor's kindness, the tea lady's sympathy, the office worker who was holding her hand, the cabbie keeping guard, it was all so confusing. Good people appearing from nowhere, rushing to her aid. And the rawness of her failure to keep her purse safe, her overwhelming sense of having let Daedio down. The pain and the shame, it was all too much. She promptly burst into tears.

The lady from the office wiped her cheeks with a hand-kerchief. 'You poor love,' she said.

'I know. What a rotten welcome to Liverpool,' said the tea lady. Turning to Dr Marcus, who was packing his torch back into his bag, she half whispered, 'Eh, Doctor, if I could slip me stocking down behind the cab, could you take a look at my varicose vein? It's killing me, it is. I know you said I had to put it up for an hour a day to drain it, but how can I? I've got a job and our kids – I never get a minute.'

The policeman's voice rose authoritatively above the others, who turned to look at him. 'Can I ask her a few questions, please, Doctor?' he said deferentially. 'There appears to be something of a pattern here. This young lady is the fifth mugging in broad daylight on the fifth day in a row. They've all been young ladies stepping off the boat and carrying a handbag or a purse.'

'Really, is that so?' said Dr Marcus with a hint of irony in his voice. 'Could you tell me then why you were inside your hut when you would have been of more use outside it, watching passengers as they disembarked, acting as a deterrent to would-be muggers? You should have been standing at the bottom of the landing, keeping your eyes peeled until everyone was safely away from the Pier Head. And why is there only one of you?'

The policeman looked confused and then had the good grace to look embarrassed.

The waitress was pulling her stocking back up and fastening her suspender, her dignity assured by the cab door and by Mary Kate, who was blocking her from public view. Dr Marcus wrote out a prescription for the waitress on his pad, ripped it off and handed it to her. 'Here, Doctor, have a cup of tea now,' she said as she retrieved the pot from the front seat of the cab.

Dr Marcus made Mary Kate lie down on the seat of his car for ten minutes, to recover from the shock. She drank her tea, which was full of sugar, in line with his instructions. Despite her trauma, she was already feeling physically better, but the shame had robbed her of her voice and her eyes remained downcast.

Slowly, the drama of the girl who had nearly been 'knocked dead' on the Pier Head subsided, and the police officer, having taken his statement, retreated to his hut. 'Right, well, I have your aunt's address,' he said to Mary Kate as he made his quick exit. 'Any news and I will come and see you, miss.'

'Aye, that'll be the day,' said the cab driver. 'Go and have a lie down first though, eh – you've had to work hard today.'

The policeman scowled in response.

'I have to go back to work now, love,' said the office worker.

Mary Kate turned to Dr Marcus and thanked him. Her face was dirt-streaked and pale. Her blue eyes shone bright with unshed tears and her hands were still shaking.

'Can you take this young lady to her destination?' the doctor asked the cabbie.

The cab driver shook his head. 'I'd love to, Doctor, I would, but the boss clocks every mile against the money at the end of my shift. If I do that, he'll think I've nicked the money.' He blushed and looked mortified.

'Don't worry,' said Dr Marcus. 'Waterloo Street isn't far. I was on my way to a lunch at the hospital, but I'll be too late now anyway. Could you wait with the young lady for a moment while I run to a phone box and make a call to Matron? She cannot abide bad manners and I'll be in trouble if I don't.'

The taxi driver saluted the doctor as though he were his senior in the army, and the doctor smiled and saluted him back. In a moment, the doctor was gone. Mary Kate watched his retreating back. Despite the warm day, he was wearing a trilby hat and had put his overcoat back on, which flapped about his legs.

'Isn't he handsome,' said the waitress. 'Everyone loves him, they do. Can't get to see him for love nor money. I reckon his list is full of women and the men can't get a look in. Right, I'm off to pop this into the chemist's. You seem all right now, love. Good luck and all that, and remember, it can only get better, eh? You know where I am if you ever want a cuppa.' She gave Mary Kate a wink, and she was gone.

Mary Kate's bottom lip trembled. There had been safety in the number of people who had gathered round, but now that it was back to her and the cab driver, she felt vulnerable once more. She removed her case from the boot of his car. 'I can walk, you know,' she said with a warble in her voice.

'No, you cannot. And anyway, Dr Marcus won't let you. He's a good man.'

Mary Kate, the most trusting of people, felt suddenly as though she would never like or trust anyone again.

'You can depend on him. Did his medical training up here, then went down south for a while and came back with a wife. He has his own practice on Princess Avenue and his reputation is bigger than he is. You are in the best hands, little lady, and there's a lot of women around here would envy you – can't say I blame them though. Good job I'm not a jealous man, eh?'

For the first time, Mary Kate felt relief wash over her. The doctor would take her to Bee's and then at last, after what felt like a very long day, she would be safe. Bee would know what to do.

Dr Marcus threw his Gladstone bag into the back of his Morris Traveller with little ceremony, removed his overcoat, folded it carefully, laid it on the back seat of the car, took off his trilby and placed it on top.

'Don't worry, Doc, I'll put her bag in the rear,' said the cab driver as he went round to the back of the car.

Mary Kate watched them both and noticed the doctor's features for the first time. His good looks were undeniable, but it was his air of kindness that was his real attraction.

His hair was the darkest brown and pushed over to the side, and his eyes were the same colour. She thought they seemed sad, mournful. He had olive skin and his face was thin and angular. His nose was almost too large for it but somehow accentuated the symmetry of his good looks, and his cheekbones were sharp enough to slice cheese. Mary Kate thought that if Granny Nola ever met him, she would want to sit him down and give him a good feed and a bowl of her own butter to take home with him.

As he walked towards her, he smiled. 'Feeling any better now? You mustn't worry. You'll feel dreadful because it was such a nasty shock, but physically you've made a full recovery. We just need to keep an eye on you. I fear it's your pride that is the most injured.'

Mary Kate couldn't quite manage a smile back, even though she tried. He was right; she was smarting from having been unable to protect herself from the thief, who had obviously listened to every word she'd said to Mrs O'Keefe and had marked her as his prey. She wanted to hit herself, never mind the thief. 'Thank you,' she mumbled as she pulled her hair back into a ponytail and tightened her band. It had become dishevelled, and it was a sign of her recovery that she wanted to look halfway presentable for her Aunty Bee. She couldn't turn up at her door looking as she did now.

'Do you need a bathroom?'

Her head shot up. Had he read her thoughts? 'I do, I'm afraid.'

'It will be the shock, and you'll want to freshen up too. I'll take you to a café. I've missed my medical lunch now, so I need feeding, otherwise I'll turn into a version of Frankenstein's monster very soon.' He opened the car door. 'In you get.'

Despite her predicament, she smiled at the thought of him turning into a monster; it was impossible to imagine.

He walked over to the cab driver and wrote something down, then joined her in the car. 'I've told him to keep an eye out and let me know if this happens again. I play golf with the chief superintendent and I'll have a word with him if it seems it's not being taken seriously.'

In the side mirror Mary Kate saw the cab driver raise his hand in farewell. If she ever had the chance, she would come back and in some way thank him for his kindness.

An hour later, Mary Kate was sitting in Trapasso's Café, her plate of egg and chips now cleared away, her face washed, her ribbons tied and her cheeks flushed once more.

'There now, doesn't everything feel a lot better?' Dr Marcus leant back in the wooden chair and lit a cigarette.

She had to admit, it did.

He slid his silver cigarette case across the yellow top of the Formica table. 'Would you like one?'

She shook her head.

He flicked the lid of his Dunhill lighter, inhaled, and with his elbows on the table, clasped his hands together and peered at her through the smoke. She smiled at him.

She felt warm inside, and it wasn't just because of his kindness, or the fried eggs and chips. She had never in her life set eyes upon a man such as he. She thought of Roshine's father, the only other doctor she knew. Big, burly and brusque. Locals would rather drink a bottle of goat blood, blessed by a tinker, before they ventured into his surgery. This doctor was nothing like him.

'Now, tell me, why are you here in this big, bad city?'

'Oh, that's an easy one to answer. My Aunty Bee has asked me to come.' She told him something of her life, about her mother's death, and Rosie, and her father, and Finn. He was entranced by her description of Tarabeg – the coast, the village, the river, the party and her slipping away in the night.

'Good Lord, it sounds like you've run away from heaven. You do know that Waterloo Road isn't the most salubrious area of Liverpool, don't you?'

Mary Kate blushed. She had no idea where it was.

'I'm not sure why your aunty would have seen that as a better place for you. I'd have thought getting more training and then finding a suitable job would have been a preferable option – it would have given you a purpose and somewhere to go. We have a lot of girls coming over to Liverpool to train as nurses, and very fine nurses they make too. I've worked with lots of them.'

Mary Kate was despondent. 'I suppose, because Aunty Bee asked me—'

'Did she? I'm not sure that was good advice. Here, let

me see the letter.' He held out his hand and Mary Kate obediently passed it over. He read it, frowned at her, folded it and handed it back, then stubbed out his cigarette in the ashtray. 'Come on then, let's go. I have a surgery starting soon.'

Mary Kate was disappointed. She'd expected a more enthusiastic response, an endorsement of the fact that Aunty Bee had meant what she said, that it was a message just for her.

A mere ten minutes later, they were on Waterloo Street. Their progress down the wide Dock Road had shown Mary Kate another world, noisy with the bustle of foundries, drays, ships and cranes. She'd blinked in the sunshine as she took it all in. They drove past some children playing on bombed-out wasteland and down a street with only one side intact; the other side had been razed to the ground. 'A direct hit during the war,' said Dr Marcus, and Mary Kate blessed herself. She wondered how many families had lost their lives.

When they turned into Waterloo Street, the sun almost disappeared. Redbrick houses, blackened by soot and coal dust from the docks, lined both sides of the narrow, cobbled road. There were children playing in the street, some only half dressed, and women leaning up against windowsills, smoking and dipping their heads to look inside the car and see who was visiting. The children began to run behind the car, chasing it and squealing, and dogs raced alongside, trying to bite the tyres.

'The dogs in Tarabeg do that too,' said Mary Kate.

'Ah, well, the dogs in Waterloo Street are as unfamiliar with cars as the dogs are in Tarabeg, I'd imagine. They'll very rarely see one around here, unless it's a Black Maria. Ah, here we are, number twenty-seven.' He slowed the car to a halt, jumped out and opened Mary Kate's door for her.

Mary Kate slid out of the car, hurried to the front door and banged on the knocker, aware that a small crowd of children was forming around her. Her heart was beating wildly with the anticipation of seeing her Aunty Bee again. She could hear her mother's voice in her ear, a more elusive memory. She swallowed hard; her mouth was dry and her eyes bright.

There were no answering footsteps on the opposite side of the door, so she knocked again.

Several of the women who'd been gossiping in the street, their hair in curlers and all wearing the ubiquitous uniform of a floral wraparound apron, slowly moved towards her. She noticed another woman, three doors down, who was kneeling on the pavement, scrubbing her step. The woman shook her head at Mary Kate as she leant back on her heels and dropped her scrubbing brush into her pail. It clattered against the side as dirty water slopped over the top. 'Cat!' she shouted over her shoulder. 'Cat, there's someone at Bee's.'

'No one's there, missus. They've left,' said a little boy with dirty hands and knees, scruffy hair, and threads hanging from his jumper. He had pushed to the front of the crowd of children. He was the smallest by far, but the most vocal.

Mary Kate felt sick. 'Gone? Gone where?'

'Cat! Come here,' an older boy shouted to a woman who was running down the street carrying a shopping bag.

'Move, would you, the lot of you,' she shouted as she approached. Waving her string bag, she clipped the older boy who'd shouted her across the head. The apron-clad women clustered around her. 'Who do you want, love?' the woman asked as she folded her arms and looked Mary Kate up and down suspiciously.

Mary Kate clung to her letter. Had she got the address wrong? Dr Marcus was standing by his car, leaning against the bonnet, keeping his eye on the dozen or so boys who had gathered around it and were bombarding him with questions.

'I'm looking for my Aunty Bee and Captain Bob and Ciaran,' said Mary Kate.

The woman looked kind enough, but she had a concerned expression on her face.

Another woman came and stood next to her. 'I'm Linda, love. Why do you want Bee?' She appeared to be waiting for Mary Kate's answer with hungry enthusiasm.

The woman the kids had called Cat laughed. 'Oh bloody hell, queen, you're a day late. They left yesterday. Off back to her beloved Tarabeg, they were. They couldn't get out fast enough. Never liked it here really, did Bee.

I'm Cat, her next-door neighbour. Are you all right? You look pale.'

Mary Kate's eyes filled with tears and the pavement slid beneath her feet. She put the flat of her hand on the door to steady herself. 'Gone to Tarabeg – are you sure?' Her words were a whisper, she could barely speak.

'Oh yeah, love, they've gone all right, and taken everything with them. Gone for good.'

Mary Kate had no chance to reply as the pavement rose to meet her.

Chapter 9

The sun bathed her upturned face as Mary Kate, her eyes shut tight, sat perched on the large white rock beside the Taramore river. The rock had absorbed all the warmth from the morning sun and Mary Kate felt it seeping into her chilled bones as she listened to the plop, plop of the salmon tails flapping about in the deeper pools. She allowed her toes to sink into the inches of ice-cold peat-coloured water until her feet rested on the cool, pebbly bottom. All she could hear was water and birdsong.

The rock had been a favourite of many generations of Malones. Over the course of thousands of years, the force of the river had worn it into an invitingly smooth seat. Decades ago, just after the seven acres through which the Taramore streamed had been bought by the Malones, Daedio's father had dragged the rock out of the river and onto the pebbly bank, helped by Daedio. The Malone children had used it as a seat ever since, sometimes just idling there, sometimes on guard while the men went out in the curragh to poach the salmon when the river ran high.

'Mary Kate! Mary Kate!' a voice called from behind her. She didn't turn. She didn't want to. She had to sit exactly where she was, there in the sun, with the sound of the river in her ears, for as long as she possibly could. To turn would be a mistake; the peace would be broken. She had to sit by the river and defy the calls, maybe forever.

It was a hot day and she'd coaxed Bid, her one-eyed dog, to the riverbank, where she'd dribbled water over his fur to cool him. She had Jacko, her donkey, with her too, as usual; otherwise he'd have escaped into the oat field at the first opportunity. He'd taken his turn to drink from the river. Mary Kate too had scooped up the water in her cupped hands. As it trickled down her throat, she thought how there was no water anywhere as cold or sweet or pure as that which ran straight down the mountains onto Malone land. She wiped her wet hands over her forehead to cool her brow.

With her eyes still closed, she reached out and wound her fingers around Jacko's rope, which was lying on the ground beside her. She held on tight and resisted his persistent tugging. The rope bit into her palm and she frowned, deciding to release him, but her fingers wouldn't let her. Bid shuffled closer to her on all fours, across the pebbles on which he'd been warming his belly, and laid his head on her lap. She smiled as her free hand stroked the damp, sun-warmed fur on his back. She was in heaven, or so she thought.

'Mary Kate! Mary Kate!' The voice again, louder and nearer now, but still she didn't turn. Bid licked her face, alerting her, urging her to look, his one eye blinking over her shoulder, his face happy. He licked her again, his tongue wet and cold, strangely cold. Jacko pulled on the rope in her hand and shook her arm; he wanted her to turn too.

'Mary Kate!'

She was losing the ability to stay in that warm, safe place, felt herself being pushed up through the layers of resistance, forced to respond. She turned half around on the rock, with a tightness in her belly, her body stiff with wariness and fear. There was an urgency to the voice that she could no longer ignore. Her legs were like lead weights and her head was almost too heavy to support. The sun was so bright, forcing her to blink, and she could only just make out the shadowy figure running towards her.

'Mary Kate!'

It was her mammy, Sarah, stumbling in her desperation to reach her, and she was being followed, chased by a woman in a black dress with wild white hair. Finn was still just a baby in her mammy's arms, and Sarah's golden-red hair was streaming out behind her as her long lemon skirt and white apron billowed about her legs in a breeze that had seemingly arrived from nowhere. The sun slipped behind a dark, ominous cloud.

'Mary Kate, come home now! Come home, quick,

please! Get up! You must come home!' Her mammy was shouting to her, seemingly unaware of the woman at her back, who was closing the distance.

Mary Kate's throat thickened. She had to warn her. She just managed to say 'Mammy!' and tried to let go of Jacko's lead rope as she did so. But Jacko wouldn't let the rope drop; it was as though it was stuck to her palm, and he kept tugging at her arm. She tried to stand, but she fell back down onto the rock. Pain split her head and as she looked up, she saw her mammy bearing down on her with tears in her eyes and distress etched across her face. She was still shouting and reaching out, but she was melting away, and the woman with the white hair had appeared above her, blocking out the sun altogether.

Mary Kate could no longer hear the voice of her beloved mammy. Her precious soft voice was ebbing away, fading to a whisper, and another replaced it as the cloud swallowed the sun and the light turned gloomy.

'Mary Kate, can you open your eyes?'

The hand holding hers belonged to the doctor who had come to help her at the dockside. He had two fingers pressed down on her wrist and was staring at the watch on his arm.

'How are you feeling now?'

She heard his words through waves of blackness. She struggled to open her eyes for longer than a few seconds, found it hard to lift her head.

As her vision adjusted, she realised she was lying on

her back. The worried face of Cat hovered somewhere over her feet.

'Oh thank bloody God. She's alive then, Doctor.'

'I think the fact that she's blinking at us would confirm that, yes. Although she is still rather confused.'

Mary Kate's gaze followed the voice and she could see the doctor was smiling. His expression changed to one of kindness and concern as he let go of her wrist and patted the back of her hand.

Cat spoke again. 'We thought you was dead, love. The doctor said you weren't, though, didn't you, Doctor?' Then, calling across the room, 'Our Betty, go and get her a glass of water.'

'Yes, it would seem I made a rather miraculous diagnosis.' Dr Marcus was smiling again.

Mary Kate turned her head and into her eyes peered the anxious eyes of a little girl aged four or five. She had a filthy face and was clutching Mary Kate's hand in her hot little fingers, her nails embedded with grime.

Betty trotted over to the sink, carrying the wet rag she'd been using to wipe Mary Kate's face. 'I can't reach,' she wailed. 'Linda is sat on the chair.'

Mary Kate lifted her head and tried to sit up. The sofa springs were sticking into her back.

'Better not do that,' said the doctor, who rose and slid a cushion under her head. 'If you don't mind, I would prefer it if you stayed lying down. Can you tell me, do you have any nausea or blurred vision?'

Mary Kate closed her eyes. 'No, just a bad headache,' she whispered, so that only he could hear her.

'Well, that's something then. But I would still prefer it if you remained on your back, to keep your blood pressure up a little, at least for the next few hours.'

Cat's face appeared again, this time almost over the doctor's shoulder. She had a glass of water in her hands. 'You've had a nasty shock, love,' she said. 'Come here, let me help you with the water.' She slipped her arm under Mary Kate's and across her back, tilted her head and held the cup to her lips. 'Is this all right, Doctor? How about I get her a nice cup of tea?'

The doctor was retrieving his stethoscope from his Gladstone bag. 'Not yet – a bit soon. I would love one though.'

'Betty, make the doctor a cuppa. Sorry, Doctor, I haven't any sugar and we only have steri milk.'

There was nothing Dr Marcus hated more in the world than sterilised milk, which never went off. He looked at his watch and pulled the earpiece of his stethoscope from one his ears. 'Actually, do you know, my afternoon surgery starts in a matter of minutes, so I don't have time, but thank you anyway.' He sat down next to Mary Kate on the sofa. 'I just need to place this on your chest,' he said.

'Me and Linda will have a cuppa, Betty,' said Cat as she laid Mary Kate's head back on the cushion and moved away to let the doctor near his patient. 'God, my nerves are shot. She scared the life out of me when she fainted. I've never seen anyone do that before. What a bang her head made on that pavement.'

She walked over to the sink. 'Come here, Betty. I'll do it meself.' She poured out the tea, then gave a cup to her daughter to take outside to Linda. She was in the back yard chatting to the women who had gathered there, wanting to know what was happening and why the doctor's car was outside.

The doctor was extraordinarily close to Mary Kate and she could feel the warmth of his body as he slipped the stethoscope under the edge of her blouse. With his face inches from hers, he looked into her eyes. 'Sorry,' he whispered. 'It's cold.' He glanced back down to concentrate and Mary Kate's heart began to pound. 'I just need to place it on your back now,' he said, and, threading his arm under her shoulders, he eased her upright.

Someone had removed Mary Kate's shoes and she pushed her feet into the sofa. She was now fully awake.

'Oh, hang on, while she's up, she can have some more water,' Cat said. 'Here you go, love, take one sip at a time.'

The water was welcome and cold. Mary Kate tried to speak but couldn't. Her head was crowded with disturbing images from home, of a sunny day by the Taramore, of her dog and her donkey, of her mammy in trouble. She felt dumb, had no idea what to say, because she was in a house full of people she had never met before and she was in pain and penniless, with nowhere to stay and no means of getting home. She might end up spending her first night in Liverpool on the streets.

Linda came in, cup in hand, and sat on a hard-backed chair at the foot of the sofa. She eyed Mary Kate cautiously, took out a tin from her apron pocket, removed some tobacco and began to roll a cigarette. 'Want a roll-up, queen?' she said to Mary Kate. 'It'll help get the blood flowing, help you to recover, like.'

Mary Kate offered her handleless mug of water to the girl she assumed was Betty. She was maybe a year older than the little girl who'd been clutching her hand, and equally as dirty. She shook her head and manged a few words. 'No, thank you. I don't smoke.'

'Oh God, did you hear that, Cat? She's as bog Irish as Bee was. Sounds just like her. How are you and Bee related exactly, love?'

The doctor returned his stethoscope to his bag and snapped the clasp shut. Mary Kate looked around the room. She could tell he was leaving and wondered what she should do. Should she leave also? Her head was still spinning as she tried to remember the events of the day. The overnight journey with Declan, the boat, the nice lady – what was her name? Mrs O'Keefe – the doctor… And then it all came rushing back. She'd been mugged, her money had been stolen and Bee had left. Tears ran down her cheeks unbidden and she took in a huge gulp of the stale air to try and stop them. But they fell as fast as summer rain and the sobs caught in her chest.

'Eh, come on, love, don't cry. It's not that bad. You need some tea and sugar now. Come on, Linda, get your fat backside off that chair and go down the road to Edith and ask her to borrow a cup of sugar. Move, Debbie, let me get closer.' Cat moved the little girl who had returned to hold Mary Kate's hand to one side, took a very grubby handkerchief out of her apron pocket and began to wipe at Mary Kate's face. 'Linda, hurry up, will you.'

Linda blew a cloud of blue smoke over Cat. 'God, Cat, keep your hair on.' She slowly raised herself from the chair.

'Is this young lady all right with you here for a little while?' The doctor had his coat on and glanced over at Mary Kate as he spoke.

'Of course she is,' Cat replied.

'Excellent.' Turning his back to Mary Kate, he slid five pounds into Cat's hand. 'She had everything stolen,' he said. 'I was driving along the Dock Road and saw it happen.'

Cat was speechless. She followed the doctor to the front door, glad that his car was parked out there and that he wouldn't have to push his way through a yard full of women and children.

At the door he said, 'I'll be back tomorrow. I'll ask the district nurse to call a little later. The money is to get her back on the ferry, and the rest is for you, for food and your generosity.'

'That's very kind, Doctor, and I won't say it isn't welcome, but I would have done it anyway.' Moments later she was back inside. 'Oi, go and get that sugar,' she said to Linda.

'Eh, just because you've made a few bob from the doctor doesn't mean you can go ordering me around. How many sugars in your tea, love?'

Linda was portly and dressed exactly like Cat, who was thin. They were wearing almost the same wraparound apron, only Linda's was green and Cat's had discoloured to an indistinguishable shade of brown. Linda's hair was an unnatural jet black, which made her pale complexion look even whiter and drained her grey eyes of almost all colour. They both wore wire curlers in their hair, held in place by headscarves tied around the back of the neck.

Cat scowled and Linda left with the sugar bowl. The back door banged behind her and Mary Kate briefly heard the sound of children playing outside. She looked at Cat through her tears. She'd tried to answer with 'Two sugars, please,' but was still confused and dazed. She shuffled to sit up straighter as Cat wiped her face.

'There, that's better then, love. Blow your nose, go on. Don't worry, it's washday tomorrow. Are you gonna tell me what's happened? You were crying for your mammy when you were out cold, so do you want me to go to the pub to use their phone and call her?'

Ten minutes later, having perked up thanks to Linda's sugar and the cup of hot sweet tea, Mary Kate did her best to explain what had happened.

'Now listen, don't you be worrying,' Cat said. 'Dr

Marcus has asked me to look after you for a couple of nights—'

'Paid you, you mean,' said Linda, throwing Cat a look that told Mary Kate she was a woman who stood no nonsense.

'Yes, well, he's given me a few bob to give you your tea and your bus fare back to the boat so you can get home. And enough for your ticket too, would you credit it. He's a saint, that doctor. He didn't want to leave you, but he had patients waiting, so he was going to call into the district nurses' home on Nelson Street and get one of them to come and check you're all right. Then tomorrow he'll come back himself.'

'Helloo,' a voice called out from the back door.

'Oh, there you go, that must be her. That was quick.' Cat turned towards the door. 'She's in here, Nurse. She's come round now. Linda's got the kettle on, so you're just in time. My God, would you believe it? It's like Lime Street station in here.'

An hour later, Mary Kate was fully upright on the sofa, her third cup of tea in her hand and a portion of chips wrapped in newspaper perched on her knees, burning her thighs through her skirt. Cat's six children had already demolished theirs, sitting cross-legged on the floor.

'Come on, eat your chips and that pickled onion, they'll do you the world of good,' said Cat. 'You'll have to sleep down here tonight, there isn't a spare inch upstairs. I've got Ben's old army coat, that'll do as a blanket to keep you warm.'

'She can always sleep at ours,' said Linda, who was screwing up the discarded chip paper into tight rolls. 'They make smashing firelighters,' she said to Mary Kate by way of explanation. 'It's the grease, gets the fire going in a flash, it does.'

Everything had been done for her: a steady refill of the tea in her hand, thanks to Betty; chips laid on her lap courtesy of Debbie, who still hadn't spoken a word; a thermometer placed in her mouth by the district nurse; and a shawl tucked around her shoulders by Cat. All Mary Kate had done was cry and wring Cat's handkerchief in despair.

Cat had demanded nothing from her. 'You cry, love,' she'd said. 'But nothing is as bad as it seems. Tomorrow, we'll have you down the Pier Head and back on the boat to your family, and all this will seem like a bad dream.'

The children had been shepherded into the scullery and Mary Kate could hear their squeals as they got washed down by Cat. The noise was constant. 'Betty, help me get these kids washed for bed. Arthur, stand still and don't be giving me none of your nonsense. Arms up. It's washday tomorrow: I want all those clothes in the basket ready to go to the wash-house. Betty, get that soap out of the water before it disappears altogether. There's no more until Saturday. You can stink, the lot of you, if we run out.'

Mary Kate allowed herself a weak smile at Linda, who had been left to watch her, and Linda smiled back.

'Cat's one of the good ones – she washes her kids every night. I can't be arsed meself. I get the bath down on a Sunday night, that's enough. How are you feeling now, love?' she asked.

Despite the racket, Cat had heard Linda from the scullery. She popped her head round the door. 'That's all, thank you, Linda. You can get home now and see to your own kids. They're the only ones still out on the street, in case you hadn't noticed, and they'll be starving hungry, the lot of them.' She scowled at Linda, then quickly smiled at Mary Kate. 'Go on, Linda, you live next door, not here – the rent man'll be charging me twice. And don't forget to take the chips out of the oven for your kids and the old man.'

Linda was not going to complain. She rose and pushed her chair back under the kitchen table. They had all bene-fitted from the doctor's generosity and she was grateful for it. She bent down at the oven door and removed a huge newspaper parcel of chips. As she reached the back door, she turned to Mary Kate. 'I'll see you tomorrow, love. You've almost fed the street tonight. Not a lot happens around here to make everyone happy, but this has. No way we could afford chips on a Monday. You'll have a good night, queen. That's Bee's sofa you're lying on – gave it to Cat when she left, she did. Only been in Cat's house a couple of days and you're on it.'

'Linda, you still 'ere?' Cat shouted through the scullery door.

With a wink, Linda was gone.

Mary Kate ran her fingers over the sofa's knotted bouclé upholstery as Linda's slippers flip-flapped down the yard. She was in the room alone, the silence more noticeable following the noise from the children only minutes before. The latch clicked and the back gate clattered shut. Mary Kate looked around her. The shovel of coal Cat had thrown on the fire as she'd moved into the scullery hissed and spat on a bed of glowing embers and the tap dripped and pinged into an enamel bowl in the sink as the clock on the mantelpiece ticked the seconds past. This was a room Mary Kate had never stepped foot in before and yet now it felt like the safest place outside of Tarabeg.

One by one, pink, scrubbed faces marched out of the scullery. First came Arthur, who had objected loudly to not having been allowed to stay out and play football on the street with Linda's sons. He scowled as he marched past Mary Kate, who he secretly blamed, opened the door at the bottom of the stairs and stomped up the wooden steps one at a time, banging as he went. Then came Edward, who waved at Mary Kate and looked sheepish, followed by Stanley, who was sobbing. 'He 'ates the soap,' said Edward, grabbing Stanley by his frayed pyjama sleeve and pulling him forward. 'Mikey, come on.'

Little Mikey shuffled out of the scullery in a nightshirt, a nappy already falling to his knees, his blond hair damp and dishevelled. He grinned at Mary Kate as he pulled his thumb from his mouth, leaving a long string of saliva attached. Mary Kate's heart constricted as she thought of Finn and she grinned back at the impish little boy. As if he'd understood, little Mikey ran over to the sofa, buried his head in her lap and threw his arms around her thighs as his feet swung off the floor.

'Oh God, come on, soft lad. Sorry, miss,' said Edward, who came back, picked up little Mikey and swung him onto his hip, with Mikey's legs wrapped around him. 'He gets tired. Sometimes Mam lets him fall asleep on her lap.'

'I don't mind,' said Mary Kate. 'He can sleep on my lap if he wants. There's room for two of us on here.' She didn't want to say, but she relished the thought of the company. Someone to look after, and the warmth of a body to comfort her. When Finn was little, she was often woken by him pulling back her candlewick bedspread and climbing into bed next to her. There was no count of the times she had fallen asleep to the rhythm of him winding a lock of her hair round and round between his forefinger and thumb.

'Do you mind?' Edward looked over his shoulder towards the scullery. Mary Kate guessed he could be no more than eight years old. Edward hadn't wanted to say anything, because Cat had whispered to them not to disturb Mary Kate, even though there was hardly any room upstairs for little Mikey, despite them sleeping top to tail.

'Leave him here.' Mary Kate hitched little Mikey up onto her lap. 'I'll say I asked. Go on.'

He grinned and ran up the stairs to the others.

Debbie and Betty came out of the scullery, each carrying one handle of a large basket of dirty clothes, which they set down by the back door.

'Thanks, girls,' said Cat. 'Go on now, loves, up you go. Say goodnight to Mary Kate.'

'Night, Mary Kate. I'm glad you're feeling better,' said Betty.

Debbie still didn't speak. She sucked her thumb, her dark brown hair tied back into a severe plait, her brown eyes twinkling mischievously.

Mary Kate wanted to scoop her up too and hold her tight. She needed that more than anything: a hug. Instead, she whispered, 'Goodnight, Betty. Goodnight, Debbie.'

Betty handed her the large, heavy overcoat she'd carried in. 'It's a bit itchy,' she said. 'It was our dad's in the war. He's dead now.'

Debbie looked sad, briefly threw her arms around Cat's waist and followed the others upstairs.

'What's our Mikey doing there?' said Cat, waiting for the door to the stairs to close and making sure the final set of footsteps had reached the top before she spoke. 'That lot, they'll be asleep in minutes, they will. They run up and down the streets all day long, and when bedtime comes I swear to God they're all out cold before Betty switches the light off.' She looked down at her youngest, already fast asleep in Mary Kate's arms. 'Look at him...'

'Do you mind if he stays with me?' asked Mary Kate.

Cat lifted a packet of cigarettes off the mantelpiece and lit one. 'Mind? God, no. There's hardly room for a mouse to fit between our kids upstairs. He comes in with me usually.' She inhaled deeply, then let the smoke exhale at a slow rate, her head back, eyes closed. 'That's better. I don't smoke as much as Linda. I can't afford to on my money – it's just a small pension from the Docks and Harbour Board.' She flopped onto the bouclé chair next to the sofa. 'So, Mary Kate, tell me, what are you doing here, just a day after your Bee left? Did you not write? Do you know what, I've heard your Bee talk about you that much, I feel like I know you, but why did you never come for a visit?'

Mary Kate instinctively knew she shouldn't mention that Bee and Captain Bob weren't married. She swallowed hard. She would have to lie to this lovely lady who had taken her in as if she was one of her own. 'I was away at school,' she stammered.

'I know that – she told me. But there was holidays, and they never took them, you know, her or Captain Bob. Never had a day off, he didn't. See all this furniture? That was theirs. Ours was falling to bits, we hardly had a chair to sit on. She said she'd ordered new things to arrive in Tarabeg for when she got home.'

Mary Kate stroked the top of little Mikey's head. Her nose filled with the freshly washed smell of him. She was recovered, her mind was working, she was making a plan.

'So, go on, tell me – what happened? Hang on, wait there.' Cat jumped to her feet. 'I've got a drop of sherry in the cupboard left over from Christmas – we'll finish it off, you and me. I've got a feeling this is going to be good.'

At the end of her tale of woe, Mary Kate took a pause and a long sip of the sherry, and announced, 'And I'm not going back. I am not going to fail. I will stay in Liverpool, earn the money back that was stolen, and more, before I go home. I won't be able to hold my head up if I don't.' She took another sip of the sherry and began to choke.

'That's your mam up there – she's telling you off and saying, "Get on that boat, Mary Kate."' Cat laughed. 'Not used to it, eh? It's all Guinness over there, isn't it? So, what are you going to do then? What kind of work do you want?'

Mary Kate took the piece of paper Mrs O'Keefe had given her with her details. She'd already told Cat about her. 'She told me she'd helped to get lots of Irish girls onto their feet – do you think she'll mind if I give her a call?'

Cat reached out and took the piece of paper. 'Nice address, Duke's Avenue, off Fullmore Park. Swanky. No, she won't mind, queen. I tell you what, she'll probably put you onto her sister's agency. There are quite a few big houses off the Aigburth Road that still have servants and I'd say around Fullmore Park would be some of the biggest. You could get a job and stay here, but I could only offer you the sofa. One of those agencies might get you a live-in job, and with your schooling, you might get taken on as a governess or something – they still have those too. Would you mind that?'

Mary Kate shook her head. 'No, I'll do anything to start with, to earn money and tide me over until I decide what I can do. I just need an angel to give me a bit of help.'

Cat ran the kitchen tap and washed the glasses. It occurred to Mary Kate that she'd been surrounded by angels all day: Mrs O'Keefe, the doctor, Cat, Linda. She didn't let her mind dwell on the mugger. Cat was talking, but her voice was fading as Mary Kate struggled to fight off the effects of the sherry. Pulling little Mikey into her, she rolled onto her side, closed her eyes and slipped down through the folds of sleep; as she did so, the face of the doctor refused to leave her thoughts.

Five minutes later, when she had finished her nightly chores and had damped down the fire, Cat pulled up the old army coat and laid it over Mary Kate and little Mikey. 'Poor love,' she said as she tucked it around them both.

The back door opened. Taking in the scene, Linda whispered, 'Can I have some of that sugar from Edith's?'

Cat handed her the cup.

'Has she decided what she's doing?'

'Yes. She's not going back. She wants to stay. I'm going to take her to the pub tomorrow morning to the phone so that she can call some woman she met on the boat. We think she might have some contacts with an agency or something. Wants to earn all the money back that was stolen before she goes home, and a bit more too.'

Linda let out a long, soft whistle. 'Well, whatever job she manages to get, it will be far from easy and even further from well paid. She'd be lucky to get seven pound a week.'

'I know. But I'm guessing it's best if she finds that out for herself.'

Linda turned back to the dark yard. 'She needs a knight in shining armour, but, pretty as she is, there aren't too many of those riding up and down the Dock Road, are there. Are you going to write to Bee?'

'Of course I am.' Cat leant against the doorframe and folded her arms. 'I was going to do that in the morning anyway. Funny day today, eh, Lin?'

'Just shows you, doesn't it. One day the same as the other and then you walk outside and find a Mary Kate fainting on the street. You see, you never know, Cat, what's around the corner. Are you alright, queen, having the house turned upside down like that?'

'Oh God, yeah. She's lovely, she is. Breath of fresh air and I wouldn't wish what's befallen her to happen to me worst enemy, but she's brightened up our day, in a funny kind of way.'

'Looks like she'll be hanging around too. Be sure to tell Bee, in case they're worrying about Mary Kate back home.'

Cat smiled and as Linda made her way down the yard, she looked up at the sky. A million stars winked down at her and she was overcome with a sense of anticipation, excitement. A shooting star shot across the summer night sky and a breeze brushed her face.

'Look at that, Lin! I reckon something is happening,' she said.

But Linda was already gone.

Chapter 10

Mrs O'Keefe laid down four sheets of newspaper on the floor, one on top of the other, in the shape of a cross, and, sliding out the tray from the bottom of Bluey's cage, emptied the sand onto the paper.

'Well, that's a right mess you made for me there, isn't it, my lad,' she said, wrinkling her nose in distaste as she folded over the paper into a tight parcel. She emptied fresh sand from a brown-paper bag onto the tray. 'There, isn't that better.'

Bluey fluttered to the end of his perch and rang his bell in reply.

Mrs O'Keefe and Bluey lived in a tall Victorian house situated halfway down Duke's Avenue, a long, leafy road in one of Liverpool's best areas. Her neighbours were sea merchants, doctors and bankers, and 'businessmen', most of whom marched down the avenue at 7 a.m. wearing bowler hats and long overcoats, carrying umbrellas and with heads bent as they made their way to one of the grand offices facing the river. The avenue had a rhythm of its own, which she'd come to know well over the years. She had never fitted in – there were no other builders on the avenue; her Pat had been the only one. 'Not one of them is any better than we are, Eileen,' Pat would chastise her when he asked her why she spent so much time alone. But how could she tell him? To join the groups of young mothers, she needed a baby, and to join the ladies that lunched, she needed to be free of her Liverpool accent. Neither option was available to her.

Grabbing hold of the chair arm for support, she rose from her knees and groaned. 'Blimey, how do I get back down for that now?' she muttered, looking at the news-paper parcel with dismay. She lifted Bluey's cage by its ring and walked over to hang it back on the stand. 'There you are, fit to be seen in public.'

Folding her arms, she gazed out of the bay window. A young woman strode past with two little boys holding her hands, one each side of her. Across the road, another young woman marched briskly along, pushing a shiny black Silver Cross pram that bounced up and down as she went.

The avenue was lined on both sides with trees and was wide enough to afford plenty of privacy from prying neighbours opposite. The wrought-iron gates to Fullmore Park stood directly across from the end of the road and it was to there that the avenue's second parade of the day always headed. By ten thirty there would be a procession of gleaming prams, pristine babies and young women wearing hats and smiles strolling around the lake, veering off around the bandstand and then back to the lake again. Watchful eyes hovered over toddlers, stopping to gossip about the new houses being erected off Aigburth Road, about how bonny the royal toddler, Prince Andrew, was and about the travelling salesman who'd been inside number seventeen for a whole hour the previous day – just like the one the previous week, who'd been selling window-scrapers from a suitcase.

Eileen O'Keefe saw them all. Sometimes she ventured into the park and overheard the snippets of conversation.

'She eats them for breakfast – it's an absolute disgrace, and her Maurice, he's been in the bank for fifteen years now, she could ruin it all for him if someone found out. It would make the *Echo*, it would.'

'I don't know where they find the energy,' said the woman she was talking to, who was leaning over her pram and straightening the covers. 'I mean, they walk from door to door all day, carting those big suitcases around. I'm sure Duke's Avenue isn't the only place they get the occasional overly warm welcome.'

Eileen often heard the best conversations when she sat on the bench by the lake.

'The park will be ruined when those new houses are built,' she'd heard one of the mothers say the previous week.

'Yes, and there will be Irish navvies everywhere,' her friend replied.

Eileen O'Keefe's face had burnt and her temper had risen – not something that happened very often. She'd got to her feet, had wanted to say something in protest, had almost said something, it was on the tip of her tongue, but both women looked over and their eyes had met hers, questioning. She failed and, feeling foolish, had turned on her heel and left.

'What was up with her?' she'd heard one of them ask.

That had been just before she left for Dublin. Her Pat would have been wounded by such comments, had he been alive.

Through her bay window she could hear the leaves rustling in the summer breeze and her heart ached. This was just the sort of day for a picnic in the park, on one of the benches by the lake, but what fun was a picnic when you were on your own? Who was there to point out the huge, vibrant rhododendrons to or to laugh with when the ducks got cheeky and forceful and mobbed you for your sandwiches? No one. The duck-pond gang, Pat used to call them. 'Come on then, let's go and be mugged for our butties,' he would say on a sunny Sunday morning when he got back from Mass.

Now there was no one, so she would eat her lunch on a tray in the sitting room, just as she always did. Her Pat was gone and had left her with a big house, a healthy bank balance and a permanent sense that she no longer belonged – not to a place, and now not to a person either.

There was a tap on the door and she turned from the window.

Deidra peeped her head round. 'Would I take the paper away, Mrs O'Keefe, would I?'

'Yes, come on in. Why do you always look as though I'm going to bite your head off, Deidra? Have I ever done that?'

Deidra smiled. 'No, Mrs O'Keefe.' She hurried over to scoop up the newspaper, almost bent in two, her eyes fixed to the floor.

Eileen O'Keefe employed three servants, one fewer than most of her neighbours, and she still thought that a ridiculous number. She often argued with her sister Lizzie about it. Lizzie was the more business-minded of the two sisters. Pat had given her money to start her own agency many years ago and she'd gone from strength to strength ever since, paying Pat back long before he died. She had her own office over a shop in Bold Street, with a painted sign above the window. Sometimes there would be a queue outside, if the Irish boat came in early, of Dublin girls clutching her details, passed on to them in a letter from a girl who had already made the journey and had been placed by Lizzie and her ladies at the agency. They stood there with eyes bloodshot from the tears they'd shed at leaving home and from the homesickness that had already set in, waiting to see her when she opened.

'Will you be wanting your coffee now, Mrs O'Keefe?'

It occurred to Eileen that Deidra only spoke in questions. Like many of the girls who arrived on the boat, she was shy, looked perpetually terrified and carried about her a sense of unworthiness. She was frightened of everything and spooked by everyone. They all were. It drove Eileen mad. 'Having girls in the house will be company for you,' Lizzie had said to her. 'Everyone in Duke's Avenue has servants. For goodness' sake, you will be the talk of the avenue, only having three. Do you think your Pat worked every day God sent to leave you on your knees, scrubbing the step?'

Her eyes always clouded over at the mention of her Pat. He had arrived as a navvy and departed this world the sole owner of O'Keefe's Builders. During the May Blitz on Liverpool, he'd taken his men down to the bombed-out streets once the air-raid sirens had ceased and helped people board up windows and doors and tried to get them safely back into their homes. At the time he died, his hands were all over the Anglican cathedral and she often wandered down to see how the building was coming along, so that she could give him all the details on her monthly trip to Dublin.

'There's more work to be done than men I can get over from home to do it,' he used to say to her. He had even employed an agent to travel along Ireland's west coast, holding meetings in pubs, seeking out men he could sign up for a life of work in Liverpool. Lizzie was right, her Pat had not worked six days a week putting Liverpool back together again, building up his business and the balance in the bank, for Eileen to have to work.

Sometimes she wished her Pat had seen her with the same eyes he'd viewed Lizzie. There was a sharpness to Lizzie that Eileen just didn't possess. Lizzie had managed the business accounts and Pat had been grateful for it. 'That's the difference between me and all the rest,' he would say to Eileen. 'I have your Lizzie. You should hear her getting the best price for a job. All I have to do is the work with me hands, and the men do the same, knowing Lizzie takes care of everything else and they will all be paid at four o'clock on a Friday, on the dot. She has the brain and I have the brawn.' He would laugh out loud at that and Eileen would laugh with him, even though he said it almost every day. The recipe was so good, they'd earned enough money to buy the house on Duke's Avenue only five years after the war was over. It had been bomb-damaged too. ''Tis a great opportunity,' Pat had said, and it was. She had the best restored house on the avenue, and as Lizzie always said, 'They would put your kitchen on the front of *Woman's Own* if they could only see it.'

She was brought back from her reverie by the sound of a polite cough from Deidra. 'Yes, I'll have the coffee now, thanks very much, Deidra.'

'And would you like a biscuit with it too?'

Another question. She smiled; it was an effort. 'Yes, please. Why not. That would be very nice.'

The door closed with barely a sound. She looked around

the room, smiled at Bluey and picked up the *Daily Post* from the table where Deidra had left it earlier that morning. The grandfather clock ticked the seconds by and began to chime the hour, the coals in the fire shifted and fell, and not for the first time she thought to herself that there was nothing quite as noisy as an empty house. If only the girls were more willing to chat, but Lizzie had warned her, 'Don't cross the boundaries. They know their place when you act like an employer. Start treating them like they're your best friend and you'll never know the last of it.'

She thought of the girl she'd met on the boat yesterday, Mary Kate, and smiled. She'd been like a breath of fresh air, had hardly stopped talking. 'Oh, I'm really sorry,' she'd said, 'Roshine says that when I was born I must have been injected with a gramophone needle.' Eileen hadn't asked who Roshine was, but the constant stream of chatter had made the journey pass much quicker.

She sat by the fire, laid the newspaper on her knee and looked into the flames. It was a damp day, despite the time of year. What else did she have to do except wait until three thirty when Lizzie would arrive, as she always did, for afternoon tea. One day she might have the courage to ask Lizzie why, if she had her Deidra and extra help too, she was so terribly lonely.

'Will the girls be there to meet you?' Bee had asked him the question once already, but he just stared down the road for the bus, his hands hidden from hers, buried in his pockets. His gaze was distant and he appeared not to have heard her.

Bee and Captain Bob were to part ways in Castlebar. They had spent the night in the hotel and there had been a silence that neither could fill. It had sucked the joy out of what had bound them together for so long, through so much adversity: the way they had stood united, defying their faith and their families, shunning the conventions that forbade them from being together, lying almost every day to keep their secret safe.

The air was heavy between them and Bee knew it for what it was; it was guilt. She had lived with it since the first night he'd entered her cottage and made love to her, and yet it occurred to her that this was the first time it had affected him.

They were standing waiting for the buses that would take her to Tarabeg and him to Ballycroy, and she felt afraid. It was as if the pull of his wife was stronger in death than it had been in life. Lying cold in her bed, no longer able to scold or insult him, she had become inoffensive, remembered only for the smattering of qualities she'd once possessed, her eyes weighted closed, the truth hidden from view. That was the way with death.

Bee stamped her feet, looked around her and thrust her own hands into the pockets of her coat. It had rained overnight. The cobbles were still damp and the weak sun struggled to rise as, partly obscured by departing clouds, it emerged like an orange globe over the market and the roofs of the shops and houses. It was early, it was market day, and the streets were already busy.

'Do you think the children will be there to meet you?' she repeated.

It was the third time of asking, but she had to say something and for the first time since they'd got together, she couldn't think what. His sparkle, his humour, his natural inquisitiveness and interest in everything and everyone were all gone.

He gazed at her and for a moment his eyes held hers, but he wasn't really looking at her; his head was elsewhere. Then he appeared to shake the thoughts from his mind as he wrapped his arms around her and pulled her into him. 'Oh, my little Bee,' he said.

But she knew he'd only done that to shield her from his thoughts. She had no more questions – it was not her way. She would wait for him to return to her; if he ever did. She knew there was a chance he might not. How could she compete with the manipulations of his eldest daughter, who'd spent the last nine years sending letters that one week forgave him for leaving her mother and the next berated him and cast him away like one of his own nets? She had played fast and loose with his emotions, tied him in knots, and all along Bee had known it was the distance that had kept the two of them safe; his inability to run to his daughter's cunning demands.

'I'm not so little any more,' she said as a means to

change the conversation, pulling away and looking up at him. She slipped her hand into his and held it fast. 'Would you look at the size of me! I was a thin woman when we left here – I'm twice the size now. No one will remember me any more. I'm big Bee, not little Bee.'

For the first time he laughed, and she was grateful that she'd reminded him of why she was there. He threw his head back and roared, and she smiled in turn, her heart soaring. She could still do it, she could still make him laugh.

It was a sound she carried with her as they went their separate ways.

Hours later, when her bus stopped on the main street in Tarabeg, Bee took a moment to relish everything around her, everything that had remained unchanged. She was home, and a lump came to her throat. She had to get to the coast and would walk it from there, but not until she had called into the Devlins' and gone across the road to Malone's to see her precious Mary Kate and Finn. Finn, who she'd not seen since he was a baby. Maybe Michael would be home and would give her a lift to the cottage and to Rory's parents. Her own cottage would not be fit to inhabit. But she would start work tomorrow and make it so, if she could, before Captain Bob returned – if he ever did.

'Jesus, wouldn't it just be so,' she said to herself as Philomena O'Donnell stepped out of the post office, stopped dead in the street and stared at her.

'Bee, heavens above, is that you?' she shouted down the road.

Before Bee could answer or escape into the Devlins', she was standing next to her.

'What are you doing here? Would you look at the size of you! You're a well-stocked woman now and that's a fact. Is Mary Kate with you? God in heaven, you've done the right thing, bringing her home. Her father has been out of his mind with the worry, so he has.'

Bee blinked as she self-consciously fastened her coat across her midriff to hide her expanding waistline. 'Philomena, will you tell me, what in God's name are you talking about?'

Chapter 11

Mary Kate snapped shut the clasp on her suitcase. She had decided to wear the best dress she'd brought with her, just in case her luck should change and Mrs O'Keefe knew someone who was looking to take on. This wasn't what she had planned. She had wanted to talk to Bee, enrol at a secretarial college, anything but clean someone's house. There was no way she could convince Roshine, Declan or anyone else that that was an adventure.

The doctor had just left, and Cat was happier now that he'd given Mary Kate a clean bill of health. 'You look much better after a good night's sleep,' he'd said after he'd looked into her eyes with the torch and taken her blood pressure again.

She was glad that today was the last time she would ever have to see him. The moment he'd walked into the kitchen her heart had done a skip and a leap, and when he touched her she'd felt her blood rise as she blushed.

There was a sadness behind his eyes and it moved her. When he looked at her and spoke, it was as though there was no one else in the room.

He'd fixed her with a smile and said, 'Well, there are two rather large bruises forming on your neck and your head. Are you going to be okay? I'm sure you don't have to dash off.'

She felt as though his eyes were boring into her soul and she wanted to get away as fast as she could. 'I'm really fine, and I have a plan,' she said.

'Ah, a plan.'

'I cannot think of anything better. I have to put right what I've done wrong. I made a stupid mistake.'

He half smiled. 'Yes, well, at least it's a mistake you can put right. Not all mistakes can be rectified quite so easily.' His eyes lost their light and she wanted to know what he was thinking.

'You ready, love? Is she all right to go then, Doctor?' Cat had taken her curlers out and had teased her hair up with a metal spike that protruded from the end of her stubbly hairbrush.

'She's as ready as she'll ever be,' said Dr Marcus. 'I have to go now. Good luck, Mary Kate.'

He held out his hand and Mary Kate took it in hers. 'Thank you. You've been a very kind man. I will pay you back the money you gave Cat just as soon as I can.'

'You don't have to do that. I was happy to help.' And with that, he'd picked up his bag and left.

As one door closed, another opened, and Linda walked in. 'Did I just miss the doctor? How are you feeling now, love?' she asked. 'You look a bit better than you did yesterday. What you going to do with her then, Cat?' She sat herself on a chair and took out her tobacco tin.

Cat smiled down at Mary Kate. 'Well, we're off to use the phone to call this Mrs O'Keefe and ask her where the agency is and if she'll put a good word in for this little lady. And then we're going to get the bus to wherever it is and go and get her signed on. You never know, they might have something right away.'

'Oh, imagine,' said Linda, 'you could be in a big posh house, like one of them on Duke's Avenue.'

'Well, let's face it,' said Cat, 'anywhere will be better than this shithole of a street.'

They were already on their way out the door when Linda called after them. 'Don't forget to post your letter to Bee, Cat.'

Mary Kate stared at the ground. 'What letter is that, Cat? Are you writing to Tarabeg?'

Cat took a deep breath, threw a scathing look at Linda and slammed the door. 'Look, love… Oh, honestly, you know what, sometimes I could throttle Linda. I am writing, but I was anyway – me and Bee, we was good mates. I'm not writing just because you're here, honest to God. I'm already missing her. I did mention though that you'd turned up at her door and that I'd taken you in. I wasn't asking her for money, if that's what you think.' She folded her arms as she walked and fixed her eyes on the red sand-stone pub at the end of the road.

'I wasn't thinking that,' Mary Kate said. 'Not at all.' In Tarabeg, palms were more likely to be crossed with goods than silver. 'I'm just worried what will happen when Bee gets home and they've been assuming I was safe with her over here.'

'Oh, don't you be worrying about that. Bee knows me – she would trust me with her life, she would. She'll let them know you'll be fine. But I'm telling you this: if they say there's no chance of work soon, you are on that boat back home or I'll have your da knocking down me door. My Ben would have insisted on that. He was a bit protective himself. Honestly, though, don't worry. I bet your da will be relieved just to know where you are and that you're safe.'

Mary Kate swallowed hard. She no longer felt quite as confident as she had when she'd boarded the boat in Dublin.

Ten minutes later, they were inside the empty pub. 'Dave, can we use your phone, love? Here's a shilling for your trouble.'

'Bloody hell, have you come into money then, Cat?' A burly man stood up from where he'd been kneeling down behind the bar, making Mary Kate jump. He was wearing a shirt with the sleeves rolled up and a brown apron.

'No, not me, love. Wish I had though. This is Bee's

niece. Turned up, she did, the day after Bee left – can you imagine that?'

'Well, that's a rotten thing to happen, queen. I thought you Irish were supposed to be the lucky ones? There you go.' He pushed a black Bakelite phone down the polished bar towards them. The bell jingled as the receiver wobbled.

'Right, love, where's your bit of paper?' said Cat.

Mary Kate extracted the slip of paper with Mrs O'Keefe's name and telephone number.

'Don't forget to ask her the address for the agency in town. If we hurry, there's a bus from the top of the Dockers' Steps in ten minutes.'

Mary Kate began to dial the number. All the time she was wondering what on earth she was going to say to the woman to whom she'd told all her grand plans, sure she would never see her again. Now, penniless and homeless, she was having to ask her for help. Tears sprang to her eyes. This was not at all how she'd imagined her life in Liverpool.

Cat felt the money in her pocket and knew, that the first moment she could, she would send a telegram to Bee, not a letter, before another misfortune befell Mary Kate.

Eileen O'Keefe had just completed the crossword in the *Daily Post* and almost jumped out of her skin when the telephone rang on the table next to her. 'Oh my giddy aunt,' she said as she pulled off her reading glasses and laid them on top of the paper. 'Why do you take your glasses off to answer the phone, you bloomin' eejit?' Pat used to say to her. She never wore her glasses in the company of anyone but Pat. 'They can't see you, can they?'

The phone didn't ring very often and when it did it was usually Lizzie to say she was going to be late or was cancelling her daily visit. As a result, Eileen had come to loathe answering the phone; she dreaded the afternoon stretching out before her without a visit from Lizzie.

'Aigburth 137, hello?' she said into the receiver, with very little enthusiasm. 'Lizzie, is that you?'

Five minutes later, she placed the handset back onto its base, just as Lizzie walked through the door.

'Who on earth were you talking to on the phone?' said Lizzie as she untied her headscarf. Inserting her ruby-red fingernails deep into her dyed chestnut hair, she pushed it upwards and then patted the back down again. 'Did someone actually ring you? What for?'

Eileen O'Keefe had been delighted to hear Mary Kate's voice. As she'd talked, describing the horror of her first twenty-four hours in Liverpool, an idea had flown into Eileen's mind. It was an indulgent notion and one that made her heart feel light. The gloom that had enveloped her disappeared in an instant. To have Mary Kate live with her, as a companion, someone to share her walks and meals with, and more. Maybe they could visit the Playhouse together, or the new cinema they were building, or go shopping in Church Street. They could take a morning walk in the park to feed the ducks and watch as the seasons changed. And Christmas... She'd be someone to go to the carol service and see the lights in town with and maybe they could book one of those coach-touring holidays. Oh, how she would love a holiday. All of these ideas, all of the things she'd done with Pat at her side and wished she could do again, filled her with warmth. But as Mary Kate continued talking, Eileen knew none of it could be. It wouldn't be right for Mary Kate, not right for a young woman who was searching for her destiny and adventure, and she could hear Pat's voice in her ear: 'No, love, let your Lizzie find her something. She's a young woman fresh off the boat, just like I was once. Don't interfere.'

Lizzie stood on the hearth and reapplied her lipstick in the mirror. She dyed her hair deep chestnut every two weeks; no grey hair would dare defy her. She had pale skin and grey eyes that snapped as she spoke. She'd worn the same shade of poppy-red lipstick all day every day for the past thirty years. 'Gives my face a bit of colour,' she said every time she reapplied it.

Eileen watched her sister, as she always did, and waited for her to stop speaking. No one interrupted Lizzie mid flow. She thought for the first time how everything about Lizzie was reduced in size: her lips, her legs, her long fingers, her waist and her capacity for human kindness.

Lizzie tightened the ties on the bow of her satin blouse in the mirror and then, with a sideways glance of self-appreciation and a final pat of the curls, she tucked her sharp pencil skirt behind her legs and sat on the chair opposite her sister, who was pouring a fresh cup of tea.

'I have someone coming to see you,' said Eileen. 'She will be here in an hour, so you will have to stay a little longer.' No one told Lizzie what she had to do – they asked – but Eileen O'Keefe was not about to brook any petulance from her younger sister.

'An hour? That's when I leave. Who is it?'

'It's a girl I met on the boat coming back from Pat's grave yesterday. She was robbed and knocked to the ground not minutes after I left her, and everything she had was taken. She was going to visit her aunt, but her aunt has returned to Ireland. Her aunt's neighbour is bringing her here. She was very good company, she spoke well and was very smart indeed. I'd say she'd be a catch for your agency, so you had better make sure you place her with the right family. And after all she's been through, I'll be checking them out myself. She doesn't know it yet, but I'm going to tell her she can stay here until you can place her.'

'Stay here? Good grief, Eileen, you mean she'll be sleeping with Deidra?'

Eileen held out the teacup and saucer. 'No, I do not. She can sleep in the guest bedroom.'

'I'm not sure I approve of that, Eileen. Why didn't you tell her to go straight to Bold Street?'

Eileen raised her head. 'Because I wanted to see her,

Lizzie, that's why. She has something about her. She's a good-looking girl, beautiful I would say, but she is also well educated. What do you think you can find for her?'

Lizzie leant over and, reaching out, took the cup and saucer from her sister. 'For goodness' sake! I place kitchen maids, cooks, housekeepers, housemaids and the like – they don't need to be a member of Mensa to do those jobs. The most she's going to earn with me is seven pounds a week. If she has such a great education, why isn't she training to be a teacher?'

Eileen frowned. 'A cleaner? Is that the best you can offer her? That's such a waste of her talent. What about a companion – do you have anyone on your books who needs a companion?'

Lizzie's eyes snapped faster and she frowned. Her tone would have been no different had her sister asked her to thrust her hand into the fire. 'A companion? No, Eileen, I don't place companions. They are for lonely people. I always think that's a bit depressing – after all, a companion is just a paid friend, isn't it? Someone to keep you company. Thank goodness you have me.'

Eileen looked over at her sister, who spent her mornings in an office staffed by five young ladies, came to her house in the early afternoon, spent the late afternoon with her daughter for her grandchildren's teatime, and the evenings with her husband. Lizzie kept everyone in compartments. No one crossed over except on specific days of the year, as arranged by Lizzie. It never occurred to her to invite her sister to visit her niece and great nephews, not unless it was Whit Monday, Christmas Day or Easter Sunday.

'But I suppose you could pay her and keep her here, if you felt you could do with someone in addition to Deidra.'

Eileen would never admit to Lizzie that she'd thought about doing just that. She took a deep breath. She must be resolute, put Mary Kate first. It would be so easy, but... No, she must not.

The door opened and Deidra's face appeared. 'There's visitors for you at the back door, Mrs O'Keefe. Shall I bring them up?'

'Oh good, they got here in plenty of time. Yes, please, Deidra.' Eileen jumped to her feet.

'How's she working out?' asked Lizzie, inclining her head towards Deidra's retreating back, not waiting for her to be fully out of earshot before she spoke. She removed her cigarettes from her handbag and lit one.

'Fine. I have yet to hear her speak when she isn't asking a question though.'

'They are paid to clean, not have opinions.' Lizzie exhaled her cigarette smoke high in the air. She had remained seated, with one arm folded across her chest and the hand holding the cigarette suspended mid air. 'Listen, I was thinking... I maybe could place your girl in a good house. We had a request in today from a professional household. The lady of the house has two little boys and she's looking for someone to help. We've placed a live-in help there already, but she said she needs a bit more assistance with the children. They've moved here, onto the avenue. How does that sound to you?'

'Better,' said Eileen. She heard footsteps coming along the corridor and whispered, 'But you can negotiate the right deal for her, and that includes where she eats and sleeps as well as how much she's paid.'

Deidra tapped on the door before she opened it.

'Well, well, well, I never thought I'd see you again so soon,' said Eileen as Mary Kate stepped nervously into the room, accompanied by a woman who seemed unable to close her mouth.

'Neither did I,' said Mary Kate. 'You would not believe what I've been through in the last twenty-four hours. This is Cat, she lives next door to my Aunt Bee, who sailed back to Ireland the day I left. Cat?'

Cat was looking around the room and had walked over to a plant on a jardinière and appeared to be staring.

Eileen smiled. 'It's an aspidistra,' she said. 'I've had it for a long time now.'

Cat found her voice. 'Do you know how long that plant would last on top of that tall thing in my house with our kids? Not even five minutes.' She looked towards Mary Kate, her eyes wide. 'Would you even believe that?' she said, pointing back to the plant.

Lizzie frowned. Eileen smiled. This was going to be fun.

One hour and two phone calls later, Lizzie pulled on her gloves. 'Well, there you go, she is expecting you at 6 p.m.'

There had been only one awkward moment, when Lizzie had asked Mary Kate to shorten her name to Mary.

Mary Kate's reply had been swift and unequivocal. 'My mammy didn't call me Mary, she called me Mary Kate, and that's my name.'

Cat had slipped her hand on top of Mary Kate's, squeezed it and smiled. 'Good for you,' she said.

Mrs O'Keefe had nodded in approval. 'Quite right,' she'd whispered over the sound of Lizzie talking into the phone.

'Don't you be late now. Best not to get off to a bad start. Jolly good luck for you that my sister met you on the boat and could vouch for you. We usually demand written testimonials.'

Mary Kate had not warmed to Lizzie and had found it difficult to understand how it was that she and Mrs O'Keefe were sisters.

'Good, well, there we go, all sorted. Perhaps you could give Cat a lift to the bus stop, Lizzie?' said Eileen.

Lizzie frowned at her sister.

'Oh, don't mind me, I can walk,' said Cat. 'I just feel a bit funny about leaving this one. But the kids will be home and wanting to know where their tea is soon, and if I leave them with Linda for much longer, she'll sell them – or even worse, knowing Linda.'

Eileen was horrified at the potential fate of Cat's children. 'Well, in that case, Lizzie will run you straight home, won't you, Lizzie.'

Lizzie was completely unused to being told what to do, and for once she was speechless. 'Come along then,' she said as she flipped her headscarf over her head like a kite and, letting it land and settle into place, tied it under her chin. 'We had better get going before my sister starts finding more things for me to do.'

There was a touch of humour in her voice, and for the first time in a long while Eileen smiled at her sister. 'Thank you, Lizzie,' she said.

'Well, it looks like all's well that ends well,' said Cat, her eyes bright, her voice full of enthusiasm as she clapped her hands together. She had really taken to Mrs O'Keefe. She was relieved she'd made the decision to remove her curlers. She nearly hadn't, wanting to keep her hair tight for the bingo that night.

'Hardly,' snapped Lizzie. 'She's lost every penny she owns. I wouldn't call that a good ending.'

Cat blushed and looked down at her hands. Now she felt foolish.

Mary Kate looked up at Mrs O'Keefe, who shook her head. 'I think you're right, Cat,' she said kindly. 'My Pat, he always used to say that everything happens for a reason, and I think, as unfortunate as yesterday was, we will know very soon what that reason was.'

Cat walked over to Mary Kate and threw her arms around her shoulders. 'You know where I am now, love. Come back and see me. If that woman doesn't want you, and she might not – they're mostly stuck-up around here

– come straight back.' She realised instantly what she'd said. 'Oh, honest to God, I don't mean you – you've been smashing.'

Mrs O'Keefe laughed. 'No offence taken, Cat. I think they're all stuck-up too.'

'Oh, for goodness' sake,' said Lizzie impatiently. 'Come along then, Cat.'

Minutes later, the front door slammed, a car engine started and Mary Kate and Eileen O'Keefe were alone.

'Let's have another pot of tea, just us two,' she said. She noted the long, deep sigh that Mary Kate gave out as she sat in front of the fire and saw the tears that filled her eyes. Her brightness in front of Lizzie, who was securing her a job, and Cat, who would be writing to her aunt, had been all bravado. 'Are you alright, love?' she asked as she placed her hand on Mary Kate's shoulder.

Mary Kate shuffled forwards in the chair to free a hand-kerchief from the pocket of her skirt. Turning a pitiful face up towards Mrs O'Keefe, she replied with one word on the end of a sob. 'No.'

Chapter 12

Lavinia Marcus turned the key and, pushing the door open with great care, tilted her head and listened. She could hear nothing but the swinging of her key fob against the wood. She let out a long sigh. Thank goodness. Joan had agreed to take the boys to the park and had clearly been as good as her word. She needed some time alone before they returned.

She hurriedly removed her gloves and hat, threw them over the chair in the hall, then did the same with her coat. She caught herself in the mirror on the hall stand as she undid the buttons on her dress. She had overdressed for the weather. She'd thought it was going to rain and in Lavinia's mind, as she was now living in the northwest of England, rain meant cold; only it hadn't rained and it was warm and clammy.

She studied her face for signs of guilt and her blue eyes stared back at her, empty. Her hair was blonde and curled around her ears, and her cheeks were soft, sharply defined like two small pillows, and as pink as her lips. She opened the vestibule door with its two stained-glass panels depicting a brace of dead pheasants, which she hated, and looked down the long hallway of her house, which she hated even more.

They were on the wrong side of the avenue, the side whose gardens faced north, and that was something Lavinia could not accept. 'Why can't we live in a smarter area?' she demanded of her husband every single night. 'How can we live on an avenue where everyone on the opposite side of the street with the south-facing gardens thinks they're a cut above us?'

Nicholas always sighed in that long-suffering way of his before he responded. 'Duke's Avenue is a smart area. The whole avenue is smart – every house. It doesn't matter what side you live on. And anyway, since when did you become such a keen gardener? I cannot live too far from my patients. I have to be nearby when I'm on call. We should really be closer to town.' He knew she would never agree to that.

'Closer to town? Are you mad? We should be out in the country. When I married you, you told me we were going to live in a smart area. You chose this practice, Nicholas – you deceived me. If you want to be in Liverpool, why don't you have a practice in a smarter area? Why did you have to take on that godawful place?'

And then the row would begin. It was always the same, and it always ended in tears. It wasn't just the house that annoyed her: there was also the way the telephone had a habit of ringing in the middle of the night with a medical emergency and someone needing his help. He shared his on-call duties with the other doctor at the practice, so he was required to be available every other night and every other weekend. If Nicholas had already been called out and the phone rang again, Lavinia had to answer it. When this happened, she routinely made him suffer in an atmosphere of silence and hostility for up to a week, with her talking to him through the boys, even though their youngest had only just started school. She prided herself on knowing how to carry a grudge.

Years ago, he would have jumped through hoops to avoid being given the silent treatment. He used to make accommodations in the form of bouquets of flowers or dinners at the golf club, but those had only mollified her to a degree, and now he'd even given up doing that. He seemed to think that just being with him and the boys should be enough to make her happy; that having a husband who was both committed to alleviating the suffering of others and able to provide a comfortable life for his own family should be sufficient. It was not.

Lavinia threw open the bedroom door and cursed that the bed wasn't made. It didn't occur to her that Joan couldn't be in two places at once, down at the park and in the house doing her chores. She let her dress slide to the floor as she removed her earrings, which she dropped onto a glass tray on the mahogany dressing table, along with her pearls and hair-combs. Flinging up the sash window, she flopped onto the bed and the feather pillows and turned her face towards the windows to catch what air there was. She could see the tops of the cherry trees swaying in the breeze, heard the gentle rustle of the leaves and the repetitive call of the wood pigeons.

Lifting her legs, she began to undo the studs on her suspender belt, flinching at the tenderness in her hips and thighs, sore from a long afternoon of lovemaking. Her fingers slipped inside her silk French knickers and she smiled. It was the wrongness, the audacity, the intense thrill of deceit that made it all so exhilarating; it was the only thing keeping her sane in that dull, dull avenue. She could never leave her husband, her prison, not without a cast-iron excuse – her parents would never forgive her. He would have to do something dreadful, and the sun would freeze before that happened. She was married to Dr Perfect, according to everyone who knew them.

She could survive, with indulgence. And Robin was her indulgence. Their hours together were limited. School having broken up was a huge inconvenience as Joan very obviously could not manage the home and the children. They ran circles around her. 'I really do need more help,' she whispered to herself.

That morning she'd been struck by a sudden thought, just before she'd set out for her assignation. Remembering that she still had the agency details from when they'd employed Joan, she'd hurried over to the bureau, pulled the lid down and begun rifling through the untidy pile of correspondence. Nicholas had his own office and desk in the house. He dealt with all of the bills and anything to do with the home and the children. He paid all of her bills too – the hairdresser, milliner and dressmaker. 'Ah, there you are,' she'd said out loud as she found a letterhead stapled to the testimonial that had arrived with Joan, along with the bill for the agency's services. Her mood had lifted. Nothing made Lavinia feel better than when she was spending money or elevating her status, and having a second girl living in, to help Joan with the boys, would certainly do that, allowing her more time to do the things she wanted.

Back from her early afternoon rendezvous now, she rolled onto her side and thought of ways she and Robin could meet more often, maybe even get away to a nice hotel. 'I need more freedom,' she repeated to herself. Her summer could be seriously curtailed if she didn't do some-thing, and soon.

She'd not been in her bedroom for ten minutes when the peal of the telephone rang up the stairs. She groaned, irritated at the thought of having to answer another call from a patient who'd confused the doctor's home tele-phone number with the one at his practice. She turned off the bath she'd started running, ran down the stairs in her slip and was immediately glad she hadn't left the phone to ring out. It was the owner of the employment agency getting back to her – not just one of her assistants – and she had good news.

'Well, actually, I have to say, this is fortuitous,' the woman said. 'My sister lives only doors from you, on the sunny side of the avenue.'

Lavinia suppressed her sigh. Everyone who lived on the other side made that point, repeatedly.

'We have the girl here with us now,' she continued. 'My sister personally recommends her. What would be a good time?'

Lavinia looked at her watch. She had her hair appointment in an hour and didn't want to be late. Looking her best was more important now than ever. 'Let's say six o'clock. Will that be too late?' she asked with unusual sweetness.

Nicholas was coming home later and later from his surgery these days. He used to make a point of being home for the boys' bathtime, running into the bathroom, rolling up his sleeves and falling to the floor. But, as ever with Nicholas, his patients had taken even that pleasure from him, a pleasure he seemed quite happy to abandon.

'Yes, six o'clock would be just fine. Her name is Mary Kate Malone.'

'Really...' Lavinia was rifling in her handbag, searching for a cigarette, half distracted. 'What a mouthful. We shall have to call her just Mary – is that acceptable?' She placed the cigarette in her mouth to free up her hand as she looked deep into her handbag for the lighter.

There was silence on the end of the phone and then the voice of the agency owner came back on. 'Er, I'm afraid not. Apparently, her full name is Mary Kate, it is not to be shortened.'

Lavinia snapped the clasp of the handbag shut, folded her arms and took a drag of her cigarette. 'Really.' She smiled and thought to herself how amusing it was that the working classes could be so protective over the most meaningless things. 'Send her at six.'

As she dressed for her hair appointment, she thought of the excuses Nicholas would make for coming home late that evening. 'My patients have very different lives to ours,' he would say, as if she couldn't possibly comprehend. 'When they have a sick baby, it's often very sick because of the conditions in which they live. Three babies registered at our surgery died last winter, two with gastroenteritis and one with pneumonia. You take the central heating and the coal fires we have for granted.'

Lavinia hated those conversations most of all. She did feel sympathetic, of course she did – she was human – but why did the living conditions of others mean she had to sacrifice her husband? 'Robin doesn't seem to be as bothered as you, and nor does he work as many hours. He also thinks a lot more of his family because, unlike you, he puts them first.' She was talking about his partner at the practice, and her secret lover too.

Nicholas never had an answer to that. Robin was a good doctor, but he didn't have quite the same bedside manner as Nicholas and was inclined to scold patients he felt were wasting his time – not something Nicholas had ever done. 'Find yourself a hobby for when the boys are at school,' he'd said to her. But Lavinia was not the type of woman one could easily placate.

She had swallowed her anger. He had moved her across the country, away from Surrey and all her smart friends with commuter husbands who worked in the City. Well, he had made his bed, now he could lie in it. She thought of his words as she walked to the hairdresser's. 'Find yourself a hobby!' She had certainly done that. Pulling her handbag further up her arm, she decided to walk down rather than up the avenue, even though it would take longer and could make her late for her appointment, not an unusual occurrence. If she walked up the avenue, she might bump into Joan bringing the boys back from the park and that just wouldn't do, not today.

Chapter 13

Eileen O'Keefe offered to walk with Mary Kate to the house for the interview. 'Just in case you feel a bit nervous on the way,' she said.

'Not at all,' Mary Kate remonstrated. 'I want to do something right and if I can make my way down the road and cross it without getting run over or mugged, that would be a huge improvement, is what I'm thinking.'

Despite the seriousness of her words, Eileen laughed; something she hadn't done for a very long time. 'If they ask you about those bruises, just tell them the truth, don't try and hide it. And also, remember that you don't have to live in – they already have someone doing that. In fact, I'd say that living out would be better. That way you can earn more money and you can sleep here.'

'But I would have to pay you for sleeping here,' Mary Kate stammered.

'No, you would not. I wouldn't let you.' Eileen was quick with her prepared retort. While Mary Kate had sobbed her heart out in front of her fire, she had thought it all through. 'It would be lovely for me and Bluey to have a bit of company at night. You can sit and watch some of that television. It's a waste, putting it on just for me. Do you know, sometimes I find I'm talking to Bluey and asking him what he thinks. It would be so much nicer if it was you – at least I'd get an answer. Let me tell you, there's nothing as miserable as laughing on your own.'

Mary Kate smiled. No one in Tarabeg had a television. There was no transmitter that reached the coast and it was widely believed that there never would be. Not that anyone in Tarabeg was remotely concerned. Who needed television when they had Mrs Doyle's telex machine in the post office, the one nod to modernity that had been made in Tarabeg since the time of the last famine – that and the opening of the Malones' shop. Most of the villagers liked it that way because Father Jerry told them they should. How could a priest do battle with the darker forces if people had a million images pumped into their homes each night and a multitude of voices spouting ungodly opinions?

Mary Kate placed her hand on the large brass handle. As she opened Mrs O'Keefe's front door, the warm, dusty air rose up from the red tarmacadam road. The sun had dipped behind the cherry trees, the last of its warmth still held in the dark red bricks of the houses and tall chimneys. She looked down the six steps and took a deep breath, her cardigan buttoned up and her shoes cleaned by Deidra on Mrs O'Keefe's instructions. She clutched her handbag, pulled the pink silk scarf Mrs O'Keefe had lent her to cover her bruising a little tighter around her neck, and prepared to leave.

The sound of a group of children shouting to each other as they raced their bikes out of the park gates and up to the top of the avenue reached their ears. Mary Kate turned and grinned, taking in their dirty, mussed hair, striped polo shirts, rapidly pedalling legs protruding from chocolate-brown shorts, and thighs burnt red by the sun. 'Last one to my gate is a big smelly poo,' she heard one boy yell.

She smiled as she remembered her own green-painted bike with the over-large wicker basket on the front, still used by Tarabeg's salmon poachers as a sign, leant up against the whitewashed shop wall, that they'd meet out on the river that night. She felt a pang of homesickness and quickly gulped it down. She had done this all on her own – run away from home, moved to another country – and had, by anyone's measure, already failed. Before she returned to Tarabeg, she had to turn her fortunes around.

Deidra came to the door. She'd been thrilled to meet Mary Kate, an Irish visitor from home. She pushed past Mrs O'Keefe with her arms and elbows, stood in front of Mary Kate and without any hesitation announced, 'When she tells you what the money is, ask for a bit more.'

Eileen O'Keefe looked at her in surprise. 'Well, you didn't do that with me, Deidra,' she said, amazed that

Deidra had actually spoken. She assumed it was because she was addressing someone her own age, from her own country.

'Aye, well, I was as green as one of the fields back home when I came here. I had no idea what I was doing at all. I will be doing just so next time, I can tell you,' she said.

'Next time?' said Eileen, her eyes wide in surprise as she folded her arms. 'What next time would that be?'

Deidra had turned her attention back to Mary Kate and reinforced her point. 'Don't take her first offer – bump it up by at least five shillings. That's what the girls who've been here a while tell me. They all do it, and they get it. They can't get enough girls over to work in the big houses in Liverpool. There's babies being born all over the place – you can't move down this street sometimes for prams and babies – and they bring work.'

'I'll try my best,' said Mary Kate.

Eileen felt a strange sense of competitiveness, as though she needed to have the last word, and decided to join in. 'And don't let her cheat you on your working hours. You want a day and a half off at the very least. Ask her to let you finish at twelve on a Saturday and have all day Sunday off. That's what the other girls who work on the avenue do. In fact, you tell her that, don't let her decide for you.'

'I will, Mrs O'Keefe.'

Eileen was grinning; this was the most excited she'd been in a long time. 'So, there you have it. Don't take the first money she offers and you tell her what hours you'll be working. Oh, would you listen to me, I just don't want you taken in and mugged in a different way. I want you back on your feet.'

Mary Kate was so grateful to them both, her bottom lip began to tremble.

'Not again!' said Eileen. 'You can cry all you like when you get back, but not now.'

'What would I have done if I hadn't met you, Mrs O'Keefe, and Cat hadn't been such a lovely woman, and if that doctor hadn't helped and offered me a lift and given Cat money like he did, and you too, Deidra. I just feel overwhelmed by it all.'

Eileen opened her arms and Mary Kate accepted her hug. 'You don't strike me as the sort to be overwhelmed by anything. Put it all behind you now – this is your new start.'

As Mrs O'Keefe hugged her, Mary Kate thought of Declan's expression as he'd stood on the dockside and waved her off. She sighed. Declan was a part of her past; he felt as distant as the miles between them, and, to her surprise, so did Tarabeg. She was about to move into her future, in a new city, and the thrill of it returned as she smoothed her skirt, straightened her hat and, with a backwards grin to Mrs O'Keefe and Deidra, strode down the steps.

*

'I would like to have every Saturday afternoon off and Sunday too, please.' Mary Kate spoke with a confidence she truly did not possess. She surprised herself.

Lavinia Marcus was seated opposite her in the sitting room. Leaning back in her chair, she considered the girl before her. 'So it's your preference not to live in, but what if we need you in the evenings, to look after the boys?'

'Well, Mrs O'Keefe's is just down the road, so I can come back in the evening, or I don't mind staying on. I'm sure we can work something out. Do you and your husband go out often together?'

Lavinia blinked quickly and shook her head. This girl was speaking to her as though she were her equal. And then, admonishing herself, she realised that that was just what the boys needed. If Nicholas raised any objections, the fact that, despite being Irish, Mary Kate had a good education and vocabulary should swing it for her. 'My husband works long hours,' she replied. 'He's a doctor. Sometimes he doesn't come home until late at night and he can be out on call.'

'Gosh, well, he has a very important job then.' Mary Kate immediately thought of Roshine and the respectability and status being a doctor's daughter had heaped on her. She thought about the doctor who'd rescued her. He was young and handsome and as far from Roshine's father as it was possible to be; he still popped into her thoughts at every moment of stillness. She almost shook herself. He was in there again.

Lavinia prickled at Mary Kate's comment about Nicholas having an important job. 'He does, yes, but sadly his patients think it's his life, not just his job, and he chooses to let them.'

Mary Kate felt a definite shift in the congeniality of the conversation and decided to change the subject. 'Can I meet the boys?' she asked with a lift in her voice.

'Good idea.' Lavinia rose from the chair. 'They are down in the kitchen with Joan. Let's go and meet them, shall we, but first let us get this clear: your job is to look after their room, their laundry, their meals, all their mending, their schoolwork and their activities. And on school days you will take them to school and collect them.'

Mary Kate did not ask what exactly she, as their mother, would be doing. She thought of Keeva and her band of boys and tried to imagine her handing over all her responsibilities to someone else. But it was none of Mary Kate's business. She was being employed to do a job and that had been explained to her. It wasn't her place to question. Her opinion was not required.

They descended a flight of steps to the lower rear kitchen and the sound of a radio and little boys arguing became louder. No one heard them approaching and the sight that greeted them made Mary Kate gasp. On the cooker a pan was boiling, its lid rattling noisily, throwing water into the flames, causing them to spit and flare and almost extinguishing them. The radio was louder than Mary Kate guessed it was supposed to be, judging by the look on her employer's face. She strode straight over to the sideboard and flicked off the dial. A wooden ironing board stood in the corner with a pile of clothes falling off it and into a basket on the floor. The table was littered with pens and ink and comics, and a scruffy black dog was gazing up longingly at a chicken that was sitting on a work surface dripping juice down the cupboard doors.

A young girl who was clearly Irish and whom Mary Kate assumed was Joan was at the sink trying to scrub down what looked to be the oldest boy. He was covered in blue ink. The girl's long red hair had been fastened into a tight bun that morning but was now spilling out all over her face.

'Joan!' Lavinia shouted, and Mary Kate ran to the cooker to switch down the flames. 'Would you look at the mess in this kitchen. Get away!' she shouted to the dog, pushing him with her foot. She opened the back door, threw him out and slammed it shut behind him.

The boy at the sink wriggled free of Joan's grip. 'Oi, don't put him outside – he likes to stay in here with us.' In seconds he'd pulled open the door and was shouting the dog to come back in.

Lavinia grabbed him by the arm and pulled him back. 'David, stop it. The dog stays outside. Your father will be home soon and if you let Jet back in, I will tell him.'

David burst into a fit of petulant tears, ran over to the table and began noisily hammering at it with his fists. A second little boy was sitting at the table and observing his brother's behaviour intently, with an amused grin on his face. He turned and looked up at Mary Kate, his mousey-brown hair flopping over his wide and mischievous blue eyes. He gave her the sweetest smile. She could see that he was the younger of the two brothers.

'He's been giving out all day, Mrs Marcus,' said Joan.

Mary Kate looked over to Joan. The name Marcus sounded so familiar. But how could it – there was no one in Tarabeg with that name. She smiled back at the little boy. 'What are you drawing there?' she said as she moved over to the table and looked over his shoulder.

The older boy seemed in every way the image of his mother, not only because of his blonde hair and blue eyes but also because of his nature. They were still arguing with each other at the back door.

'Have you never heard the saying "children should be seen and not heard"? That applies to you, young man, as you are a child and I am your mother. Be quiet and stop arguing with me right now or I will tell your father and make sure he deals with you when he comes home.'

The wails became louder and angrier and the younger boy's smile became a trembling bottom lip. Mary Kate realised that he was scared.

Joan, who'd been standing there staring at Mary Kate, suddenly remembered the boiling potatoes. Turning to the cooker, she lifted the heavy pan onto a metal trivet on the table, spilling some of the water on the way.

'Joan, why is supper only half prepared?' Lavinia asked.

'I'm nearly done, missus. The doctor, he will be home soon. He rang when you were out this afternoon to say he would be in for his tea, and the boys, they haven't had their food yet.'

'For goodness' sake, why not? They are supposed to have their supper at five o'clock on the dot.'

Joan looked close to tears. 'I haven't had time, that's why,' she wailed as she grabbed at her apron and dashed it against her face. 'David has been giving me the run-around all day.'

Mary Kate felt uncomfortable. They had only been in the kitchen for moments and now two people were crying and a dog was barking incessantly outside. She was already removing her cardigan. 'Here, let me help. I'll mash the potatoes for you.' She threw Joan a sympathetic smile and squeezed her hand. 'We can have the tea ready in minutes – that chicken looks to me like it's already cooked.'

It took her a moment to notice that David had stopped yelling and the room had fallen quiet. The only noise was the dog barking out in the garden. It was only when the younger son said, 'Hello, Daddy,' that Mary Kate smiled and looked up – straight into the face of the doctor who had saved her.

His eyes were kind and full of curiosity as he took in the scene before him. 'Hello, Jack,' he said as he moved forwards, dropped his case on the floor and, removing his hat, planted a kiss on Jack's head and ruffled his hair.

His eyes never left Mary Kate's, and over the top of Jack's head he said, 'Hello.'

Mary Kate felt as though the room was moving. Her breath caught in her throat and she was almost unable to reply. She swallowed hard. 'Oh, hello, I've er... I've come for a—' She didn't get the chance to explain any more as Lavinia jumped in.

'She was sent here by the agency, Nicholas. As you can see, Joan just can't cope. The girl is hopeless – just take a look at this kitchen and the mess. The boys haven't even been fed or bathed yet.'

Nicholas Marcus walked over to his eldest son and scooped him up into his arms. 'What's up, David? Why are you so upset?'

David kicked against his father's thighs and wriggled. 'Let me down. I wasn't crying – I'm not a baby.'

Nicholas let him slip to the floor.

'You can pick me up if you like, Daddy,' said Jack in a voice so small, it was barely audible.

Lavinia folded her arms and her husband moved towards her and kissed the cool powdered cheek she'd proffered. 'Look, I'm going upstairs – I need another aspirin after all of this. Mary Kate, if you can agree to what we talked about earlier, can you start on Thursday morning?'

'Hang on a minute.' Nicholas Marcus's voice, still gentle, sounded concerned. 'We haven't even discussed this, Lavinia. I have no idea what's happening here – what is going on?'

'That, Nicholas, is because you are never here to discuss anything with. I have taken this decision. Mary Kate, we will see you on Thursday morning at seven.' Lavinia turned on her heel and, pushing past Nicholas, made for the door.

'Eight.' Mary Kate's voice cut through the room.

'I beg your pardon?' Lavinia Marcus turned around and her eyes locked onto Mary Kate's and flashed with impatience.

Mary Kate blushed and then just as quickly went pale. 'I begin at eight.'

Lavinia Marcus's mouth dropped open and then swiftly closed again. There was very obviously something she wanted to say, but she decided against it. 'Very well, you start at eight and stay until seven.'

'In that case,' said Mary Kate, 'and I hope you don't mind me bringing this up, we need to discuss my pay. If you want me to work eleven hours a day, I will need another ten shillings on top of what we agreed.'

She held her breath. This would go one of two ways: she would either exit the kitchen the same way as the dog or be taken on. Her face flared and she couldn't meet the eyes of Dr Marcus, who she knew was staring at her and grinning in mild amusement.

Lavinia looked as though she was about to explode. 'I'm really not sure the kitchen is the place for this discussion. However, very well. If they are your terms, I agree.'

'Thank you,' said Mary Kate. 'I know I haven't started

yet, but I'll just stay and help Joan here tonight. She looks exhausted and I can learn the ropes whilst I'm at it.'

'Jolly good idea.' And Lavinia, without another word to her husband, flounced out of the kitchen, up the stairs and back to the sitting room.

Neither the boys, Mary Kate nor Joan said anything; the only sound was the deep sigh that came from Nicholas Marcus. The sitting room door banged shut.

Jack was the first to speak. 'Daddy, can I let Jet back in now? He hasn't had his tea either.'

Dr Marcus nodded and Jack ran to the back door and shouted, 'Jet, come on, boy.'

David, much to Mary Kate's surprise, made his way towards the stairs. 'Mummy's upset, I can tell. And, Daddy, tell her we don't need anyone else…' He pointed his finger straight at Mary Kate's face. 'She can go home. I'm going to see Mummy.' And before his father could reprimand him, he ran up the stairs shouting, 'Mummy, Mummy, are you all right?'

'Come along, Jack, I suggest we do the same,' said Dr Marcus. 'Leave Jet down here. You know how Mummy hates him being up in the house.' He lifted his son into his arms. 'Ring the bell when supper is ready, if you don't mind, Joan. I'll bring the boys down myself.' Turning to Mary Kate, he said, 'Are you fully recovered now?'

Joan's mouth fell open and she looked as though she was about to faint.

Mary Kate nodded, avoiding his eyes. Her stomach

flipped as he spoke. She mentally remonstrated with herself, lifted her head high and looked at him straight on, then immediately regretted it. He was studying her face, looking at her with intense curiosity. 'I am, thank you.'

'And did your aunt's neighbour look after you well? Are you going to be sharing a room with Joan?'

Another question. Where would she start with the answers? 'No, I am living with Mrs O'Keefe, who is across the road and I met her on the boat and she was such a lovely lady, and Cat, she did look after me, but I wanted to come to Mrs O'Keefe's, and her sister owns the agency and she called around when I was there and your wife had already just rung looking for someone, but I had no idea it was you.'

'Whoa!' Dr Marcus, grinning, put up his hand to halt her volley of words. 'This sounds like a long story. Let's talk about it another time, shall we? In the meantime, welcome, Mary Kate. I hope you don't regret this.' He pulled Jack up higher into his arms and turned to the door.

As he left, Jack smiled at her over his father's shoulder, but she couldn't smile back. Something had happened and she wasn't sure what. It had made her skin prickle and her mouth dry. Every nerve in her body was tingling, and there was one thing she was sure of: she would not sleep tonight. She was already playing his last words over in her mind. The sound of his voice alone churned her emotions and brought feelings to the surface she never knew existed.

'Here you go.' Joan's voice broke into her thoughts, and Mary Kate turned as Joan slapped a wooden implement into her hand. 'Get mashing then.'

Mary Kate's room was the smallest guest room in the house. Mrs O'Keefe had shown her the other three, which were large and airy and not like any bedroom that Mary Kate had ever seen before, and then they'd climbed the stairs to the top of the house, where Deidra's room was. Mary Kate's was on the first floor, below Deidra's but not much bigger. Mary Kate had thought it a tactful decision to choose the smallest room. Deirdra was someone she did not want to offend.

As she prepared for bed, she thought back to the previous night and her fitful sleep at Cat's house. It was dark outside and she threw up the large sash window to let what breeze there was into the room. With her hands on the windowsill, she dipped, put her head and torso outside and peered down the avenue. She could see what she thought must be the chimney of the Marcus house further down, peeping up above the treetops.

The night sounds were very different from her room back in Tarabeg. No river rushing past in the background. No splashing salmon or hooting owl. Instead there was what sounded like the cry of a distressed baby but which Deidra had already taught her was actually a cat. There were no cats in Tarabeg.

She dipped back inside. 'You're a noisy one,' she whispered to the cat as she pattered across the lino floor and, freshly bathed, slipped between the pair of cool linen sheets. She stared up at the ceiling, at the fringed pink lampshade hanging from the central plaster rose, and thought what a beautiful sound the Tarabeg river made and why had she never noticed how lovely it was. There was no time to search for an answer as she melted into the depths of her first deep sleep since leaving Tarabeg.

Lavinia Marcus had tried to entice Nicholas to make love to her, but he was asleep before her lips had reached his soft lower belly. The rhythm of his breathing became slow and heavy and she knew she'd lost. She moved to her own side of the bed, plumped the goose-down pillows, placated herself with the memory of her assignation earlier and felt the burning, tense knot of frustration settle in her groin.

The room was dark and the only sound other than Nicholas breathing was the distant trundle of the last bus heading down Aigburth Road, the occasional rustle of the leaves and the caterwauling of the huge ginger tom from next door as he squared up to protect his territory.

She pushed the covers off and kicked her legs out of the bed as she wondered who she was becoming. Each boundary she pushed fell at the touch of her manicured fingers. It had all been so simple. It had taken minimal ingenuity to deceive and, surprisingly, given that his wife wasn't altogether a headscarf-wearing frump, it had taken even less effort to entice Robin into an affair. Oh, how easily that boundary had been breached. She smiled at the memory of that day, and of the subsequent days and alternate weekends since.

It was the wickedness, the illicit nature of the affair that thrilled her. She was high on the oxygen of sex and duplicity. The lies came easily, and of course she relished having men desire her and tell her how beautiful and irresistible she was. She was the modern-day Cleopatra of her own suburb. She grinned in the dark as she thought of the women she lunched with, played bridge with and met at the golf club on the odd occasion Nicholas found the time to take her there. She finally gave in to sleep, wondered how many of their husbands were safe and, as it was so easy, who she would reel in next. Her affair with Robin was too risky. Far too close to home, but she wasn't willing to let him go yet. She would be more careful next time.

Chapter 14

Bridget McAndrew sat with the pen poised over the paper. 'So I am to reply that you are long dead, is that right?'

Daedio wriggled himself further up the bed. 'Aye, say I died of the plague, a rat bite. No, I know, tell them I was cursed, fell down a bog hole and was never seen again, that Seamus is still searching for me and that Nola is beside herself with the grief.'

Bridget snorted with laughter. 'Well, that could very well have happened to you after many a night in Paddy's, and sure, I think it did once or twice, did it not?'

Daedio rubbed his chin and had the grace to look shamefaced. 'It did. If Annie hadn't been stood in the doorway, listening out for me, she would never have heard my screams. I wouldn't even be here today, God rest her soul.'

Bridget laid the pen back down again. 'Daedio, listen while I tell ye, I'm not sure they have the same notions in America as we do here. Do they even have bog holes or faeries over there? Or are they just here in Ireland? Have any of your lot, in their letters home, ever once mentioned the faeries or the bog holes?'

Daedio looked dismayed. 'The letters home were about New York and Brooklyn. About bridges being built and dollars being made. About a general store called Macy's, which Nola said must be just like Malone's. What shall we say then? We'd better get a move on, Nola will be back up the boreen within the hour.'

'How about this then: Dear Joe Junior of Brooklyn, America, thank you very much for your letter enquiring as to the whereabouts of Mr P.T. Malone. I am replying to you from the post office in Tarabeg and I am very sorry to inform you that he died some twenty years ago, leaving nothing to anyone. The man was a drunk and a tramp and lived out in barns and on the charity of others—'

'Don't go too far – you make me sound like Matty Maughan,' said Daedio, his voice loaded with indignation.

Harmless Matty Maughan had moved into the village when his relative, Shona, and her grandson Jay had moved out. He walked from farm to farm, carrying his food in a cloth bundle tied to the end of a stick and perched on his shoulder, and had no more than his next meal to his name. Ostensibly he helped with harvests and other odd jobs. In fact he did very little, but he was never turned out of a cow byre or a pig pen and he lived off the scraps of food that were given readily, along with a kind word, at nearly every door. No one in Tarabeg remembered how

Matty was related to Shona or Jay, they only knew that he kept his distance from them both.

'I know I am. I'm using Matty as an example, and I'm thinking, if they ever come here looking for you, we can get Matty to pretend he's you. He can say that he didn't die, just went wandering, and returned at the same time the American did.'

Daedio flopped back onto his pillows. 'Matty can barely speak. The poteen has addled his brain.'

Bridget smiled. 'I know. Why do you think he was the first person to come into me mind? 'Twas an easy comparison for me to make.'

Daedio picked up his mug of tea and nursed it to his chest as he glared into the flames of the fire, which was always lit, no matter the time of year. 'If I meet our Joe in heaven, I'm going to beat the fecking living daylights out of the bastard. Our Joe couldn't write, no more than the rest of us could, and that, Bridget, is the reason I know there is no fecking will. The person who wrote this letter is not related to our Joe, and now, God help us, we have a murderer from America, who found out about the money in jail, sending an assassin here to claim it. What right-minded person would think it was still here after all this time? He's chancing his luck, he is – a chancer, nothing more – and it's trouble our Joe is heaping on us from his bloody grave, the fecking eejit.'

He waved his fist at the ceiling. 'Just you wait until I'm up there, Joe – bringing all this worry on my shoulders.

Go on then, Bridget, do a Matty letter, 'tis our only hope. I'll make sure he's the best fed on this farm next time he calls. Jesus, I'll give him me own bed for the night, so I will. Go on, write, tell him that's who I was. Does Mrs Doyle know?'

'Oh, she does that. I've told her there will be the finest crate of whiskey in it for her after this.'

Daedio grimaced.

'Take that scowl off your face. You got seven acres out of it, your grandson built the best shop in the west, and you are sitting on the best farmed hill in the country. They can't take none of that from you, and you still have a fortune hidden somewhere. What in God's name is up with you?'

Bridget began to write as Daedio supped his tea. What was up with him was that he knew there was a great deal of money hidden behind the bricks of his fireplace. He knew why whoever it was Joe had confided in had passed the information on and why a chancer was writing to him. The money, the ill-gotten gains of a bank robbery, had obviously cooled with time, over in America, and someone was coming to fetch it. A letter was their first shot, but Daedio was quite sure that if whoever it was from Brooklyn knew how much money there was, and Annie had told him it was a lot, the letter would be just the first salvo in their treasure hunt.

★

Teresa hurried to the oven when she caught sight of Father Jerry running up the path to the presbytery, and with one swift tug she removed the steaming apple pie. 'Go and get yourself ready now, Father, I have your dinner almost on the table,' she shouted as soon as the door was opened. 'Who was it that made you late tonight then? Do they not think you are a shadow of yourself by the time the Angelus arrives and that you don't have a breath left in your body for nothing other than to eat your tea?'

'I will be down in ten minutes, Teresa.' And with no other explanation, he was gone.

Teresa wiped her floury hands on the tea towel and watched him go with suspicion. He was usually quick to volunteer the news from the Angelus. The talk had been fervent since Mary Kate had run away from home, and the gossip, well, that was wild. He was hiding something from her.

Father Jerry closed the door to his room behind him. He was not about to discuss with Teresa his conversation with Bee. Bee had attended the Angelus and he had left her in no doubt how he felt about her having lived in sin in Liverpool for so many years. If it had been a welcome Bee was after, she was in for a serious disappointment and he had told her so. He had expected her back home to repent the error of her ways within the year, not after nearly ten. As he hung up his cloak and surplice, he pondered on Bee's words. He was still smarting at her lack of contrition and how she'd fought back when he'd pointed out to her all that she'd done that was sinful.

'What was I supposed to do? Live my life here in Tarabeg along with nothing but the memory of my murdered sister and dead niece, working every hour I was sent on this earth just to put bread on the table? Living the same life, day after day – is that what God had planned for me, Father? Is that why he took my Rory in the way he did, drowned him out at sea so that I had to struggle just that bit harder? Did he?' Her face was flushed and she was on the verge of tears.

Father Jerry turned his head away and began to scrabble around in the side of his cassock. He hated these conversations with strong women like Bee. He hated tears. By the time most Irishwomen reached Bee's age, the tears were usually long spent, replaced with the realisation that they changed nothing, that they themselves had nothing, and that the full weight of the Church and society would bear down on them should they try to do anything about that.

Bee looked towards the door. She wanted to escape from the Church of the Sacred Heart. Her throat was thick with holy smoke and the anxiety that had beset her since the death of Captain Bob's wife. 'Anyway, Father, you might not have to worry about my soul being sent to purgatory any longer. I've had neither sight nor sound of Captain Bob since he left me to travel to Ballycroy. I came back to the house all on me own.'

'Yes, well, he has his own family to put first now, Bee,

now that the poor woman, his wife in the eyes of God, is dead.'

The blood rushed to Bee's face and her temper flared. She swallowed down the bile that had risen to her throat and took a deep breath before she spoke. 'Father, since when did you become a man with such little understanding? I well know you didn't approve of the fact that Captain Bob and I were living in sin, but you were never like this. I never expected your blessing, but I thought you – the man who preaches against theft but poaches when the salmon are in, and who drinks in Paddy's bar even when it's closed on a Sunday, taking the Guinness – would be a little more understanding.'

Father Jerry was embarrassed as he wiped his brow with the neatly folded white handkerchief he'd extracted from his cassock. 'I've had a duty to be vigilant since evil began to stalk our village, Bee. You of all people should know that, after the terrible murder of your own sister and then the awful shock of Sarah passing over as she did. 'Twas partly my fault. I made too many excuses, allowed too much to fall from my grasp.' He leant over and almost hissed in her face. 'I lost control of this village, so I did, and in my negligence, someone else slipped in. Do you not understand? Are ye forcing me to speak his name out loud?'

Bee could see the distress in his eyes, but she would not be put off her stride. 'You didn't murder Angela or kill Sarah and you cannot use what happed to them to blame yourself, or anyone else, or take your anger out on me. And anyway, whatever you say, Captain Bob's daughters were worse than the old scold and yet he never missed a week when he kept them comfortable, nor their mother. They all had the best, while we lived a frugal life in Liverpool. But none of that matters now. I think they may have won – you have probably got your way, Father, because I've not heard a word.'

Father Jerry looked at Bee askance. He could hardly believe what she was saying and they were still standing in God's house. 'Sure, the funeral hasn't even taken place yet. Have a bit of decency about you, Bee, would you. He has duties to attend to, obligations to meet.'

Bee did feel chastened. She knew how she sounded, and unfamiliar tears threatened. She was the strong one; she had carried them through the past ten years. Without Captain Bob at her side, she felt lost, besieged, alone.

She walked behind Father Jerry to the church door and it occurred to her that he was in a hurry to get away from her.

'As it happens, I'm not here to talk about Captain Bob. I've come to ask something of you and you can make of it what you will. Michael is in a mighty temper and he's packing his bag right now ready to head to Liverpool and fetch Mary Kate home. Rosie is beside herself; she thinks it will be a disaster if he does that, thinks Mary Kate will just dig her heels in further, and that if he leaves her be, she'll come back of her own accord. Nola and

Seamus are on their way down the hill to talk to him, but it seems to me like he has the Devil himself in him, he's been giving out so much.'

They were outside on the gravel path now. Father Jerry pulled the heavy church doors closed behind him and they stood in the graveyard in the evening light. He looked up towards the lights of the presbytery, where he knew Teresa would be preparing his supper. His stomach rumbled. The lights were on in the Devlins' too; the bar was open, and he would be heading there after his supper. As soon as he returned home he would fall to his knees and pray for forgiveness. The keys of St Patrick brushed against his bare thigh, reminding him of his obligation. He, in all of Ireland, was the priest to hold the secret chest, the scroll and the keys. He had felt that Tarabeg was blessed. That St Patrick regarded their village above all others he had visited. Only a few people knew about the treasure in Father Jerry's care: himself, the Bishop of Galway, and the Vatican. He had proved himself unworthy once; it would not happen again.

'I've heard Liverpool is a terrible place altogether – I know priests who are over there. I think Michael's doing the right thing, going to fetch her home.'

'Well, if you think he's doing the right thing, you don't know Mary Kate very well.' And with that, Bee turned on her heel and headed towards the Malones'.

Father Jerry stood watching her, his hand resting on the gravestone of Sarah Malone.

*

Bee didn't look back as she turned the corner and hurried towards the Malones'. Despite her mission to plea for help for Rosie and Mary Kate, her thoughts were full of Captain Bob. He would have known how to deal with Michael right now. There hadn't been a decision made by either one of them in the last ten years that hadn't seen the other involved in it, and yet now, in the face of the momentous occasion of the death of his wife and the beginning of their long-awaited freedom, he hadn't even sent a telex from Ballycroy to let her know what was going on.

On top of this, her quiet homecoming had been anything but. The gossip from Ballycroy was beginning to filter into Tarabeg, and it was only Mary Kate having run away that had deflected the attention from her, allowing her a measure of freedom to go about her business. At night she lay awake wondering what would happen if the village did find out the truth about her life over the past ten years. What if Captain Bob didn't come back? What options did she have? Could she live in a village where her sins would fuel the gossip for years to come and never be forgotten; where she would be shunned and excluded from everything as if she were a pariah?

She now realised that Father Jerry must have been behind Michael's decision not to allow Mary Kate to visit. It was obvious from the father's manner. Michael would never have been so cruel. They had liked Captain

Bob well enough when she'd lived in Tarabeg, when he'd kept up the pretence of returning home to his wife. As long as the villagers had had a reasonable charade to cling to, providing a veneer of respectability that had not challenged their own hypocrisy or threatened their place in heaven, all had been well.

The day she'd arrived home, she'd stood in her cottage doorway looking out at the ocean, well aware of what her options were. She would not return to scratching a living from the land and the sea and the grace of God. She would not walk the mile to the village each night and resume her work in Paddy's bar for as long as her bones would allow. She would not, when the day arrived, live off charity or beg for her son to send pounds or dollars to the post office. 'I may be coming to join you sooner than I thought,' she sobbed to her dead sister and her dead niece. As black thoughts filled her mind, the clouds blocked out the sun and the shadows lurking in the corners of the cottage drifted towards her.

Rosie was standing at the end of the bed and Finn was on the chair beside the scrubbed pine table under the bedroom window. The lemon-yellow curtains decorated with sprigs of pink flowers lifted and dropped in the light breeze, and the red and orange fuchsias and dog roses in the jug were already beginning to wilt. So was Finn.

His legs swung under the chair as he looked about him

and tried to blot out his father's remonstrations and Rosie's pleading. He was supposed to be over in the Devlins' house, playing with the boys. Keeva had tried her best to make him stay – 'Would you look, Finn, Aunty Josie and I have made your favourite chocolate cake, and Uncle Paddy, he wants—' But her words had fallen on deaf ears.

'I'll be back, Aunty Keeva. Mrs McAndrew said Daddy's losing his mind and I want to go and watch.'

He had indeed sat and watched as his daddy roared for all of half an hour, and now he was bored. If that had really been his father losing his mind, it had been slightly alarming but nothing more than that. He'd seen him shout plenty of times before. Finn ran his hands though his mop of golden-red hair and sighed, wondering how he could sneak back over the road to the cake. His biggest concern being whether there'd be any left. He didn't want to become the next object of his father's wrath, didn't dare move, regretted coming back to watch.

'What do you expect me to do, Rosie? She has left me a note telling me she is running away to Bee and then Bee turns up here, having seen neither hide nor hair of her. Her mother will be weeping in her grave, and if you really thought of her as your daughter, you would be weeping too, not trying to stop me.'

Rosie pursed her lips to stop the words from escaping. God forgive him, was the only thought that passed through her mind. She took a breath, looked towards Finnbar, whom she had tried to remove once already, and decided to try again. 'Finn, would you please go across the road to Aunty Keeva's and play with the boys. It will be light for hours yet. Go on, I'll let you go to bed late tonight.'

To Rosie's surprise, he didn't need to be asked twice. Finn slipped off the chair and ran out of the room, straight past her and Michael. As his departing steps faded, Rosie sat down on the side of the bed. 'Michael, what will you do if she says no, she won't come back? Are you going to drag her home?'

'If I have to, I will.' Michael was now at the press, yanking open drawers and removing clean shirts. He stormed into Mary Kate's bedroom once again, and Rosie heard drawers banging in there. He came back into the room, carrying the box containing the emerald heart given to Sarah by Daedio. 'She didn't even take this – that's how little her mother means to her,' he said, opening the drawer of the pine table in their room and throwing it inside. 'I'm her father, for God's sake – she will do as I say. I am going. The girl has lost her senses.' He picked up the shirts and threw them into the open case on the bed.

'But, Michael, she's a strong-willed young woman with a good education – she won't just do as she is told.'

Michael shoved his hands into his trouser pockets and went over to the window that looked out across the road to the Devlins' butcher's shop and bar. Not for the first time, he wondered why, when he and Sarah had built the cottage, they hadn't put the main bedroom to the back and looked out at the view of the river and mountains.

They'd been in such a hurry to build, to start their life, and he'd thought he'd made such a good job, but it was a big error, depriving him and Sarah of the most special view in the world, especially given the hours they used to spend in bed, talking, talking, talking and making love.

He was standing in the room where his Sarah had died in childbirth: he had failed her then and he was failing her now. The children bound them forever, but now he had lost their daughter and she was possibly in danger. He felt the same anguish he imagined Sarah would feel if she were still alive and he wanted to bend double with the pain of having let her down. How could he explain to Rosie that it was as if Sarah were packing the case for him, there, in the room where she'd died; he could feel her, and as he turned, he would not have registered a flicker of surprise to find her standing right next to him, folding his shirts. She would be with him, supporting him; she was Mary Kate's mother. Rosie was trying to prevent him from going, but Sarah would have been pushing him out the door.

He took a deep breath and turned, calmer. How could he say the words, 'You are not a mother yourself, Rosie, you just don't understand.' His temper was almost spent, but not quite.

'Mary Kate can talk the back legs off Jacko and that's a fact. She can persuade anyone to do anything and that is just what she'll do in Liverpool. She's an innocent, Rosie, from this village, and she's spent her whole life wrapping me around her little finger. But by God, not this time. Now she will do as I say and come back home. She didn't leave here alone, Rosie, someone helped her, and when I find out who it was, I'll be kicking him down the road, all the way to Ballina.'

'Don't be ridiculous. No one helped her. She's strong-willed enough to do it herself. She probably booked a cab from Galway with the money Daedio gave her.'

Rosie had no idea why she was protecting Declan. She had seen the way he looked at Mary Kate since she'd grown from a girl into a beautiful woman. It had happened over the course of the last year and what a transformation it had been. One that had stabbed at Rosie's heart. Mary Kate had shed her gangly limbs and too-thin face and evolved into the likeness of her mother. Sarah's face and eyes stared back at her every day Mary Kate was in the house.

Michael returned to the bed and slammed the case shut. 'If Bee is here, Mary Kate is alone in Liverpool. I have a father's responsibility to go and fetch her and I have Father Jerry's blessing. It defeats me why I don't have yours.'

'Oh, you do have mine, Michael. It's Mary Kate you have to convince, not me—'

'Hello!'

They both heard Bee's voice shouting up the stairs from the kitchen. Rosie jumped up from the side of the bed.

'It's Bee, she could have news,' said Michael, racing down the stairs to find out.

Rosie was hot on his heels.

'Bee, do you have news?' Michael was short of a greeting, Mary Kate being the only thing on his mind.

'Lovely to see you, would you like some tea?' asked Rosie as she lifted the kettle and carried it to the tap.

Bee half nodded to Rosie and looked straight to Michael. 'I do. I have a telegram from my next-door neighbour, Cat. I've just collected it from Mrs Doyle's. God in heaven, Michael, she was attacked in Liverpool, and, thank God, Cat took her in.'

Bee held out the telegram for Michael, who sank onto the settle to read it. A heart-rending noise had come from somewhere deep within him at the word 'attacked'; it tore at Rosie and she moved to the settle to sit next to him, placing her arm around his shoulders and at the same time shaking her head and thinking, *Mary Kate, what have you done?*

The decision was made. The news Bee had brought changed everything. Rosie sighed. She now had to play her part and help her husband, not fight him. She'd been wrong and he was right: travelling to Liverpool and bringing her back was the right thing to do. Her place as his wife was to pull with him, to make it easier for him, not place obstacles in his way.

'I'll make you some tea and cut up some bread and cheese and then you head off in the car. You can make the early morning crossing and be in Liverpool for the afternoon. Does Captain Bob know the sailing times, Bee?

Here, sit down.' Rosie sprang to her feet and pulled out a chair for Bee, who sank down with a weary sigh.

Rosie did a double-take and glanced back at Bee as she removed the bread crock and cheese from the press. Bee looked pale, troubled. They were all worried about Mary Kate, but she thought there must be something else. Vibrant, happy, strong Bee seemed dark about the eyes.

'Well, he would know them, that's for sure, but as I haven't heard from him let alone seen him, I can't ask him.'

Rosie saw the tears in Bee's eyes and her heart contracted in a spontaneous burst of sympathy. If anyone knew the pain of love, it was Rosie, who met it and felt it every day. Turning to her husband, she said, 'Right, Michael, go upstairs and finish packing. Bee, stay here with me tonight. Let us open a bottle of Michael's best porter whilst he's gone and you can tell me all that's going on because I think there's lots to tell.'

She was swamped with guilt. They'd been so preoccupied with Mary Kate's disappearance, driving over to Galway to see Roshine and her parents, a task that had taken a whole day and night, they'd forgotten to speak to Bee in any depth. Mary Kate had left Tarabeg and had been attacked in Liverpool. Rosie blessed herself and slipped the rosaries though her fingers; she was now determined to put things right.

As Michael rose to collect his case from the bedroom, he caught Rosie's hand. 'Thank you,' he whispered, squeezing her fingers and laying the softest and longest kiss on her cheek.

It was a gesture full of a tenderness the like of which she hadn't known since the day they were married. She had long felt that every kiss, every touch, was something he had done and known before and was repeating for the memory of someone else. For Sarah. Every time they made love, it was as if he was going through the motions with his body while at the same time, behind his always closed eyes, he was making love to Sarah. Rosie knew it and hoped that every time was the last time and that one day he would make love to her.

She blinked back an unexpected tear and, filled with gratitude and love, placed a hand on the side of his cheek. 'Go. Go and bring your daughter home.'

'Our daughter,' he whispered.

Her heart lifted and her spirit soared. That one kiss, that one gesture, those few words had restored her happiness, her reason to be a part of the Malones.

Chapter 15

Michael parked his car in the Dublin port car park and removed his bag from the back. The weather had broken without warning and the wind had turned wild. The hinges on his car door creaked in protest as he opened it. 'Jesus, feck,' he hissed as he tried to grab the handle and stop the door from being ripped off. The wind fought him and almost won as it whipped across the empty car park, pulling leaves and branches from the trees, tipping over old wooden Guinness barrels planted with purple fuchsias and scattering the flowers and soil like open graves. Holding onto his cap, he raced across to the ticket office. A wooden board that shouted 'Ice Cream and Cigarettes Sold Here' swung precariously as he ducked past, and he turned, alarmed, as he heard it crash onto the pavement.

It had been raining for the past hour of his journey, slowing him down and making it difficult for him to see as his windscreen wipers did battle with the torrential downpour. The roads had become treacherous in the first rain following the prolonged spell of hot weather. It didn't help that it was still dark, the dawn slow to break on account of the storm, and he was tired from having driven all through the night.

He tried to light a cigarette, but the match would not catch and the tissue-thin paper became soaked. He threw the wet tobacco to the ground and shoved the packet back into his pocket. His frustration at the slowness of the journey had made him bad-tempered enough; this was now exacerbated by the sign that greeted him as he reached the ticket office: 'All Sailings Cancelled Until Further Notice Due to Bad Weather.'

'Nicholas, what time is it?'

There was no reply.

'Nicholas?' She tried again.

Lavinia Marcus woke to the sound of her husband brushing his teeth in the bathroom. Joan was shouting at David downstairs. Footsteps that could only belong to nimble little Jack pattered past her bedroom door. They stopped suddenly as a tiny voice whispered, 'Mummy, are you awake?'

She almost answered, but then, thinking better of it, remained silent. The boys were not allowed into her room without checking first. She heard his faint little sigh of disappointment, then the bare footed patter continued down the stairs and he called through to the back kitchen, 'Joan, has Daddy gone to work yet?'

There was no response other than a grumble from Joan and the growl of a fractious David.

Lavinia sighed, mildly irritated. Her oyster silk night-dress had become twisted around her waist during the night and, wriggling, she pulled it down tight over her thighs as she shrugged the thin straps up onto her shoulders and rolled onto her back. The memory of attempting to entice Nicholas into making love to her the previous evening returned as she stared at his naked back, half bent over the sink while he rinsed his mouth.

'I'm off to lunch today with the Doctors' Wives Benevolence Group, so I won't be around if you call,' she shouted from the bed.

Nicholas appeared at the door, wiping his face clean with a towel. 'I doubt I will have time to call,' he said. 'Robin has something to do in town today and has asked me to cover from twelve until two thirty, alone. I'll be flat out. No lunch for me, I'm afraid.' He threw the towel into the laundry basket and walked to the wardrobe as she turned her face to the wall.

Two and a half hours, she thought to herself. Does Robin think that's all I'm worth – two and a half hours?

'Maybe you and I should go out tomorrow, now that you have extra help, with Mary Kate. What do you think?' he said.

'We are going out,' said Lavinia as she slithered out of bed. 'We're going to a party, Joan is babysitting. Can't you remember anything, Nicholas?'

She slammed the bathroom door behind her and Nicholas stood and stared for a long moment, his brow furrowed, before he slipped the shirt he was holding over his arms.

Mary Kate came downstairs early, but Eileen O'Keefe was already in the sitting room, in her dressing gown; she appeared to be waiting for Mary Kate. 'I knew it,' she said. 'You did a great thing, making her pay you more money, but now you're going to get there early and work for free.'

Mary Kate smiled. 'I feel sorry for the girl, Joan. I think she's from Mayo, and, Holy Mother, she has her hands full with that David.'

'I think I've seen her, walking past with the pair of them,' said Eileen. 'Does she have darkish red hair she wears swept up on top?'

Mary Kate nodded. 'She does, and lovely big dark eyes. She has the features of a family from the coast. Looking at her made me feel homesick – it was like meeting one of my own tribe.'

'One of those boys does appear to be a handful,' said Eileen. 'Now, come on, Deidra is getting breakfast ready for all of us down in the kitchen. She usually brings it up to me in the dining room, but do you know, last night I asked myself, why? It's warmer in the kitchen anyway.'

Eileen failed to mention that she knew she would have to find a way to keep a balance in the house. She had seen Deidra in a new light and she didn't want her to leave them; she wanted a happy house, and for the first time in a long while, she thought she might have one again. 'We will keep your supper here for you tonight for when you get home, so don't worry if they don't feed you. You won't starve. I think we'll be having a nice bit of ham on the bone, and salad with some Jersey Royals, I heard they landed in Liverpool yesterday.'

They were on their way down the stairs and had almost reached the kitchen.

'Jersey Royals, what are they?' asked Mary Kate.

'Call yourself Irish and you don't know what a potato is?' said Eileen as she opened the kitchen door.

Deidra was filling the teapot as they both walked in and she looked up and smiled. Happy that, for the first time since she'd arrived in England, she would not be eating breakfast alone.

The sun was bright and the day was already very warm as Mary Kate made her way down the avenue.

'Oh Jesus and Mary, 'twill be a hot one today,' Deidra had said before she left and it looked like she was right. Mary Kate hummed a song from home as she walked. Her heart felt light and her head clear. Things were far from perfect – she had lost her money and didn't have a penny to her name – but now, thanks to the kindness of Mrs O'Keefe, she would soon be able to save. She was on a path to putting things right and it felt good.

As she approached the front steps to the house, she saw Nicholas Marcus heading to his car, which was parked in the driveway at the side. His jacket was slung over one arm, he was carrying his Gladstone bag, and in his free hand he held a half-bitten slice of buttered toast.

'Morning,' he shouted, lifting his hat with the toast hand and placing his bag in the back of the car. He walked towards her. 'Mary Kate, I just want to tell you that my wife doesn't know that I gave you a lift to your aunt's, or even that I've met you before. Would you mind keeping that between us?'

Mary Kate was immediately apologetic. 'N... no, of course not. I wasn't going to mention it at all.'

His sigh was heavy with relief. He knew Lavinia would be furious with him if she found out. She was prone to bouts of jealousy and as Mary Kate was such an attractive young woman, she would accuse him of having an ulterior motive, of that he was sure. At the very least, she would berate him for having spent time attending to someone who wasn't officially his responsibility. She spent a lot of time doing that.

Mary Kate blushed, embarrassed at the possibility that his kindness to her had caused him problems, and made to walk past him and up the steps to the front door.

'Thank you,' he said. 'David is being David this morning,

and Jack, well, he's just being the sensitive soul he always is. If you have a bit of attention or affection to spare, he could do with some. Everyone spends so much time keeping David happy.'

'Of course I will.' She smiled, and for some reason her heart was beating madly.

'Thank you. I really appreciate it. I don't know how this happened or how you got here, Mary Kate, but you couldn't be more welcome.'

There was something in his tone that alerted her, made her look back. He was sliding into his seat and starting his car. She knew what he'd said, but that was not what he'd meant – there was something deeper behind his words. As he reached the gateposts, he put his arm out of the window and raised his hand in farewell. She stood and watched, replaying yet again the expression she'd seen in his eyes that first evening she'd gone to the house, the way he had looked at her, the smile that lifted the corner of his mouth when he'd spoken to her. This morning, the fresh encounter and that memory made her feel weak at the knees.

She was about to raise her own hand and return his farewell wave when the door flew open to reveal Lavinia Marcus, standing there in a long oyster silk dressing gown, her face free of make-up, her blonde curls in disarray, and a cigarette in her hand.

'Oh, it's you. Thank goodness. Joan has just about lost control in the kitchen again. Go on down, would you. Oh and, Mary Kate, in future, go round to the tradesmen's entrance, not the front door.' Without another word, she picked up the tea tray she'd laid on the hall table before opening the door and marched up the stairs, leaving it to Mary Kate to lean forward and, grabbing hold of the central brass knob, close the door.

'Good morning to you, Mrs Marcus,' she whispered as the door clicked shut.

Lavinia Marcus had not exaggerated: the scene that greeted her was chaotic.

'Oh, thank all the saints in heaven – you came,' said Joan as Mary Kate walked in through the door. 'Did she tell you about not using the front door?' She was in the middle of combing Jack's hair; he was sitting on a kitchen chair, wincing.

'She did. I won't do it again.'

'Oh, don't be apologising to me now. I couldn't care less if you came in down the chimney, but that one, she thinks she's Princess Margaret, so she does. Did she chew your head off?'

Mary Kate walked over and took the comb from Joan. 'There you go, you're free now. The boys are mine.'

Joan did not look displeased. 'Jesus, Mary and Joseph, I have no idea where you came from, but I've never been so glad to see anyone in my life. Where are you from?'

'Tarabeg,' said Mary Kate. 'What about you?'

'Well, what would you know, Tarabeg, eh? I'm from Clew Bay, but I know Tarabeg well enough.'

Within minutes of being freed from the boys' demands, Joan had laid breakfast for them all.

Mary Kate sat the boys down, now spick and span. 'I've had my breakfast already,' she said.

'Well now, you be telling Deidra you'll be having it here with the boys and me.'

'Do you know Deidra?' Mary Kate was surprised, and then almost chastised herself. Why wouldn't they know each other? Everyone in Mayo knew each other indirectly, and the Irish diaspora in Liverpool had to be close.

'Oh, sure, we all know each other. On a Friday or Saturday night we go into town together. You will have to come along with us. We take the bus. Do you dance?'

'I learnt to at the convent.'

Joan threw her head back and laughed. 'We all learnt at the convent, but it's not like that here. You'll have your eyes opened, so you will.'

In no time at all, Mary Kate had the boys organised and ready for the park. 'Will you show me your room first?' she asked. 'We have to make sure it's tidy and clean before we leave.'

David looked as though the sky had fallen in and landed on the kitchen floor. Jack nodded enthusiastically. 'We have a sitting room too, and me and Daddy, we have a big board on the floor for our battle.'

It took over an hour and a half to tidy their room. Jack helped Mary Kate with all of it, while David sat on his bed and refused. Mary Kate gave him a very simple choice. 'You can have it your way or my way, David. Either you help or I take Jack to the park on his own and you stay here.'

He looked up from his comic, a sneer on his face. 'You wouldn't dare do that – I'll tell Mummy.'

Just as he spoke, Mary Kate heard the front door slam. Walking over to the window, she looked down. A taxi was waiting on the street. Mrs Marcus said something to the driver, ducked in and was gone in a flash.

She turned back from the window. 'Well, that was your mammy leaving. You are free to tell her if you want, but that won't be until later. In the meantime, you still have two choices: help, or stay here.'

Jack was scooping up books from the floor beside David's bed; once his arms were full, he was then inserting them into the empty gaps in the bookcase. It took a few minutes, but eventually David slipped off the bed and onto the floor.

'Come here, Jack – you're putting them back all wrong. *The Last of the Mohicans* goes on the top.'

Mary Kate smiled. 'Good boy, David,' she said as she stroked his hair.

He didn't quite reach a smile, but the expression on his face was softer.

'I have a brother who's only a bit older than you. His name is Finn and he's just like you.'

The moment was lost as David snapped back, 'I'm not Irish. The Irish are dirty, all the boys around here say so.'

Mary Kate smarted. His words had hit her like a slap

to her face. She'd never heard anyone say an unkind word that encompassed the entire population of her country. Swallowing hard, she replied, 'The only dirtiness I have come across since I arrived in Liverpool, David, has been here, in this house. More specifically, in your room.'

David opened his mouth to speak and then closed it again without saying anything. This girl was not like Joan; he was not going to be able to make her cry or shout in indignation or anger. He could see that and he didn't like it. 'I'm going to tell Mummy to get rid of you,' he said quietly.

Mary Kate pretended not to hear and instead turned her attention to the boys' sitting room, where Jack had lined up his soldiers in columns on a huge board laid out on the floor.

She didn't get a chance to talk to Joan until later in the afternoon. The boys were in the garden with two other boys from down the street who had called and asked were they allowed out to play. Mary Kate wasn't sure of her ground, so she invited the visitors to play in the garden, much to the delight of the dog, who never left Jack's side. She took them out a tray of squash and biscuits, then collapsed into the kitchen chair to enjoy a cup of tea with Joan.

'How did you manage before I got here?' she asked. 'You haven't stopped and I've been with the boys all day.'

'The boys only broke up from school last Friday,' said Joan. 'It wasn't too bad before, but I have all the cleaning to do as well. It wasn't easy. She's out all the time, so she is. Never here to help with the boys.'

'Where does she go?'

Joan looked behind her to see were the boys near the door before she replied. 'Feck knows, but she comes back smiling. Not like the poor doctor. God in heaven, I have no idea where the man gets the energy from. Works every day God sends and, sure, if you speak to any of his patients, they say he's the best doctor in all of Liverpool.'

'I know – he looked after me after I was attacked.' Mary Kate had explained all about her mugging and Cat when she'd helped Joan hang out the washing earlier.

'Well, you know what I'm talking about then,' said Joan. 'The missus, she gives him an awful time. The man has no peace. She doesn't deserve him.'

'Where is she now?'

'I have not the faintest idea. I never do. She tells me nothing. I just have to run her house and her children – why would anyone tell me anything.' Joan looked up at the huge clock on the wall and leapt to her feet. 'I promised Jack I'd make him biscuits. I had better get a move on.'

Mary Kate listened to the boys' shrieks, which sounded like Finn playing with Keeva's sons on the bridge, and she was swamped with homesickness. This place, the boys, her emotions, all that was happening – it was too much for her, she realised. She had seen and met almost as many people in Liverpool as there were in Tarabeg.

★

Lavinia sat on the side of the bed and pulled on her stockings. Robin handed her a lit cigarette. There were two glasses on the bedside tables, drained of whiskey and soda, and the room smelt strongly of alcohol fumes, cigarette smoke and sex. The quilted pink satin eiderdown and woollen blankets were trailing off the end of the bed onto the floor and diffused daylight filtered through the long net curtains.

Lavinia's hotel of choice was the Adelphi, but Robin had booked a room in a different hotel on Mount Pleasant, only yards from the Adelphi, which had displeased her. Their hastily discarded clothes were spread across the floor. As she stood to fasten her suspenders, he leant over and slapped her bare buttocks revealed by her slip.

'That was bloody good, eh?' He grinned and lay back against the pillows.

'Actually,' said Lavinia as she took the proffered cigarette, 'it's been better. You having to leave at two o'clock to get back to work doesn't give us much time, does it?'

'Steady on, Lavinia. What about your poor husband? I've had to leave him running the show. Have a bit of sympathy for the old chap.'

She lay back against the pillow next to him and rolled onto her side. 'I dare you,' she said.

He exhaled his smoke and turned his face sideways. His dark hair had the first signs of grey appearing at the sides, his eyes were the palest blue, almost grey, and his lips, neither thin nor full, were pulled into a quizzical grin. He's one of those bloody men who gets better looking with age, she had often thought. But his eyes were shallow, untrustworthy; unusual eyes for a doctor.

'You dare me what?' he said, his eyes now twinkling.

She kissed his lips slowly and between breaths said, 'I dare you to take the weekend off.'

Robin spluttered. 'How can I do that? Besides, we are both at the Thompsons' party tomorrow.'

'I know, but can't you have a course starting on Saturday – one that's being held in a very nice hotel somewhere? We could have dinner and spend a whole night together. We both know that sex in the morning is the best, and we're missing out.'

She slipped her hand down and cupped him, and instantly, although it had been only half an hour since their last bout of passionate lovemaking, he began to swell against her. With a sense of urgency, he stubbed out his cigarette in the ashtray at the side of the bed, curled one hand behind her neck and the other under her buttocks, and pulled her towards him.

'Hang on,' she said, placing the flat of her hand against his chest. 'I need to hear a "yes" first.'

'Yes,' he groaned. 'Yes. Now come here.' He pulled her towards him, pushed his thigh between hers, lifted her up and slipped into her. 'You are insatiable,' he said as, with little preamble, he thrust himself inside her, guessing that she wouldn't complain.

She let out a small yelp, fastened her arms across his back and bit down hard into his shoulder. He moaned with pleasure. The clock on the bedside table came into view. It was two thirty-five. She had won. There was no way she would allow him to short-change her by sparing her only the time he had allocated. She imagined her husband, alone, struggling for a little longer with his precious patients, and the thought made her smile.

Chapter 16

When Joe Malone finally received a reply from Tarabeg, it was not the news he'd been hoping for. It seemed his great-granddaddy's relatives had mysteriously vanished from Tarabeg Hill, but that only made him more determined to go and see the place for himself. In recent weeks, Joe had visited the offices of Messrs Collins, Murphy, Browne and Sons on a number of occasions, to discuss the situation, and had formed a bond with Mr Browne. Though their lives were worlds apart, there was a historic connection between them, and it intrigued them both. He decided to ask Mr Browne's advice.

'Well, there's only one thing for it,' Mr Browne said. 'You must take the mountain to Mohammed. You must go over there yourself and find your inheritance. I always think it's the best way: to speak to people face to face. Look a man in the eye when you ask a question if you want an honest answer.'

Mr Browne sat back in his chair and crossed his legs in

front of him. A self-satisfied expression settled on his face as he joined his hands together. It had been an immense relief to discover that Joe Malone had no interest in Messrs Collins, Murphy, Browne and Sons other than the profit it made and thereby his share. The last thing Mr Browne needed at this stage in his life was for the sleeping partner to wake. Things were going to proceed just as they always had. He found the prospect of change abhorrent and con-sidered himself far too old to contemplate new ways. He secretly hoped that Mr Malone might take a liking to the old country, to the place so many Irish Americans still referred to as home.

'I don't think I have any choice,' said Joe. 'I had better start making arrangements.'

'Oh indeed, you don't have to worry about that. Miss Carroll will sort everything.'

Mr Browne summoned Miss Carroll into his office in his customary manner: he picked up the gold-plated tele-phone, rattled the handset up and down a few times and then spoke into it in a deep voice that was totally unlike the one he'd used with Joe. 'Miss Carroll, would you step inside, please.'

Joe grinned. Mr Browne's formal ways had begun to amuse him.

Miss Carroll, who had to be sixty if she was a day, turned the brass door handle and came into the office, her head held high. She was wearing shoes far too high for a woman her age. Her lipstick was too red and bled into the deep lines etched into her upper lip; it would have looked better on the lips of one of the younger women in the typing pool he'd been introduced to when he was first shown around the office. The typing pool had been the only element of the business to rouse Joe's interest. He could not have found the world of law-making more stuffy or boring if he tried.

Miss Carroll and Joe had already made their introductions before the meeting with Mr Browne had begun and, much to his delight, she had served him his espresso coffee just as he liked it. She was a woman who prided herself on her attention to detail. She knew every client, their likes and dislikes, what they drank, the ages of their children, and the details of their various medical complaints. Miss Carroll was a pro and she knew it.

As Joe had relaxed in a plush purple velvet chair opposite Miss Carroll's own mini version of Mr Browne's oak desk, waiting for Mr Browne's client meeting to finish, he'd told her about the frustrating situation regarding Tarabeg. 'What was the name of the village?' she'd asked him, flipping over a sheet of her ring-bound notepad, which Joe could see was filled from top to bottom with incomprehensible shorthand. She found a clean sheet and wrote the name down quickly. When she'd finished, she chewed the end of her pencil thoughtfully, leaving behind a ring of red lipstick like a watermark. Then she laid the pencil back down on the pad and smiled up at him, just as Mr Browne opened his door and ushered out his previous client.

Now, as the wood-panelled office door clicked shut, Joe swivelled around in his chair to acknowledge Miss Carroll's arrival. As she crossed the acreage of deep-pile carpet to the desk, he took in her old-fashioned tightly waved hairstyle and was once again reminded of an older version of Wallis Simpson, the American socialite who had married an English king for love; it occurred to him that this was possibly a similarity that she both enjoyed and cultivated.

'Ah, Miss Carroll.' Mr Browne looked up from his desk. 'We need to book a ticket for Mr Malone to fly to Ireland, as soon as possible, please. First class, of course. On the account of Collins, Murphy and Browne.'

Miss Carroll nodded and smiled benignly, giving nothing away. She stood under the central light in her dove-grey mid-calf dress and three strings of pearls sitting perfectly in place, her pad in one hand and her HB pencil poised in the other, just in case she might be required to take a letter. She turned and addressed Joe directly. 'Please excuse me, Mr Browne,' she said. 'Mr Malone, following our earlier conversation, and while you were taking your meeting with Mr Browne, I took the liberty of researching a more efficient way of communicating with Tarabeg. Letters can be so unreliable when sent abroad. I do hope you don't mind.'

She glanced nervously towards Mr Browne from under her lashes. He nodded almost imperceptibly, a look of mild curiosity on his face.

Joe smiled. 'I see. And did you have any success?'

Mr Browne, his interest piqued, sat forwards in his chair and rested his elbows on the table. Only Miss Carroll and Mr Browne knew that the day she retired of her own free will would be the day he'd be forced to do the same. He couldn't possibly manage without her and although it remained unspoken, they both understood it. In the meantime, she continued to play the servant to his master, even though it was quite obvious to all that the roles had been reversed many years since.

'There is a telex machine in the village post office. In fact, if you would like to come with me to our telex room, we could send a massage right now. It could be answered almost immediately. If there is one way to discover the whereabouts of any Malones still residing in Tarabeg, it will be via the post office.'

Joe almost leapt out of his seat. 'Miss Carroll, you are one angel,' he said and he marched over and hugged her so tight, a small birdlike noise squeaked out from somewhere within his embrace.

Later that evening, Joe headed over to his mother's house for his supper. 'I have no idea how that place makes any money and I feel indecent that we are the beneficiaries,' he said to her as she heaped pieces of fried chicken onto his plate.

On the day he had returned from the will-reading and told her that they were the sleeping partner and share- holders in the most successful law firm in Brooklyn, she had needed to sit down. When he'd told her of the fortune waiting in a village no one had ever heard of before, she needed a drink. Tonight, just as she had each time he returned from meeting Mr Browne, her words rapidly turned to despair.

'To think, your father might not have worked himself into the ground and be dead and buried if he'd known that money was sitting there, in that law firm, and that it was all his by rights.'

She was really speaking to Rocket, stroking his muzzle, looking deep into his eyes. Rocket, aware of her pain, nuzzled his mouth against her palm and licked her.

Joe reached across the kitchen table and squeezed his mother's hand. He had never been very good with words and didn't trust himself to say the right thing.

'What did you say in the telex?' she asked as she tore her eyes away from Rocket and focused on her son. 'Eat your chicken before it goes cold.'

Joe picked up the freshly ironed white napkin from the side of his plate and tucked it into the neck of his shirt as he glanced at her own empty plate. She'd lost twenty pounds since his father had died; it was hit and miss whether she ate the food she served up at supper.

'I just said that I was Joe Malone the fourth, looking for the family of my late father, the Malones, who were last known to be in residence on Tarabeg Hill. And to please inform them that I'll be arriving soon. That was all. Nothing else to say.'

His mother gave a short harrumph. 'You know, your daddy never stopped talking about them and yet he wouldn't know any of them, not if they all knocked on the door together, carrying a sack of potatoes with leprechauns sat on their shoulders. He wouldn't have had a clue. Never even seen a photograph of one of them. I could never understand it. Did you get a reply to the telex?'

Joe shook his head. 'Not yet, but Miss Carroll is going to keep an eye out for me.'

His mother stood and walked out of the room, returning seconds later with the dog-biscuit tin.

'Ma, eat the chicken instead – it tastes better.' Joe grinned and was relieved to see his mother manage a smile back.

Arthritic Rocket dragged himself to his feet and as she stood before her, his tail thumped repetitively against the table leg.

'Well, I think you are wasting your time. You've inherited enough here, with the firm, and you don't need to lift a finger, so why would you want to be going all the way over there? Enough is enough. What's the point? Do you really think the money will still be there? You must be mad. It will be long gone. Who would keep that amount of money for all of those years? No, whoever got their hands on that little lot bought the first ticket to America and carried those dollars back here.'

Rocket licked his chops. He could no longer jump for his treats and as Mrs Malone bent and placed a Milk-Bone biscuit in his mouth, Joe decided to drop the conversation.

He heaped mashed potatoes and corn onto his plate. He would tell Enzo to call round for his supper each night, as he'd promised.

It took Mrs Doyle only seconds to rip the telex out of the machine and place it into her apron pocket.

'Who is that for?' asked Keeva.

'No one. No one at all,' said Mrs Doyle. 'You be minding your own business now, Keeva, as well as the shop. I'm off over the road to Ellen's.'

Keeva had been brushing the post-office floorboards. She had worked there since she was a young girl as Mrs Doyle's assistant, though she knew the time was approaching when she and Tig would need to assume responsibility for the Devlin family business. In the meantime, however, Josie and Paddy continued to run the butcher's shop and the bar and to keep an eye on her brood of carrot-topped scallywags during the school holidays.

She watched with mild curiosity as Mrs Doyle hurried across the street. '"No one", my backside,' she muttered to herself but was distracted from her thoughts as the bell rang once again and Philomena O'Donnell bustled in.

'Keeva, have you an airmail letter?' she said as she closed the door behind her.

'Philomena, it's a post office. I haven't. Would a pound of rashers do instead?'

Philomena stood and stared. Keeva waited for the laugh,

but it never came. 'Why in God's name would I be coming here for the rashers? 'Tis an airmail letter I'm after, Keeva.'

Keeva sighed, denied her amusement for the afternoon. She lifted the wooden countertop and made her way round to the other side, squinting through the afternoon sunshine and the dust from the mud road to see Mrs Doyle heading through the door of Ellen Carey's tailor's shop.

Ellen was sitting at her sewing machine in the window when Mrs Doyle burst in; she'd just waved to Philomena as she went past. 'What's up with you? Your knicker elastic gone again?' Ellen lifted the foot of the sewing machine and removed the dress she'd been sewing.

'Jesus, no, it's much more serious than that.'

Mrs Doyle slipped the bolt across the top of the door, peeped out through the lace curtain to check who had seen her entering, and removed the telex from her pocket. She handed it to Ellen, who rose slowly from her chair. Threads of fabric, cotton and a cascade of metal sewing pins slid from her lap and bounced off the wooden floor as she read, but she appeared not to notice.

Handing the telex back to Mrs Doyle, she pushed her glasses back up to the bridge of her nose, folded her arms and said, 'Annie said this day might come, in the hour before she died. She knew, so she did. God in heaven, it has come to pass. She never said that a murdering criminal would be coming, though, did she?'

'Aye, she said it to all of us,' said Mrs Doyle, not wanting

Ellen to claim the upper hand. 'And I remember what she said we should do if we were here when it happened. And it's only gone and happened, hasn't it. Bloody Joe Malone. Do you remember what Annie said we had to do?'

Ellen was affronted. She'd been the closest to Annie Malone and she remembered her instructions as though she'd been told them only yesterday. She could recall Annie's words almost to the letter.

'"If anyone claiming to be from Joe Malone's family comes from America to Tarabeg, make sure they never set foot on Tarabeg Hill." Of course I remember. I was there, just like you, was I not. She said that if someone from America came knocking on the door, Daedio would hand over the flamin' lot because he would be scared witless, and that we would have to stop him. She said Joe Malone had loose lips and would have told someone in prison that he'd sent the box with the money to Tarabeg, and that no one on this earth would keep that a secret. Nola, Seamus and Michael have no idea that we know where the money came from for the shop, and it has to stay that way. We can't be letting Annie down.'

Ellen pulled her shawl across her front and held it with both hands. Her small, almost black eyes shone with purpose. Her good friend Annie had been gone many years, but not in spirit. She still visited Ellen in her kitchen at night, keeping her company as she drank her last glass of whiskey before she headed to bed. 'Will you take one yourself, Annie,' she often said. But Annie never replied.

Just sat in the chair on the other side of the fire and told her all the future secrets of Tarabeg.

'I knew something was happening. Annie was here last night and she was telling me to be ready. Who needs Philomena O'Donnell for the news when I have Annie?'

Mrs Doyle gasped and put her hand across her mouth, her eyes wide. 'Jesus, she knew already? Before the telex arrived?'

'Aye, so she did. Didn't she always know everything before anyone else? She is the only woman who ever lived in Mayo that the tinker Shona was afraid of. Annie knew she would need us one day to help her and that's why she never went and has been here all this time, keeping me company, waiting for the day. And now, Mrs Doyle, as God is my judge, that day has arrived. And you know what we have to do, don't you? She gave us our instructions, sure enough. She truly had the sight, that one, and there is only one other person who has it now.'

Mrs Doyle blessed herself at the mention of the sight and, slipping her hands into the pocket of her skirt, felt the reassuring beads of her rosary. Guilt was never too far from the surface for Mrs Doyle.

'Shall I be running to fetch Bridget with Teresa on me own, or will you be coming with me?' asked Ellen.

Mrs Doyle bristled. She had never been as close to Annie as the others, but she was not going to be left out. 'Jesus, you think I'm going back to the post office to miss out on this? If it hadn't been for my telex machine, sure,

Annie or not, you would be none the wiser, would you? Keeva can manage. I'll be coming with you.'

Moments later, they were both heading to the presbytery to persuade Teresa Gallagher to get out her car and run them to Bridget's farm. Trouble was on its way to Tarabeg and it would be down to them, the only people who knew what was happening, guided by the spirit world, to do something about it.

Chapter 17

'How many more weeks till this lot go back to school?' asked Cat as she filled up old pop bottles with water from the tap. In preparation for the outing, she'd taken out her curlers and had fastened her hair into pin curls around her ears, using silver clips. Under her usual faded flowery apron, she wore her best summer frock; its once yellow skirt billowed out at the sides.

Linda was sitting at the table on one of Bee's old kitchen chairs, thinly spreading Shippam's beef paste on slices of white bread. She piled them up, one sandwich on top of the other, then cut each one in half and wrapped them in greaseproof paper. 'Three more weeks to go, and you're gonna love every minute,' she said.

The cigarette perched on her bottom lip wobbled as she spoke. As she looked up, silver flakes of ash cascaded onto the beef paste. 'Oh buggerin' 'ell,' she said and used her fingernail to scoop out the bigger flakes. Losing patience, she slapped a slice of bread on top.

Betty was standing beside her, watching and helping. 'Sshh,' Linda said, placing her finger on her lips, 'don't tell anyone. Our Tommy can have that one.'

Betty smiled up at her as Linda placed the packets of sandwiches in a knitted string bag.

'Anyway, Cat, stop your moaning. I'm looking forward to this. A nice day out in the park for all of us and the kids. Barb down the bottom got a bag of flour off the back of a ship the night before last and the bloody sultanas to go with it as well. Her old man was on the night shift down on the *Clarence*. Split the sack with the night watchman, he did. She took the half sack round to his wife's house in the pram yesterday after the klaxon went. Anyway, who cares how she got it – it's scones for the bloody lot of us. It's gonna be a great day, Cat. The best day of the summer.'

Cat turned the tap off and smiled. Linda had been talking about the scones ever since the flour had arrived in Barb's outhouse. Not one to be selfish, Barb had filled up a few flour bins just in time for the annual day out. There was no charabanc – they couldn't afford it. Nor could they afford the train from Lime Street to New Brighton for a day on the beach. Instead, the whole of Waterloo Street was heading off to make camp among the rhododendron bushes in the park, as near to the lake as possible. They would transport their picnic in boxes and bags balanced across the handlebars of prams, with old tablecloths laid on the bottoms for spreading out on the grass to sit on. Suntan lotion was made by mixing olive oil and lemon juice. All they needed was the bus fare for the advance party of the younger children; the women with good shoes and prams walked there with the food.

Despite the simplicity of the day out, the kids had been scrubbed to within an inch of their lives. Pumps had been blancoed and dried overnight, and Sun-San sandals washed; shirts and dresses were clean and cardigans had been darned, their threads knitted back in.

'I'm not going to be put to shame by dirty kids,' said Cat as she passed a worn grey flannel across the mucky faces of a row of wincing children. 'Right, Linda, that's the last. Let's get the prams loaded up. It'll be time to come home if we don't get going soon.'

She walked over to the mantelpiece, picked up her lipstick and had just begun to apply it in the mirror when there was a bang on the door.

'Flamin' hell, who's that at the front door?' asked Linda.

Cat looked at the door as though it had spoken Mandarin. No one ever knocked on the front door. 'Can't have been the door. The only person to have done that since I've lived here was Mary Kate, God love her. They must use their front doors a lot in Ireland.'

The banging sounded again.

'Who is it, Mam?' shouted Arthur, breaking ranks with the rest of the scrubbed kids and racing to the door.

'Have you paid your rent, Cat?'

Cat looked confused. 'Of course I bleedin' have,' she

said, clicking the top back onto her lipstick and returning it to the mantelpiece. 'I had that money from the doctor, so I was bang on time this week.'

'Well, who is it then?' Linda was apprehensive, as she always was at the sound of sudden loud bangs, having lived through the May Blitz.

'I can't reach,' Arthur yelled as he jumped up and down in an attempt to grab the door handle.

'Come here, you.' Cat walked to the door, pushed away the cluster of protesting children who had gathered round, and opened it wide.

'Hello, love, who are you?' she asked the man standing in front of her.

He removed his cap. 'Good morning. A soft day it is,' he said. 'I'm Michael Malone, a relative of Bee's. I've come for my daughter, Mary Kate.'

'Bloody hell,' shouted Linda from the kitchen, 'we'll 'ave the whole flaming family here by this time next week.'

Cat invited him in, and he was greeted by the sight of a gang of well-behaved children standing in a row. She explained the situation. 'I can't take you to see Mary Kate until tonight, Michael,' she said. 'It's the kids' summer holiday.'

'And nothing is bloody stopping us 'avin' our day out,' said Linda, by way of a warning, should Cat decide to change their plans. She was packing the bottom tray of the Silver Cross pram in the kitchen doorway leading to the back yard.

Cat shot her a look. She'd been instantly taken by Michael Malone. His almost black wavy hair, his dark eyes, the earthy smell of him, the height and width of him – it was all having a strange and long-forgotten effect.

'You can wait here if you like, until we get back. Make yourself a cuppa. I haven't got much in, but there's a shop at the end of the road on the corner…' Her voice trailed off. There wasn't much in because every penny of her meagre pension and family allowance had been spent on the day out. She felt ashamed that a visitor had arrived at her door and all she had in was the picnic and the few potatoes and eggs she would use to make egg and chips for them all when they returned.

Michael glanced around the small kitchen and down at the children, who were looking up at him expectantly. His eyes lingered on the red of Cat's lips. No one in Tarabeg wore lipstick unless they were going to a dance. It was ten o'clock in the morning and Cat's lips were as red as an apple and looked twice as delicious. Tearing his eyes away, he said, 'I really need to find my daughter. She ran away, did she tell you that? I've been out of my mind with the worry.'

As Cat watched him anxiously rotating his cap in his hands, she felt a stab of pity. Men in Waterloo Street were largely absent, and when they were at home, it was to sleep off a skinful. The public house at the end of the road was their refuge, somewhere children weren't allowed, and Cat's husband had been no different. He'd not been a bad man, but he was a docker and he did pass the pub on his way home from the top of the Dockers' Steps.

'I can give you the address of Mrs O'Keefe's if you like,' she said. 'It's two buses away, though, and you might get lost.' She was disappointed but had no idea why. This man had stepped into her kitchen only moments ago and the only thing she knew, transferred to her in a code by the thumping of her heart, was that she didn't want him to step back out again. 'You really don't have to worry about Mary Kate – as right as rain, she is, isn't she, Linda?'

Linda looked up from her kneeling position on the floor, where she was fastening the buckles on a row of Sunny-San sandals. The children were already bored with the arrival of Michael and keen to return to the preparations for their departure. Stanley could barely contain his excitement; the thought of the lake and so much green grass taunted him. 'Mam, stop, we've got to go now,' he pleaded, looking up at Michael, who was causing the delay, with resentment in his eyes.

Cat dropped her hand down by her side and waved it discreetly, wafting away his complaint, silently instructing him to shush.

'Come here, Stanley,' said Linda. 'Give us your foot. We're leaving now, aren't we, Cat?' She threw Michael a look that left no doubt as to what she was thinking. He had arrived at a bad moment and their children's special day out would not be delayed as a result. She grabbed the back of the chair and with much fuss pulled herself up onto her feet. 'Right, that's you lot ready,' she announced to the line of anxious faces.

Michael turned to Cat, who felt her dress being tugged by a pair of very small hands.

'Mrs O'Keefe had Mary Kate a job sorted and she was as right as rain, wasn't she, Linda? The house isn't easy to find and I can't make the kids late – they don't get to go to the park very often,' she lied, grasping the little hand and holding it tight. 'And anyway, if you just wait here for us, you can have a kip on the sofa. You must be tired after all that travelling – I know Mary Kate was, wasn't she, Lin? And as soon as I get back, Linda will have my kids and I'll take you on the bus. Won't you, Linda?' She gave Linda a look that said, 'Don't you dare argue with me?'

'Oh, aye, I will,' said Linda, looking confused.

'But your letter said she'd been attacked. Was she hurt?'

'Just her pride, love.' Linda fastened her headscarf under her chin. 'That's all. But she'll be a wiser person after it and a bit more careful where she flashes her cash next time.'

Michael wiped his brow with the back of his hand and sighed. 'She has a wilful nature, does Mary Kate, when she gets something into her mind. I imagined all sorts, I did. She lost her mammy, Bee's niece—'

'Ah, don't be worrying, love,' said Cat, touched by the rawness of his emotions and wanting to reassure him even more. 'She came to our house and she's as right as rain.'

'I think I'll...' Michael hesitated. He'd been about to say he would find the bus and make his way to Mrs

O'Keefe's, when Debbie walked up to him and slipped her hand into his.

'Would you like to come with us on the picnic?' she asked.

Michael looked down into her face. She reminded him of Mary Kate as a child.

'Sorry,' whispered Cat. 'She doesn't have a dad. She misses him.'

'You too?' said Michael, glancing up at her. 'Are you a widow too?'

Cat shrugged. Being a widow was the defining fact of her life, for her and her children. They were the fatherless family, the family who'd been left on their own.

Half an hour later, Michael found himself wandering down the Dock Road in a caravan of women and children, pushing a pram, singing songs he'd never heard of until minutes before, and he wondered just how that had happened.

Nola was up an hour earlier than usual, almost before the cock crowed. She'd been baking sweet pastry for a pie as well as extra bread. The kitchen door stood wide open to the lush green of Tarabeg Hill, which had all but crossed the threshold and taken root in the compressed earth of the cottage floor. She still had the curlers she'd slept in fastened tight, kept in place by the paisley silk headscarf one of her children had sent from America at

Christmas. She wished they would save their money and buy a ticket home instead of sending presents.

At this time of the morning, as she baked to the tune of Daedio's rising snores, she indulged herself with thoughts of all the children she had borne. All but one of them had gone off to live and work in America and she had long since accepted that she would never set her eyes upon them again. She blessed herself and thanked God for leaving her Michael in Tarabeg. Early on there had been promises – 'We will be home soon, Mammy' – but those had faded as the pursuit of the American dream had eaten up their time and resources. She knew she would never hear her children's voices again, or meet her grandchildren. All she had were the memories of their births and childhoods; the letters announcing new grandchildren; and the annual photographs, smiling out at her from black-and-white serrated-edged postcards with 'Moyle's Photographic Studio, Brooklyn' etched across the corner.

The antics and tears of her children, all born in that cottage, and the laughter that once filled it, lived on in Nola as she went about her morning chores. As she rolled out her pastry, she often saw the eyes of her four-year-old daughter peeping over the wood of the table, hands gripping and lifting her onto her tiptoes, smiling, hoping that Nola would hold out the bowl for her to dip her finger into. And Nola, with a smile on her lips, would whisper, 'Sshh now, don't you be telling the others, do you hear me?'

This hour of baking was Nola's hour of secret tears,

the only time of the day she allowed the pain in her heart to rest unchecked. 'Please God, don't let Mary Kate be another,' she whispered. She blessed herself as she swayed back and forth over the table, rolling out the pastry with a rolling pin carved from a branch many years ago by Daedio for his new wife, Annie, her mother-in-law.

She went about her business with the minimum of fuss while Daedio slept on his bed in front of the fire, and Seamus, in no hurry to alter the farming hours he'd kept to his whole life, took his full hour in bed. Outside, in the old house, Pete Shevlin had opened the door and unchained the dogs, who had cantered as far as the cottage door and were now looking in, heads high, ears pert, tails wagging, hopeful.

Wiping her hands on her apron, Nola reached for the dish of leftover scraps from the evening before and, walking to the door, threw them straight onto the dew-soaked grass. She leant against the doorframe and crossed her arms, nursing the empty dish against her as the dogs devoured the scraps within seconds. She loved to watch her food being eaten, even the leftovers of charred potato peel and cabbage with a smattering of cold gravy. The dogs looked up gratefully before they sloped off down the hill to engage in their favourite pastime of terrorising any car, cart or cyclist that dared to pass their boreen on their way between the coast and the heart of Tarabeg.

'Is that baking for Bee?' Daedio's morning voice called out from behind her and she automatically walked to the range to place the bowl in the sink and pour him his tea from the large black cast-iron pot.

'It is, aye. 'Tis the right thing to do – the poor woman is having a desperate time, doing up that cottage all alone. She hasn't only the years of the weather and the damage it has done, and God knows, that's bad enough, but she has all those memories to be dealing with too. She must be heavy with the sadness, being where her own sister was murdered by that evil feck of a husband. Rosie and I decided, after the Angelus last night, this was the least I could do, and Rosie, she will be going straight up there tonight.'

'Tell her not to worry, Nola.' Daedio reached out to take his old stained and chipped earthenware mug from her. 'Is there a drop of whiskey in this, to get the blood flowing? I won't be able to get me legs going without it.' He placed the mug to his lips, sniffed at the rising steam and winked through the haze.

Nola placed her hands in her pockets, sighed and then grinned. 'Aye, well, if you are after a drop, so am I, but don't be telling that son of yours. He chooses the strangest things to be pious about, as if a drop did anyone any harm.' She cast a cautionary glance towards the bedroom door as she made her way to the press and extracted a bottle of Powers.

Five minutes later, she was sitting on the end of Daedio's bed, nursing her own mug. 'Ah, that's better,' she said, sharing a rare smile with him. They coexisted in an atmosphere of faux animosity; everyone knew they'd both be lost without the other to fire up each day with provocative humour and complaints.

Daedio rested his mug on his lap, lifted his cap off the bedpost, pushed back the stray strands of silver hair and placed it on his head. As he did, he noted the faraway look in Nola's eyes. She thought he slept in the mornings as she went about her routine. In fact he was usually awake well before either she or Seamus entered the kitchen, but he knew that the time alone, in the peace of the morning, was precious to her. Out of the corner of his eye, he caught the tears, heard the sniffs; like her, he could feel the memories, and they haunted him too, but he could never tell her. The guilt weighed heavy on his bed. There was money, lots of it, packed behind the chimney stones and if he'd used it, his grandchildren would never have had to leave. As it was, he'd given each of them a wallet full of dollars and bought their tickets to sail away and find their fortunes. He'd given Michael and Sarah enough to make their way in Tarabeg too, and Nola knew that. Annie, long gone, had known it too.

'Don't you be worrying about Bee. Captain Bob will be back. A man needs time to know which way the wind blows. He'll be thinking it all through and as long as he hasn't taken to drink or lost his mind, he'll be back. Praise God, Bee has returned – that doesn't often happen.'

Nola tipped her own mug and drained the last of the whiskey and sugar. 'Pass me that,' she said, choosing not to comment on Daedio's words of wisdom. 'Let me rinse them before Seamus gets up. You know what his nose is like, he'll smell it a mile off.'

Daedio grinned and handed over his mug. 'I won't breathe a word,' he whispered.

''Tis not your words I'm bothered about,' said Nola. ''Tis your fumes. As rancid as your breath.'

When Seamus emerged from his bed, Nola was almost done. She loaded the basket for Bee and issued instructions as he packed away his usual breakfast of rashers, eggs and a double doorstep of freshly fried bread, soaking up the last of the mixture of black-speckled dripping and bacon fat. 'Take it to Bee as soon as you can, Seamus,' she said. 'Rosie says she's been working on the cottage all on her own, hasn't asked for help from anyone. Rosie said as much to Keeva, and Tig went down on his bike to see her yesterday and fixed the thatch while he was there. He said there was a pile of old wood in the cowshed from when Rory had first thatched it and he took the heather with him on the back of the cart, which was handy. Rory's parents are well enough, but too old to even reach the bottom of the boreen from their own cottage, let alone be trudging up to Bee's.'

Seamus was enjoying his breakfast and was only half listening.

'Seamus, are you hearing me? Or is it only your rashers and yer big fat belly you are interested in?'

Daedio lay back on his pillows, slurping his third mug

of strong sweet tea, minus the whiskey. He'd been deep in thought, as he had been most days since the arrival of the letter from America. Mary Kate had run away from home and Michael straight after her. He'd been staring into the fire; all he saw these days was the face of Shona the tinker dancing among the flames. Her hair floated and flickered and the black coals of her eyes burnt back out at him.

He turned and blinked the smoke away. 'I wish I could come with you, Seamus, or go down and help Bee,' he said. 'No matter what she says, she can't be feeling right. Bridget says she left Tarabeg too soon after Sarah died. Said she should have got used to Sarah's death before she ran off. She's come back home having never lived here without her. There will be only ghosts waiting for her in that cottage – Rory, Angela and Sarah. Ghosts and heart-break, that's all.'

'Aye, and she had Tig visit too,' said Seamus as his tongue protruded and licked away the egg yolk running down his chin. A wet cloth slapped him in the face, thrown by Nola for the same purpose.

Daedio shook his head. 'She is a woman who has lived through too much death too soon, and none of it natural, all of it sudden. That kind of death is the hardest for any-one to deal with, and Bridget says you can't run away, as tempting as it may be.'

Nola stood with her hands on her hips, staring at Daedio with incredulity as he regaled them with his monologue. She had also been out of sorts since the day Mary Kate ran away. 'Said all that, did Bridget? Well I never, and here was me sending Seamus off down there with the basket and baking her a pie because I thought she would be as bright as a new penny.'

Seamus had wiped his mouth. Getting to his feet now, he picked up the basket. As soon as the tension began to rise between Daedio and Nola and he sensed a fight was brewing, his own inclination was to flee. 'Right, I'll have a quick word with Pete in the old house first. The bull is gone. Broke through the fence of whin I spent yesterday dragging all the way down on the back of the horse, and he's roaming feck knows where. I'll be off to Bee straight after and do what I can. I'll call into the Devlins' first and pick her up some rashers. 'Tis a strange state of affairs altogether, what with the death over in Ballycroy and no one having seen yer man.'

Nola slipped a cover over the basket. Her pillowy cheeks, crisscrossed with tiny red veins from the heat of the fire and the range, were more flushed than usual following the extra baking and the stealthy whiskey in the tea. 'She's at first Mass every morning, Father tells me. Something is up, Seamus, but I can't go myself – I have Teresa, Bridget and Ellen coming up here today, visiting Daedio. We are picking and then bottling the wild redcurrants and I can't leave it or the birds will have robbed the flaming lot by sundown. I hope the bull isn't roaming in the fields around Crewhorn – we'll be up there in the afternoon.' She set the basket on the floor by the door.

'I hope he fecking is.' Daedio winked at Seamus, who was slipping on his jacket and cap. And for the first time in days, since the news of Mary Kate's departure, father and son laughed together.

Seamus was more than happy to take the gifts down to Bee. The fruit harvest was one for the women and he was never involved. With two more weeks of fine weather, it would soon be time for the main harvest, at which point the press in the kitchen and the store out in the old house would be full of every kind of picked and preserved fruit, including the jars of deep purple elderberry syrup that they drizzled over warm, sweet pastry in the dark winter months when the fields and hedgerows were frozen hard.

'Did Nola send you?' asked Bee.

Seamus stood at Bee's kitchen table, rested the wicker basket on it and removed an elderberry and apple pie wrapped in a gingham cloth. The pie was still warm and a strong aroma of freshly baked buttery pastry and sweet elderberry juice filled the room. As he looked down at Bee, who had not risen from the table as he entered the cottage, he extracted a dish of butter, six eggs protected in a parcel of straw, and several handfuls of potatoes and other vegetables.

He pulled out a stool from under the table opposite where Bee was sitting and, without waiting to be asked, lowered himself onto it. 'I came to see if there is anything I can do to be helping you,' he said. 'We had no idea you were here – you've been as quiet as a mouse and we thought that was because Captain Bob was with you and you were, well, keeping your head down, what with Mary Kate running to Liverpool as she has and the death out at Ballycroy… But Rosie, Keeva and Tig, they tell us you are all alone.'

Bee stood up, her face closed. Her hair was tied up in a knot at the top and strands hung down the sides of her face. Her eyes were wide and haunted; she'd always been a good-looking woman, but today she looked every day of her forty-plus years.

It took Seamus a moment to realise that Bridget was right. This was not the Bee who'd left Tarabeg ten years ago. That Bee, despite the loss she'd suffered and the load she'd had to bear, had fight left in her. Before Sarah's death, Bee had always been so full of life; if a smile or laughter was missing in a room, a joke from Bee was always quick to make them reappear.

She looked up sharply, her eyes flickering with anger as the words flew from her tongue. She had assumed Rosie would keep her own counsel. 'Does the whole village know now then? That I, a harlot of a woman, has had her comeuppance. Laughing, are they all? I expect the scold of Tarabeg, Philomena O'Donnell, has it in the *Mayo News*, does she? Father Jerry will be using me as proof that sinners never win, citing me in sermons from his pulpit soon enough.'

Her anger spent, she sighed and looked embarrassed.

Seamus, the most gentle of all men, had only ever shown her kindness, and Tig, he had pedalled down on his bike the moment he knew she was alone, which was no easy feat for a man with one leg markedly shorter than the other.

She placed the flat of both hands on the scrubbed table. Before she'd left Tarabeg, she'd oiled it and wrapped it in thickly soaked oilcloth, and she was glad she had. Once she'd removed the cloth and given the table the most basic clean, it had gleamed back at her, unharmed. It had been her sister's, and after Angela's murderer of a husband had scarpered, Bee had rescued it, strapping it to the turf cart, hitching up the donkey and taking it to her own house. It was made from wood that had surfaced in the bay, supposedly from a sunken Spanish galleon. She and Angela had changed Sarah's nappies on that table, and Ciaran's too. She and Angela and Sarah had laughed and cried at the table, and it was where Angela had been laid out for her wake. It had been Angela's pride and joy, and it would be Bee's too, until the day Mary Kate married.

'Here, let me make you some tea – you won't be leaving without it,' she said. 'I may be the talk of the village and on my way to hell, but I still have my manners.'

'Bee, Bee, this is nonsense.' Seamus's tone was soothing. He removed his cap and laid it with care on the table in front of him, playing for time, choosing his words carefully as he clasped his hands together and fixed Bee with a steady gaze.

'I was at the house when Michael left for Dublin.

I wasn't my best. I suppose you've heard all about it. Do you know about the letter I had from my neighbour Cat too?' She looked alarmed and spoke rapidly, as though she was waiting for Seamus to condemn her.

He smiled. 'I do, and it seems to me it was a very good letter altogether – once you got past the part about Mary Kate being attacked, losing all her money, having to be seen to by a doctor, finding herself penniless and lost in a sinful city like Liverpool, and you having already left when she got there. When you put all that to one side, she has what she went for: a job and her independence. It being our Mary Kate, she has just gone about things in a very headstrong and unusual way.'

Bee snorted and turned back from the old range. She would have to get used to that again, after her years with a gas cooker. It was probably the only thing from Liverpool she would miss; that and Cat's chatter, and, it had dawned on her, her friendship.

'You can say that again,' she said. 'She has Sarah's spirit – her happy ways, her absolute belief that no one and nothing will fail her, that all will be well – and her father's streak for striding out and seeking a new opportunity. The trouble is, the only person who can't see that is Michael himself, and, would you believe it, Mary Kate. Why did we never guess that the child of Michael and Sarah would be one to go her own way?'

She walked over to the table and placed the steaming pot onto the metal trivet, along with two mugs. 'Do ye have any milk in that basket of tricks?' she asked with a smile, relieved that the Seamus sat in her kitchen held no condemnation in his voice, no Bible in his hands.

'I do that.' He lifted the metal jug out and placed it on the table. 'I have something else, but it has to be our secret.' He winked and from the inside pocket of his jacket extracted a small bottle of whiskey. Pulling out the straw stopper, he slopped two generous helpings into the tea. 'Don't be telling our Nola – she doesn't approve of whiskey in the tea before four.'

Five minutes later, Bee was topping up the pot, pouring them both a second mug and looking very much better. The whiskey had had a medicinal effect. Her blood flowed, her cheeks were flushed and her humour had returned. She let out a deep sigh as she poured the milk into her mug.

Seamus was glad to see her shoulders relax and her natural colour restored. 'That's better. Now at least you look more like the Bee we knew.'

She smiled. She couldn't argue with him. She hadn't eaten since the previous day and the whiskey was warming her through.

'Listen here while I tell ye, Bee.' Seamus tipped the remainder of the bottle into their mugs. 'I've come for another reason altogether.'

He was more nervous about revealing his next message, and Bee, sensing this, despite the whiskey, stopped dead, her mug halfway to her lips, and looked deep into his eyes.

It struck him that they were Sarah's eyes, filled with apprehension, even fear. For the first time, he realised she was scared. He took a deep breath. 'Keeva's been telling me she'd be happy to go with you to Ballycroy, help you find out what's going on. Why don't you do that?' He exhaled, unaware that he had been holding his breath.

Bee leant forward and splayed her hands out before her as though using the table for support. Her legs felt weak and her head spun. She opened her mouth and closed it again before swallowing hard. As she looked at him, he saw that this time her eyes were filled with tears.

'Seamus, I don't know what to do. I haven't heard a thing. He left me at Castlebar, at the bus, and there's not been a single word since. Every day I call into Mrs Doyle's and think there will be something, a message, a call booked, a telex on that fecking machine of hers, something, anything – but there's nothing. There has not been a day since the night Angela was murdered that I have been without him or we haven't spoken.' She blushed and averted her eyes. 'He has slept next to me every single night. Seamus, I fall asleep in his arms and I wake in them.'

Her voice broke and distress settled on her features. 'He's virtually brought Ciaran up and… and now I think he's gone, because never, ever, if that was not the God's honest truth, would he leave it that long without even speaking to me. He knows how I'll be feeling. 'Tis unbelievable, impossible to imagine, but I have to face the truth because it's staring me right here in the face. He's gone, Seamus.

I wake up every morning and I expect to hear him coming through the door, but he doesn't. It's over. Instead of his wife's death bringing us together, it has torn us apart. He's gone, Seamus. His daughters have won. He cannot leave them and they won't let him. 'Tis just me now. Angela has gone, Sarah's gone and even Mary Kate has gone. And Ciaran is at sea for months yet. There is only me, Seamus. I have to face it: I am all alone in this world and I always will be.'

Her voice had become increasingly tearful. Removing a handkerchief from her apron pocket, she blew her nose as she turned her gaze out of the door Seamus had left open and across the beach to the bay. A pillar of morning sunlight fell into the cottage and the ocean was calm; the fishermen were long gone, their sails having disappeared around the headland in the direction of Blacksod Bay. She had sat in just the same spot and watched them cast off before she left for Mass.

Seamus spared Bee's embarrassment by gazing into his tea. He didn't speak as she began to cry, wanting to give her the privacy and time to compose herself. But now her tears were turning into soft sobs of anguish and they pulled at his heart, so he did what came naturally to him, what he had done with Nola every time one of their children had emigrated to America, when Michael had left for the war, when Sarah died. He recognised those sobs; they were rooted in fathomless grief.

He carried his stool to the opposite side of the table,

placed it next to Bee and said, 'Here, come on now, Bee. Here, here.' He put his arms around her shoulders and she turned and buried her face in his chest, letting the coarse wool of his jacket absorb the pain of her loss. He stroked her hair, trying to ease her heartbreak.

He looked towards the door and out across to the ocean reflecting the azure blue of the summer sky. Life had moved on, despite the sadness and the tragedies. It had moved on, and so had Bee, to Liverpool, and now she was back again and facing her ghosts. Bridget was right, Bridget was always right. A shiver ran down his spine as he realised Bee had spent ten years in exile with Captain Bob. Had she cried? Had she mourned? Maybe these tears were long overdue. Maybe Captain Bob had some of his own tears to shed now that he was home in Ballycroy. Maybe his homecoming had been equally unnerving. Captain Bob, the genial man, the capable man, the solid man, who always came to the aid of others.

The air tightened as Seamus heard the faintest shuffling in the room behind his whispered words of comfort. An icy chill fell on the back of his hand as he stroked Bee's hair and he knew it for what it was as tears of grateful acknowledgement filled his own eyes. It was Angela, and through him, she placed a warm hand on her sister's back. He had felt and heard the ghosts slip from the shadows and join them and as Bee sobbed her tears of desperate anguish, he whispered to Angela, 'Help her. Help her.'

Chapter 18

'Mam, can we take a boat out on the lake?' Arthur was standing in front of Cat, his face, clean on arrival, now smeared with dirt, his nose running, his eyes as bright as his chatter was fast. His fingers grabbed her skirt as though it were a bell cord and tugged.

'Arthur, your filthy hands – look at my skirt.' Cat reached down and took his hand in hers as she cast her eyes towards the boating lake. The sun shimmered and the swans floated among the water lilies and rushes, and her heart lifted in a way it hadn't since Ben had died. It was a rare good day. 'How much is it, love?' she asked, squatting down and ruffling his hair.

The children always ran to Cat when they wanted something that required spending money. She was perceived as soft compared to the other mothers. The boys had sent Arthur – she knew that, and she could see them watching hopefully.

'Not now, Arthur,' shouted Linda, who had heard the

exchange from where she was sitting on one of the old tablecloths, unwrapping the parcels of greaseproof paper and laying out the sandwiches.

Disappointment washed over Arthur's face as he looked up at Cat, mouthing the word 'Please'.

'Do something useful, Arthur. Go and tell the boys to stop playing football now, and tell the girls too. It's time to eat these butties before they all curl up and the wasps get them, bleedin' things.' Linda flicked her hands across the sandwiches once more, waging a losing battle against the persistent wasps.

'Go on, Arthur,' said Cat. 'Tell the boys I'll see about the boats when everyone has eaten.'

Arthur broke into a smile. From his mam, everyone knew that was a yes. 'Can I have a jam butty, Aunty Linda?' he asked as he ran to the edge of the cloth. 'I don't like paste.'

'You can, love, once you've got everyone else over here. I'll keep one back for you.'

And with that, Arthur sprinted off across the grass towards the two rhododendron bushes being used as goals. Having now seen the picnic, his stomach rumbled and his mouth watered. On many days, lunch for the kids on Waterloo Street was a slice of bread dipped in dripping or sprinkled with sugar. Today, it was sandwiches and cakes.

'I'll fetch the girls, Arthur,' shouted Cat as she looked towards the rose garden. Its small stone folly had been transformed by the girls into a palace and a palace garden in which resided a large number of princesses who all pushed prams and nursed real babies, with not a husband in sight. An elderly lady stooped and, lifting a rose, inhaled deeply. Cat hoped the girls weren't spoiling her walk.

'Thought you'd be wanting to go and fetch the lads,' said Linda with a grin as she inclined her head towards the rhododendrons. Michael was standing in the middle of the pitch, instructing the boys, having taken the role of referee.

Cat grinned back. 'He is lovely, isn't he? I'll have to try and find a way to keep him for a day or two at our house.' She laughed, aware that she was half joking, half speaking her thoughts out loud.

It appeared that she was now laughing alone when Linda replied, 'Aye, he is a fine-looking man. He was also once married to Bee's niece and we both know that because Bee told us often enough that he is now married to a teacher called Rosie. We know all about Michael, don't we, Cat. He's a married man who's had his share of tragedy and you can keep your bloody eyes off if you don't want any trouble, because you and your kids have been through enough, and you manage just fine without any man.' She flattened out a sheet of greaseproof paper as though she was trying to iron it onto the cloth with her hands and it crackled in response.

Cat's heart sank and her smile faded. It was as though a cloud had passed over the park and blocked out the sun. 'Thanks a lot, Lin. You really know how to spoil a day. Anyway, he hadn't even crossed my mind. I've been too busy playing rounders.'

Linda glanced up at her from under her heavy lids and frowned. She opened the battered handbag she'd bought from a jumble sale, which was on the grass next to her, extracted a tin of tobacco and took out a roll-up she'd made earlier.

'And what if I did like him – which I don't, by the way. A girl can dream, can't she?' Cat squatted down. Arthur had trodden on the cloth and she pulled it out by the corners and smoothed it.

Linda was unequivocal in her response. 'No, Cat, she cannot. Women like you and me are fools if we dream about anything other than washing nappies, feeding the kids, meeting the rent, paying the food – and the club, if there's anything left over – and praying every flamin' week that it doesn't rain on washday. Because that, my girl, is our lot in life, and the only way you get through it is to know it and accept it. Dreaming is for fools. Dream and you become miserable and, like as not, land yourself in a whole load of trouble.'

Cat sprang to her feet and folded her arms. 'Oh yeah, and I suppose you would know, wouldn't you, Linda. Dreamt for a husband like your old man, did you? That useless waste of space. The answer to your dreams, was he? At least my Ben knew where he lived and didn't give his address as the Anchor Pub when he was asked. Happy with your lot, are you? Really? Because given you spend most of your time in our house, it doesn't seem that way to me.' She glared at Linda, her jaw jutting upwards, her eyes blazing. She could tell within seconds that Linda wasn't going to take her on.

It was as though Cat hadn't spoken at all. Linda simply continued separating out the piles of sandwiches. 'Betty Dunsthorne, she's only gone and sent dripping butties. I told her, it's a special day. Good job we've got plenty of jam and paste.'

To distract herself and to contain her disappointment and anger, Cat placed her hand over her eyes to shield the sun as she scanned the middle distance for the girls.

Linda was having none of it. She and Cat rarely argued and she would not take her on or allow the day to be ruined. She had fired her warning and there was nothing more she could do; the rest was up to Cat. 'Pass me that packet of butties from the bottom of Susan's pram there, would you. Let's see if she even bothered to spread any marge on. As tight as a duck's arse, that one.' She made a fancy arrangement out of the stacks of sandwiches she'd unwrapped.

'Jesus, you're a barrel of flamin' laughs today.' Cat retrieved the sandwiches and dropped them on the cloth. Without another word, she turned on her heel and headed towards the princesses in the fairy castle over in the rose garden, with Linda's words ringing in her ears.

Half an hour later, most of the food was gone.

'That was the most delicious cake I have ever tasted,' Michael lied as he downed the last mouthful.

The sandwiches and cake had been plentiful, and they had sung 'Happy Birthday' to the five birthday-girls and -boys. Michael had noted the poor quality of the food, suddenly realising that in Tarabeg they ate like kings. Why had he never noticed that? he wondered as he finished the last crumbs of the cake. On the day before he left Tarabeg, Nola had been complaining how sick she was of the fresh salmon he poached and that it was time to kill a pig. Did the children sitting on the cloth even know what salmon tasted like? He fancied that the white Liverpool marge cake needed a bit of Nola's fresh thick yellow butter in it.

'There's some left if you want another slice,' said Cat, lifting the plate and offering it to him.

The boys had wolfed down their food and were running back to the makeshift football pitch. Refuelling was the only acceptable reason for stopping play. Summer-long matches were usually played out in the streets and on the bombed-out wasteland. The luxury of green grass beneath their badly soled shoes was one they would enjoy until the parkie came to tell them he was about to lock the gates.

'Are you coming, Michael?' they yelled over their shoulders as they ran.

'I will. I'm on me way after the tea,' he shouted.

He and Cat had carried two trays from the wooden hut at the side of the lake and Michael had left a deposit for the china. It had been his suggestion – not something they normally treated themselves to on the birthday picnic. Cat was happy to hide the now cold bottles of tea under a sheet on the bottom of the pram, having been kept warm by the legs of the babies on the way to the park; they'd been made with sterilised milk so they didn't curdle or turn. She'd enjoyed every minute of her conversation with Michael as they walked around the lake and back to camp, where they found Linda propped up against a tree stump, fast asleep.

Cat poured Michael another cup from the pot, without asking. Anything to keep him there a little longer.

'You have great boys and they are the devils with the football,' he said.

She smiled. 'They talk about nothing else and they play it every day, all summer long. They start the match on the day school breaks up and it keeps going until September. The street with the highest number of goals wins and then we have a bit of a party in the winner's street. It keeps them happy, I suppose. I think the goal score for our street is at sixty-four this summer – the highest ever, Arthur tells me. They all love the Liverpool manager, Bill Shankly.' She heaped the sugar into his tea.

'It must be hard for them,' said Michael, pulling his gaze from the boys and turning to her, looking her straight in the eye, 'having no da. And hard for you, being on your own. I lost my wife, my Sarah, too. I know how it feels.'

Cat didn't reply but instead made a great fuss of tipping

her spilt tea from the flower-patterned saucer back into her cup.

Michael's face burnt at her sudden silence. Her down-cast eyes told him all he needed to know: she still missed Ben and he had probably overstepped his place. He raised the cup to his lips and regretted his words. 'Thank you for the tea,' he said, desperate to bury the offending remarks.

'But you married again – I remember Bee telling me. Rosie, was it? She's the one who wrote the letters to Bee.'

Michael shuffled his legs into a more comfortable posi-tion. 'Sure. Rosie, aye. I wasn't trying to make out I was alone now, just that I know what it's like, to lose some-one, that's all.'

Cat attempted a smile, but Michael noted that it didn't reach her eyes. The only sound was the gentle snoring of Linda, still slumped against the tree, her chin on her chest.

Cat was sitting half on the cloth, half off, her legs tucked beneath her. Leaning to her side, she picked a blade of grass, slipped it between her lips and twirled it round. Michael was transfixed. He flushed again, his heartbeat speeded up and he swallowed his tea down almost in one gulp. This proud and hard-working woman, who didn't have two halfpennies to rub together, was an enigma to him and quite unlike any woman he knew in Ireland.

She turned away to the lake and he had the advantage of her side profile. Her hair sat on her shoulders, her com-plexion was unlined, her nose slightly upturned, her red lips bringing a warm glow to her cheeks. She moved to a more comfortable position, her stockinged legs stretched out on the grass, the now discarded sandals lying under the tree next to Linda. Her hand moved down to her toes and began to massage them back into life; they were red from the ill-fitting sandals and from walking around the lake for the tea, and numb with pins and needles from being tucked beneath her for so long. He wanted to reach out, to move her hand away and slide his own hand along the American tan nylon, feeling the slip of it beneath his fingers, all the way up to the clasps of the suspender belt he could see protruding through the thin fabric of her skirt, and then beyond.

'The boys want to go out on the lake in a boat.' She turned back to him abruptly, and there was no mistaking that she knew. Her eyes had received the messages transmitted from his. She smiled and this time it was warm and beckoning.

'Would you like me to go out on the lake with them? I have a boat meself at home.' His voice was thick with lust; he floundered over his words and with a cough moved swiftly on. 'Well, not a boat exactly – a curragh, for fishing the salmon on the river.'

The sound of a cheer filled the air. Stanley was leaping up and down and the other boys were patting his back. He'd obviously scored a goal. The thwack of leather on willow drifted over from a cricket match taking place on the opposite side of the park. The buzz of a bee on a nearby flower, in competition with the snores of Linda, drew Cat's attention. 'Arthur was keen for the lake earlier,' she said. She didn't want to add that she had checked out the prices while he was buying the tea. It was sixpence per boat and that was sixpence they didn't have.

Michael jumped to his feet. 'Tell you what I'm thinking – I'll go and ask them who wants to go and it will be my treat. You have fed me and looked after me, and everyone else too, as well as my Mary Kate. 'Tis my turn to do a bit.'

The snoring stopped. Michael thought he heard a snort, but Linda didn't appear to have woken up.

Cat jumped up too. 'Well, if you don't mind. I'm a bit nervous, like, because I don't swim.'

Michael dusted his trousers down and avoided her gaze. He had a boat, right enough, but he could no more swim than Cat could. 'They'll be as right as rain with me. Sure, I fish on the river most days – I know how to handle water, I do.'

'Oh, that's such a relief.' Cat smiled up at him. 'They'll love it.'

'Come on then,' he whispered, glancing at Linda and the sleeping babies, anxious not to wake them. 'Let's round them up.'

Only five of the boys went with Michael. The remainder were stuck between believing boating was for girls and a reluctance to stop playing football. The five boys ran down to the lake ahead of Cat and Michael and whooped for joy as they pointed excitedly to each other and at the island in the centre.

'I bet we can't reach that far,' said one of the boys to Stanley.

'I bet we can,' shouted Stanley. 'Can't we, Michael?'

'Oh aye, sure, and we can row all the way around it too.'

Cat laughed out loud. 'They used to love it with Ciaran. He was the eldest boy in the street and Stanley wants to follow him to sea – if he doesn't get taken on by Bill Shankly, that is.'

It was a scene of normal, uncomplicated happiness as Cat waved off Michael and the boys from the landing. 'Remember you are in boat twenty-one,' she shouted as Michael pulled away. 'When your time is up, the man will shout you in through the loudhailer. Listen out, Arthur.' She carried on waving as they rowed out into the middle of the lake, then made her way back to the camp under the trees to wake Linda.

It was the goal that did it – or rather the fact that Stanley saw the goal from the middle of the lake, forgot where he was, joined in the cheers and excitement, leapt to his feet, punched the air, and yelled, 'Goal!'

'Stanley, sit down! Would you sit,' said Michael, who'd rowed almost as far as the island.

But it was too late. Stanley landed on the side of the boat, and as Michael stood to steady the rocking, the other boys got frightened, leapt to their feet, and made the situation worse.

The boat rocked wildly from side to side. Michael, his

hands grabbing the edges, shouted, 'Jesus, sit down! Sit down now or we'll all be in.'

Those were the last words he spoke for some time as, with a large splash and many screams of panic from the five little boys, everyone tumbled into the water. The boat, very calmly and slowly, slipped beneath the surface of the lake.

Chapter 19

'What in God's name would you do with this heat? It feels to me like there's a thunderstorm on the way,' Joan exclaimed as she sliced a freshly cooked ham for the supper. 'Will you be staying to eat tonight or what?' she asked Mary Kate, who was ironing the boys' freshly laundered clothes as the sweat dripped from her brow.

Mary Kate lifted her arm to her forehead and wiped the strands of sticky hair away. She wondered whether Mrs O'Keefe would let her have a bath when she returned to the house. Back home in Tarabeg, there was no end of hot water, heated by the fire and the range in the kitchen. She remembered how, every Sunday, Granny Nola and Seamus came down the hill to the house for a bath, and her heart folded.

'No, I won't be, thanks, Joan. Mrs O'Keefe and Deidra are keeping mine ready for me again.'

Joan glanced up, the knife in her hand poised in mid air. 'Will ye be coming back again tomorrow?' she asked, her voice full of doubt. 'Only I wouldn't blame you if you weren't. David has been a right little sod.'

Mary Kate folded the last pair of shorts. 'I will be back, and don't worry about David. It's a battle of the wills and he's determined to win, only he won't, I will, and the sooner he realises that, the better. I'm surrounded by little boys with more cunning than he has, back in Tarabeg.'

As she placed the clothes into the wicker basket ready to take up to the boys' room, she sighed. David had yet again done everything he could to make life difficult. He had let Jet out of the back gate and the dog had run away, sending Jack into the kitchen crying. Her late afternoon had been spent racing up and down the back entry shouting for Jet, whom she and Jack had eventually found in the park. She'd led the dog home by the collar, only to be met by Mrs Marcus stepping out of a taxi.

'Mummy, Mummy,' shouted Jack, hurtling himself at her and throwing his arms around her waist.

'Jack, my skirt! Your hands are filthy – get off.' She unpeeled his hands from around her waist and pushed him away. As she did, her eyes fell on Mary Kate, still crouched, holding on to Jet by his collar. 'I thought I had employed you to look after my children, not the dog. Where is David?' She snapped her handbag closed after putting her purse back inside. The taxi driver shot Mary Kate and Jack a look of deep sympathy as he pulled away from the kerb.

'He's in the kitchen with Joan and the boys from next

door. The dog... escaped, so I had to find him.' She resisted the urge to tell her it had been David who'd set him free, creating almost an hour of work for her and a distressed Jack.

'Well, next time, leave the dog. If he wants to run off, he can. It was my husband's idea to have a dog, not mine. Bring these up to my dressing room later, would you. And, Jack, it is time for your bath.' She deposited a box and a bag on the ground and, turning on her heel, headed up the steps to the house.

Mary Kate looked Jet square in the eye. 'Don't you dare even think about running away when I let go of your collar to pick up those bags, do you hear me? You just sit there. Jack, watch him, will you.'

Jet wagged his tail and sat on the ground next to Jack, his ears pricked, ready for his next instruction. She picked up the bags with one hand and said to the dog and Jack, 'Come on, both of you, it's time for your tea. Joan has a nice bit of ham for you.'

It was as if Jet understood English; he followed her and Jack tamely around to the back door, only to be greeted by David fighting with the neighbours' son.

It had been a difficult day, and if she were to survive, she would have to find a way to cope, to bring harmony into a house which appeared to be totally devoid of parents. Even so, David seemed to have exhausted his naughty streak by supper, and she said as much to Joan once the boys had sat down to eat.

'He's just hungry,' Joan replied. 'He's been able to run about more now that you're here. When it was just me, we went to the park every morning, but most of the time they were stuck in the kitchen while I had to get on with the jobs. I swear by all that is holy, Dr Marcus has no idea that she spends almost every day out of the house. On Sundays she puts on a different show altogether.' She raised her eyes to the ceiling, in the general direction of Mrs Marcus.

'Are you cooking their supper tonight too?' asked Mary Kate.

'No, they're both off out to a party. But sometimes he doesn't get home in time and when that happens, run for your life – you cannot imagine the way she gives out to the poor man. He was supposed to be home early tonight, he told me when he came down for some toast this morning, but I'll believe that when I see it.'

Mary Kate glanced up at the large kitchen clock suspended high on the wall over the back door. 'I can't be late or I'll have Mrs O'Keefe giving out to me. What do we do with the boys then, if she goes out?'

Joan shredded the ham from the bone, and as the steam and the smell rose, Mary Kate's tummy rumbled. Joan wiped her hands on her apron. 'After they've eaten, they can go up to the boys' sitting room and watch the TV. Dr Marcus always goes in as soon as he gets home and spends half an hour with them, and it's always him who puts them to bed. Loves those boys, he does. If he's going to be late and miss it, he will always ring first.'

'Right, well, while they're finishing their supper, I'll take this basket upstairs, shall I? Oh, and these flamin' parcels she gave me.' Mary Kate balanced the basket of ironing on her hip, gripped the handles of the box and the bag in her hand, and struggled through the door to the stairs.

'A note was delivered for her an hour ago,' Joan said. 'I put it on the hall table – just check it's gone and she has it, would you? The boy who brought it said it was urgent.'

The letter tray on the hall table was empty. As Mary Kate reached the first-floor landing, she heard the water being run in the bathroom. Loud music from the radio spilt out from the main bedroom, along with a sweet, heady aroma. She thought it must be Mrs Marcus running a bath before her party. She filled her nostrils with the fragrance and smiled; perfume was a novelty to Mary Kate.

Turning the brass handle on the white panelled door, she walked straight into the dressing room opposite the bedroom to deposit the bags. In the dimly lit room, what met her was disarray: clothes scattered across the floor, dresses half on hangers, a coat hanging from the corner of a French cheval mirror in the corner and stockings trailing over the edge of a stack of hat boxes. The room was the size of Deidra's bedroom at Mrs O'Keefe's, but without the window.

Mary Kate fumbled on the wall for the brass light switch, with half an intention of tidying a bit of space in which to leave the bags. The central ceiling light flickered into life, revealing that the room was in a worse mess than the shaft of light from the landing had led her to believe.

'Where do I put them?' she asked herself. She spotted a pale pink velvet chair in the corner opposite the mirror. It was clear, with a small heap of clothes piled alongside it, as though someone had pushed them off the chair to make space to sit down. But there was something on the chair; an open note rested on the pink velvet.

'Here we go,' she said as she crossed the room.

She lifted the note to set the parcels down on the chair and had every intention of placing the note on top of them, but her eyes were drawn to three words that leapt off the page: 'my little kitten'.

Her skin prickled and tightened as she glanced over her shoulder. The music had filled the room and, apart from the splashing of water in the bathroom and Mrs Marcus humming along to Neil Sedaka, she was alone. Her eyes returned to the note and her hand trembled as she read.

Hotel booked, my little kitten. I will collect you from the junction with Aigburth Road at 9.30 a.m. tomorrow. I've booked us into the restaurant in the hotel and I've taken a room with a romantic view – only the best for you.

Forgive me if I deliberately ignore you tonight – better to not raise the slightest suspicion. Pity me, having to avoid you, when all I will want to do is wrap my arms around you and feel your beautiful silky skin beneath my fingers.

As I look at you, I will see you not in your cocktail dress but naked, happy, lying in bed next to me, just as you so often do.

Mary Kate's face flamed with guilt and embarrassment and the letter fell to the floor. 'Oh God, you wicked girl,' she muttered to herself as she placed the bags on the chair and stooped to retrieve the note.

If she put the note on top of the bags, Mrs Marcus would know that she'd read it. The realisation of what the note revealed was filtering through. Mrs Marcus was having an affair. Mary Kate and Roshine had heard of such things. She knew they happened. One of the girls at the convent had had just such a catastrophe occur in her family and she'd disappeared from the school overnight, with her father collecting her in his car. Not a word was spoken, but Mary Kate remembered his stony, ashen face and the shame of his tearful daughter as, with her head bent low, she slunk off down the stairs into the hallway and out of the door her father held open. The whispers had flown around the dorm like wildfire: her mother had had an affair with the cowman and run away to Roscommon, where no one knew them. In that moment, it occurred to Mary Kate: was that what Bee had done?

Was Mrs Marcus having an affair with a cowman or a man like Captain Bob? Was it more common than she thought? What if lovely Dr Marcus should read it? His heart would be broken – what then?

She was about to slip the note under the bags, to make

it appear as though she hadn't noticed it at all and had simply dumped the parcels on top of it.

'And just why are you a wicked girl?' A voice came from behind her and she screamed as she jumped around to look into the wryly smiling face of Dr Marcus.

Her mouth opened and closed, and the note in her hand burnt her fingers. She could think of nothing to say as she quickly hid her hands behind her back, trying to conceal the note. She wanted to throw it to the floor and kick it under a pile of the scattered clothes, but it was as if it were glued to her fingers.

'Well, wickedness is a great sin, is it not?'

She could see now that he was half joking; he couldn't keep the mirth from his eyes. He hadn't noticed the note – his gaze was fixed on her face.

'What is this terrible thing you have done, Mary Kate?'

The Neil Sedaka song had finished, to be replaced by 'Three Steps to Heaven', and she heard the gurgle of the bathwater disappearing down the plughole. Mrs Marcus would be in there any moment to collect her clothes – maybe she'd want to wear whatever was in the parcels she'd bought today. Mary Kate's heart beat faster and beads of perspiration sprang up along her top lip. She blinked furiously, her mind racing, looking for a way out of the predicament she was in, but she could find none. She was trapped. Mrs Marcus and the despicable cowman were about to be exposed and Dr Marcus would be put through the shame of finding out, all because of her.

A quizzical look crossed Dr Marcus's face as he tucked his hands into his pockets and nonchalantly leant against the wall.

The thought went through her mind that he was the most attractive man she had ever met. Her emotions were in such turmoil, her mind froze.

'Come on then, Mary Kate. I'm waiting,' he said, and she could see that his eyes were laughing at her.

'Well... it was a thought, Dr Marcus, not something I have done as such. Like, just a thought I had. It was nothing, really.' Her hands unconsciously gripped the note harder and her heart sank as the sound of crinkling paper filled the space between them.

'Oh, a wicked thought indeed? I like that even more.' His mouth lifted at the corners and broke into a wide grin, which had the effect of melting her heart.

Mary Kate felt faint with relief. He was smiling. She could get out of this. 'Well, I am entitled to keep my own thoughts private,' she said as she flicked her hair over her ears with her free hand and pulled the hand with the note further up her back.

'You are indeed – as are we all,' he said. Changing the subject, he pushed himself away from the wall and smoothed his grey flannel trousers. 'How have my boys been today? Did they behave themselves?'

Mary Kate had no idea where the words came from as she blurted out, 'No, they did not. Well, actually, Jack was an angel, and David, he was a little devil, but I will get the better of him, I can tell you. He will be behaving like an angel too, just give me a week. I was thinking of paying a visit to see Cat and taking them with me. Would that be all right with you?'

She was chatting nervously, consciously diverting his attention, wary of his reply, well aware that the neighbourhood Cat lived in was a million miles from Fullmore Park. She hadn't intended to do any such thing – the notion had just flown into her head. 'I haven't asked Mrs Marcus yet,' she said, 'but I thought that as you know where and what I mean when I talk about visiting Cat, 'twould be better to ask you first.'

The sound of the radio, a dog barking out in the road, the bathwater draining, and the squeak of a door opening and closing filled the long moment of silence and she imagined she could see the thoughts flickering behind his eyes as his smile turned into a frown. 'I think it might be best...' His words were spoken slowly, ponderously. He took a breath, blinked, folded his arms across his chest, repeated himself. 'I think it might be best if you just tell my wife you're taking them to visit a friend of yours. Don't tell her where – although I'm sure she won't ask.' A cloud had crossed his face and he looked sad, lost, vulnerable.

She stared into his eyes and realised that she knew exactly what she was doing. It thrilled her. And his eyes were speaking back.

Neither moved and the moment seemed to last forever,

until the voice of Mrs Marcus rang out. 'Nicholas, is that you?'

'Coming, darling.' Looking embarrassed, he took a deep breath and straightened his shoulders. He seemed pale and tired. 'I have to go,' he said wryly.

'Yes, me too. I have to put the boys' clothes away.'

Mary Kate followed him out of the room and stood on the landing, holding her breath as he closed the bedroom door behind him. A waft of Midnight in Paris drifted out. The latch clicked and she waited for a moment, stood stock still. She heard the sound of muffled voices, the opening and shutting of a drawer, and then, turning on her heel, she tiptoed back into the dressing room. She would return the note to the chair and deposit the parcels on top.

Her heart was beating against her ribcage like a trapped bird and as she re-entered the dressing room, her breath was shallow; she was terrified of being heard. A floorboard creaked and she banged her toe against the protruding foot of the cheval mirror as she bent to pick up the parcels. The top box slipped and she cursed under her breath as she moved back to the chair and bent to replace the note.

This time when the voice behind her called her name, she thought she might faint. The words trickled down her spine.

'Mary Kate, would you pass me that note, please.'

Chapter 20

Mary Kate froze as she looked down at the note in her hand.

'Mary Kate, please.' A muscle in his cheek had begun twitching uncontrollably as he held out his hand. His face was void of all colour. 'The note – I take it it doesn't belong to you, as you were hiding it behind your back and looking extremely guilty, if I may say?'

Mary Kate was speechless. She still clung onto the note, which was now vibrating wildly in her trembling hand. She was too scared to look up. Her tongue stuck fast to the roof of her mouth while her eyes stared at the note, willing it to disappear in a puff of smoke.

This cannot be happening, she thought to herself. She was reminded of the occasions she'd been sent to stand outside Sister Magdalena's office, which had been bad enough, but this was a million times worse. Had she really still been at St Catherine's only a matter of weeks ago? She blinked furiously and tried to swallow. Oh God, Roshine, help me, she thought, but her old partner in crime was as good as a thousand miles away now. Mary Kate was in this mess alone.

Dr Marcus's voice cut through her panicked thoughts once more. 'Would you pass it to me then, please. Is it addressed to my wife? I can see by your reaction that it is something you would rather I didn't see.' His voice sounded softer now. She detected no anger, only a hint of sadness.

She knew the contents of the note would tear the Marcus household apart, would destroy everything – the home, the children and him. How would he survive the shame if it should get out? She felt lightheaded and, closing her eyes, reached out her free hand to the cheval to steady herself.

A beam of pink light shone down from the fringed lampshade overhead, directly onto the letter, and exposed the menacing message. The back ink danced before her eyes and all she could see through her blurred vision were the taunting, incriminating words: 'little kitten... naked... in bed next to me...'

'Oh God,' she groaned, and felt the note being tugged from her fingers by his outstretched hand.

She opened her eyes wide to see him scanning the page. It was a moment that felt like a lifetime and her feet, rooted to the spot, only just supported her as her knees began to shake violently.

Dr Marcus looked confused as he turned the note over, seemingly studying the handwriting or maybe checking that it really was addressed to his wife. He turned it back over and Mary Kate flinched to see the pain flashing across his face. His lips tightened into a line and the colour rose once more, his cheeks now bright red. His jaw was set rigid. His eyes reached the bottom of the page, then lifted, dazed, and locked onto hers, pinning her to the spot. She felt more humiliated than she had ever been in her life. The crime she'd committed, the words on the page, the like of which she'd never seen before, and now this, being caught.

'Where did you find it?' he asked. There was no emotion in his voice; it was controlled and low, each word spoken with cold precision.

She gulped, opened her mouth to speak, found she could not. No sound came. She blinked, raised her shaking arm and pointed to the chair.

He walked over to the bags. 'Come here, please. Show me, quickly, then put it back as it was. I assume that was what you were doing? We don't have much time – her nails must be nearly dry, so she'll be in here in a moment. Now, Mary Kate.'

She returned to the moment with a jolt, took the few steps to the chair and lifted the bags. 'There,' she said.

He laid the letter on the velvet chair and looked up. 'Was it like this?'

She shook her head and, bending down, turned the note over to face the right way up.

'She barely tried to conceal it this time.' He spat the words out, the first sign of his anger, and then, composing himself once more, he turned to Mary Kate. 'Could you go back downstairs to the boys now, please,' he said and stood aside to allow her past.

She still didn't speak; she couldn't. Everything in that house had now changed and it was all her fault and she'd only been there two days. Without another word, she stumbled past him and fled down the stairs to the kitchen.

It was empty. She'd heard Joan on the first-floor landing with the boys. The TV hissed and crackled as it warmed up and Joan had tried to tune in the aerial to make the picture clearer so that they could watch. It really wouldn't matter what she put on for them: these were their last moments of normality. A bomb was about to fall into the middle of their world and they had no idea. Only Mary Kate could hear it whistling down the staircase in slow motion from the room above. Any moment now, she would hear – they would all hear – the impact.

She felt physically sick and ran the cold tap at the sink and began to splash her face. She wanted to run out the door and down the street to Mrs O'Keefe, collect her bags and get herself to Dublin and Tarabeg as fast as was possible. 'Oh, Declan, what have I done?' For a fleeting moment, a life with Declan appeared a blissful option. Peace and predictability suddenly seemed very attractive. 'God in heaven, what is wrong with you?' she asked herself as she cupped her hands under the icy flow and slurped the water down, a habit she'd picked up at home, drinking from the Taramore, and had yet to lose.

She looked to the back door. Should she flee – leave without a word to anyone and save her skin? She couldn't face it. Would Mrs Marcus come down the stairs and hit her? Would Dr Marcus kill Mrs Marcus?

She heard David talking to Joan. Maybe she should stay. She should warn Joan at the very least; she owed her that. She could tell Joan to run to Mrs O'Keefe's – she was sure Mrs O'Keefe would let her sleep with Deidra while she sorted herself another position – but then she would have to tell Joan about the note and, worse, what she had done, her part in the destruction of the Marcus household. What if he actually murdered her upstairs, in cold blood, while her nail varnish was still drying? If only she hadn't picked up the letter, Dr Marcus would be none the wiser. Whatever was about to happen in this house, it was all her fault.

A door upstairs slammed, hard, and she jolted with the force of it as her cupped hands covered her mouth. 'Holy Mary, Mother of God, be with us now and in our—'

'What in God's name is up with you?' asked Joan as she walked into the kitchen and unfastened her apron. 'Jesus, you look as though you've seen a ghost. And saying your Hail Marys... Have you seen a ghost, or what? I wouldn't be surprised. I sometimes think I see a little girl running around in here, but she's gone so quick, I can't be sure, like.'

Mary Kate couldn't speak; she was trembling and terri-fied. Any second now, she expected Mrs Marcus to storm down the stairs, fists flying, and grab Mary Kate's hair, kick her shins. She'd seen two girls do that once in the playground at school and it had half scared her to death. Now it would be herself who was being attacked – for the second time in days. Mrs Marcus would be demanding to know what she had done by reading her mail and Dr Marcus would be hot on her heels to tell her she was an ungrateful busybody because Mrs Marcus would have told him that's what she was.

'Mary Kate, what the hell is wrong?' asked Joan.

But Mary Kate had no time to reply because Dr Marcus was shouting down the stairs. 'Joan, could you ask Mary Kate to bring some hot chocolate up for the boys. I will put them to bed myself before Mrs Marcus and I leave for the evening.'

Mary Kate looked towards the back kitchen door, astonished. 'What?' she said. 'What did he just say? Hot chocolate? Did he just say that?'

Joan was already taking the milk out of the fridge. 'Yes, Jesus and all the saints in heaven, have you never heard of hot chocolate? What kind of life did you lead in that boarding school? They have it everywhere over here.' She turned the dial on the radio and music filled the kitchen.

Mary Kate shook the thoughts from her head. At the very least, she imagined Mrs Marcus lying dead and bleeding on the bedroom floor, and here was Dr Marcus, as cool as a cucumber, asking for hot chocolate, and Joan singing along to Cliff Richard's 'Travellin' Light' on the radio. Was Dr Marcus really a madman, pretending to act normally while he worked out how to dispose of his wife's corpse?

'Yes, of course I've heard of it.'

'Oh right, well that's good then, because I haven't eaten my supper yet and I'm starving, so I am, and this is my programme on the radio now. Don't you just love Cliff Richard? God, I dream of the man. I imagine every day what I would do if I met him outside the Co-op on Aigburth Road.'

Mary Kate had one ear trained on the stairs and the other on Joan, who was measuring spoons of drinking chocolate into a pan of almost boiling milk. She wanted to ask her what she would do if she did meet Cliff Richard outside the Co-op, but she couldn't concentrate enough on what she was saying.

The milk spat as Joan poured it out of the enamel pan and into an earthenware jug. 'You can take it up now,' she said, glancing at the kitchen clock. 'Anyway, would you look at that – you have ten minutes until you knock off, so you've just enough time. Oh, would you listen, it's Cliff with the Shadows, they play this all the time at the dances in town, and everyone knows all the words and you should see the fellas dancing to it too.'

Mary Kate knew she wouldn't be able to knock on the boys' door; she had her hands full, balancing the tray with the jug of hot chocolate, two mugs and a plate of biscuits. But she needn't have worried. It was as though

Dr Marcus had been waiting to hear her footsteps on the stairs. The door was flung open and he stood before her.

'Are you putting the boys to bed, Nicholas?' Mrs Marcus shouted down the stairs.

Mary Kate froze. At least Mrs Marcus was alive – and able to speak.

'Yes, dear,' he shouted back up the stairwell, and, turning to Mary Kate, 'Ah, excellent. Would you just wait here while I take it in to them.'

She couldn't speak, just nodded in response, her mouth half open, her pulse still racing, her instinct to flee attempting to pull her back down the stairs. As well as being angry with herself, she felt desperately sorry for him. You poor man, she thought as she watched him give the boys their hot chocolate and ruffle their hair with such tenderness. Jack was sitting on the floor, moving his soldiers into position, and David had his eyes glued to the screen, watching a donkey that talked. Both boys took their mugs from him. He laid down the plate of biscuits on the low coffee table between them, spoke a few words that Mary Kate couldn't hear and made his way back to the door, shutting it behind him.

He placed his index finger on his lips, urging her not to speak, and, looking around him, opened the sitting-room door and ushered Mary Kate inside. As he laid his hand on the small of her back to guide her through the door, it was as though an electric shock coursed through her.

She wanted to turn around and throw her arms around him, an impulse she fought, for once.

He stood against the door, his hands behind his back, and took a deep breath. She was standing beside the chair she'd sat in on the evening she'd been interviewed, just a few short days ago. 'Mary Kate, I have to be quick. I know you read the letter – I could tell from your face.'

Mary Kate swallowed hard. She'd been about to deny that she had read it, as much to save his own embarrassment as to keep her job – assuming the house hadn't fallen apart by the following morning when she turned up for work.

'My wife doesn't know that both you and I are aware of the contents of the letter. I have the boys to consider, things to think about, and reacting now would do nothing but cause them great upset and distress. God knows, they have enough to deal with as it is: a half-absent mother and the hours I work on top of that. Mrs Marcus is apparently away for the weekend. I have to spend that time deciding what I'm going to do, how I'm going to deal with this. I'm also working this weekend, and so I wondered if you wouldn't mind working too. Joan has Sunday off. I know you've said you'd like Sundays off too and ordinarily my wife would be here – it's the one day she does spend with the boys when I'm on call. But apparently not any more. If I'm called out, I can't leave the boys in the house on their own. It would appear my partner at the practice is away for the weekend too.'

His voice was laced with sarcasm. Mary Kate could tell that there was more to this than even she knew. He paced around the room as he spoke, rubbing his hands through his hair, his eyes blinking, as though he was surveying his own thoughts, preparing to speak them out loud. He stopped and turned to her, his expression anguished.

'I would understand if you never wanted to come here again. Believe me, I wouldn't blame you. This is just another thing, another situation I have to deal with. It's not the first time – there have been others...' He hesitated, as if trying to fully comprehend what it was he was about to say. 'Just never quite so close to home.'

She had no idea what he meant, but it was plain he was in a great deal of pain. Again, she resisted the urge to run to him and throw her arms around him. 'Of course I will be here,' she said.

Relief flooded his face and his voice caught as he thanked her. 'I really appreciate that, and I won't forget it. You have already been so kind with the boys. Jack just asked me as I left him to make sure you come back tomorrow. He's had the best days in a long while, and that means more than anything to me, given everything the boys have to put up with.'

Neither of them said anything, the silence between them conveying all that needed to be communicated. Mary Kate managed a half smile of reassurance and understanding; she wanted him to know that she was on his side, would help him all she could.

Mrs Marcus's voice shrieked down the stairs and shattered the moment between them. 'Nicholas, can you come and zip up my dress, please.'

His eyes rolled heavenwards. 'I have to go. Can we speak in the morning?'

'Yes. Please don't worry, I'll be here,' she said, feeling a twinge of jealousy at the thought of him zipping up the dress of the woman who had lain naked in someone else's bed. She suppressed the emotion, which was not her place, and said, 'It was my fault, Dr Marcus. I read something I shouldn't and I am so, so sorry.'

He was on his way to the door, but he turned and took hold of both her hands. 'Mary Kate, please don't be. This is possibly the best thing that could have happened – it just doesn't feel that way right now. This... this situation... it's not the first time. We had to leave Surrey and move here, to a new practice. My decision...'

His voice trailed off as he turned his head to catch something David was saying to Jack behind their sitting room door. Reassured that the boys were not about to leave the room, he turned to Mary Kate and looked deep into her eyes. 'Something is about to happen, to change, I feel it, and I think it might be something true and real and for the better. I just have to sort out this godawful mess – my mess.'

Her heart stopped. He was talking to her, about her – she knew it. She watched his back as he sprinted up the next flight of stairs, grabbing the swan-neck bannister and hauling himself up two at a time, his face set and grim.

And then she reprimanded herself. *Stop, you eejit. You thought Bee was sending you an invitation to come and live in Liverpool and look where that got you. Get over yourself.* She left the room and went back down the stairs to the strains of the Everly Brothers and Joan singing along at the top of her voice, mangling the words, something about someone not wanting her love any more.

Chapter 21

Mrs Doyle took the call to book the taxi from Shannon Airport herself. Despite the number of years Keeva had worked at the post office, she was expressly forbidden to answer the phone, the existence of which was, to many in the village, still a novelty twenty years after the exchange had been installed. 'Only in the case of fire, flood or famine, if I'm caught short or if I'm away over the road and can't get to it meself,' Mrs Doyle had emphatically told her on more than one occasion.

Today was no exception. Mrs Doyle left Keeva stacking the shelf of tourist knick-knacks and bustled back behind the counter, removing the flowery overalls she wore for the dusty jobs and thrusting them into Keeva's hand. 'Oh now, who would this be ringing me on such a lovely afternoon?' she exclaimed as she banged the counter lid down behind her. Taking a deep breath, she inserted her black Bakelite ear- and mouthpiece and inserted a plug into the flashing light on the board. Being responsible for the local telephone exchange and telex gave Mrs Doyle a status she enjoyed to the full.

'Tarabeg here,' she said with an air of affected authority as she made the connection. 'Hello, yes, it is, it is, this is indeed Tarabeg post office and it is Mrs Doyle herself speaking to you here. How may I help you?'

Keeva returned to her task of replenishing the display of souvenirs aimed at the tourists and the new influx of Germans who bought licences from the land owner, Captain Carter, to fish salmon in the Taramore River. The number of people visiting from America was also on the increase, and so were the profits.

Mrs Doyle was often miffed that Keeva never appeared to want to witness her efficiency on the telephone in action. It was when she was at her finest. If the post office was busy, she could command an audience of very impressed village women when she answered a call. Keeva had need to hide her grin. The high-pitched, important-sounding voice that was so unlike Mrs Doyle's normal voice and manner got her every time, and it was all she could do to stop herself from laughing out loud.

Teresa Gallagher opened the door and Mrs Doyle placed her finger to her lips. Teresa, fully acquainted with the telephone etiquette, tiptoed across to Keeva as best she could, her stick beating out a gentle tattoo on the floorboards. Mrs Doyle continued, sounding even more self-important, delighted that she now had an audience. The telephone didn't ring very often.

'Yes, that is quite right, I do book the taxi service, as well as everything else around here, it would seem. Hospital appointments, a visit to the Vatican, it's all down to me. That will be Porick ye will be after now, but he doesn't have a phone, you see, that is why you have to call here. And I would say 'tis an exaggeration altogether to say that he has a car. No, I wouldn't call it that, 'tis more a place where the chickens live, and I don't think it even has all the tyres, does it, Keeva?'

She turned from the phone to Keeva, who shook her head solemnly. 'He borrows a tyre from Paddy,' said Keeva. 'He can't get too far in it, though, because it doesn't quite fit. I'd say as far as Belmullet and back, but that would be it now.'

'Ah, did ye hear that?' said Mrs Doyle into the mouthpiece. 'That would be Keeva, my assistant, who is married to Tig, Paddy's son. So you see, she would know. But don't you be worrying, Miss... what did you say your name was? If you book it with me, something or someone will be there to meet you. You won't be waiting – well, not for too long anyway, and if ye are, there is a very nice café now at the airport and they tell me they serve a lovely cup of tea. What did you say your name was?'

'Who is she talking to?' asked Teresa. 'The Pope? It can't be anyone else with that la-di-da voice.'

'I have no idea at all,' said Keeva. 'I thought it might be Michael at first, asking about the shop. He's in Liverpool.'

'So I hear,' said Teresa. 'Chasing after Mary Kate.' She

tutted and shook her head. 'What a wayward girl she is, and here was me hoping she'd be wanting to take over the Sunday school from me. I saw Bee at Mass yesterday – the only regret she has was that she wasn't still in Liverpool when Mary Kate got there. I passed that on to Father Jerry, straight after Mass.'

'Oh, Teresa, stop. The world is moving on. Tarabeg isn't for all of us, as well you know. She is the daughter of Michael and Sarah, for heaven's sake – she was always going to leave. And Michael was an eejit putting his foot down. Drove her away, so he did, and Rosie and Bee both agree. Ah well, would you look at that – speak of an angel and his wife appears.'

The door opened and in stepped Rosie with Bee in tow. It was now Teresa's turn to place her index finger on her lips; raising her eyebrows, she indicated that Mrs Doyle was on the telephone. Rosie and Bee also did the tiptoe walk across to Keeva, the creaking of the floorboards making far more noise than their shoes normally would.

'I was just popping in to see was there any news from Michael,' Rosie said.

'Or is there any for me?' asked Bee hopefully. Rosie squeezed her hand.

'What do you know – I was just asking the very same thing,' said Teresa.

'I'm sorry to disappoint you, ladies,' said Keeva, 'but it sounds like it's someone who wants to book a taxi from the airport to Tarabeg.'

'Well now, who would that be?' said Teresa. 'There's been no one up at the presbytery with news of a relative coming home.'

'I have no idea. We haven't heard of anyone in the bar either.' Keeva placed the last ashtray with a map of Mayo in its centre on the shelf and picked up the empty packing chest. 'Tea, is it, ladies?'

Rosie and Bee replied in chorus and followed Keeva into the back. But Teresa walked over to Mrs Doyle. The look Mrs Doyle slipped her told her all she needed to know. This was it. Joe Malone really was despatching one of his descendants to collect the money he'd sent to Tarabeg all those years ago. Bridget's letter had not been enough, and the telex from America earlier in the week had not been a hoax.

Over in New York, Miss Carroll moved the phone away from her ear and looked at the handset. She could barely understand what was being said to her and began to feel nervous. 'I wish to book a cab to meet a Mr Joe Malone at Shannon Airport. His plane lands at nine o'clock on Saturday morning. Will this be acceptable, or shall I call a taxi firm in Cork?'

'Oh Jesus, no, don't you be doing that at all – devils, they are, the lot of them, and if they can get away with charging ye ten shilling over the odds, they will. We will be there to meet him. Mr Joe Malone, did you say it was?'

'I did indeed,' said Miss Carroll. 'I wonder if, whilst I have you on the telephone, you could help me with something else. We are trying to track down the Malone family of Tarabeg Hill – would you be aware of their whereabouts? Mr Malone is related to them.'

Mrs Doyle gave a good impression of acting surprised. 'The Malones, you say? Ah now, there haven't been any Malones on Tarabeg Hill since the war, I would be saying.' She gesticulated wildly to Teresa and pointed at the phone as the clatter of china and chatter in the kitchen told her that Rosie, Bee and Keeva were busy in the kitchen. 'It's about Joe Malone,' she mouthed.

'I knew it,' Teresa whispered back, and pressed her head closer to Mrs Doyle's.

They could almost hear Miss Carroll's frown. 'Well, that is very sad indeed. I do hope Mr Malone's journey will not be in vain after all this time and planning. He is very keen indeed to make contact with his relatives.'

'Carroll? Did you say you were a Carroll?' said Mrs Doyle. 'Now, there were Carrolls running the post office in Belmullet and they moved to Brooklyn nearly fifteen years ago, I would say. It was just after the war they went. Been in Belmullet since before the famine, they had. Would they be related to yourself? How are they doing? We haven't heard a word since the day they left and we often wonder.'

It was agreed that Teresa Gallagher would make the run to the airport in Father Jerry's car. Whether or not he would let her take it overnight was a moot point. Between them they decided that if he objected, Teresa would suffer a lapse of memory and drive off in it anyway, while Father Jerry was drinking in Paddy's bar, having claimed to Teresa, as he always did, that he was off visiting the sick. Two wrongs would very definitely make a right.

The older women had gathered around Daedio's bed not two hours after the call from America came through. Teresa had arrived with Ellen, and Bridget with Mrs Doyle.

'But Teresa can hardly feckin' walk,' said Daedio as they discussed the plan.

'I can walk better than you and that's a fact,' Teresa said. 'And besides, I don't need to walk – I'm driving. I'll stay at my sister's overnight and then make the run back in one trip the following day. There won't be much I don't know about Joe Malone by the time we get back here.'

Mrs Doyle shuffled in her seat. This was not a satisfactory state of affairs. Her privileged position as postmistress ensured that she was always the one ahead of the news. 'I could always ask Sam to collect him in the mail van,' she offered.

Teresa drew herself up to her full height and adjusted her hatpin. She was the only visitor not to have removed her hat. 'And how does that work?' she said in a scathing voice, looking at Mrs Doyle over the top of her wire-framed spectacles. 'Shall we ask Sam to bring him all the way to the farm as well, straight to the door? And how do we protect the postman, asking him to collect a man who is the descendant of a known murderer? He may not be safe.'

'You might not be safe either,' said Daedio, 'and anyway, Joe was no murderer, he was a bank robber.'

'Well, he died in prison, and that's what they do to murderers in America. It was very suspicious altogether, if you ask me,' said Ellen.

Everyone in the room blessed themselves and was silent for a moment.

'I really don't think you'll be safe in a car with an American stranger for all of those hours,' said Daedio, looking more concerned by the moment. 'Joe never told us about any children, so the man can't be from this family. They say America is a place where the Devil runs free in the streets.'

'I will be collecting him because that is the only way we'll know who he is, what his intentions are and how he knows about the money. We are one step ahead of him. Tell me, what murderer would harm an old woman with a stick who was giving him a seat all the way to where he wanted to go? Besides, do you see this…?' Teresa brandished her hatpin. 'Straight in his neck, that would be. I'd stab him and I'd ram it all the way home. Spies did more on less during the war. I'll be safe all right. I'm not sure how I'll keep my hat on after though.'

They were all speechless and everyone took a sip of their whiskey-laced tea while they allowed the image of Teresa murdering an innocent American visitor in Father Jerry's car to exit their minds.

'How much money is there, Daedio?' said Bridget.

'I wish I knew. I've never unwrapped it since the day Annie rolled it all up into fat cigars and stacked them in the chimney.'

'It can't be that much, surely to God. Shall we count it?' said Mrs Doyle. 'I'm used to money, seeing as how I handle it every day.'

'That would be a start,' said Bridget.

'Aye, maybe I should give him half of it when he comes and not tell him about the other half,' said Daedio.

'That's not what Annie wants,' said Bridget.

They all turned to the only woman in the village with the sight.

'Annie came to me last night and she told me that Mary Kate will be in need of that money one day, and the seven acres it bought as well. She said the money will stay just where it is.'

They all gasped.

'Did she say anything else?' Daedio asked.

'Aye, she did. She said for you to stop giving out to Nola all the time and to behave yourself. Oh, and she also said to remember to cover the sign up over Michael's shop door and to get Pete Shevlin to drag the whins down to the bottom of the boreen and block the turning up the hill, and then to put the bull on the boreen. If you do that, the American will never be able to find the farm.'

'Well, if ever I needed proof that Annie is still with us,' Daedio said, 'that was it just there. Organising us all and telling us what to do. Every word that ever fell out of that woman's mouth was a right one.'

'Where's the money?' Mrs Doyle got up from the seat and brushed down her skirt.

''Tis there. See? That loose brick.'

Mrs Doyle ran her hand along the wall and felt one of the large lime-painted bricks slightly jutting out.

Half an hour later, she was still pulling rolls of dollars out of the wall cavity created by Annie as Bridget threw the tea slops out of the front door onto the grass and filled the mugs with neat whiskey. Teetotaller Teresa, who had placed her hand protectively over her mug and shaken her head with a disapproving sniff when the whiskey had been added to the tea, mouthing, 'Not for me, thank you', was now the first to hold out her mug when Bridget unplugged the straw stopper from the top of the bottle. As they continued to count, they all needed it.

Chapter 22

Mrs O'Keefe and Deidra could tell that there was something amiss the second a subdued Mary Kate arrived home from the Marcuses'. She walked straight through the kitchen and disappeared into the bathroom.

'I've been waiting for you. Are you coming to the dance or not?' Deidra's words went unanswered as the bathroom door closed. 'That does not look good,' she whispered to Mrs O'Keefe as she placed her purse into her beaded clutch-bag ready to leave for her night out.

'Indeed,' said Eileen O'Keefe. A frown crossed her face and she instantly decided that she wouldn't pry. She would allow Mary Kate the time to settle and then, if she felt comfortable enough, she was sure Mary Kate would tell her what was wrong. 'Don't ask her anything else, she will tell us soon enough,' she whispered to Deidra.

It was dancing night and Deidra's toes were already tapping on the terracotta tiles she'd mopped less than an hour ago. She was beside herself with excitement and a glum Mary Kate had not suppressed her mood.

'Will ye be coming with me, Mary Kate?' she asked again, as soon as Mary Kate surfaced. She was quivering with excitement in her pale lemon summer dress, smooth stockings and white slingback sandals with kitten heels. Her auburn hair had been brushed out and fell softly around her shoulders as she tucked her bag under her arm. Deidra felt like a movie star and it showed in her eyes, which were glistening with anticipation. 'I can lend you one of my frocks. I have three now, since I began earning me own money. Come on, would you? You can be ready in ten minutes. Sure, you're gorgeous – all you need to do is change your dress.'

Mary Kate smiled wistfully. Going dancing... Wasn't that just what she had dreamt of doing once she'd made her escape from Tarabeg? Hadn't she imagined herself in a fine dress – one she owned, not one she'd borrowed – being twirled around a dancehall by a good-looking young man? Right now though, it was the last thing she, her aching feet or her buzzing head wanted. Much as she'd tried, she hadn't been able to shake Dr Marcus from her thoughts on her walk back up the avenue.

Mary Kate smiled. 'I will so, Deidra. It's just that it's my first week and all that,' she said apologetically.

Deidra's face softened. 'I know. My first week I could just about drag myself up the stairs away to my bed. One night I lay down for a minute with all my clothes on, closed my eyes and never woke up till Mrs O'Keefe shook me the next morning. She thought I was dead. Imagine!'

Deidra's laugh made Mary Kate smile and on impulse she threw her arms around her shoulders and hugged her. 'I'm sorry,' she whispered and she swallowed down the lump in her throat that had appeared from nowhere.

'Oh sure, don't be saying sorry to me. I've Joan waiting at the bus stop now. You'll not be getting away with it next week, mind,' she shouted as she crashed out of the back door so loudly, it must have been heard in every house on Duke's Avenue.

Eileen O'Keefe and Mary Kate spent the night in the sitting room. The black-and-white television in the corner was on good form, apart from the occasional snowstorm, which prompted Eileen to jump up and start playing with the aerial protruding from the top of the set. 'Tell me when it gets better,' she said to Mary Kate as she stood on a chair behind the television.

'Up a bit,' said Mary Kate. 'Over to Bluey. There, stop.'

With the aerial half pushed through the wire of Bluey's cage, which was suspended in front of the window, they were entertained to the point where Mary Kate could sit back in the chair and allow herself to think. There were no demands for conversation and for that she was grateful. The only comments from Mrs O'Keefe were statements rather than questions – 'Would you look at the state of him!' – as the images flickered across the screen.

They'd eaten lamb chops for supper and even though

Mary Kate felt sick as a result of the day's events, she found she was hungry and devoured the lot. Bluey sang along to the advert for Palmolive soap and they both laughed as he objected to the aerial protruding into his cage. He pecked at it in annoyance and tried to push it out, using the top of his beak.

'He won't electrocute himself, will he?' asked Mary Kate.

'Oh heavens, no. If there was the slightest possibility of that, he would have been burnt to a crisp years ago. One night I had to put it all the way in and he sat on it, caused terrible interference he did and wouldn't let me take it back out again.'

Mary Kate felt the tension she hadn't even been aware of leave her shoulders.

Eileen was pouring another cup of tea from the pot when, noting that Mary Kate was now well rested and well fed, she decided to take the plunge. 'I'm assuming today wasn't a very good day then?' She looked up from under her heavy lids and could see the colour drain from Mary Kate's face. 'You don't have to tell me if you don't want to, and it isn't my place to pry. Just to remember, though, the first week in any new job is very hard – it's the same for everyone.'

Mary Kate sat forwards on her seat and accepted the tea. She really wanted to confide in Mrs O'Keefe. The words were nudging at her lips, desperate to escape. She could trust Mrs O'Keefe – the woman was a saint, her home a haven of kindness and generosity. She sipped her tea and made the decision to keep her own counsel. It was not her place to speak and tell anyone the Marcuses' business. Least said, soonest mended, she thought to herself as she put the cup down on the saucer.

But the events of the day had been too much for a girl from Tarabeg who had only ever witnessed drama when the tinkers came and cast a curse or when Murphy's pig escaped and went on a rampage around the churchyard.

She set her cup and saucer on the table, straightened her back, brushed her hair away from her face with both hands, placed her hands in her lap, turned to Mrs O'Keefe and blurted out, 'There's trouble in the Marcus house. All is not what it seems down there.' And within five minutes she'd told Mrs O'Keefe almost everything.

'Goodness me,' said Eileen, 'what a terrible experience for you. We need something stronger than tea – let me get us a drop of sherry out of the sideboard. What did the letter say exactly?' she asked as she fumbled with the key to the door.

Mary Kate blushed, took the deepest breath and told her.

Eileen poured two glasses of sherry almost to the brim and carried the tray over to the chairs. 'I'm going to fetch the bottle,' she said. 'I think we need it after that.'

An hour later, when they had analysed every aspect of the day, Mrs O'Keefe decided it was time for dishes and bed, but not before she'd dropped a word of warning in Mary Kate's ear. 'The minute something is awry in that house that you aren't comfortable with, you come straight down here. Hang up your pinny and get out of that door. Do you hear me?'

'I do. It's not as if you live far away, is it?' Mary Kate smiled.

'True enough. I don't want your family saying I got you a job in a house of ill repute, that wouldn't do at all, and anyway, my sister would be mortified. When I tell her about this tomorrow, she will pull you out, that's for sure.'

She rose and began to stack the dishes onto the tray. Minutes later, they were in the downstairs kitchen. 'You wash and I'll dry,' she said.

'I'll wait up for Deidra to come home,' said Mary Kate. 'That's if you don't mind.'

Eileen tutted and shook her head as she removed a clean tea towel from the kitchen drawer. 'That girl is always giddy the morning after a night in the Cabbage Hall. She spends half the day singing songs and dancing around the furniture, she does.'

Mary Kate ran the tap into the enamel bowl and added the detergent. Soon she was up to her elbows in suds and up to her neck in steam.

'We will have that to put up with while I talk to my sister about what's happened to you down there. You shouldn't have had to read that note. What kind of woman is she, for goodness' sake?'

Mary Kate was alarmed. The thought of Mrs O'Keefe telling her sister to pull her out of the Marcus house made her heart sink and she surprised herself when the reason dawned on her; it was the thought that she might never see Dr Marcus again. 'Oh, I'll be fine going back. I get the impression Mrs Marcus is never there. The doctor, he is the loveliest, kindest man and you should see the way he is with the boys – loves them, he does, it's obvious from the way he is with them.'

Eileen stretched up and slipped a plate into the rack on the wall above the sink. 'Aye, well, isn't it a pity his wife can't behave in the same way.' She cast Mary Kate a sideways glance. It was the tone of Mary Kate's voice that had alerted her, a tone she had used herself when talking about her Pat all those years ago. 'Mary Kate, I mean it – be careful. Do your job, that's all. Don't become involved. You are there to help with the boys and the house, not their marriage. I have no idea what he will do. I know what my Pat would have done if he'd caught me carrying on, and I can tell you this, it wouldn't have had a happy ending. Out on the street on my ear, I would have been.'

'I can't believe people behave like that,' said Mary Kate, handing over the second plate. 'That their marriage vows can be put aside without a thought for the pain of others.'

'Oh well, I'm afraid that's because you've been brought up in the shadow of the Catholic Church. People do. There is no accounting for passion and the things it makes people do and that's the truth of it. Lust and love – kingdoms have been lost for it, and when you consider what that one down there is getting up to' – she jabbed her thumb in the direction of the Marcus house – 'you can well believe it.'

'It's so hot,' said Mary Kate as she ran the cold tap and splashed water onto her face. 'I think I'll go and meet Deidra at the bus stop. I've been running around and indoors for most of the day.' She knew the area was safe enough and well lit and the bus stop was down the opposite end to the park gates.

'Well now, you take care. I'm off to my bed. Don't let Deidra sing when she gets home, and for God's sake don't let her come up the road swinging around the lampposts with her imaginary Fred Astaire. Ginger Rogers she is not.'

Mary Kate slipped out of the house, instructions still ringing in her ears.

'And don't forget to lock the back door either.'

The night air was refreshingly cool and she tilted her face to catch the gentle breeze.

She had to pass the Marcus house on the opposite side of the road to reach the bus stop. As she approached their gate, her heart began to pound at the thought of Dr Marcus. The words he'd spoken, the look in his eyes. The instant bond she had felt between them, as though they were equals. It was as if they'd been fated to meet, meant to be; she'd been sent there, propelled to Liverpool, for a reason and maybe he was it. Maybe she was meant to be there in his hour of need, to help him.

She could see the master bedroom light was on, so they were obviously home. She crossed the wide road, her footsteps light, and leant against one of the tall laurel bushes that marked the perimeter of the Marcus property. As she gazed down the drive towards the house, about to move away and continue towards the bus stop, she noticed the red glow of a cigarette end and she realised it was Dr Marcus sitting on the bonnet of his car, smoking.

He pushed himself up off the car and whispered, 'Is that you?'

Mary Kate stepped out of the shadows and stood at the entrance to the drive. 'If you meant me, then yes.' She smiled, filled with a confidence she had been unaware she possessed.

He did not smile back. His face was set and serious-looking.

'How was your evening?' she asked.

He put his cigarette in his mouth and took a long pull before turning his head sideways and exhaling in the direction of the breeze. 'I've had better.' He threw his cigarette to the ground and stubbed it out with the toe of his shoe.

There was a frisson between them and she knew she wasn't imagining it. They were standing only a few feet apart and her eyes fixed on his white shirt, open at the neck, dark hair curling over the edges. In the dim, silvery moonlight she could see the pulse throbbing in the side of his neck as he glanced up towards the bedroom window.

He turned back to her, his hands thrust deep into his pockets.

'Did you…? Did you…?' She couldn't form the words, couldn't frame the question, but she wanted to know. She realised that this was the question that had been burning into her brain all evening. Had he…? Would he…? When would he let his wife know what he had read?

He finished the question for her. 'Did I tell my partner at the practice what a cheating cad he is? No, I didn't. Did I tell my wife that if she doesn't behave like a good mother to our children, I will leave her? No. Did I even tell her that there is a young woman I have been inexplicably drawn to since the second I looked into her eyes and that ever since that moment I haven't been able to get either her or those eyes out of my mind? No, Mary Kate, I did not, because that makes me as guilty as my wife. Or do you believe there is a difference between thought and deed? Because, truly, I don't. What my wife has done in deed has been no worse than what I have done in thought.'

Mary Kate gasped as she struggled to comprehend who and what he was talking about. Surely he couldn't mean her? Not Mary Kate. Her mouth dropped open and her hand flew to her throat.

'You do know who and what I am talking about, don't you?'

Mary Kate shook her head, dumbfounded. But, like waves encroaching the shore, the truth gradually washed over her.

He continued regardless. 'The moment I saw you in my house, before you started to work for us, I thought it must be fate. What else could it be? You arrive in Liverpool and within seconds, just seconds, I happen to be driving past and I put you back together, and then the next evening you are here, in my home, and I am more drawn to you than I have been to anyone in my life. I want to see you, know you. I haven't been able to stop thinking about you all evening.'

He tapped his finger on the side of his head. 'You may have left my sight, but you have taken root in here. I'm talking about you, Mary Kate. It's you. I should be enraged, as the wronged husband, and yet the weight of my guilt, my feelings for you, the thoughts in my head, they are stronger than the anger I feel towards my wife.'

Mary Kate swallowed hard and thought she must be dreaming. This could not be happening. She tried again to speak, but there was no need for words as in a stride he was in front of her and holding both of her elbows. For this she was grateful because if he hadn't done that there was a strong possibility she'd have fallen over. She looked up, met his gaze and smiled. And then she began to giggle, and she couldn't stop.

'Are you laughing at me?' he asked, taking a step back. 'Have I got this all wrong? Is it not the same for you?' He sounded incredulous.

Mary Kate stopped laughing. 'No, no. I was laughing because I'm happy, because I cannot believe how this is all happening. It's like I'm at a film or something, watching someone else's story. I can hardly keep up with my own life, it's all moving so fast. Last week, I had never heard of you or you of me, and I'd never set foot in Liverpool even, and now... now this?'

She lifted her arms in a gesture of bemusement and he caught her hands and pulled her into him. His hands cradled her face and he looked deep into her eyes. 'This is real,' he whispered, his voice thick with emotion. 'This is what I've been missing for all of my life... You.'

She placed the tips of her fingers onto his lips and traced them, as though the words were written in an emotional braille and she had to feel them to understand them. Her brow furrowed. 'What do we do?' she asked and then answered her own question. 'There isn't anything we can do, is there?' Her eyes scanned his face, her knees weak.

'Yes, there is.' His hungry mouth found hers and he pulled her back into the shadow of the hedge.

She responded, equally desperate to feel his body close to hers, to taste his lips. She gasped as his hands slipped down her back and their bodies fused; he pulled her deep into him, his urgency and passion burning into her. She was drowning in the moment, her body reacting without reason or control. His hands slid through her hair and around her waist and as he moved from her lips to her neck, she tilted her head and groaned, surprising herself at the sound that had escaped from her.

Abruptly, he pushed her away. 'No, no, I must stop,'

he said as he took both of her hands into his and pressed them together. 'This isn't right, I can't do this to you. We have to stop.'

Mary Kate dragged herself back into the present and was about to protest, but she never got that far. She wished the earth would open up and swallow her as the voice of Lavinia Marcus spoke out.

'Well, well, well. Back so soon, Mary Kate.'

Chapter 23

Cat was hanging Michael's clothes out on the line when Linda popped her head over the wall.

'How is Michael now?'

Cat pegged his trousers by the bottoms. 'He's in a right state – he's never had his stomach pumped before, or been in a hospital or an ambulance. I think it's his pride that's hurt the most though, that the kids could swim and he couldn't.'

'No shame in that,' said Linda. 'I can't and neither can you. Our kids are lucky, being taken to the new baths by the school every week.'

'But these clothes, honest to God, I can't get the smell of the lake water out of them.'

'Send your kids round to me,' said Linda. 'They can sleep at ours. He'll need to go in the kids' bed – he's so tall. And mind, I said the kids' bed, not yours.'

Cat grinned. 'Go and wash your mouth out, Lin. The poor man has had a nasty shock. He's never worn a hospital gown before either and that's all he has until this lot are dry. They sent him back in the ambulance wearing that and an army blanket.'

Linda's head disappeared behind the wall only to reappear with her own basket of wet clothes to hang up. 'Well, one thing's for sure, Cat, no one's going to trust us to take the kids to the park ever again. And by the morning, if Michael spends the night at your house, you'll be the talk of the streets, and every woman around here will be as jealous as hell.'

Cat winked and grinned, enjoying the fact that a good-looking if slightly poorly man was spending the night in her house.

'Especially when you're walking like a cowboy in the morning, eh?'

Both women laughed.

Linda took a cigarette from behind her ear and then the matches from her apron pocket to light it. She'd already put her curlers back in and as she bent to take the flame, Cat saw the redness on her scalp where the hair was stretched.

As she puffed out, Linda said, 'Tell you what, I'm thinking of writing to Bee to ask her who she's sending over next and if I can have him. For God's sake, Captain Bob was a bit of a dish, in a homely way. She was bloody lucky. And you have the hunk lying on your sofa. Mary Kate is lovely too. I'll tell her, I don't mind if the fella she sends for me has a bit of a belly, as long as he's discreet.' Linda cackled as she picked up her washing basket.

When she'd finished, she said, 'Be careful, Cat. Don't go doing anything I wouldn't. The last thing you need is another mouth to feed, or a broken heart either, for that matter.'

'Oh, don't you worry about me.' Cat clipped the peg bag onto her apron waist tie. 'I'm fine. There's nothing life can throw at me that's worse than what I've already been through.'

Michael opened his eyes as Cat entered the room and untied her apron.

'How are you feeling now, love?' she asked as she threw it over the back of the kitchen chair.

The boys had fallen in, surfaced and swum to the island. Michael had failed to surface and it was only the quick action of the boys and the park keeper that had saved his life. He'd swallowed a great deal of water and a couple of fish by the feel of his stomach, which the doctor at the hospital told him had to be pumped out.

'It's my pride that's taken a beating,' he said. 'Those kids were smashing little swimmers, and me, I sank like a stone. Did me wallet survive the dunking?'

'It did.' Cat had laid out the wallet and its contents on the mantelpiece to dry. She was surprised at the number of twenty-pound notes. 'I thought everyone in Ireland was supposed to be poor,' she said.

Michael didn't answer. 'Take one of those notes and go and fetch us a bottle of porter and some food,' he said. 'Now they've pumped my stomach out, I could eat a horse.'

'Pie and chips?' asked Cat, smiling.

'Aye, and for all the kids too.'

'Well, this is becoming a habit,' said Cat. 'I'm going to send you back to Ireland with my address to hand out. If everyone who comes here gets hurt, needs help and buys chips for tea, I want them all to stop here first.'

Michael reached out and grabbed Cat's hand. 'I know now what good company our Mary Kate was in and I'm grateful for it. I want you to know that.'

'Oh, get away. You're Bee's family – she was my mate for years and that's what mates do.'

Half an hour later, Michael heard whoops of delight coming through the walls from next door. He assumed that meant Cat had just walked into Linda's with a card-board box full of chips and pies. A moment later, she was back in her own house with him.

'I was cold to the bone, so I hope you don't mind me lighting the fire,' he said.

'Don't be daft.' Cat plated up the pies and chips and poured two glasses of porter. 'A hot meal, a drink and a fire, that's what you need to put you right. Bottoms up.' She clinked her glass against his and flopped down next to him on the springy and very lumpy sofa.

As she put the glass to her lips, their eyes met and she knew absolutely what the night would hold. For the first time since Ben died, she was ready.

They were halfway down the bottle, empty plates discarded on the hearth, and she couldn't even remember what it was they were talking about when he set his glass down on the floor, leant back up, removed her glass from her fingers, placed it on the floor, took her face in both his hands and kissed her.

In the seconds it took him to place her glass down, her heart beat wildly, her breath shortened and the air in the room stood still. She kissed him back as passionately as he kissed her, and when he stood and reached down his hands, she took them and willingly allowed him to lead her.

They got as far as the stone floor by the kitchen door, and there, in the grip of a passion she'd never known – he in just the gown he'd been lent by the hospital, and she undressing in a flash – they made love.

'Oh God,' gasped Cat, 'that wasn't supposed to happen.'

'Wasn't it?' Michael grinned, and to her surprise, Cat found herself laughing long and hard, in a way she couldn't remember doing for many years.

'Come here,' he said as he helped her up off the floor, and immediately began kissing her neck. 'Let's try somewhere comfortable next time.'

Cat hesitated for a moment before she led him up the stairs. She really wasn't sure that her legs would hold her up all the way.

She lost count of how many times they made love during the night. She was intoxicated, high on her own sensuality; for the first time in three years, she felt like a woman, like Cat the person and not Cat the widow, the mother, the one who had to hold everything together. This special night was just for her.

It was as dawn broke and Michael snored gently, his naked limbs splayed out half on and half off her, that the sadness crept in. The first weak grey shafts of light fell onto the bed through the gap in the curtains and she turned her head to watch his sleeping face. The pain in her heart felt like a tightening band.

Ben filled her thoughts. He'd not been in her mind all that afternoon or through the night – his longest absence since the day of his death – but he'd slipped back in now, and there he was. The nights they'd shared in that bed, making babies, delivering babies, kissing and loving their babies, talking, worrying, planning into the small hours, hoping, dreaming of a better life. And here she was with no Ben, no better life, struggling hand to mouth, day to day, and now with another woman's husband in her bed.

She was swamped by a self-pity she couldn't dismiss. Life was so hard, so unbearably hard for every woman in Waterloo Street, but for her, the only woman on her own, it was doubly so. She had no one to send out to fetch in the coal, no one to carry back the bags of shopping, no one to help when a soot-fall came down the chimney, no one to bring home a wage and no one to share the middle of the night with. No physical warmth, no one to whom she could voice her darkest fears or with whom she could share the pleasures of the children. And this, with

Michael, had not made it better. It had brought home to her how alone she was. It had made it worse.

She lay on her side and sobbed.

Michael woke. 'Hey… There, there. What's going on? I wasn't that bad, was I?'

In between her sobs, she giggled and wiped at her eyes with the corner of the sheet. 'God, you make me laugh. No, it's not you. I was just remembering Ben and feeling a bit sorry for myself. It's nothing to do with you – really, I'm sorry.'

Michael scooped her pale, frail form into his dark, work-hardened arms, moved her onto her side and hugged her tight into his chest. He kissed first her eyelids, then her cheeks. 'You don't have to be saying sorry to me, not ever. I truly know how it is. Jesus, I've cried more nights than I can remember since Sarah died.'

'I never knew it would go on for so long,' she said in a voice so soft and so full of pain, he felt his own heart break a little in sympathy. 'They said it would get easier after a year.'

He kissed the side of her face as she spoke, not wanting to interrupt her, propped himself up on one elbow and looked down at her. 'Listen, I don't know who's been telling you all that fecking shite, but it won't ever stop. Well, it hasn't for me anyway. If it was real, if you were truly in love, I don't think it ever will. Oh aye, you can find distractions and you can learn to cope with it, but when it's just you and the night, here in your room, when the world is sleeping and no one knows or cares whether you're also sleeping or not, that's when it's the hardest of all. And you should let it out – there's no shame in a few tears.'

Not wanting to break the moment or move out of his arms, Cat lifted the corner of the sheet and blew her nose into it. 'But you... you married again, didn't you.'

'Aye. I'm a man, and the fact is, men are fecking useless without a woman. I had Mary Kate and Finn, I'd been almost out of my mind and I'd scared everyone half to death I was so wasted by the grief. But Rosie, she loved me. I know now that she always had. She helped look after the kids and she was always, well, just there. It was like coming in from a hard day at work, taking off the boots and putting on a pair of well-worn slippers when I married Rosie. It was all just... I suppose it was right. It just all fitted together.'

He glanced over towards the upended cardboard box that served as a table and the empty ashtray and box of matches next to it. 'I suppose I soaked my fags in the lake, did I?'

Cat laughed again. 'Yes, you did, but I bought you a packet from the pub when I got the port.'

'What a magnificent woman you are altogether,' Michael exclaimed. 'Imagine, if I wasn't a married man, I don't think I would be leaving here, so I wouldn't.'

Cat was kneeling on the bed, striking the match for Michael to light his cigarette, and as he exhaled and flopped back onto the pillow, he failed to catch the sadness in her eyes. In the morning he would be gone, and somewhere in the farthest corner of her mind had flickered the hope she hadn't known was there. That he might stay. That Mary Kate wouldn't want to leave Liverpool. That they would find a way to get to know one another better. But it had all truly been a fantasy.

As he smoked, they lay there in silence, his free hand slipped beneath her shoulders and stroking her arm. His own thoughts wandered to places that only made sense in his dreams. He imagined living there, in that house on Waterloo Street, and knew it was impossible. It was not his fate. His fate lay in Tarabeg, with his children and Rosie, and he would have to return there soon.

He turned to Cat and his eyes travelled over her face, feasting, drinking in her expression, her upturned nose, her now flushed cheekbones, her mussed hair, bruised lips and after-sex glow that radiated contentment. He smiled as her eyes questioned the intensity of his gaze.

The room was filling with morning sunlight as once more his hands began to roam over her aching, love-sore body. Bending his head, his tongue circled her nipples and as he moved his hands to her upturned knees, her legs fell wide and parted, yielding willingly as his fingers caressed and aroused her once more. She felt insatiable, that he could do that forever and she would never want him to stop.

Halting, he leant over and kissed her nose.

She smiled back up at him. 'What?' she whispered.

He stared deep into her eyes, his expression altered, sombre, and as her image burnt onto his memory, they both luxuriated in the moment. It felt as though time had stopped. Her head was light and almost dizzy and nothing else in the entire world mattered but the two of them.

The church bells rang out for first mass as the clock struck six o'clock, exactly as they did in Tarabeg every morning. Michael turned towards the window and the spire towering over the rooftops, and the peal of the bells transported him all the way across the Irish Sea and landed his thoughts back in Tarabeg.

Cat felt him slipping away. Stretching up, she kissed his nose and pulled him back to her, smiling, beckoning, imploring. She lifted her head and put the tip of her tongue between his lips, reached up with her hands and turned his face to hers.

He was back. He kissed her lips and neck, and as he lowered his mouth to explore her body, with the bells ringing in the distance and the two of them feeling as close to heaven as mortals could get, they both knew it would be for the very last time.

Chapter 24

Rosie alighted from the bus in Ballycroy with Keeva at her side.

Keeva linked her arm through Rosie's. 'There is only one bus back,' she said, 'so we have time, but we can't miss it or Tig will be out of his mind with the worry. He doesn't like me leaving Tarabeg unless he's there to look after me. Do you know which house it is?'

'I don't,' said Rosie. 'I haven't a clue. And do you know, it just occurred to me I don't know anyone who would. Captain Bob and Bee were always very secretive.'

'Well, there's the pub, Carey's. Everyone in Tarabeg says that Carey's is where you find everything out. Seems to me that will be a good place to start.'

'Do you mind walking into a pub in broad daylight?' asked Rosie.

Keeva laughed. 'Rosie, I live in a pub. Come on, you follow me.'

Twenty minutes later, Rosie and Keeva were walking

with confidence to the address they'd been given. But when they reached the gate they both stopped dead in their tracks. Before them stood the most ominous-looking cottage either had ever seen. It had dirty windows, flaking paint, and dead flowers in the window box, and the front was overgrown with tufts of wild grass and a tree that clung dejectedly to the wall above the front door. The cottage faced the sea and was next to a filleting shed.

'This can't be it,' said Keeva. 'He was always so particular.'

Rosie looked at the piece of paper in her hand. 'It is. This is it.'

Both stood and for a moment considered walking away.

'Shall we go?' said Keeva, already taking a step back.

'No, don't be daft, we can't come all this way and not ask. What would we say to Bee?'

'Nothing. She doesn't even know we're here.'

'Leave it to me, I'll do the talking,' said Rosie.

'That's fine by me,' said Keeva. 'After what the pot man in Carey's has just told us about Captain Bob's daughter and her affliction, I'm quite keen to get that bus home as soon as possible. He said we wouldn't get through the door anyway.' She tightened her grip on the handbag Josie had lent her for the day, as if she was worried it might be ripped away from her at any moment.

Rosie was reading the roughly scribbled map the landlord had given them, hoping beyond the odds that they'd taken a wrong turn. 'Aye, but I'm more worried about what he said about Captain Bob and the fact that no one has seen him since the day of the funeral. Do you think he knew that everyone other than his eldest daughter had already left for America?'

Keeva shook her head in disbelief and dismay. 'Bee never said. And surely, if he's gone away somewhere, he would have called to see Bee and tell her. The landlord said he was in a bad way altogether, keen to leave. I'm worried for Bee. There is something not quite right and I want to know what it is, for Bee's sake as much as his.' Her hair, neatly tied back into a tail any pony would envy, swished behind her as she looked from Rosie to the house and back again.

'Right, well, here goes then. With a bit of luck, he might be in there and be wanting to come back with us. Imagine! Wouldn't that be just grand.' Rosie took a deep breath and pushed back her shoulders. 'Come on then, let's get on with it. We'll find nothing good stood here gawping.'

The gate was broken and to open it Rosie had to lift it and shove hard. It creaked in protest, opening just enough to allow her and Keeva to squeeze through.

'God, when was the last time someone came through that?' hissed Keeva, hesitantly following Rosie up the path. As she looked up at the lone upstairs window she saw a net curtain fall into place. Their arrival had been noted by someone.

'Will I knock?' whispered Rosie as they reached the door.

'How else will we get in? It might be locked,' Keeva whispered back.

'Yes, but there might be some benefit in an element of surprise, do you not think? If we just step inside, like?'

'Rosie, you aren't in a fecking film. Just open the door. I don't like this place, it gives me the creeps. No wonder he upped and left for Liverpool.'

As Keeva pulled her cardigan tighter across her chest, Rosie reached out to the latch. But before her hand could make contact, the door was flung open and there before them stood the most forbidding woman they had ever laid eyes on. Her hair resembled a bird's nest perched on the top of her head, pins protruding like twigs and escaped wisps forming an unruly halo. Her face was round and ruddy and she was dressed from top to toe in a high-necked, long-sleeved black dress, tied at the waist with a strip of leather. Her eyes were narrow and she squinted at them, all the while keeping one hand on the door, rocking it back and forth as though at any moment she would slam it in their faces, as fast as she had opened it.

There was a crow on the tiled roof. Surveying the scene below, it lifted its head and cawed a warning, sending a shiver down Keeva's spine. She looked behind her to check had anyone seen them turn into the short boreen that led to the house. She could still see the main road, such as it was. It was empty; no one had seen them. Her heart pounded and she wondered why she'd agreed to come. But of course she knew the answer. Bee's pain was as visible as if she was wearing it for all to see, and Keeva and Rosie were determined that her pride would not prevent them from finding out just what had happened to Captain Bob.

'This is a house of mourning. What do you want? Who are you?' the voice barked.

Rosie recoiled. The woman's tone was aggressive, not at all like that of someone in mourning, and her wide-set eyes and flat features bore no trace of a welcoming smile. Rosie stammered her response. 'I'm sorry for your troubles. I am enquiring about the whereabouts of a work friend of my husband's – Captain Bob. We haven't seen him for some time and we are calling to see is he about and well?'

The woman peered intently into Rosie's face. 'I'm his daughter, Nell. I can tell you all you need to know. Are you *her*? Because if you are, you can get off our land, and if you don't, I'll be taking the gun to you, I will, and I know how.'

Rosie glanced nervously at Keeva, who slipped her arm through Rosie's in a gesture of protection and unity.

'Am I who?' asked Rosie with more confidence than she felt.

'The woman from Liverpool. Are you her? Because if you are, you can't take my daddy – he has to stay, because everyone has gone now, so go away, will you.' She reached behind the door and brought out a long-barrelled shotgun, the type kept on farms for shooting wildlife and pigs.

Keeva squeezed Rosie's arm and moved a step closer to her side. Captain Bob had clearly kept Bee's identity secret from his wife and daughters, and they instantly understood why.

'I've never been to Liverpool,' said Rosie. 'My husband is there though.' She felt inclined to bless herself and then it dawned on her that she wasn't telling a lie; right now, Michael was in Liverpool. 'He wants to know if Captain Bob is well enough as they haven't seen anything of him. He was expected back to work, you know. How is he? Will I be giving my husband good news?'

She didn't know where the words came from; they were unplanned and she was almost impressed at how easily they fell from her lips.

Nell appeared satisfied with Rosie's answer. Her gaze travelled the full length of the two women, both of whom were well dressed. Rosie had an air about her that took the sting out of Nell's aggressiveness.

'Why aren't you in Liverpool?' she asked.

Rosie and Keeva could both tell there was something not quite right. Nell was the afflicted one. Then Rosie had a brainwave; she decided to play the authority card. 'I'm a schoolteacher,' she said. 'My husband works in Liverpool, but I can't leave my job here.'

'A headmistress,' added Keeva, straightaway understanding what Rosie was up to. Both left out the fact that they were from Tarabeg. Rosie and Keeva's instincts were in perfect accord and they had no need to confer.

On hearing that, Nell immediately set down the gun and opened the door wide, in fear and awe at having such a person as her visitor. 'You can step inside,' she said. 'Don't be standing in the doorway now in case anyone sees you and thinks I have no manners and left a headmistress on the doorstep. But you can't be seeing Captain Bob. He's taken to his bed with grief since Mammy's death and he won't be going back to work, or anywhere else for that matter. He doesn't want to. He can't. He has to stay here with me now.'

Rosie and Keeva took in the appearance of the cottage as she spoke. It was as dirty and untidy on the inside as it was outside. Although the day was bright, the thickly ingrained weather and salt smears on the windows meant the light struggled to reach into the room, creating a gloomy and oppressive atmosphere. The truckle bed near the fire was unmade and the furniture was sparse. In the corner near the scullery sink stood some fifty dark brown, long-necked bottles which Keeva recognised as having once held porter. She guessed they would be from the wake. The branches of the overgrown tree pushed against the pane next to the door, making a high-pitched screeching noise as they swayed, setting Keeva's nerves on edge. They both looked towards a hissing from the fire grate, where two peat bricks smouldered in the hearth. A pot simmered on the black cast-iron griddle, emitting a smell of cabbage and potatoes.

'We are both sorry for your troubles,' said Rosie. 'Was

it a shock to you or had you been nursing your mammy at home?' She felt the best way was to humour Nell, to try and appeal to her better nature, if she had one.

'It was the biggest shock of me life. We was here, peeling the potatoes, and then she was on the floor. She died in the hospital.'

Rosie tutted. 'That must have been an awful shock for you all. Are you all alone?' She already knew the answers to her questions from the pot man but was trying to coax Nell into admitting that she was there by herself. Bee had told her there was more than one daughter, but she had no idea how many or what their names were.

'Gone,' hissed Nell, her face darkening. 'They all ran off, every one of them, as soon as they got the chance. Helped each other, they did, without Mammy's say-so. They went to Daddy's sister and she won't send them back, even though I've written and asked her.'

'Oh dear, that's a shame for you,' said Rosie. Before the words had left her mouth, they heard a bang from upstairs. 'Who's that?' she asked gently. 'Is that Captain Bob?'

Nell looked to the ceiling. 'It may be. He can't have visitors though. He can wait for me until you've gone. He's looking after me now – he has to. The priest says that if I'm on my own, I'll have to go to the asylum in the convent, and Mammy told me it's a bad place. She always said to me that if I ran away like the others, she would find me and put me there.'

Nell had become very distressed as she spoke. Her nose was running and the tears poured from her eyes.

'You look exhausted, Nell. Would you like me to make you some tea?' asked Rosie. 'It must have been awful for you, having to deal with everything all by yourself. You must be run off your feet as well, with your loss, and your daddy needing so much help too.' She placed her arm around Nell's shoulders, guided her to the chair beside the fire and eased her down.

Nell stared into the fire and began talking. 'Took the boat, they did, and not one of them told me or Mammy when they were off. Mammy was told by the Regans – their daughter left on the same boat, and they knew all about it, but they didn't tell us a thing until the boat had sailed and it was too late. I thought they might have gone to Liverpool. Could you ask your husband has he seen any Tooleys? They might not have gone to America at all. Daddy wants to go away again, but he can't leave me on my own.'

Keeva gestured at the ceiling with her finger and mouthed to Rosie, 'You talk, I'll look.'

Rosie spoke in a brighter and louder voice as Keeva silently depressed the latch on the door that led to the stairs. 'Oh look, you have the mint drying by the fire – did you grow it in the garden? It's my favourite, mint tea. We sell it in the shop too. Bridget said it's the best thing for people with gastric problems, to aid the digestion.' She clanged the kettle onto the griddle, making as much noise as possible while Keeva climbed the first stairs.

'What shop?' said Nell, pulling her gaze from the fire. 'I thought your husband was a seaman like Daddy.'

'Oh, he is, he is. It's my relatives' shop. Here, let me make you some mint tea. Should we take some up to your daddy?'

'No!' Nell was not to be diverted. 'I will take him some when you've gone. You can't see Daddy.'

'Of course, forgive me. You have a lot on here – it isn't my place to disturb your routine. But I'm so glad I came, because now I can tell my husband that all is well. Here you go, drink the tea and take a rest.'

She held out the tin mug full of mint leaves and boiling water. It was obvious that all was not well in this house and her heart felt as though it was gripped in a hand of ice. Danger was nearby, but she didn't know where or in what form it would appear.

'Did you manage to get to the hospital yourself before your mammy died?' she asked, sitting herself down in the chair opposite Nell, who appeared to have forgotten about Keeva.

Rosie hoped Keeva would hurry back down soon or else she'd be running out of questions to keep Nell distracted. But Keeva had other things on her mind as she entered the room space at the top of the stairs.

'Oh Mother of God,' she exclaimed when she opened the door.

The smell hit her in the face with the force of a slap and she slammed the palm of her hand to her mouth in an attempt to filter out the worst of it. She was frozen to the spot, unable to move as her eyes adjusted to both the light and the sight before her.

Thinner than she remembered him, Captain Bob looked towards her, a shrunken man with bloodshot, pleading eyes.

'Keeva, is that you? Help me,' he gasped. 'God in heaven, help me, please.'

Joe Malone paced up and down outside the airport terminal, waiting for his taxi as instructed. Just as he was about to give up and go in search of a telephone to call Miss Carroll, he spotted a pale blue 1935 Austin 7 motoring towards him with the top down. It was almost too late when he realised that whoever it was who was driving – hidden beneath goggles and a hat tied down with a headscarf – would not be able to stop in time. With a single leap he saved his own life by diving four feet to the side. Unfortunately, his landing was not so graceful: his suitcase hit the corner of the pavement, taking him with it, and its lock snapped, spilling his belongings in front of him.

Teresa Gallagher clambered out of the car as fast as her stiff legs and her stick would allow. 'What were you doing, standing in the way like that?' she said as she attempted to crouch down on the ground beside him. 'Do ye have a death wish or what?'

It was clearly going be too much of a struggle to lower

herself any further, so instead she gripped the top of her stick with both hands and held herself steady in an upright position. 'I'm sorry, I can't get down to help ye,' she said. 'I can't walk too well.'

Joe was already up on his feet, scooping his belongings back into his case. 'You can't drive too well either,' he snapped.

'Well now, there aren't many who hold that opinion in Tarabeg,' she lied. 'Would ye be wanting a lift or not, because I would be saying that if ye do, a little more politeness would be required. 'Tis a long drive and I won't be looking forward to sitting next to a scold like yourself all that way. A Malone, are you? I think I can tell.'

Teresa understated her point. She wasn't about to tell this young man that the reason she'd forgotten to brake was that the sight of him had transported her back over sixty years and for the briefest moment she'd thought it was the young Daedio standing there. The man she had carried a torch for but whom Annie had won. This was no chancer or murderer; this man really was a great-great-nephew of Daedio Malone.

Joe flushed with embarrassment. He brushed the dust off his trousers and, forcing the lid of his suitcase shut, his belongings still spilling out of the sides, he held out his hand to Teresa. 'I do apologise. Joe Malone at your service, ma'am.'

He wondered why it was he was apologising and why, under her unflinching gaze, he felt as if he'd just done something very wrong indeed. It was like he was back in the classroom.

Teresa belted along the lanes in Father Jerry's car, all the while extracting as much information as she could from the young man sitting next to her. That didn't stop her from waving at other car drivers and bicycle riders as they passed. Her right hand was off the wheel more than it was on it. When she raised her hand in greeting yet again, this time to an elderly gentleman on a bike, Joe couldn't resist making a comment.

'Gosh, do you know every person in all of Ireland?' he asked.

Teresa stuck her hand out to signal as she turned onto the road to Mayo. 'Of course not,' she said. 'Only those worth knowing.'

'Oh, right.' Joe pushed his hair back off his face. 'I hope you don't mind me saying, it's just that you've waved to every single person we've passed so far.'

Teresa shot him a sharp sideways look. 'Sure, why would I not. They are only being polite, saying hello. Do you not do that in America?'

Joe shook his head, knowing how the answer would make America look.

'Where would you be staying?' she asked. 'I take it that's where you will want to be dropped off?'

Joe smiled. 'Oh, it's all the way to Tarabeg for me. I was told the place isn't exactly busy and that I'd be able to find a room in the village.'

Teresa laughed. 'Well, you might have, if the salmon weren't in and the village wasn't full of fishermen. You won't be finding anything in Tarabeg. There's no hotel as such.'

He looked crestfallen.

'I'm afraid Galway will be the best bet.'

'No.' His voice was firm. He turned to face her, his jaw jutting out, his eyes steely with resolve. He wore no hat, which surprised her. 'Miss Gallagher, I have come all this way to see Tarabeg and to carry out my daddy's dying wishes. He never planned to see Galway. He only spoke of the place his daddy had told him he must return to one day, but he died before he ever got the chance. I don't care if I have to sleep on the street, I am going to Tarabeg, for my pa.'

For a reason he couldn't explain, a lump came to his throat. He turned back to look at the road and a group of passing schoolchildren waved to him.

Teresa had heard the break in his voice and instantly felt sorry for him. She couldn't imagine not being able to watch the sun rise over the Taramore River and across the Nephin Beg when she woke up of a morning. She was ashamed of herself for having tried to trick someone out of visiting the one village on earth that was closest to heaven itself. 'Why would I want a holiday,' she asked her sister every time she tried to persuade her to visit her nieces and nephews in America, 'when I live in the best place on earth? Wouldn't it just be a waste of my time and money? Sure, I'd only be disappointed, and who wants to pay for that?'

Joe coughed, and, removing his handkerchief from his pocket, blew his nose. The metal corner of his leather suitcase dug into his knee and he pulled it upright and rested his chin on the top as he waved back to the schoolchildren.

Teresa was swamped with guilt. The matron who had never married and had never mourned the lack of a husband but had always wondered what it would mean to have a son felt a tug on her heartstrings for the tired and lost young man sitting next to her.

Annie's warnings or not, decoy plans, blockading whin and fierce-looking bull notwithstanding, Teresa Gallagher was taking this young man to see Daedio. But she needed to talk to Daedio and the others first. 'The teacher, Declan Feenan, is away on his holidays,' she said. 'I have the keys to his house – he won't mind one bit if you stay there. You can eat with us at the presbytery tonight and then I'll drop you off. And tomorrow I will take you to see the people I think are your family. How does that sound?'

He grinned. 'Are you sure Mr Feenan won't mind?'

Teresa was surprised. 'Why would he mind? He's not sleeping in the bed himself – of course he won't.'

She crunched the gears as she turned a corner and hit a rock beside the verge, sending the car into a swerve right across the road. Joe grabbed the top of the door.

As she straightened and regained control, she shouted,

'You, young man, are the living image of your relatives and you have every right to know who they are. They will have a bed for you too, once they've met you and I've explained everything to them. I could tell who you were the minute I saw you standing outside the airport. Daedio Malone is your great-great-uncle. He lives on Tarabeg Farm and that's where I'll be taking you.'

Keeva crept across the room, unable to remove her hand from her face in case she made a noise that would alert Nell downstairs.

Captain Bob was tied to a chair next to the window. The smell in the room was almost overpowering. 'Keeva,' his voice croaked in a coarse whisper. 'Thank God you've come. Is Bee with you?'

'Did Nell do this?' whispered Keeva, horrified, her eyes roaming over the chair.

Captain Bob could move his legs, and there was enough rope to allow him to half stand, but he couldn't go far because both arms were firmly tied down.

'Untie me,' he croaked. 'She did it while I was asleep, the night after the funeral. I told her I was leaving the following morning and that I'd be coming back for her, but she didn't believe me. She trusts no one and she's terrified of being left on her own here, in case the priest comes with the guard to take her away. Is Bee with you?'

Keeva's eyes locked onto his as she shook her head. His

beard was as long and unkempt as his hair. His clothes were dirty and food-stained and he wore no socks or shoes.

'For the love of God,' she whispered, her eyes filling with tears. Wasting no time, she bent over him and with shaking hands, trying to make as little noise as possible, she began to pull at the ropes that bound him.

Downstairs, Rosie continued to jump from topic to topic, talking fast, trying to hold Nell's attention.

'Is there anything at all I can be doing to help you?' she said. 'Do you have a message from Captain Bob for me to send? Maybe if you tell him I'm here, he might want to say a few words.' She hoped her voice still sounded natural and not abnormally loud.

Nell shot Rosie a suspicious look. 'You don't have to be telling anyone I can't manage. I do. I don't want anyone calling here to the house.'

Rosie knew that Nell was tolerating her presence because, like all women in Ireland, she was afraid of authority and wanted to make sure that Rosie, as a headmistress, would see her on her best behaviour. She needed Rosie to believe she could cope. The Church and the schools, the priests and the teachers, operated in concert with each other, using fear to control and dominate the lives of everyone in rural Ireland, especially women. A woman had no status and could be disappeared overnight. A letter from the priest could mean a packed suitcase and fifty years of hard labour in a laundry for a woman deemed to have transgressed in some obscure or even unexplained way.

'I'm needing nothing,' said Nell. 'Daddy is staying now – you can tell your husband that. My job now Mammy has gone is to look after this house and Daddy.' A startled look suddenly crossed her face. 'The lady… the other lady, where is she?' She looked to the front door and began to rise from her chair.

'Oh, she went outside to find the midden,' said Rosie, her eyes darting to the door that led to the staircase.

Suddenly they were both alerted to the sound of clattering feet on the stairs. With a roar, Captain Bob almost fell through the door. He was finding it difficult to walk, having not moved his legs for days. 'Where's Bee?' he asked as he staggered towards Rosie and grabbed onto her arms.

'She didn't know where you were – she thought you'd left her.'

Sobs filled the air and they all turned towards the chair, where Nell was rocking and crying.

Rosie put her hand on Captain Bob's arm. 'She's scared,' she said. 'Don't shout at her. She's scared of being left on her own. Let me talk to her. Bee wouldn't want to see her like this. She is your responsibility now that her mammy has died, but we can sort that out. We're going to have to come back for her. She can live in Angela's cottage – it's still empty. I know Bee would agree, and besides, she would have more company in Tarabeg.'

Keeva chimed in. 'She can't have much company here or someone would have noticed you being tied up like that.'

'No one comes here,' said Captain Bob. 'Her mammy

drove everyone away, using nothing more than the lash of her tongue.'

Rosie knelt down by the side of Nell's chair and laid both of her hands on top of Nell's. 'Nell...' she whispered. 'Nell, stop crying now. I have news for you. You are coming to Tarabeg with us. We will come back for you in the next few days. Your daddy has to come with us, but don't be afraid, we'll be back. In the car next time, and you will come too.'

It took over an hour before Nell was properly calm and reassured of their intentions.

'I'm sorry, Daddy,' she said to Captain Bob. 'I was scared to be on my own and without any money. I was scared the priest would come and send me away.'

Captain Bob hugged his daughter. 'I don't blame you. You didn't understand,' he said. 'But for feck's sake, Nell, why did you tie my arms when I was sleeping? Where in the name of God did you learn to do that?'

'Mammy,' she replied. 'Mammy did it to me when you left, to stop me coming after you.'

The room fell quiet as Captain Bob stood and embraced his daughter once again. 'Nell, oh, Nell,' he said, 'you were always the best.'

'We will be calling into the priest to tell him we're coming back for you,' said Rosie, 'so don't you be worrying about him.' And although she was concerned for Nell, her heart sang at the prospect of reuniting Captain Bob and Bee.

Keeva found a bicycle in the filleting shed, dusted it down and made her way back into Ballycroy to see was there a taxi to take them home, but there was none to be had. Despite being a larger village than Tarabeg, booking a taxi was still a major event that required much discussion and preparation, via the postmistress, who was as interested in the affairs of others as Mrs Doyle.

'The bus it is then,' said Rosie, exhausted and disappointed. She had spent the time clearing the scullery and preparing a meal from what there was in the press, while Captain Bob dug up some of the potatoes, cabbages and carrots his wife had planted.

Keeva leant the bike against the wall and lifted a brown-paper packet out of the basket.

'What's that?' asked Rosie.

'I called into the butcher's and picked up a packet of rashers, a couple of trotters and half a chicken for Nell, in case there was nothing in, and the last loaf of boxty bread in the shop.'

'God love you. I can put the chicken in the stew pot I've just made up for her, the trotters will keep on the cold shelf in the press until tomorrow and I can cook the rashers now for her with some fried potatoes.'

'You're making my mouth water,' said Captain Bob. 'With so little food in, I was half thinking of staying and sending you on with a message for Bee. But Nell is well provisioned now.'

Nell had been unresponsive at first, but she'd warmed

to Rosie's encouragement and had helped her with the cleaning. All the time, Rosie spoke to her of Tarabeg and Angela's cottage, praying in her quiet moments that they could make it work.

They left behind a calmer, smiling Nell, a cottage filled with the smell of chicken roasting and a promise that they would be back for her before the week was out.

Chapter 25

Mary Kate opened her eyes with a start and instantly remembered that something was very wrong. The sash window was pushed up as far as it would reach, and above the deafening dawn chorus of the birds in the garden outside she could hear the squeal of brakes from the bus at the end of the road, the rattle of bottles in the milk cart and the clip-clopping of its horse's hooves as it moved along Duke's Avenue. A feeling of foreboding washed over her. The world in which all was well and perfectly normal suddenly slipped away as the events of the previous evening pierced her consciousness. She gasped with the force of it. 'Oh God in heaven, no.' She closed her eyes and pulled the covers over her head.

Deidra's room was above hers and Mary Kate heard the thud of her feet landing on her bedside rug, then the padding along as she crossed the room and headed for the bathroom. Deidra never missed the 6 a.m. Mass, even when she'd been to a dance the evening before. It was the one promise to her mammy she'd kept since she left home. She was back in the house for ten past seven to prepare breakfast and start the day.

Deidra had shown both surprise and concern for Mary Kate's soul when Mary Kate had refused to join her. 'You can't be missing Mass,' she'd said. 'What would yer mammy say if she knew? Oh, Mary Kate, just because you've left Ireland doesn't mean you've left your soul behind, you know.'

A weight settled on Mary Kate's heart. She swung her legs out of bed and decided that everything that was happening must be because she hadn't been to Mass since she left home. Tossing back the bedcovers, she dressed hurriedly and intercepted Deidra at the bottom of the stairs.

'I'm coming with you,' she said.

'Oh, well now, isn't that nice. And no wonder, I would be saying, after what I saw last night.' Deidra sniffed and moved on ahead of Mary Kate and down the stairs.

As they rounded the street corner, Deidra pulled on her white cotton summer gloves and the girls fell into step, walking quickly, almost marching, their shoes tapping briskly on the pavement.

'Well, are you going to be telling me what happened last night then? Because you sure as hell weren't waiting for me at the bus stop when I got back, and what I saw was a right commotion going on in the Marcuses' driveway. Mrs O'Keefe was making herself cocoa in the back kitchen and she was very surprised indeed that you weren't with me and wanted me to be going back out to look for you.'

Their feet pounded harder as the church bells rang out and tugged them along. Mary Kate's hand flew to her mouth. 'Oh no,' she wailed, not breaking her step.

Deidra shot her a sideways glance and leant over. Although there was no one near them, she hissed her next words, in the belief that if sinful words were whispered, God might not hear them. 'I saw it all as I walked back from the bus stop, and you right in the middle of it all. What the feck was going on?'

Mary Kate stammered. 'Well—'

'Well what? I saw Mrs Marcus giving out in the middle of the driveway and I could hardly believe my eyes. She's a different sort from most of the women around Fullmore Park – she really is a one. Always out in the taxis and the cars. Him, the poor man, looked lost, he did. And then I saw you. Did they send for you or what?'

Mary Kate took a deep breath. So Deidra hadn't seen her and Dr Marcus, a married man, kissing in the bright moonlight. She was almost faint with relief. 'No, I was walking past, to come and meet you, and they called me over. They, er, lost the dog. He got out and the boys were upset and I helped them to look for him and then Mrs Marcus blamed Dr Marcus and they had one almighty row.'

Mary Kate didn't know where the words had come from, and without Deidra noticing, she blessed herself.

They turned sharply between the tall red sandstone pillars and up the steps to the church doors. Mary Kate wondered if they would crash shut behind her as she stepped over the threshold of God's holy house.

'Well, what a state of affairs, and fancy them involving you like that. I swear to God, the people back home have better manners, so they do.' Deidra didn't like to be late and hurried towards her usual seat without turning around. She dipped her knee to the cross, slipped into the pew and knelt down.

Mary Kate was pale with shock. Her eyes stung and filled with tears and she wondered if that was because she'd become unaccustomed to the holy smoke. She entwined her fingers in her lap, as much to stop them from shaking as anything else. 'Oh Lord, what have I done?' were the only prayers she managed to say, followed by, 'Please forgive me, Father, for I have sinned.' As she sat on the carved wooden pew and looked up to the statue of Our Lady, the words of the sermon floated over her head. A terrible truth pounded to the beat of her pulse. She had wanted him to kiss her. She had enjoyed him kissing her. She had kissed him back, and in those few seconds she'd felt as though she might die from happiness.

Her head was spinning, consumed with thoughts of Dr Marcus and his words to his wife. As the priest spoke, she drifted back to the previous evening. The solid, peaceful silence in the church gave her the space and time. Even though she was surrounded by people, their shuffle of prayer cushions, their sniffles and coughs, and the chanting from the altar, she was entirely alone because God was not speaking to Mary Kate.

'You have no idea about right and wrong, Lavinia,' Dr Marcus had snapped at his wife, 'so I don't think you're one to make any judgements here.'

Lavinia Marcus had folded her arms, placed one foot in front of the other and rocked her hips as she sneered at Mary Kate. 'Oh I am, Nicholas. I am. And I know this, that if you wanted to deceive your wife, you could have chosen someone with a bit of class and not a cheap girl from the bogs.'

Lavinia Marcus's words had stung so hard, Mary Kate had felt as though she'd been slapped across the face. She took a sharp intake of breath.

'How dare you.' Dr Marcus's arms were ramrod straight, down by his sides, and his fists were clenched. His words sounded controlled, but his voice shook with anger. 'Do not dare to stand there and judge this kind-hearted girl as though you are some form of angel. You are so lacking in morality, you're not fit to polish her shoes. You, Lavinia, belong in the gutter. You disgust me.'

It was Lavinia Marcus's turn to look surprised. She had clearly assumed that her husband would be mortified at having been caught kissing a service maid from Ireland. She seemed to be expecting him to grovel or at least express contrition. She blinked and the smile fell from her face. 'Nicholas, you don't seem to be aware what's going on here. I've just caught you red-handed, you stupid man. Have you lost your mind?' She gave a thin, shrill laugh.

'Have I? I don't know, Lavinia. Has it been lost for some time?' He lunged towards his wife and she stepped backwards in shock. 'I think I lost my mind when I allowed you to behave like less than a mother to our two boys, less than a wife to me, less than a decent human being. You are a self-obsessed woman, Lavinia, interested only in yourself.'

Lavinia Marcus let out another piercing, incredulous laugh. 'Me, self-obsessed? Not you, the precious doctor who's so desperate for attention he cannot tear himself away from his patients, ever? Me? Oh, don't make me laugh, Nicholas. Now get upstairs and we can discuss this further once you've explained yourself.' She had regained her confidence and was wielding her words like a boxer dishing out punches. 'As for you, madam…' She pointed to Mary Kate. 'I shall be on the telephone to the agency first thing in the morning and I shall be telling them exactly what has happened here tonight, you little trollop. You will never find work in Liverpool again.'

Mary Kate gasped, the horror of the situation sinking in. 'No!' she said. 'I haven't done anything.' She started to shake and, despite herself, tears began to roll down her cheeks.

'You haven't done anything?' Lavinia Marcus was on the attack. 'My husband might be gutless, but he knows where his priorities lie – he has his wife, his family and his reputation to worry about. He will come to his senses.

As for you...' She rolled her eyes in disgust at Mary Kate. 'I saw you from the landing window. Sneaking into the driveway, walking up to my husband at this time of night – you knew exactly what you were up to, didn't you – and then pulling him into the bushes. What were you after: a bun in the oven, a means to a financial end, a bit of blackmail? I've heard all about girls like you – there are homes for the likes of you, spewing out unwanted babies all over Liverpool. I am far from stupid, my girl. I know your type. You were after money, thought you could use my husband to change your family fortunes, didn't you? Now get off my driveway. And as I said, first thing in the morning, I am on the telephone.'

Dr Marcus reached out and grabbed his wife's wrists.

'Get off me, Nicholas, you're hurting me,' she squealed, shaking her arms and attempting to take a step back.

'I read a letter today, Lavinia,' he said and his voice was so low, Mary Kate could only just make out the words.

His wife appeared not to be listening as she tried in vain to break free from his grip.

'It was from Robin, my partner. If you pick up any phone tomorrow, I shall be straight round to his house and showing the letter to Susan. Would you like that?'

Lavinia stopped her struggling and stared at her husband. 'You would not dare,' she spluttered. The fight went out of her and she stood stock still. 'The letter...' she gasped. 'What letter? What are you talking about?'

Even Mary Kate could see the way her mind was

working. She was trying to remember if and where she'd left any incriminating evidence.

'The letter in which Robin talks about you being naked in his bed,' he replied, again calmly and void of emotion. Then he added the words that made Lavinia Marcus look at him in horror. 'Mary Kate has read it too. We both have, together.'

If he had slapped her across the face, she couldn't have looked more stunned. Her knees appeared to be only just holding her up and she seemed to shrink before Mary Kate's eyes.

'Yes, Mary Kate and I. You say or do one thing to harm her and she has my permission to make sure every home on this avenue knows exactly what kind of woman you are. Do you understand? Robin will be a ruined man and as you are his patient, I will make sure he gets struck off for misconduct. A ruined man. He will never work again. You attempt to destroy Mary Kate and I will bring it back to you, ten times over. When I have finished with Robin, I will ensure I post the letter straight to your parents. Make threats, Lavinia, and you're on dangerous ground.'

'You wouldn't. You wouldn't dare.' She glanced furiously back from Mary Kate to her husband and it was obvious she was weighing up the consequences of her actions.

'And then...'

Mary Kate looked at Dr Marcus, who appeared to be thinking on his feet.

'And then I shall submit the letter as evidence when I divorce you for adultery. You will have nothing left, Lavinia, and neither will Robin. Harm this young woman and you will regret it.'

'Oh, Nicholas...' Lavinia seemed to be crying. 'Let's go inside and talk about this, please, darling.' She ran her hand down her husband's arm and looked pleadingly into his eyes.

Even with her minimal experience of the world, Mary Kate could see that Lavinia Marcus was acting.

'You wouldn't want to upset dear Susan and cause problems for her and Robin, would you? And besides, we would be the talk of Fullmore Park, and the children's lives would be ruined.'

Mary Kate saw him hesitate at the mention of the boys. So did his wife, and she seized on it.

'Nicholas...' Her voice had altered from scathing to pleading in a heartbeat. 'We have both just made a terrible mistake, a misjudgement. We can sort this out, the two of us. None of this will make any difference to you and me, to our family. We are special, aren't we, my darling? Nothing, absolutely not a single moment with Robin, can compare to what we have. He was just a dalliance, darling – nothing that we can't put right with a little effort.'

Mary Kate's heart constricted as her emotions did battle. Lavinia Marcus had slipped her hands around the back of her husband's neck and was attempting to move his lips closer to hers.

'Come along, darling, let's go to bed and make up after this dreadful row.'

For a brief moment, Mary Kate thought she was about to witness Dr Marcus kissing his wife, minutes after he'd kissed her, her own lips still tender from the pressure of his. She could smell his expensive musky aftershave on her own skin, she could taste him, and she felt sick to the pit of her stomach.

Dr Marcus responded with what sounded like a growl. In hindsight, as Mary Kate sat there in church, picking over each minute of the scene, she realised it had been a growl of anger. She was grateful to him for that, and for having preserved her own dignity in the presence of his wife. He took hold of his wife's hands and with a single tug broke them from their clasp around his neck and pushed her backwards. Lavinia Marcus resisted, tried to reach his lips with hers. It was the act of a desperate woman. The heel of her evening shoe snapped and the sound filled the air like a gunshot as she staggered backwards.

'Do not play games with me, Lavinia. I don't want to return to our bedroom with you ever again. I will see Mary Kate safely home. Come here, my lovely,' he said to Mary Kate and as he turned, his face filled with concern at the sight of her. She was visibly shaking.

Mary Kate saw the disbelief etched on his wife's face. Her sneer reappeared, but she was blocked from Mary Kate's view by Dr Marcus, who reached out his hand to steady her.

Mary Kate remained frozen to the spot. He put his arm around her shoulders and led her towards the gate. She managed to place one foot in front of the other. He spoke as they walked, neither turning around. Both of them heard the uneven crunch of the gravel as Mrs Marcus limped back to the house.

'I'll walk you home. Return in the morning as normal and I'll be waiting for you. We will sort this out.'

'Don't walk down the avenue with me,' said Mary Kate as they reached the gate. 'I don't want us to be seen together. Deidra will be back on the bus soon – it's best if I go by myself.'

'Are you sure?' He glanced behind him at the sound of his front door slamming.

'I am, I really am. You go and calm her down – she seemed hysterical. This isn't right. You and I can't do that again.' She spoke the words, but her heart broke as she did so.

'And I can no longer live in this sham of a marriage,' he replied. 'This has happened so many times before. It's the reason we moved here, why we uprooted the boys, to be away from her parents lest they found out about her last affair down south. My wife gets bored easily and I forgive too easily, but no longer. Not now that I have met you. The worm has turned.'

As he walked away from her, down the drive and towards the house, Mary Kate stole one last glance. Her eyes were drawn to the red glow of Lavinia Marcus's cigarette butt, discarded on the driveway. She stood watching it until it died away.

Mary Kate felt a sharp prod in her thigh and was dragged away from the events of last night by Deidra, who was on her knees. Mary Kate slipped from the bench beside her and dipped her head. 'Father, forgive us,' she chanted, having no idea where she would go or what she would do once she left the church. She heard the creak of the wooden church doors and turned round to see who it was coming in to Mass so late.

Mrs O'Keefe stood framed in the doorway. Mary Kate was in no doubt that it was her she was looking for.

Chapter 26

Deidra and Mary Kate were the first out of the doors and down the steps to leave Mass, before the priest had even reached them.

'Deidra, you run on ahead and get the kettle on,' Eileen O'Keefe said. 'I have an urgent message for Mary Kate. Go on and shut your mouth or you'll be catching flies out here.'

Deidra blinked hard and closed her mouth. Her pigtail plaits hung down, one each side of her straw hat. 'I will. And the toast?' she asked as she hurried away, back up the avenue.

Mary Kate didn't dare speak as both she and Mrs O'Keefe watched Deidra's departing back.

'Well, my girl,' said Mrs O'Keefe. 'I suppose I should have known. A young woman with looks and a way like yours was always going to be out of the ordinary. I suppose it was mad of me to think you would just slip into service – you have far more about you, and anyone who cares to look can see it.'

She spoke wistfully, sadly. Mary Kate reminded her so much of herself and her impetuous youth. The heady, passionate days of her courtship, when she'd married the man of her dreams after mere weeks, despite everyone telling her what a mistake she was making. The same man she now missed so much, she had a permanent pain between her ribs. She knew, without any doubt, that if she herself had worked as a housemaid, she'd have lasted only a few days too. Her voice was soft now, coaxing.

'Dr Marcus came to the house just after you left for Mass. He asked me to give you this.' She opened her handbag and extracted a pale blue envelope with Mary Kate's name written across the front in black cursive script and underlined.

The congregation was still filing out of the church behind and around them. Some were making their way to the bus stop, others were walking back along the avenue to their homes or places of work. Many, like Deidra, would be rushing back to carefully lay aside their gloves, hats and best hand-me-down cardigans and replace them with aprons and caps ready for a hard day on their knees. Mary Kate hadn't worn gloves, hadn't had time to collect them, being in such a rush to catch Deidra. She held out a trembling hand to take the letter.

'Here, let's sit on the wall.' Mrs O'Keefe took hold of Mary Kate's arm and led her to the low red sandstone wall that surrounded the church. It was still stained with the rusty tears left by the removal of the railings for the war effort.

Mary Kate could hear nothing but a loud buzzing in her head as she tore open the letter. She knew her fate was contained therein. Knew that she was about to be sacked, or perhaps worse, if he'd been unable to quell the wrath of his shamed wife. This letter was to warn her that he and his wife had patched up their differences and that he'd been unable to prevent her from picking up the telephone and destroying Mary Kate's reputation in just a few short sentences. She would never be able to return home. She had behaved abominably – even Roshine would struggle to understand her plight.

Mary Kate stared at the folded sheet of paper. Cast as a harlot. Ruined. What would she do? Where would she go? Everything was so normal around her: Deidra at home making tea and toast, people on their way to work, while she was probably about to have to return to Mrs O'Keefe's to pack her bag. After such a short time she'd be homeless and penniless once more, and hurt too, but this time the injury was not visible and all the more painful for that.

Mrs O'Keefe had risen to greet a member of the congregation whom she knew. 'Yes, I do find life difficult without him still,' Mary Kate heard her say. 'But I do enjoy visiting the grave once a month.'

She stared at the words in front of her and tried to make sense of them as they swam before her tear-filled eyes.

Dearest Mary Kate,

I have little time to write this as it would appear that I am alone at the practice today and will have two surgeries to deal with, not one.

Lavinia has left me and, as you must know after last night, I am not sorry about that. I am only sad for Susan, the wife of my partner, Robin, who is an innocent in all of this. She will be badly hurt as her world collapses around her. Lavinia refused to spare her.

The boys are with Joan. She is entirely unaware of what has happened. I will understand if you never want to return to the house or see either myself or the boys again. I cannot say I would blame you, but please know that what will sustain me through today is the slim chance that when I return this evening you might be there waiting.

I want nothing more than to talk to you, just to talk and explain my actions and feelings towards you. As I write these words, I have no expectation that you will want to hear me out. I cannot and do not presume anything. I expect nothing whatsoever from you after we have spoken. All I can do is hope and pray that you will be there when I return.

Yours,
Nicholas

Mary Kate's tears plopped onto the words, wet the ink and ran down the page. She folded the sheet, held it to her and took deep breaths. She didn't even have to think about her response. She knew without any doubt that she would be there waiting for him. If he'd asked her to do that a million times, she would.

Mrs O'Keefe sat back down next to her on the wall. 'Now, looking at the state of you, I don't think there's much point in me asking if everything's all right, is there?'

Mary Kate dipped her head, her eyes fixed on the letter.

'Is it about her? I hope to God she isn't trying to lay any blame on you for her disgusting behaviour, because if she is...' Mrs O'Keefe pulled her brown leather handbag up onto her lap, where it landed with a thump, undid the top clasp and began moving its contents from one end to the other. She lifted out a packet of Trill birdseed and held it in the air with one hand, as she rummaged with the other.

Mary Kate took a deep breath and swiped at her eyes and nose with the back of her hand. 'No, she isn't,' she said in a voice choked with tears. 'She's left him.'

'Ah, here it is.' Mrs O'Keefe pressed a clean, folded, lace-edged handkerchief into Mary Kate's hand. 'Well, that's a scandal in the avenue if she has, and made worse by the fact that he's a doctor. Everyone will be talking about it in no time. Mind you, everyone in the avenue likes him and no one in their right mind likes her, not even the postman, so he'll survive it, just about. It's the boys I feel sorry for. Are you going back there? Because I am quite serious, you can only do that if Joan is still there and there are two of you. You cannot go back there alone.'

Her voice had dropped slightly with her words of caution.

Mary Kate wiped away the last of her tears and nodded in reply, not trusting herself to speak.

The look on her face, the determination in her eyes, told Eileen O'Keefe all she needed to know. 'Oh dear God, you're in love with him, aren't you?'

Mary Kate had no idea what being in love entailed. What she did know was that she wanted to run to the house right then and look after his boys and count the minutes until he returned home. If that was what love was about, then, yes, she must be in love with him.

Nicholas Marcus worked flat out through the morning and was relieved to have finished both lists by one thirty. He was desperately sorry that some of his patients had waited as long as two hours to see him. The cup of tea his receptionist, Bella, had brought him at 11 a.m. stood cold on his desk. He picked it up, took a sip, winced and placed it back on the saucer. Elbows on his desk, he rubbed the balls of his palms into his eyes and struggled to keep his head up. He had finally fallen asleep at five that morning, to be woken at six thirty by the boys demanding to know where Mummy was.

The night had been long and torturous. Lavinia, keen to blame and punish him, had reached the point where she had to face her own failings and indiscretions. Unable to do so, she'd left the house in the early hours, apparently fully intending to carry out her threats. Nicholas felt as though he'd been holding his breath ever since, waiting for worst to befall him.

'Why do you think I took a lover?' She'd stood in front of him, one hand on her hips, the other jabbing a lit cigarette towards his face. 'You leave me, a woman like me, for hours on end, giving all of your time to your precious patients, and you expect me to just sit here all day like some grateful maid, awaiting your return. You are as dull as dishwater, Nicholas, and if you had anything about you, you would understand that I have needs too.'

She had taken off her dress, and as Nicholas sat on the end of the bed listening to her monologue, it struck him that, in body only, Lavinia was beautiful. Everything about her was perfect. Her long, shapely legs, enhanced by her silk stockings and suspenders, her breasts hardly touched by the hungry mouths of their sons were still firm and, like her belly, blemish-free. He remembered that throughout her pregnancies, which she had resented from beginning to end, she had lathered her body in lanoline oil three times a day, examining every inch of her skin for the first sign of stretch marks.

She strode to the ashtray by the side of the bed, bent down, removed her shoes and threw first one and then the other across the room.

'Are you getting into bed?' he asked.

'Yes, I am. Have you any objection?'

'Yes,' he answered quietly. 'I'll sleep in the spare bedroom. It's over, Lavinia. I will leave in the morning.'

Her mouth opened and closed, her eyes blinked in astonishment. 'You? Leave?' Nicholas watched as the realisation of what that meant flashed across her face. 'You are not leaving me in this prison with those boys.'

She marched out of the bedroom, across the landing to the dressing room, and returned in a summer dress he had never seen before.

'What are you doing?' he asked. He had not raised his voice once for fear of waking the boys, but she had no such concerns.

'I'll tell you what I am doing,' she said loudly. 'I'm going to Robin and Susan's house. When she knows what her husband has been up to, she'll be out the door. There is something you don't understand, Nicholas: Robin loves me, he's obsessed with me. He told me only the other day that he has never met or known a woman like me – and by the way, he meant that in the most intimate terms.'

Nicholas flinched. 'Lavinia, you can't do that to Susan. Meet Robin alone, talk to him if you must, but there's no need to hurt anyone else. Susan doesn't deserve that.'

Lavinia rooted about in her handbag, her head down as she spoke. 'Doesn't she? If she were half the wife she should have been, her husband would have had no need to look elsewhere. I will be back for my things tomorrow.'

Nicholas heard her calling for a taxi from the telephone on the landing. Ten minutes later, she was gone. As the taxi pulled away, he felt bad for Susan. He picked up the phone himself and dialled Robin's number. After a short while, a thick, sleepy voice answered.

'What's up?' Robin asked as soon as he recognised Nicholas's voice. 'I'm not the one on call, you are.'

Nicholas took a long breath. He wanted to say, 'I usually am, given that you make so many excuses to avoid your own on calls,' but instead he simply said, in a calm, low voice, 'Lavinia is on her way to your house. I think you need to prepare Susan.' And before Robin could ask him any more, he replaced the receiver.

He considered asking Bella for a fresh cup of tea. He wondered if she would resign the moment the news of the scandal hit the surgery. A long waiting list was not going to be the worst of his embarrassment or discomfort. There would be more pain and chaos to follow.

Without Bella buzzing to warn him, the door to his surgery opened and Robin walked in, his complexion as white as the notepad Nicholas had been scribbling on all morning. Nicholas folded his arms and sat back in his seat, surprised that he felt no animosity towards the man with whom he shared not only a medical practice and patients but also, seemingly, his wife. They had never been close, but he didn't envy anyone who found themselves subjected to Lavinia's wrath, as Robin clearly had. A path had been embarked upon which they all now needed to see to the end, and there were no soft edges.

Robin was not so forgiving. His eyes looked red

against his sallow, tired skin. 'Your wife has destroyed my marriage.' He almost spat out the words.

Nicholas sat forwards in surprise. 'My wife has? I think the saying goes that it takes two to tango – am I right?'

He picked up his pen and began signing the wad of repeat prescriptions Bella had placed on his desk earlier. He knew she'd be waiting for them, having instructed his patients to collect them at lunchtime. He didn't want to keep them hanging around. He cast his eyes over Bella's writing. She always wrote out the drug requirements herself, having first checked the notes. He double-checked the dosage, and the pharmacist did a third check. Bella never made a mistake; if she were to resign today, he wasn't sure he'd be able to cope. He might have to ask for advice from his friend Dr Gaskell at St Angelus, where he occasionally helped out on the receiving ward. He read the next prescription. It was for Mrs Hooper, whose senility was becoming difficult for her husband to manage: 'Valium, 5 mg TDS.' That was correct. He signed it and then spoke.

'Most of the patients I've seen this morning were yours, by the way. And while you're here, I think it's time for Mrs Whitley to be admitted to St Angelus.' He slipped the signed prescription for Mrs Hooper back into her notes and added them to the checked pile. 'I've given her daughter another prescription for painkillers this morning, but she can't manage much longer. At the very least, she needs professional nursing care and some peace. A house with five young children is no environment for a terminally ill woman.' And then he added in a softer voice, 'It should have been organised some time ago.'

Robin looked down and checked his nails. He was ignoring Nicholas.

It was as if Nicholas had been given an electric shock: it suddenly occurred to him that he'd spent the best part of the last decade living with a woman who didn't care about her family and working with a man who cared even less for his patients.

Robin collapsed onto a patient's chair opposite the desk and wearily rubbed his hands through his hair. Nicholas almost felt sorry for him. 'Would you like me to organise it this afternoon? I can telephone Dr Gaskell and arrange a bed for her for next week?'

Robin had the good grace to look ashamed now that the problem had been solved and Nicholas had offered to do the work. 'Please,' he said weakly.

Nicholas had never heard him sound so deflated. He decided to change the subject. 'How is Susan?' he asked. She was the innocent victim in all of this and it was her he truly felt sorry for.

'How do you think? She was in bits and she's taken the children to her parents'. I am instructed to follow this evening and then I'll have the joy of dealing with her father. She refuses to divorce me, and her father is to be in charge of how my marriage proceeds. You do know he owns our house? Susan is the one with the money. On Monday it's the AGM at the golf club and I have all the votes required to make me captain, but that won't be happening now. The scandal will lose me the support.' He rubbed his hands despondently across his eyes.

'Where is Lavinia?' Nicholas almost whispered his question. Robin was clearly there for a reason and Nicholas still had a lot to do before he could set off on his home visits to patients too sick to attend the surgery. After that he had a hospital visit and then his afternoon surgery, which was meant to finish at six but rarely did so before seven.

'How the hell do I know where she is?' Robin sat upright in the chair and clasped his hands in front, propelling himself forward by his elbows. His shirt was crumpled and his tie appeared to have been knotted in a hurry. 'She told Susan bloody everything, Nicholas, do you understand that? That you knew, that she'd told you everything too and that you couldn't care less. Is that true?'

Nicholas nodded.

'She said she'd caught you at it with a new maid.'

'No!' Nicholas almost shouted his denial. 'That bit is not true. We were not "at it" and never have been.'

'She's gone,' said Robin, 'and she isn't coming back. I think she expected Susan to do the same, but Susan isn't like that. She's Catholic for one thing, and divorce is something she would never in a million years agree to, and neither would her family. You're the lucky bastard – you're free. Now, thanks to your wife, I have to live the rest of my life apologising and feeling grateful to my wife.'

'Where is Lavinia?' Nicholas repeated, convinced Robin would know.

'Er, she said she'd be going to the house while you were at work to collect her things. And then... well, I'm meeting her at the hotel we used.'

Nicholas was mildly surprised that not a flash of shame touched Robin's cheeks as he spoke.

'She said she was leaving Liverpool for good, called the house this morning – thank God it was after Susan had left.'

'Well, that's something, I suppose.' Nicholas returned to his prescriptions and looked at his watch.

Robin peered at him though narrowed eyes as though he were mad. 'Nicholas, if all this gets out, we're ruined. We'll be hauled in front of the Liverpool Medical Council and they may even take the practice from us.'

Nicholas nodded and bit the top of his pen. 'We'll have to keep all this as civilised as possible, won't we? We should be able to avoid double ruin and scandal if one of us leaves the practice and as I am not the one who had an affair with another man's wife, I don't think it should be me.'

Robin stared back at him long and hard, but Nicholas meant every word. His emotions were controlled, but his anger was simmering just below the surface, as it had been throughout his marriage to Lavinia and his partnership with Robin. He'd been deceived by both of them and his blood ran hot. He looked down at the silver letter-opener on his desk, picked it up and let it slip backwards and forwards through his fingers.

'You will have to buy me out,' Robin said. 'I want my damned investment back.'

'Of course you do. You want a lot, Robin: my wife, Susan's money, less time on call, perfect patients, the golf club... You're full of demands – you and Lavinia are actually well suited. It's a pity Susan has decided she's better off staying married. You and Lavinia would have made a wonderful couple – you're far more her type than I ever was. Of course I'll buy you out. I wouldn't want you to lose everything. I'll get a locum in to cover, until I find a new partner. I'll ask Bella to have your brass name plaque removed this afternoon and sent to your house. Please, Robin, don't ever return here again.'

Robin had not expected this. 'Fucking hell, I may have dallied with your wife, but she is one evil woman to have acted in this way. What drove her to come to the house like that? And what am I going to say to Susan's father? Being unfaithful is one thing – he's bloody done it himself, I swear – but losing the practice, he won't forgive that.'

'I have no idea,' said Nicholas. 'I've never met him. Maybe you could ask Lavinia for her advice when you meet her this afternoon.' He pushed the chair back with his legs. 'I'll get my solicitor to write to you,' he said, and without another word he picked up the pile of checked prescriptions, stood up and walked out of the room.

Chapter 27

Joan was in a pickle when Mary Kate arrived at the house. She dashed out of the back door to meet her before she reached the kitchen, so the boys couldn't hear what she had to say. 'It's mayhem, no one has told me a thing. She isn't even here. She was here last night – I heard her kicking off in one of her tempers upstairs – but this morning, puff, she's gone. Something is going on and I have no idea what it is. Have you?'

The noise of the radio and the boys chattering over their breakfast masked her whispered words as she glanced back over her shoulder, her hands firmly placed on her hips, legs apart, lips pursed.

Mary Kate felt like a fish, her mouth opening and closing, not knowing what to say.

'I know you do,' hissed Joan accusingly. 'He told me you might not be here today. What did he mean – how did he know that?'

'I... I...'

Mary Kate was saved by Jack running out, swinging his precious teddy by one arm and shouting, 'Mary Kate, I saw you! Can we go to the park now?'

Saved by the child, Mary Kate took the boys and the dog to the park while Joan went about her normal chores. She cleaned the kitchen, washed the floor and filled up the twin-tub in the scullery, all the time worrying, shaking her head, thinking about how pale Dr Marcus had looked that morning, and muttering to herself, 'There's trouble coming, it's in my waters, I can feel it.' As she connected the grey hose from the scullery tap, dropped the end into the twin-tub and switched the tap on, she yelped, 'Oh Holy Mother, I need to go again.'

With the washing basket on her hip, she was just about to run up the stairs to collect the washing from the boys' room and make their beds when she heard a shout from the hallway.

'I'm here to collect my belongings.' It was Lavinia Marcus. She crashed the front door open and dropped her handbag onto the floor. 'And then you can fuel the gossip mills and tell your network of Irish skivvies up and down the avenue that I have left.'

Joan gasped. 'Left?' She almost ran into the hallway, the basket on her hip bashing against the wall. 'What do you mean, Mrs Marcus? On a holiday, is it?'

This was not an unreasonable question. It had been three years since Dr Marcus had been able to take a holiday with the family. It was the summer and Mrs Marcus was often off somewhere alone.

'No, not a holiday, Joan. I'm leaving, for good. Where are the boys?'

Joan could barely speak. 'For good? But… but what about the boys?'

Mrs Marcus laughed out loud. 'They are all yours, dear Joan, but don't worry, only until the cars arrive. We're leaving for my parents' for the rest of the holidays and then I'm sorting out a boarding school, or Mummy is. There's one near Box Hill, where my parents live in Surrey. We won't be back, Joan, but Dr Marcus will still need you, I'm sure.'

'Box Hill?' Joan was dumbfounded. The information was coming at her faster than she could absorb it and she felt as though the floor was shifting beneath her feet.

Lavinia Marcus began to trip up the stairs, her tight pencil skirt limiting the reach of her knees and forcing her to take short, stubby steps and grasp the bannister to help her up. Her ankles swung side to side, which made her look quite ridiculous – like a penguin, Joan thought.

'I spoke to Mummy this morning. They can't wait for the boys to arrive. I'll be back out of that door the minute I've packed. God, I cannot wait to get out of the north and back to civilisation.'

Joan was crestfallen. 'Is Surrey far?' she asked. Her heart was pounding and she felt close to tears, but Lavinia Marcus didn't answer her or notice.

'We have two cars arriving, one for the cases and one for us. You pack for the boys.' She glanced at her watch. 'I had better get a move on. Where are the boys now?'

'They're out with Mary Kate,' said Joan innocently.

Lavinia Marcus had almost reached the top of the stairs. Gripping the bannister, she stopped dead and turned back to Joan. 'They are out with who?' She began to come back down again, one step at a time, much quicker than going up. Just as her heels clicked on the large black-and-white-checked tiles of the hallway, the front door opened.

'Tell Joan how the ducks all ganged up and chased you, David,' Mary Kate shouted from the pathway. She laughed and the boys ran into the hallway ahead of her.

Mary Kate stepped into the pillar of sunlight that had landed in the hallway as the door opened and dropped Jet's lead into the Moorcroft bowl in the middle of the circular table.

But the merriment was short-lived as, without another word, the boys shouted in unison, 'Mummy!' just as Lavinia Marcus closed the short distance between the foot of the stairs and the table, her kitten heels clicking the countdown: five, four, three, two…

When she reached the table, she slapped Mary Kate so hard across the face, Mary Kate staggered backwards. Her head jerked so violently, it hit the frame of the open door.

Joan screamed, the boys were frozen to the spot in fear, and the dog skulked back out onto the driveway and lay down whimpering on the warm gravel.

Mrs Marcus hissed in Mary Kate's face, 'And what gives you the right to walk through my front door? Hands all over my husband, feet all over my mat – is it my bed next? My, my, you are a quick worker, aren't you. Barely stepped off the boat and you have everything you came to England for.'

Jack began to cry and his voice was a thin wail. 'Mummy, Mummy, don't hurt Mary Kate, please.'

Lavinia Marcus ignored him and continued with her rant. 'Think you can both blackmail me, do you? Well, let me tell you this, one day you will hear from me again. The likes of you, a girl from the bogs, will never have the upper hand over someone like me. Do you understand that? We've been keeping your sort in place forever and it isn't going to stop with a fanciful chit who doesn't know her place. *Do you understand?* I will make you pay, and when I do, you'll wish you had never been born.'

Her face was so close that Mary Kate could feel fine flecks of spittle landing on her cheek. The warm, sickly aroma of stale perfume from Lavinia's linen jacket flooded the space between them. Mary Kate's eyes blazed in defiance. She didn't speak – her face stung and the pain of the bang made it feel as if her head were splitting in two – but her eyes did the talking. For a split second, she saw doubt cross Lavinia Marcus's face, a question in her eye.

Turning, Mrs Marcus grabbed both stunned boys by the shoulders. 'Come along, boys. Gather up your toys – you can help pack. Just a few each. We are done here.

Granny and Granddad are waiting to spoil you rotten, just like they did me when I was a little girl.'

'Is Jet coming with us?' Jack's voice was quiet. His eyes hadn't left Mary Kate's face and he looked terrified.

Jet, panting in distress, was gazing in through the front door, desperate for water, searching for his best friend, Jack.

'No, he is not. You know very well that Granny doesn't like dogs. Come along, up the stairs now. Joan, start packing the boys' room and stop gawping. Oh, and bring me some tea first. I'll get the boys started.'

Mary Kate and Joan stood and watched helplessly as she grasped the boys' hands, one in each of hers, and almost dragged them to their room on the top floor. Lavinia led the way; the boys, struggling to avoid her swinging feet, scrambled up a step behind her.

The heat of her anger almost consumed Mary Kate. With one hand nursing her cheek, she turned to Joan, who was in shock, her face drained of blood and her bottom lip trembling. There was something she had to do.

'Hold it together, Joan,' she whispered. 'Let's do what we have to do and then when she's gone, I'll tell you everything, I promise. Sorry, but there's something I need to do. You fetch her tea – I have to go upstairs.'

Joan gasped and her hand flew to her mouth in horror.

'Go, Joan, or she'll be down here giving out to you.'

Glancing up the stairwell to check that Lavinia Marcus was on the top floor, Mary Kate left Joan and took the stairs two at a time to the first landing. From upstairs, she heard little voices protesting.

'Is Daddy coming?'

'I'm not going to Grandma's house without my soldiers, am I? Daddy won't know what to do with the battle, Mummy.'

'Mummy, what about my comics?'

She couldn't hear Lavinia's answers, but when the wailing started, that told her all she needed to know. Aware that she didn't have the time to think about whether what she was doing was right or not, she slipped into the dressing room, edged past the cheval mirror and lifted the boxes on the chair. The note was still there.

She reached out and tucked it into her pocket, then turned to exit the room. She was too late. Her heart stopped as she heard Lavinia's footsteps crashing down the wooden stairs leading to the nursery floor and Joan's room. She would either turn right along the short landing and go into the bedroom, or she'd take the first left into the dressing room. If it was left, Mary Kate was done for.

She looked about her. The only place to hide was among the racks of clothes, but she would be discovered if Lavinia was packing. The footsteps came closer and her heart was beating so fast, she thought she might faint. They stopped right outside the door and Lavinia shouted over the bannister, 'Joan, hurry up with that tea. I have to draw a bath. Sort the boys out, will you.' And with that, she continued past the door.

The second Mary Kate heard the brass taps turn and the water clank through the pipes, she tiptoed out of the room. She was on the last stair as Lavinia Marcus stormed out of the bathroom and into the dressing room, unaware that Mary Kate had left only seconds before.

One frenetic hour later, Joan walked into the kitchen balancing a tray between unsteady hands. On a plate lay a raw steak and next to it a bowl of ice cubes.

'Here, try this, it's supposed to work wonders on a black eye.' Joan lifted the slab of meat with her fingertips and swung it in the air in front of Mary Kate's face. Her hands were still shaking and the steak quivered. She looked as though she'd shed a few tears herself – her face was as red and blotchy as the steak.

Mary Kate, on the other hand, had remained composed in the face of Lavinia Marcus's rage, too angry to flinch.

'Tip your head back, go on,' said Joan. 'And then, while the steak's working, I'll make us some tea and you can tell us what's going on. Honest to God, by all that's holy, Mary Kate, nothing has been right since the second you walked through that door.'

'It's not my fault,' Mary Kate protested. She lifted her head and the steak slipped.

'Keep your head back and your mouth shut,' said Joan as she replaced her dubious cure.

Half of the steak rested against Mary Kate's lips and

the smell of blood made her feel sick. 'Oh, Jesus, I can't do this,' she squealed. She threw the steak back down, picked up one of the ice cubes and held it in place.

Joan had taken the tray and put a pot of tea on it. She sat down next to her. 'I can't believe what's going on. The boys have gone. What is there to do? I still have Jack's shirts in the basket to iron – he's gone without them. And look...' She leapt out of her seat and retrieved Jack's teddy from the hall table, where he'd left it when the drivers were lifting the cases into the car. 'He will be lost without his teddy. Do you think she'll send the car back for it?'

'Do you?' asked Mary Kate, in a tone that gave Joan her answer.

Joan handed Mary Kate her tea and in a much quieter voice said, 'What is going on? Will you tell me, please? I know you're involved.'

Mary Kate dropped the ice cube into the bowl, where it landed with a clink, and gracefully took the tea. 'I will. Come on, sit back down.'

Joan slid onto the chair, clutching the teddy. As she did so, there was an enormous bang on the back door. 'Mother of God, is there no peace? Oh, it'll be the driver for the teddy. See! Ye of little faith.' A grin crossed Joan's face. 'Or maybe they're back?'

'What, knocking on their own back door? I don't think so, Joan.'

Mary Kate removed her handkerchief from up her

sleeve and wiped her face. It stared back at her, smeared in blood. She was dipping the handkerchief into the iced water ready for a second wipe when Joan opened the door. Her hand hovered in mid air as she heard a voice she recognised.

'Is my daughter Mary Kate here, please? I've come to take her home.'

And without further ado, Michael, Deidra, Mrs O'Keefe and Cat walked into the kitchen.

Chapter 28

'I'm not coming.' Mary Kate was unequivocal in her response.

Mary Kate, her father, Mrs O'Keefe and Cat were sitting around the Marcuses' kitchen table, having been through the routine of making small talk. Deidra and Joan were at the sink, rinsing cups and preparing tea, communicating with each other via raised eyebrows and sighs.

'You have to, Mary Kate,' said Michael. 'I cannot leave you here in Liverpool on your own.'

'I'm not on my own, Daddy. I'm living with Mrs O'Keefe and I'm working here, for Dr Marcus, his wife and his family.' She crossed her fingers under the table and shot a look to Joan. Who sent a disapproving look back that said, 'You are a terrible person, Mary Kate, and you will rot in hell for that.'

Eileen O'Keefe sat with her hands in her lap, staring down, doing battle with herself, her suspicions and all that she knew. She gave a big sigh.

'I'm sorry, Mrs O'Keefe. You shouldn't be involved in all this,' said Michael. 'You hardly know us and it is a great imposition on your time and your hospitality.'

'No, not at all,' she replied. 'I've lived alone since the death of my husband, Mr Malone. I was more than happy for Mary Kate to live with Deidra and me.'

'Well, if I might say so, she's a very lucky lady to have landed on her feet like that and I will give thanks in prayer for the rest of me life that she met you.'

Eileen smiled. He reminded her of her husband. Irishmen were all the same when it boiled down to it – proud, reactionary and passionate. 'Mr Malone, the thing is, over the years I have met lots of fathers from Ireland on the boat. All coming over to look for their daughters. And as you can see, I employ one such girl myself.' She smiled at Deidra. 'In fact, Deidra's own father turned up on my doorstep – isn't that right, Deidra?'

Deidra blushed. 'Yes, Mrs O'Keefe.'

'The fact is, Mr Malone, Deidra's father was convinced that Deidra had landed herself in the path of temptation and sin – those were his words. That she was working as a maid in a house of ill repute. Now, he was quickly disabused of that notion, but do you see my point? You have seen my house. The fear rarely matches up to the reality, in my experience.'

Michael removed his cap, laid it on his knees and began to twist it around. Unbeknown to him, Cat's eyes never left his face. She was sitting almost forgotten at the furthest corner of the table, silently chanting, 'Stay. Stay. Stay.' A thrill ran through her. There was a chance he would. She could see he was weighing things up, wavering. She remembered the gentle touch of his thumbs against her hips as he effortlessly lifted her body onto his. Her thighs ached and she could feel the bruises on her breasts, made by his lips only hours before, pressing against the fabric of her dress. Her life could alter beyond all recognition. She could love again – she knew it. She could live more than half a life. She was ready.

Michael, shamefaced, looked about the room. 'I feel like a fool altogether,' he said. 'I came over here ready to pick you up and put you under my arm and drag you back if I had to.'

''Tis not your fault, Daddy,' said Mary Kate, feeling that she was winning, that the will of room was on her side, easing her father back to the Mersey and the boat journey home, leaving her anchored there in Liverpool.

She would not go; she could not. Because, while everyone was talking, in the midst of all the chaos, all she could do was count down the hours until Dr Marcus was due home. She could not, however hard she tried, prevent her mind from wandering to their kiss and the thrill that had coursed through her. She could still recall the feel, the taste, the smell of him. She closed her eyes and swayed in her seat with the sheer ecstatic headiness brought on by nothing more than the memory.

'Mary Kate…' It was Deidra. 'Do you want your tea?

Is the missus out, Joan?' she said as she laid the tea tray on the table.

Joan's face was set. She would not go into the confessional and tell Father Kenny that she had lied. She would not. She glared at Mary Kate.

'She is, Deidra. Taken the boys shopping for clothes,' said Mary Kate, her fingers crossed again.

'Aha, it was them. I thought it was, going down the avenue in a car when I was upstairs,' said Deidra.

Mary Kate wanted to jump up and kiss her.

'What happened to your eye?' asked Cat, who'd noticed the swelling and could feel her opportunity to ensnare Michael slipping away.

'Honestly, Cat, have you seen Jet?'

Jet lifted his head from his basket by the fire.

'I'd just brought him back from his walk, taken his lead off, and when I put it in the bowl on the table, he turned round and ran back out of the door. So I gave chase and the doorframe tried to stop me. I swear to God, he tried to flick the door shut with his paw before I moved.'

They all laughed. Jet's ears dropped flat to his head, his eyes looking from one to the other in confusion. Joan almost dropped the tray. Never in her entire life had she seen someone lie so much and so fast. She glanced up at the ceiling, expecting to see it collapse on top of them.

Michael placed his hands on the table and eased himself up. 'I should be going,' he said. 'I don't want to inconvenience you any longer, Mrs O'Keefe. Might Mary

Kate be permitted to come to the Pier Head with me?' he asked Joan, who he assumed was the housekeeper and Mary Kate's superior.

Joan nodded. 'No need to be asking me,' she said. 'No one cares what happens in this house. I think I'll go to the films this afternoon – and why not.'

Everyone laughed, as though Joan were joking. Joan leant halfway across the table, arms outstretched, wiping away the crumbs from the packet of biscuits she'd arranged in a fan on a plate and no one had touched. Only she and Mary Kate knew the truth. She'd already looked up the time of the matinee in the previous night's *Echo* while Mary Kate was bathing her eye in raw meat, and she was deadly serious.

Cat pushed back her chair. It was back to loneliness and isolation for her. As she stood up, she realised with a guilty jolt that she'd been prepared to steal a man from his family in order to spare her that future, if only for one more day.

Mary Kate phoned a cab from the house, and Eileen O'Keefe, Deidra, Cat and Michael walked down to the end of the drive.

'If you come back to Liverpool again, Mr Malone, you will be very welcome,' said Eileen.

'Can I give you some money for her keep?' asked Michael, looking embarrassed.

Eileen reached out her hand and placed it on top of his. 'No, you cannot,' she said. 'Her company and good humour are payment enough. Life has been a lot more interesting since Mary Kate arrived, isn't that right, Deidra?'

She and Deidra walked away, laughing, and Michael turned to face Cat.

'Well, you are one woman I won't allow to turn me down.'

Hearing those words, Cat's heart did a somersault beneath her ribs.

Michael held out his wallet. 'Here – you have no man behind you; life must be an awful struggle – take this.' He extracted a wad of notes and held them out to Cat.

She turned to the side, desperately trying to blink back her tears. Wanting the money for her family, needing to hold onto her self-respect even more. The words almost killed her as she spoke them. 'No way. I don't want your money.' She half laughed as she wiped her eyes with the back of her hands, just about holding it together.

'What's the matter?' he asked. 'Are you crying?'

'No, God, it's always the same in the summer when I'm out in the country. It's the seeds, they get in my eyes or something.'

Michael glanced down the tree-lined avenue. 'You call this the country?' He began to laugh.

Cat looked embarrassed.

'I'm sorry,' he said. 'It's just that in Tarabeg things are very different.' He could see the offer of money had embarrassed her and closed his wallet, feeling like a fool.

'Anyway,' she said in a much perkier voice, 'I thought all the Irish were as poor as church mice.'

'Well now, many are, to be fair, but when you earn money, sure there's nothing to spend it on, so most have enough and no one who has a good farm should ever go hungry. The famine taught the Irish that, if nothing else.'

'Mary Kate will be here in a second,' said Cat. 'If it's all right with you, I'll go and catch the bus. There's a stop at the end of the avenue. You two have some time on your own.'

Michael made to object, but he did want some time alone with Mary Kate. 'That's good of you,' he said. 'Come here.' He held out his arms and Cat willingly fell into them, for one last time.

'Take care, you,' she said into his jacket. Despite the dunking in the lake, she could smell things that were strange to her. Another woman's kitchen, earth and the sea. As she took in a deep breath she inhaled the musky male smell of him that lurked underneath and committed it to memory.

'It's you that needs to take care. And don't think you've seen the last of me – you haven't,' he said as he slipped his arms around her waist and almost lifted her off the ground.

Forgetting where they were for a second, Cat lifted her face and placed her hand on his shoulders, and he kissed her. As she walked down the avenue with her head held high, she was aware of his eyes on her back and she was grateful that now her tears could fall freely.

Mary Kate turned the front-door handle and was greeted by the sight of her father kissing Cat. Retracing her steps, she retreated inside and closed the door.

Joan was polishing the hall table, rushing through her chores, ready to take the rest of the afternoon off. 'Isn't the taxi on its way?' she asked.

'Aye. I forgot my gloves – I think I left them in my coat at Mass.'

'Did you?' Joan looked up suspiciously as she tucked the duster into her belt. 'Mary Kate, I still don't know what's going on. You've told me nothing. Aren't I the one who should know above everyone else?' She picked up one of Jack's toy soldiers from the floor. 'Oh God, would you look at that. He must have been trying to take it with him.' Tears stuck in her throat as she slipped the toy soldier into her pocket. 'Dr Marcus has to chase after those boys and bring them back here,' she said. 'I can't bear to think of them where they aren't looked after properly and that woman doesn't have a notion what to do.'

Mary Kate could hear the sound of the bus pulling away. 'I'll go and see Da off. You watch your film and let's talk later.' She stepped back outside to see her father standing by himself in the driveway, staring after the bus, oblivious to her approaching footsteps.

The corner table next to the window in the Pier Head café was free and Mary Kate filled her lungs with the sea air as the seagulls screeched and swooped overhead. It reminded her of Dublin and the day she'd left Ireland.

'When do you think you'll be home?' asked Michael.

They'd bought his ticket and had almost an hour to wait before the next sailing.

'I have no idea, Da. What is it you want me to come home for? There's nothing for me.'

'That's not true. Rosie tells me that Declan is sweet on you.'

Mary Kate put her hands to her forehead. 'Da, Declan is a lovely man, but I've known him since I was a child and if I marry him, I just carry on the pattern of life in Tarabeg. It's not like that any more. Things are changing, you know. Women go to university and have opinions now and everything.'

Michael grinned. 'Not being one of that sort has never stopped you having an opinion, Mary Kate. Look…' He swivelled the saucer in front of him around and around. 'Just be a good girl. Remember your catechisms, go to Mass every day and confession as often as you have to. Say your prayers every night. And listen to Mrs O'Keefe – she's a good woman. She may not be Irish, but she was married to an Irishman for long enough. Don't eat too many of the pick 'n' mix in that shop called Woolworths because Mrs Doyle has heard about one girl who came over who was addicted to them and all her teeth fell out in a year. But most of all, Mary Kate, honour your chastity. Keep yourself pure for when you do come home to marry. And let's hope Declan it is, when you finally get fed up of cleaning other people's dirt and come home to Tarabeg.'

Mary Kate placed her cup in her saucer and looked him square in the eye. 'Da, I will be as good and honest and true as you are yourself, I promise you that.'

Cat hopped onto the bus and walked down the aisle to the back seat. She knew she had some change in her purse. She felt stupid and angry at her own pride. She had no food in the house and would have to borrow a halfpenny from each of her neighbours to get enough money together to buy some potatoes and maybe half a sausage for each of the kids. If Linda was making gravy, she would send a bit round in a jug with one of her kids to pour on top. There wouldn't be enough for her as well, but she could manage on a bit of toast. Haven't I had enough practice, she thought.

The money Michael had offered her had looked as if it would cover a year's rent. Turning to stare out the window, she saw a woman pushing a pram with a child sitting on the front, eating an ice cream. She wished she were that woman and that she could buy her children ice cream. Ice cream and new shoes for school. Her next hurdle. School starting in two weeks and not a clue how she would afford to buy them. She would have to put the kids before her pride and contact the social and scour the jumble sales. Despair curled like a cat and settled in the pit of her stomach.

The bus conductor walked towards her, gripping the corded brown rope that ran the length of the bus, his grey peaked cap ducking to peer out of the window as he weaved his way down, his ticket machine banging against the metal rails on the backs of the seats. 'Tickets, please,' he shouted, even though she was the only passenger on the lower deck.

She shuffled in her seat and slipped her hand into her coat pocket to remove her purse.

'God in heaven,' she gasped as a flurry of twenty-pound notes fluttered to the floor.

Joan had returned from the film delirious and with the songs buzzing around in her head. 'When did you get back?' she said to Mary Kate as she unfastened her coat and hung it on the back of the kitchen door. 'Did your daddy get a boat in good time? Fancy him coming all this way and going back without you. Most of the girls just go home to save the trouble of the fight. The number of fathers I've seen marching down this avenue with a couple of brothers in tow, all of 'em ready to give someone a good kicking and with nothing more than flapping shoe leather on their feet and a letter in their hands. Sent by the priests to save their daughters' souls. God love them, I don't think some of them eat from the moment they leave until they get back. You should see the state of the girls when their menfolk turn up at the door – ashamed, they are, and cry all the way back to the Pier Head. Some of them have been to a dance. One night in heaven it is and then dragged back to the bogs. I think that's worse than never having been to Liverpool at all. Not me though. My old man never gave one feck where I was, as long as the money kept arriving. Now, I need to make some pastry. We can have a pie tonight.'

'I've done it,' said Mary Kate. 'And I've made a syrup pudding. Don't tell Dr Marcus, but that steak you put over my eye – I chopped it up to put in the pie.'

Joan gasped. 'You did not!'

'Well, it couldn't go to waste, could it. I gave it a good wash first and browned it off in the pan.'

They both heard the front door open and looked at each other, standing stock still. Fear crept across Joan's face, anticipation across Mary Kate's.

'What do we do?' whispered Joan. 'Do you think he knows?'

Mary Kate rose from the chair. 'That she's left and has taken the children? I think he knows she's left, but I'm not sure about the rest.'

'Oh God, who's going to tell him? I need the toilet, so I do. I can't tell him.'

'I'll go up,' said Mary Kate. 'You stay here and carry on. Don't come up until I say, Joan.' Acting and appearing much older than her years, Mary Kate walked up the stairs with her head held high and her back straight, to the man she knew was hoping it would be her and not Joan coming to greet him.

His face lit up as he placed his hat and keys on the table. 'Well, there's a sight for sore eyes. Has she really gone? I've heard nothing all day.' He glanced up the stairs to the boys' sitting room, half hopeful, half terrified to hear the answer.

Mary Kate had decided there was no point in holding back; she had to tell him. 'She has, Dr Marcus.'

He held up his hand. 'Mary Kate, it's Nicholas.'

She hesitated, frowned. A look of deep pity crept into her eyes and her stomach churned. There'd been no one to guide her to this moment, no one to advise her how to cross the bridge between being a girl fresh out of school and a woman about to deliver the hardest message to the kindest man. She'd planned to have Bee as her guide, her mother's aunt, because somewhere deep within she yearned to be closer to her mother, the mother she struggled to remember except in her dreams, which were vivid and detailed. Mary Kate had felt compelled to leave Tarabeg, but for what she didn't know. Was this it? This moment? Was she meant to be here for this?

'What is it, Mary Kate? What's wrong? Please don't think that I'm upset that she's left. You have no idea how awful the past few years have been, and for the boys too. She stopped caring about any of us a long time ago. The harder we tried, the more distant she became. I've spent all day thinking about how different life will be when I can stop worrying about pleasing Lavinia and can concentrate on my sons instead. At last I'll have the chance to make their lives more fun and less anxious.'

He placed both his hands on the table and leant forward, his head down. Mary Kate's heart folded with pity. He probably hadn't slept the night before. She walked over to where he was standing and wanted to put her arm around his shoulders, to hold him steady for when she delivered the news.

'I am so sorry, Nicholas, but she's taken the boys with her.'

Her words hit him with the force of a bullet. His head jerked up violently and turned to the stairs. 'Jack, too? But he really needs his daddy! He's such a sensitive soul and no one else really understands him.'

He was moving towards the stairs, his hand out ready to grip the bannister. 'David is more robust, he's always been the sporty one, but Jack... I'm the only one he talks to.' His words finished on a croak. Mary Kate could see he was at breaking point.

'Our battle...' he said, and began to run up the stairs to the boys' sitting room.

There on the board were the tin soldiers and tanks and the papier-mâché trees, just as they'd left it the night before. A note in large, childish scrawl lay in the middle of it:

Sorry, Daddy, I think I've been bad.
  Jack xx

Nicholas bent and retrieved it. He folded it carefully before tucking it into his shirt pocket. His eyes filled with tears and, turning to Mary Kate, he asked, 'Will I ever see them again, do you think?'

In her heart, Mary Kate knew the answer and it was no. 'Of course you will – by this time next week, I would imagine.'

She didn't know who moved first, whether or not it was she who took the few steps towards him, but within moments he was in her arms, not she in his. She stroked his hair and led him to the boys' sofa, and as they sat there, he laid his head on her shoulder and she kissed the top of it as he sobbed.

Chapter 29

Mrs Doyle was at the bus stop in Tarabeg to meet Keeva, Rosie and Captain Bob as they alighted from the Ballycroy bus. 'Oh, there you are at last. I had a call from the pot man in Carey's,' she said. 'He saw you getting on the bus, so he did, and I thought, well now, where do I start? And then I thought, with the most important message of all, of course. Michael is on his way home. He rang me from the Pier Head in Liverpool, and mysterious tinker that he is, he would not tell me if Mary Kate was with him.'

'Ah well, I'm guessing now that's because he thinks that the first people to know should be the likes of Nola, Seamus and meself,' said Rosie.

The insult flew straight over Mrs Doyle's head, who appeared quite giddy. And then she saw Captain Bob getting off the bus behind Keeva. 'Well, well, we haven't seen you around these parts for a long time, Captain,' she said. 'I'm going to start having to write everything down at this rate – there's so much happening. I have Ellen making me a new frock for the harvest dance – imagine! Oh God, isn't it just going to be the best night we ever saw in Tarabeg, Rosie.' And with that, she headed straight back to Ellen's to carry the news that Rosie was home and that Captain Bob was in tow.

'A new frock? Ellen hasn't made her a new frock since the Pope died and she went to Rome. The place has gone mad while we've been in Ballycroy,' said Keeva as she and Rosie parted at the crossroads. Keeva was heading for home and the Devlins' bar, and Rosie was going to the shop.

A pack of boys, Finn among them, came running out to greet Keeva. Whooping and laughing, they almost pulled her handbag from her arm to see had she returned from her adventure in Ballycroy with treats.

'Back down, the lot of you. You're like a pack of wolves,' she shouted. 'I have licorice laces, but the only person to get one will be Finn as he's the only one not acting like a half-starved animal.'

Captain Bob laughed at the sight of them. Turning to the Taramore behind them, he said to Rosie, 'Would you look at the river – it makes your heart sing. I'd forgotten what it looked and smelt like. This must be the finest air in all of Ireland.'

Rosie followed his gaze. 'It is a special river, but then this is a special place. I saw it in Ballycroy today. 'Tis funny how you have to step outside of what you're used to before you realise how lucky you are.'

'I've missed this place, Rosie. Ten years in Liverpool has been too long away, but we had no choice in the matter.'

Rosie began to untie the knot of her green, fern-patterned headscarf from under her chin. 'Well, that's all different now, Bob. You're free to make the choices you want. There's nothing and no one to hold you back now. There's only Nell and it seems to me we can do for her what Tarabeg does best – we can all rally round.' She folded the headscarf into a neat square and slipped it into her coat pocket. 'As I say, 'tis all down to you now.'

Captain Bob's gaze had not left the river. 'You go inside, Rosie. I'll be back with you in five minutes. There's something I need to think about before I see Bee. I'm just a man, Rosie, I need a bit of time to meself, to empty my head.' And with that, he strode out across the land at the back of the Malones' and down to the pebbled shore of the Taramore.

Rosie's heart sank.

She entered the shop via the back door, having seen that there were no customers in the front. 'Peggy!' she shouted as she hung up her coat.

There was no reply.

'Peggy!' she shouted again.

There was the sound of running footsteps on the floor-boards above her head. Rosie stood at the bottom of the stairs and waited. Moments later, Peggy appeared on the top step, in full make-up and wearing a dress that Rosie knew to be one of Sarah's. It was from a wardrobe she had never touched. She was waiting for the day when Michael decided himself that it was time to clear out the memories once and for all. Peggy looked shamefaced.

'Peggy, what in God's name are you doing?'

'Oh God, I'm sorry. I thought if Michael didn't come from Liverpool until after the harvest party, you might let me wear this. He would never know, would he?'

It was the emerald-green dress Sarah had worn for the opening party for the shop, the year Mary Kate was born, the night everyone thought Shona Maughan had cast a curse on the Malones.

Rosie stood dumbfounded as memories of a night long forgotten washed over her, and there was something else too, something she couldn't attribute, a sense of foreboding, a warning, a bad feeling. She shook her head. It was just seeing the dress again that had done it, and the memory of herself, a younger Rosie, trembling, walking through the crowd with Keeva, to stand next to Sarah with Mary Kate in her arms. She could almost have been there now. She could smell the night air, could see the moon and the dust on the road as Shona and Jay Maughan's caravan pulled into their midst. She could feel the force of Bridge repelling Shona's curse with one of her own.

She shook herself out of her reverie. 'Peggy,' she hissed, 'I have Captain Bob with me, who has not been home for nearly ten years. He's down at the Taramore. Get that dress off and get down here now or so help me God, I will tell Mr Malone, because he, Peggy, will be giving out to you like never before if he even hears about you running around in that dress. It was Sarah's, you stupid girl.'

She almost spat out the last words. She never lost her temper and felt instantly guilty.

Peggy was left in no doubt as to the anger simmering inside Rosie. Her face dropped and she gave a little squeal. 'Oh Jesus, Holy Mother, I'm sorry,' as she ran along the landing to change back into her own clothes.

Rosie suddenly felt drained. 'I need a drink,' she said to herself. 'The place has gone mad.'

Much to Rosie's surprise, Captain Bob arrived at the back door dripping wet and shivering.

'What in God's name were you doing?' she asked as she fetched him a towel from the shelf above the range. 'No one goes in the river unless it's by accident.'

'I couldn't stop myself,' he said as he dried his hair. 'I needed to, and it worked.'

The kitchen was filled with baskets and boxes of end-of-summer fruit that had been gathered that day by Josie and the boys from the fields and hedgerows and was now waiting to be stewed or pickled. Peggy had come down and was now standing at the range, frying potatoes and making tea. Finn was still across the road in the Devlins', refusing to leave his friends and return home.

'Does that feel better now?' Rosie asked Captain Bob after he'd eaten his fill of the stew that Peggy had simmered in the pot and watched like a hawk since early that morning.

'It does, and I'm thanking you for everything, Rosie. And yourself now, Peggy – that was a fine-tasting stew. I have not the words to tell you how grateful I am. But now, do I look presentable enough not to scare the life out of Bee?'

'Of course you do. The soaking in the Taramore has worked wonders, and who would have thought that Michael's clothes would fit you so well, eh?' She placed the flat of her hands on the table and the chair legs scratched on the flags as she rose. 'You and Bee can decide what to do about Nell, when you've both sorted yourselves out.'

'I truly had no idea Nell was on her own,' said Captain Bob as he replaced the captain's hat he refused to part with, despite it needing a wash. 'It would never fit me again,' he said as he gently teased it back out of Rosie's hands.

'The scold of a woman told me they were all still at home and she needed money to feed them. Nell told me, she never wrote to one of them and they never wrote to her. Nell was born afflicted, but she's really harmless and was the only one with a heart. She would have untied me eventually, when she wasn't so upset. She was scared that she would be taken away by the nuns and bless her, she's right. They would have come for her and that's a fact. Nell always got upset when she was little. She tied her big sister up in the filleting shed once. She was only doing what I would have loved to have done to the little madam, given half the chance. Maybe if I had scolded her at the time, I might have been saved.'

Rosie had her drink in her hand and had taken a sip while he was talking. Despite the trauma and exhaustion of the day, she found this amusing and unable to contain her laughter, it sprayed him. 'Look what you've done,' he exclaimed. 'All over my clean shirt.'

Rosie laughed again. 'Get out of here, would you,' she said as they walked to the door. 'I have my husband coming back tomorrow and there's a deal of stuff I need to get ready for him when he arrives. I cannot believe the amount of news I have to tell him. He has an American cousin here turning the village on its head and he's barely left.'

'It all happens in Tarabeg.' Captain Bob laughed as he kissed Rosie on the cheek. 'Meself, I'm desperate to meet the American. He must be a good-looking fella, all right, if he's got Mrs Doyle in a spin.'

'Take the bike,' said Rosie. 'No one is needing it tonight.'

With a raise of his hat, Captain Bob pulled the bike away from the wall and pedalled down the road towards the coast.

Captain Bob sang to himself as he cycled along the road. The red evening sun cast long shadows of Crewhorn across the sprawling deep-amber peat bogs to his left and his own shadow cycled through the fields beside him. He could hear nothing but the repetitive squeak of its wheels as he rode. In the few fields where the soil was fertile enough, the crops stood high and swayed in the breeze. The harvest would be happening in the coming days and the land was at its most bountiful; this time of year was always alive with anticipation and urgency. It was something he'd forgotten during his years in Liverpool.

His heart lifted as he came closer and for the first time heard the sound of the ocean hitting the shore.

Bee saw him before he saw her. She was walking down the road towards the village for the Angelus Mass. She went for the conversation, the company and the sense of community and belonging; she had little else to sustain her during the long days she spent in her cottage, just the memories of her years with Captain Bob, and thoughts of her late sister and niece. At least when she left Mass she felt lifted, renewed, ready to take on the loneliness and battle through the following day.

She thought at first it was an illusion, her mind playing tricks, and then he did something that every Irishman on a bike did when he saw someone walking along the road: he lifted his cap and wobbled as he gripped one handle-bar. As she waved back, the sob caught in her throat and her walk became a run.

Moments later, the bike crashed to the ground, the wheels still spinning, as they collided, he laughing while she cried out loud and held him tight.

As he swung her around, her feet lifting from the ground, the sky flaming red above them and the ocean crashing against the rocks behind them, he popped the question she thought he could never ask, 'Oh, my little Bee, will you be my wife?'

Seamus and Nola rode up the boreen to the farm with Finn in the back of the cart. 'Would you look at the state of him,' said Nola, trying to suppress her laughter.

Seamus glanced over his shoulder. Finn was lying on his back, his hands behind his head, his head resting on a small pile of folded sacks, staring up at the twilight sky.

'He hasn't a care in the world, that fella,' said Seamus. 'He has everything before him and nothing to worry about behind him.' He lifted the reins, gave a light crack and made a noise in the side of his mouth that the horse knew meant trot on faster.

Nola snorted. 'Aye, nothing but a dead mother, a murdered grandmother, a sister who's run off and broken everyone's heart in the process, and a family cursed by the gypsies.'

'That's the trouble with you, Nola,' said Seamus. 'You always talk about the bad things that happened. Me, I'm looking to the lad's future.'

'Oh, you are so bloody perfect, Seamus. You're getting like your father, and all I will say is, the day that happens, God help you. Anyway, it won't be me looking after you – I don't have long left.'

Seamus looked sharply to his wife. 'There you go again,

always giving me the bad news. What would you want to say that for?'

The light was fading, the sun had disappeared and the moon had climbed above the Taramore River and was beginning its ascent towards the mountains.

'Because I won't make old bones. And don't be giving out to me – I know what a sinful thing that is to say. But, Seamus, I've spent half of my life looking after Daedio and who is there to look after us? Sarah's gone, Michael would be worse than useless, always working, and we aren't Rosie's blood. Mary Kate has gone, and if you think for one moment that Michael will bring her back, you are as mad as he is. She wants to live her life on one of those new motorways, that's what Father Jerry said, and what Mary Kate wants, she gets. Don't you know that? No, once Daedio goes, that's us on our own and I don't much like the thought of it.'

'You just miss having people around the place,' said Seamus.

The horse turned the bend and they began the last and steepest stretch to the top.

'I do. It's why I kidnap this little fella so often. What's the point of me if I have no one to cook for and fuss over. There is none, I tell you, and before we can blink our eyes, he'll be off too, after Mary Kate, to Liverpool or America. I may as well not be here. That's when I will go, when he's off.'

Seamus placed his hand on his wife's knee. 'Shush now,

you still have me. I need feeding, and so do Pete and Daedio.'

'Aye, you ungrateful lot of feckers, a curse is what you lot are.' Nola wiped her eyes with her handkerchief as Seamus roared with laughter.

The horse, smelling the hay in the manger Pete had prepared already, did his usual fifty-yard dash to the old house and his stable. Finn, who always thought this was the best part of the journey, squatted down, facing forwards and grabbed both sides of the cart, yelling, 'Faster! Faster!'

As they turned the corner, Seamus knew instantly that something was amiss because Porick came out of the house with a pot in his hand and took a drink from it. 'Whoa,' he shouted as he pulled the horse to a standstill. 'Porick, 'tis a delight to see you and a mystery too,' he said.

'Aye, I would think so,' said Porick. 'And there's more – you have a houseful in there and a visitor from America too.'

Nola got down from the cart faster than she had done in ten years or more. She put out her hand and Finn grabbed it and leapfrogged over the edge of the cart.

The three of them entered the cottage and were stunned into silence to see Joe Malone, looking as though he'd been there all his life, sitting on the end of Daedio's bed. He jumped to his feet and extended his hand. 'Joe Malone. It's my pleasure, ma'am, sir.'

Chapter 30

Joe slept in Michael's old bed – Nola wouldn't hear of him sleeping anywhere else – and sat in Annie's rocking chair, also on Nola's instructions. He only left Daedio's side when Teresa arrived at the bottom of the boreen to chauffeur him around. She introduced him to everyone they met and paraded him around Tarabeg as if he were her own creation. And, of course, she took him to Mass.

Father Jerry had noticed Teresa's absences and distractedness. He minded and he let Paddy know so when he called in for his afternoon pint of Guinness.

'Sure, it can't be right that a fella can be that good-looking, can it? I'm not sure what God thought he was doing putting such temptation in the way of all the women in Tarabeg,' he said as soon as he walked in.

Teresa had hurtled past him in the car an hour earlier, tooting the horn and raising one hand in the air, the chiffon scarf around her hat billowing behind. Joe sat beside her and Ellen was in the back, ramrod straight and with her hands in her lap, a smug look of self-importance on her face as she scanned the lanes and boreens she'd spent her entire life tramping up and down on foot. Viewing them from the plush leather back seat of Father Jerry's car gave her a whole new perspective.

Between them, Nola, Teresa, Ellen, Bridget and sometimes Josie had formed a protective matronly cordon around Tarabeg's American sensation. Their defences were designed to deter even the most determined young women from getting anywhere near him, however well armed with bottles of perming solution.

'I suppose,' said Father Jerry with a sniff, 'we take what beauty the good Lord gives us, and he sends men like Joe to test us.'

'Aye, Father, that would be so,' said Paddy, happy that Father Jerry had answered his own question. 'He's certainly testing us this time. Sent the women in this village into a blind tizzy, the American has. They say Malones' has sold out of all manner of cosmetics. The shelves are empty, Roise tells me, with not a bottle of Coty L'Aimant or a pink shimmer lipstick in sight. And she has no more coming in for weeks and everyone is going wild because Michael's on his way home already and they can't give him an order to fetch more. No one has a notion what's happening, nor even if Mary Kate is coming back with him or not.'

Josie bustled in to the back bar from the butcher's shop at the front. 'Is that you, Father?' she shouted. She dipped her bulky frame through the curtain with difficulty. 'I thought it was. Well, I'll be saying this now, if Mary Kate does come back to Tarabeg, every girl in this village will have been perming her hair in vain. There's not one of them can hold a candle to her when it comes to the looks. Isn't that why Declan is all soft in the head for her?'

Father Jerry took the Guinness Paddy was holding out to him in his familiar pot. 'I thought it was the music the women in this village were all mad for? That and getting across to Ballycroy for the dancing every full moon. Isn't it hard work enough trying to keep everyone on the straight and narrow without this distraction right in the heart of our own village.'

Paddy narrowed his eyes as he wiped the drips of Guinness from the bar. 'Are you out of sorts, Father? Have the mice been at your wooden leg again?'

Father Jerry sipped the foam off the top of his pint. 'Not at all. There's nothing wrong with me.'

'Well, don't forget to thank the Lord for that then, when you next take Mass. Joe is just a relative visiting the Malones from America. It's not Daedio's fault that the man looks and talks like a film star, is it?'

Father Jerry took his pint and carried it to the window. The rhythm of life in Tarabeg was moving into a different phase and things were about to change. The summer was coming to an end and the harvest was imminent. As always at this time, there was tension in the air. Would the rain hold off? Would the sun continue to shine? Would the thresher work? How many people would come down from the hills to help? And this year there was an extra dimension. Mary Kate had gone, the American had arrived, Michael was in a temper that had sent him wild. Father Jerry knew that whatever it was that was afflicting the village, Mary Kate was at the heart of it. Blessing himself, he asked God to bring her safely home.

Nola was on her way to the creamery, to make and salt extra butter for harvest week. 'You keep that miserable eejit company, would you?' she asked of Joe as she made them both tea before she left.

'I'll be happy to,' said Joe. 'I hear Michael will be home tonight. I was going to call on him later, and Teresa offered to take me, but I reckon that might not be a good idea. I'll go tomorrow instead.'

Nola placed her hands on her hips and shook her head. 'You know, I want to be mad with Mary Kate, but I just can't be. I cannot see her coming home with her father tonight, however hard he tried to persuade her. She is the cut of her mother and she will not be told by anyone what it is she has to do. My guess is she'll be in Liverpool still.'

'Does that upset you?' asked Joe, intrigued by all he had heard about the wilful Mary Kate.

'Not at all. She'll come home one day. She has a nature for the place, and those that do can try as hard as they like, but it cannot be got rid of. They say it's always there, that Ireland never stops trying to pull its lost children home. Hopefully she'll be back before that one meets his maker.' She inclined her head towards Daedio, who was having his second sleep. 'Michael was away at war for five long years. My guess is that Mary Kate will be away for just as long.'

Joe walked over to the press and picked up one of the many photographs Nola kept on the shelves. 'Is this her?' he asked, holding the picture out to Nola.

'Aye, it is, on her last day at school. It was a grand day, apart from Seamus farting as loud as the bull in the middle of Sister Magdalena's speech. Aye, it was grand. A beautiful colleen, is she not.'

Joe put it back. 'She is very beautiful indeed. I would have liked to have met her.'

'Ah well, patience is all that's needed. Right, the butter won't churn itself, I'm off. Don't let that old maggot give you the runaround – he's been doing it to me for years. I tell everyone he'll be at *my* funeral, not me at his.'

Joe thrust his hands into his pockets and looked down at Daedio asleep in his bed in front of the fire. They had talked into the small hours every night since he'd arrived in Tarabeg, and he wondered had that tired him out. Sometimes Seamus sat with them: three men united by a deep, ineffable bond. There was an easiness to their conversation, which flowed as though Joe had been born in Tarabeg. He was familiar with all the major events in

Daedio's life, laughed at the jokes between him and Nola and felt so close to them all, even though he'd known them less than a week. It was an unworldly experience. He had served in the marines, lived in Brooklyn, met many people in his life, but never had he experienced this immediate sense of belonging or such unquestioning acceptance.

Daedio opened his eyes and Joe grinned.

'Has she gone?' Daedio whispered, glancing towards the scullery door.

'She has,' said Joe. 'I thought you were pretending.'

'Thank God for that. I thought she would never leave, and you kept asking her questions.' Daedio shuffled up the bed and banged his pillow back into place. 'Seamus won't be back for hours either. Right, come and sit yerself down. I have news for ye, and I've been beside myself, waiting for the right moment to tell ye.'

Joe could tell by the change of tempo that this was the conversation he'd been waiting for. This was it: the moment.

Seamus was down in the village. The harvest was due and he was meeting with Paddy to decide how many barrels they would need to buy in. 'Needs a few days to settle,' he'd said to Joe.

The planning of the harvest party was in full swing, but this time with a difference. People from far and wide and anyone with the remotest connection to Joe Malone's great-grand-daddy were being flushed out from neighbouring villages. And that included a surprising number of nonagenarians even older than Daedio. The guard who'd caught a ten-year-old Joe Senior scrumping in Lord Carter's orchards was coming – he remembered letting Joe keep some of the apples and had even given him a lift back to the farm. Also keen to meet Joe's great-grandson was the lady who'd once danced at the hall with Joe. He had kissed her in the moonlight as the sound of the water rushing down the mountainside into the Taramore rang in her ears. He whispered sweet nothings, undid her blouse, slipped his fingers inside her many vests and promised her that at the next dance he'd be waiting and would expect more. She had dressed herself up and made her way to the dance hall every full moon for months afterwards before anyone had the heart to tell her he'd left for America. 'I don't bear a grudge,' she'd said when she was told about the party for Joe Junior. 'Anyway, Joe Senior is long dead, God rest his soul. A poor and miserable life as a young widow I would have had, wouldn't I now. I'll be there.'

Young women from as far away as across the Nephin Beg were delirious at the prospect of meeting a young, rich, handsome American in a Mayo village. For those lacking the money or permission to travel, it was as if America had come to them. None was more excited than Peggy, who was still wondering what to wear. She spent her days at the Malones' shop wishing she could move the till from the counter to the window to better keep her eye on the road for a glimpse of the handsome Joe being chauffeured around by Teresa.

'Get us a drink, will you?' said Daedio. ''Tis my belief no conversation about money can be held without a drink in your hand. 'Tisn't right.'

Joe had very quickly become used to the Malone house. When he thought about Brooklyn, all he heard was traffic, noise and a pace of life that didn't suit him. 'This sounds serious,' he said as he removed from the press the glasses he'd got into the habit of drying and placing there for Nola every night.

'Oh, it is. I haven't had many conversations in my life as serious as this one,' said Daedio. 'Get the whiskey, not the porter. You're going to need it.'

Five minutes later, with a glass in his hand, Joe sat back in the rocking chair and gave it a push with his feet to set the rockers moving.

Daedio began. 'Now, your great-granddaddy, when he was in jail, he sent something here to me. It was a box. A box full of money, a great deal of money. He said in a letter that someone would come for it, but that was some seventy years ago and I thought it had been forgotten altogether. But now here you are. It's yours.'

Joe stared into his drink. 'I know,' he said.

Suddenly, the rockers on his chair came to a standstill with a jolt and he felt as if he was being pushed forwards. The whiskey slopped over the rim of his glass. 'What the hell…?' he said, glancing round to the back of his chair to see who'd stopped it.

Daedio waved his hand. 'Oh, don't be worrying about

that, 'tis only Annie. She's never left. Waiting for me, she is.'

Joe looked into Daedio's eyes and could tell he was serious.

'Don't you have visitors from the other side in America?'

Joe swallowed hard. 'Er, no. Not at all.'

'You don't say! Well, imagine. I wonder why not?'

Joe knew why not. 'Because it's noisy and sophisticated, and I guess there's nowhere to hide?'

'Aye, that'll be it,' said Daedio, satisfied with the answer, and they both grinned as the chair began to rock again. 'Don't worry, you'll get used to her if you stay much longer. Anyway, what do you mean, you know? You see that brick in the wall, if you move it, you'll find all the money there – well, most of it. I will admit there have been times I've had to er… avail myself of some of it – when Michael and Sarah first married, and when Michael needed money to set up his shop. And the first time was when I used it to buy those seven acres so we could drive Shona Maughan off the land and out of the village. But as God is my judge, we only counted it when we got your letter, and I'd be saying we haven't spent much, not compared with what's there.'

'I know,' said Joe again. 'That's why I'm here. Joe Senior left a will and it has only just reached maturity. I only found out myself recently. There is more to his story though. Your brother was no ordinary thief or jailbird, Daedio – did you know that?'

Daedio was all ears. He was so focused on Joe Junior's revelations, he didn't even take a sip of his whiskey.

'My great-granddaddy did what he did in anger. He robbed the payroll truck to get back at the firm for the way they treated the Irishmen they employed to build their roads and bridges. The conditions were appalling – you cannot imagine it. Those men dropped dead with the heat in summer and slipped on the ice and broke bones and necks in the winter. And as if that wasn't bad enough, there were no payouts for the families. That was why Joe Senior robbed the payroll. He wanted to use the money to try and make those men's lives easier. Problem was, he got caught.'

'Aye, but he got the money here, to Tarabeg Farm.'

'That's true. He was pretty smart there. The chances of anyone finding it here on this hill were just about zero, I'd say.' Joe paused and gave a small smile. 'I know about the money, but I don't want it.'

Daedio took a sip of his whiskey before saying in a much quieter voice, 'What do you mean, you don't want it?'

Joe leant forward, stopped the rockers himself and looked at Daedio square on. 'Daedio, I am a very wealthy man, thanks to Great-Granddaddy. I'm a sleeping partner in one of the biggest law firms in New York, and every month they just keep giving me money for doing nothing. Great-Granddaddy bought shares back when they were setting up the law firm to help the people coming over from Ireland, and now I've inherited all the dividends that have accrued since way back. It's much more than what was sent to you. I want the Tarabeg money to stay here. It can be yours to do with as you wish. I have more than enough.'

Daedio looked like he was about to faint. With rheumy eyes and a gummy smile, he stared up at the rocking chair. 'I reckon I may live another ten years now. Annie, you are going to have to wait.' He laughed and, lifting up his glass, clinked it with Joe's.

'I have something else to say that might surprise you,' said Joe. 'I've made a decision. I'm not going back to Brooklyn. I want to live here, in Tarabeg. Can I stay here with you until I find somewhere suitable to buy?'

'What about your mammy?' Daedio rasped, his eyes full of tears.

'Oh, she won't move, but I'll go back four times a year for holidays, and for board meetings at the law firm, even if I won't have a clue what they're talking about. And Mammy can visit here.'

Daedio lay back on his pillows and smiled. 'I cannot even begin to tell you why,' he said, 'but you have just made an old man very happy.' And with that, the glass slowly slipped from his fingers. He closed his eyes and, this time, fell asleep for real.

Chapter 31

'Go on, Peggy, you've done now. Away home. Keeva is keeping Finn tonight.'

Peggy blushed; she knew the importance of that statement. Rosie blushed too. She had missed her husband in more ways than one. Soon he would be home and he'd have come to a resolution over Mary Kate, because she knew for sure that he wouldn't be returning to Tarabeg without one. With his mind still at last, she wanted to show him what he'd missed.

Once the door was closed on Peggy, she ran upstairs, pulled out her favourite negligée that she'd bought, amid deep blushes, for her honeymoon many years ago and hadn't worn since, and ran back downstairs to bathe. When Michael walked in through that door, she would make his homecoming one to remember.

Two hours later, Rosie opened the door of the old range and placed Michael's dinner inside. A new electric oven had been installed and Rosie loved it, but Michael refused to remove the range and Rosie had to admit it had its uses, such as now, when the heat from the fire kept the old oven just warm enough.

It was late and, despite Mrs Doyle's message, there was no sign of Michael. Disappointed, she took herself up to the bedroom. She sat at the dressing table in her gossamer negligée, brushing her auburn hair until it shone, listening to snatches of conversation from Paddy's bar across the road each time the door opened and closed.

She returned the silver-backed brush to the green-frosted-glass dressing-table tray, all of which had once been Sarah's. 'Do you not feel a bit odd, lying in a dead woman's bed?' Philomena O'Donnell had asked her shortly after she and Michael had married.

Her answer had been, 'No. I don't feel Sarah there at all, and besides, I have a job to do, looking after the children and Michael. I don't worry about ghosts.'

She opened the drawer of the table, took out the box Michael had thrown in it, and placed the emerald heart around her neck. It nestled in the hollow of her throat as her fingers caressed it, the stone absorbing the light. She looked in the drawer and found a lipstick that had belonged to Sarah and which she'd not thrown away. It had retained its deep red colour, despite being a little hard and waxy. Unlike some of the other women in the village, Rosie didn't have any rouge, so she dabbed the lipstick onto her cheeks and rubbed it in. Sitting back on the stool, she admired the effect. She smiled, pleased with her reflection, and wondered why she'd never worn rouge before. It accentuated the freckles across the bridge of her nose and made them look attractive.

The house was so silent, she could hear herself think. Her house, her home, her Michael. All she had ever wanted. 'Rosie Malone,' she whispered, 'smile, you got the life you dreamed of.'

She decided to apply the lipstick to her lips as well. Although she'd never done it herself, she'd seen Keeva do it often enough. She started on the bottom lip and worked her way along and round, up to the top, tracing her Cupid's bow. And then her heart stopped dead. Over her shoulder, staring into the mirror next to her, was the haunting reflection of Sarah, as beautiful as the day she died.

Rosie's hand began to shake, smearing the lipstick around the side of her mouth. She dropped it on the dressing table. Her eyes filled with tears and the image blurred. She blinked and as quick as she had arrived, Sarah was gone. But the feeling of dread she'd brought with her remained. Rosie hurriedly unfastened the clasp and pressed the emerald heart back into the box and into the drawer, just as she heard Michael shouting, 'Rosie! Rosie!' as he ran up the stairs.

'I'm home.'

He exploded into the room, removed his jacket, threw it onto the chair and then leapt onto the bed and lay prone with his shoes on and his arms folded across his chest. 'Get you,' he said as he caught her reflection in the mirror. 'Are you wearing lipstick? It doesn't suit you, makes you look pale, as if you've seen a ghost.'

Rosie crossed the room and sat on the edge of the bed. 'Well?' she said. In the back of her mind a thought niggled that he hadn't even noticed the negligée and her naked body beneath. She had wanted to feel womanly, appear desirable. She suddenly felt ridiculous.

'I found her,' he said, in a much more subdued tone of voice, 'and she isn't coming home, not yet. She's looking after a family in a very swanky doctor's house. Rosie, I will give her until Christmas, I would say, before she's back here, begging Declan to take her to the dance. Is there any food?' He looked up at her pleadingly.

She couldn't help it. Even though her pulse was only just returning to normal after she'd caught sight of Sarah, she smiled back at him. 'Shall I bring it to you up here?'

As she lifted her dressing gown from the back of the door and made her way downstairs, Michael rose from the bed and, crossing to the window, looked over to Paddy's bar to see Father Jerry slipping through the door. His mind wandered to Cat and the night they had spent together. He had been cleansed of his sin, but the guilt lay heavy on his heart.

Father Jerry had been leaving the churchyard after the Angelus when Michael had driven into Tarabeg. 'Michael, are you coming across to Paddy's to tell me all the news?'

he asked as he clicked the church gate closed after him. 'Have you Mary Kate with you?'

'No, Father, I have not.'

Father Jerry looked disappointed, but before he could respond, Michael said, 'Father, will you take my confession?' He removed his cap and held it against his chest.

Father Jerry searched his eyes and seeing his sin and guilt cowering there, had turned on his heel without another word and walked back up the church path.

Ten minutes later, her dressing gown tied tight across her negligée, Rosie carried in a tray with a bowl of steaming stew and the pint of Guinness that Tig, having seen Michael's car arrive, had sent over. 'This will revive you,' she said as she pushed the door open.

But there was no reply. Michael was under the covers, fast asleep, his clothes in a pile on the floor.

Mary Kate's return to the Marcus house on Sunday evening took some explaining. Mrs O'Keefe was far from happy about it. 'He's in bits,' Mary Kate said. 'Mrs Marcus has left and taken the children with her, and I have to go back, just to see is he all right. He'll have been on call all day, and it's Joan's night off.'

'This is not what I promised your father,' Mrs O'Keefe said as she tipped up a cardboard box of Trill with a huge picture of a canary on the front and filled the budgie feeder with millet.

'Mrs O'Keefe, I'm not a fool. I will not do anything that would bring shame on my family or you. I just want to see that he is all right.'

'Go on then. You have one hour, and don't be later than that, mind. I don't want to be going out at this time of night looking for you, do you hear me?'

Mary Kate already had her hand on the door. 'I do and I will be,' she said. Without another word, she flew down the steps and along the avenue.

When she burst in through the back door, he was waiting for her in the kitchen, as they'd arranged.

'Oh, you're here. How are you?' she asked as she walked up to him.

Joan had cleared up the kitchen after supper. Without the children there, it was spotless.

Nicholas was standing with his back against the sink. Without saying a word, he opened his arms, and Mary Kate ran willingly into them. He didn't kiss her or even try to; he just held her close and stroked her long hair, which hung down her back.

After a moment he said, 'I don't imagine you have long. Let's sit down.' He led her over to the chairs and cupped both of her hands in his. 'I've spoken to my in-laws,' he said and she detected anger in his voice. 'They've told me they'll fight me in every court in the land if they have to, and that they'll name you if I try to divorce my wife. They seem to think that Lavinia is an angel and that I deceived her, and they said things about you that I would never repeat. Mary Kate, for the sake of your reputation and your future happiness, you must return to Ireland, now.'

Mary Kate pulled her hands away and sat up straight. 'No, I will not. This cannot be right,' she said. 'You've done nothing wrong. Mrs Marcus has behaved abominably – she's turned your life upside down, and the boys' lives too.'

Nicholas reached out and took her hands again. 'Mary Kate, I have no proof and neither does she, but I imagine a divorce-court judge would believe the word of a wife and mother forced to run from her own home before he'd believe the word of the sort of man she'll make me out to be. Robin will never confess to having had an affair with my wife.'

He lowered his head and let it rest on her shoulder. 'There is no other way to protect you. You have to leave and never return. I will have to pick up the pieces here. If she's really vindictive, she might even try and get me struck off. I cannot have you associated with any of that. With my dying breath, I will protect you and your reputation.'

Mary Kate kissed the top of his head. 'You do have proof,' she whispered.

'I don't. It will boil down to her word against mine.'

'Not with this.' Mary Kate put her hands on his shoulders, gently pushed him away and removed the letter from her pocket.

Nicholas recognised it immediately. 'She never took it?' he gasped as he took it from her.

'No. She turned the place upside down looking for it, but I got there first.'

Realisation softened his features and the first hint of a smile lifted the corners of his mouth. 'I can use this to see my boys, to fight for them,' he said, and she could see his thoughts racing. 'Will you stay? Will you wait?' He reached out and stroked her cheek. 'Can I dare to ask you to wait until this is all over?'

At first Mary Kate couldn't reply. She just nodded, tears pouring down her face as she clasped one hand over his and kissed his palm. 'You can and I will,' she said. 'It's all a mess, but I know we can find a way, because if there wasn't a way, we wouldn't have been put together like this. It must have been meant to happen.'

'Come here,' he said. Reaching out, he slid her across onto his knee. Her hands circled his neck and his hands circled her waist. 'I will do everything in my power to make you my wife. Everything. You're right: we need to take one day at a time, and each day will bring us a step closer. Are you sure, Mary Kate? It could take a long time. I wouldn't blame you if you wanted to run a million miles from me and here.'

'Am I sure?' she repeated, mimicking him. Then she bent her head and kissed him, leaving him in no doubt that she would wait for as long as it took.

Chapter 32

It was just before dawn when Joe and Seamus carried a singing Daedio from the back of the cart into the house. He was still holding his mug in his hand, half filled with porter, and he refused to be parted from it even when they'd settled him into his bed. He sank back gratefully into his soft pillows. 'You can take the pot when I've finished,' he said to Seamus with a prolonged chuckle. 'That old bat will only give out to me in the morning if I spill it on the blanket in me sleep.' He inclined his head towards the bedroom door through which Nola had just weaved her unsteady way, having slept all the way up the hill with her head resting on Seamus's shoulder.

Daedio had been transported on Joe's knee, with Joe sitting on the back of the turf cart, his long legs hung over the edge and resting on the wheel mounts to stop his feet from dragging along the ground. Even so, his legs slipped off each time the wheels fell into a rut. Daedio sang to

Joe all the way up Tarabeg Hill and Joe committed every second of the magical night to memory.

The house was silhouetted against the brooding harvest moon, its orange light shot through with wisps of dark cloud as it rested above the crest of the hill, waiting to see them safely home before it dipped below the line of trees. The dew was already heavy on the ferns up the side of the boreen and Joe's trousers were wet through by the time they reached the top.

'You drank more than was good for you tonight, Daddy. You should be slowing down, a man of your grand age,' said Seamus as he filled a pot with water for Nola.

The sound of a crash filled the room and Seamus dropped the mug into the sink and ran to the bedroom. When he emerged, he was laughing. 'Sure, I cannot even remember the last time Nola went to bed fully dressed,' he said. 'Not unless I'd dragged her there.'

On this occasion, Joe was not embarrassed. In the relatively short time he'd become accustomed to the ways of the villagers. They lived close to the earth and took every aspect of life in their stride, including the more intimate ones.

Daedio's shoulders heaved as he fought to contain his laughter. 'Did ye see Teresa Gallagher? Oh my, I won't forget the sight of that woman drunk for as long as I live. Once we got two down her, 'twas easy to keep going, and when she grabbed Paddy for a kiss, I thought Josie was going to clobber her.'

Seamus shook his head as he poked the fire and threw on half a dozen peat bricks. 'There's a chill in the air tonight,' he said. 'It will be the weather turning. What makes me smile tonight, Daedio, is seeing that harvest safely in. Tomorrow, Pete and I will store the last of it into the barns and then I can take the pigs to Castlebar.'

Daedio was still clinging onto the porter mug. 'I nearly danced, tonight, Seamus,' he said, grinning up at his son. 'Me legs had a life of their own. Do you remember Mammy and me and the way we used to dance at harvest? We were the last to stop, always. Mammy used to say that if she could dance every night of her life, she would. Oh, she loved the fiddlers and the music all right.'

Bending down, Seamus placed his hands on either side of his father's bed. The room flickered as the flames roared up the chimney like chained dogs and Daedio's eyes shone up at him. 'Daddy, I'm sure Mammy is dancing every night with the angels, and they'll be a lot better at it than you.'

He lifted his father's cap and flopped it back down on his head in an affectionate gesture. 'Now give me that mug. We don't want to wake up to a row in the morning, do we. Harvest dance or not, the cows don't know that and we still have to be up soon. And Joe wants to be away to his bed already. Michael, Rosie and Finn are all tucked up, Paddy has taken the barrels in and everyone is heading safely home. All is well in Tarabeg. 'Tis only you and I, the last two men to be awake still.'

'I'm still awake,' said Joe. 'I'll sit with him awhile, Seamus. You go off to your bed and Nola. If you can trust an American, I think it's time I helped out a bit around here, until I can get my own place. I'll start by helping with the cows.'

Seamus rose, placing one hand in the small of his back and flinching. 'Well now, isn't that grand, and I won't pretend my back won't benefit.'

'I wish Mary Kate had been there,' said Daedio, his expression turning sad.

Seamus's heart constricted in response. He had missed his granddaughter too. 'I said the same to Michael and he said she'll be back long before the next harvest, Daedio. He's been to see her, he knows what he's talking about. That was the best we've ever had, thanks be to God, and yourself there, Joe,' he said. 'You turned the head of every woman in the village.'

'Feck, you did that alright,' said Daedio, perking up. 'I thought Ellen was going to faint when you danced with her, and did you see the frock on Mrs Doyle! She told me she was wearing a brassiere for the first time in her life, she did, and asked me did I want to see it. I said no, why the hell would I? Drunk as Matty Maughan she was. I've never seen that woman drink so much, and that's saying something, it is. I said to her, come here, Mrs Doyle and give me a kiss first. Feck, she's never kissed a man in her life – she nearly fainted, so she did.' His shoulders began to shake at the memory.

Seamus blew out the candle in the hurricane lamp by the door as he made his way to bed. The kitchen was dark now, save for the firelight and the glow from the lamp that Joe had lit in Michael's old room.

Joe rose and poured himself a glass of porter from the press, casting a nervous glance over his shoulder at Seamus's door. 'Do you want a top-up?' he whispered to Daedio.

Daedio grinned and held up his mug. ''Twas grand to see you and Michael getting along so well at the party,' he said, 'but be careful with the poaching – those fellas know how to run. When are they taking you?'

'Tomorrow night. Michael tells me that if I want to live in Tarabeg, I have to catch a salmon the size of my leg before I'm accepted.'

Exhausted from laughing, Daedio collapsed against his pillows. 'Aye, that would be the way,' he said. 'I was glad to see Michael in such good spirits. He's happy that Mary Kate will be home soon. She was never one for clearing up her own mess, so she won't last long cleaning up after other people, and that's a fact. I'll give her until Christmas, so I will. Joe, tell me, did I see you kissing Peggy?'

Joe raised his eyebrows. 'No, sir, you did not. What you saw was Peggy throwing her arms around my neck and heaving herself up until she planted her lips square on my own.'

'Oh feck, she will live on that until the next harvest,' said Daedio. 'She'll be telling everyone tomorrow she's getting married. She loves the film stars, you see, and the poor girl, I don't think she's ever even seen a film. Did you see if Michael danced with Rosie?'

Joe furrowed his brow as he tried to remember. 'I saw Tig and Keeva sitting on the hay bales like a pair of lovebirds while they were watching the children dancing.'

Daedio snorted. 'Those two, they're indecent. Paddy says that sometimes they're that desperate in the day, they disappear into the walk-in fridge. Imagine! And after all this time. I have no notion what is wrong with them at all.'

Joe took a sip of his drink. 'I didn't see Michael and Rosie, now you come to mention it. Michael spent most of his night with myself – I think maybe he thought he had to chaperone me, seeing as how I was a visitor. He didn't need to do that, though, I had a great deal of company. In fact, now that I think about it, Rosie told me she was going back into the house to fetch a cardigan, but I don't remember her coming back out again.'

'Maybe she's sad that Mary Kate didn't come back home,' said Daedio.

One of the peat bricks tumbled into the grate and sent a shower of sparks flying.

'To think, Bee and Captain Bob too. The smile on Father Jerry's face when Captain Bob announced they're to be married. I'll tell you all about their story tomorrow.' Daedio slipped further down his bed, still staring into the fire, the heat stinging his eyes. Joe slipped his hand into his pocket and took out the emerald heart he had been wanting to show Daedio since the day he arrived. He slipped the gold chain through his fingers as the emerald swung and captured the flames.

'Daedio, have you ever seen this before?' he asked. Joe thought he caught the flash of a reflection of white hair and dark eyes. He blinked; it was gone and just as quickly Daedio was fast asleep.

He leant forward to take the mug and pull the cover over Daedio's shoulders, and as he did so he felt a surge of affection for the old man as he smiled contentedly in his sleep.

It was the rocking of the chair that roused Daedio from his slumbers, and when he woke he instantly knew why.

'Is that you, Annie?' he whispered.

The flames had died, the light in Michael's room was out and Joe had closed the door. The ashes still glowed red and he could make out the outline of the woman he had loved for all of his life sitting in the rocking chair.

'It is, Daedio. I've come to take you over to the other side. It's time now.'

Daedio's eyes filled with tears. Despite all the times he'd thought he wanted to go, wanted to be with his Annie, he was scared, unready. 'Will they just find me here when they come in in the morning?' he asked.

There was a silence and then the chair rocked again before she spoke. 'They will. And just think what they will say, that your last night was one of the best you ever had. I was dancing too, so I was. I tried to get you up on your legs.'

'I felt it,' he whispered. 'I nearly made it. I nearly danced with you, Annie.' He tried to smile, but he couldn't, his throat felt tight. 'Mary Kate, she isn't home yet – can I not wait for her, Annie?'

He tried to move, but his legs felt like lead weights and his arms pressed heavy on his chest.

'She isn't coming home, Daedio. It will be a long time yet before Mary Kate returns to Tarabeg, and there is much that needs to happen before then. Mary Kate will have to make her way back to Tarabeg of her own free will. She'll have pain of her own to face before that day comes. There is nothing we can do to help or change that.'

Panic washed over Daedio; he didn't want his beloved Mary Kate to suffer. 'Let me stay a while, Annie. Let me see her one more time, will you, please, and then I'll come.'

But even as he asked the question, he understood. Annie had said it would be a long while, and he was already an old man; time was running out for him. 'Please, Annie. Annie...'

But all he could hear was the rocking of the chair, back and forth.

Glossary of Irish terms

boreen	narrow country lane
boxty	bread made with grated potato and flour
colleen	girl or young woman
curragh	small wickerwork boat or coracle
Garda	the Irish police force
poteen	illegal home-brewed alcohol, made from potatoes
whin	gorse

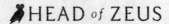